LOVERS' REUNION

The *hula* Emma had chosen told a much-loved island legend. A thrill of recognition shimmied down Gideon's spine as she began to dance, for the tale was one he remembered all too well. It was the story she had told him; the romantic yet tragic tale of a forbidden love affair between a Hawaiian princess and her commoner lover.

In Emma's movements, Gideon saw the palm trees swaying in the sultry breeze. In her gently undulating hips was the rolling motion of the breakers that pounded the cove where the lovers had first met. With a flick of her fingertips to the left and right, she scattered handfuls of tiny stars across the sweeping sky, while with but a sweeping gesture of her slender arms she embraced the full, round circle of the shining moon, who had kept watch over the beautiful maiden and her handsome sweetheart while they made love on the warm sand.

Time turned back for Gideon in that moment. Seven years vanished as if they'd never been. He held his breath, transfixed, for it seemed as if Emma was telling the poignant story of their own first meeting with her dancing, as if she was describing the tender passion they'd shared beneath the sea-grape tree, only to be parted by distance, time, and the cruel whims of fate.

As her violet eyes lifted to his, a tremulously sweet smile curved her lips for an instant, then her sooty lashes dropped, and she quickly turned her head away. A thrill ran through him in that moment, for he knew that no matter what, she loved him still. Loved him . . . as, God help him, he loved her.

"Neri creates a sumptuous love story!"
—Kathe Robin, *Romantic Times*

"Savor the magic!"
—Arnette Lamb, author of *Border Lord*

PENELOPE NERI

This Stolen Moment

ZEBRA BOOKS
KENSINGTON PUBLISHING CORP.

A Legend . . .

So great was the chieftain's anger,
When he heard of her defiance,
That his voice made mountains tremble.
"Go!" he bade his warriors. "Find her!
Find the maid, wahine kapu—
From her birth, pledged to another—
Slay the one who dared defile her . . . !"

Soon, the maiden heard them coming,
Knew that they would slay her loved one—
"Go!" she pleaded. "Quickly! Flee them!"
But he would not leave his sweetheart
To endure her father's anger.
"While I yet have breath within me
I shall not be parted from thee.
Let them come. Yes! Let them take me—
Sweet one, I shall not forsake thee!"

As the warriors drew nearer
Hand in hand, the lovers fled them,
Running—not toward the mountains,
Nor to the sacred place of refuge—
But into the perilous currents,
Where the waters swirled and eddied.
As the sun set, as the moon rose,
Shared one last kiss of aloha.

There it was her father found them,
When the sun rose with the dawning.
And his grief made mountains tremble
For he knew he could not part them—
Knew the gods had blessed the lovers—
For twin rocks rose from the waters,
Where no rocks had stood before then.

—P.N.

One

1859

*Kawaiihae Landing, the "Big Island" of Hawaii,
The Sandwich Isles*

"Yee—haaa! Swim, you old devil!"

"Hold him, Mo'o! *Hold him! Hold him!* Watch out for his horns!"

With a grin to show he'd heard the yell of his calabash uncle—his honorary uncle—Gideon Kane gritted his teeth and again maneuvered his agile bronco through the crashing surf, half towing, half crowding the wild-eyed steer at the end of his lariat through the swells and out to the waiting longboats.

Sweat streamed from his forehead, kept out of his eyes by the rolled bandanna he wore tied about his forehead like an Indian. A battered woven hat with a curled brim shaded his deep-blue eyes against the dazzling light that bounced blinding sunbursts off the Pacific, while chaps of goatskin buffeted his inner thighs against a brine-stiffened saddle.

He was headed for the waiting longboat, where the steer he was towing behind his horse would be lashed to the gunwales by its horns, then rowed out to the steamship *Mariposa,* bobbing at anchor beyond the reef. The *Mariposa*'s captain was leaning over the taffrail and enjoying a pipe as he watched the *paniolos*—as the Hawaiian cowboys were called—swimming the longhorns out to his vessel. Aboard, other crew members waited for the little vessels to come alongside, ready to lower sailcloth slings for slipping under the steers' bellies. A winch then hoisted the cattle onto the *Mariposa*'s decks for the five-day sea voyage to the bustling sea port of Honolulu and the feeding pens and slaughter houses there.

The lading was a lengthy, arduous, and extremely dangerous business for the cowboys, but it was one Gideon relished, testing as it did his mettle both as a man and a seasoned hand. Very conscious that, as the only son of wealthy cattle baron Jacob Kane, a great deal was expected of him, ever since he could sit a horse Gideon had nursed a burning desire to prove himself his father's equal. If he succeeded, perhaps his father would reconsider his decision to send him off to America to complete his education.

Lately, however, he'd felt as if he were racing against an invisible clock that was inexorably marking off the days, hours, minutes, then finally the seconds left of the life he knew and loved, gobbling them up with every tick and tock. Up long before dawn each day, when the moon still carved a foamy crescent from the lightening charcoal sky, he and the other hands had completed the arduous *hoohulu pipi,* the roundup, gathering a herd of fractious beeves from the remote hiding places they favored, be it deep in grassy canyons, in far-flung tangles of cactus and mesquite, or in barren black lava wastes, then driving the herd down from the ranch's inland grazing to the coast.

They'd arrived dusty, exhausted, and famished late yesterday afternoon at the landing known as Kawaiihae, on the arid western shores of the biggest of the Sandwich Isles, the island of Hawaii. A few hours sleep, then he and the other hands had been up once again. It was yet dark and only a dull sulphur glow on the horizon had foretold the coming of dawn as Gideon gulped down a cup of strong island-grown Kona coffee and a hasty swallow of jerked beef and bread before selecting and cutting his first steer from the holding pen. Since daybreak, he'd lost count of the number of steers he'd personally battled to the waiting longboats.

Setting his jaw, Gideon gripped Akamai's sides even tighter with his knees and heels as the game cow-pony breasted the rolling surf, thinking there'd be many more hours of equally arduous labor before he and the other hands could rest again as he chivied the struggling steer alongside. All around him, Spanish or Mexican *vaqueros,* drawn from ranches in New Mexico or Texas, native-born cowboys, or second-generation Chinese, Portuguese, or various combinations of the same, did likewise, performing their difficult tasks with the economy of movement, strength, and skill that were all marks of the true professional, making as they did the whole procedure look deceptively easy to the casual eye. Pride filled Gideon. His father's *paniolos* were the best cowboys in the world—and they knew it! They worked longer and harder than most men ever dreamed of working, herding several thousand of the orneriest longhorns to be found on the toughest ranges anywhere, and they did it all without a word of complaint. Yet, when they rolled themselves into their bedrolls about the fire that night and plummeted into a few meager hours deep and well-deserved slumber, Gideon's father would be the last to follow suit and find his own bed. Well loved and respected by all of his men, the title *"Makua"*—the Hawaiian word for father or mother—had not been casually bestowed upon Jacob Kane, Gideon reflected. On the contrary, his father had more than earned it. So, he wondered in frustration, how did you prove to such a man that four more years of education for his only son would be wasted, not to mention unwanted? Gideon scowled, drawing a grin from Alika as he rode past him. His father had been everywhere—America, China, the South Seas—and done just about everything, it seemed. Consequently, he fully expected—nay, insisted—that his only son do likewise, before settling down to run the ranch in his footsteps.

"You must leave here to see something of the wide and wonderful world God has given us, my boy," he'd told Gideon one crisp morning as they worked side by side at the sawmill, shirt-sleeves rolled up to the elbows as they sawed planks of beauti-fully grained *koa* wood. Jacob had chosen the tree they'd felled himself, and planned to use its timber in the construction of a wooden house in which one of his ranch hands would live with his family. "If you never leave these islands, you'll grow old and dissatisfied, always wondering if there was something better out there that you missed. And—whether you believe me or not—someday that doubt will start to chafe at you, like an over-starched collar or a pesky mosquito bite, itching you raw. Get an education, Son. Learn about the fine American stock you sprang from. See the world. Experience all the wonders life has to offer. Get to know the family we have in Boston, and learn the ropes of our shipping and whaling concerns there. Then, when you're ready to settle down, and come home to us to stay, your mother and I will welcome you back with open hearts and open arms."

Gideon had scowled, quite certain his father didn't know what he was talking about. "And what if Harvard won't accept me?" he'd asked, trying—with little success—to hide the note of hope in his voice.

Jacob Kane had only smiled and reached out to ruffle his son's black hair as if he'd been eight, instead of almost eighteen. Though Gideon chose to ignore it, they both knew his excellent examination marks that spring had virtually guaranteed his ac-ceptance at any college he chose to attend. His Punahou profes-sors' glowing letters of recommendation and his family's fine reputation would ensure his acceptance. "Never fear, they'll ac-cept you, my boy, you'll see. Have faith, Gideon—in the good Lord, if not in your own abilities!" his father had added.

His steer securely lashed to a longboat's gunwales, Gideon thrust the conversation from his mind and concentrated on swim-ming his horse back to shore for another steer, instead, veering sharply away from the holding pens and the milling, snorting herd when he saw his father beckoning to him, vigorously waving a paper in his hand—surely one of the letters from Boston the *Mariposa* had delivered that morning? His heart sank. A heavy feeling of foreboding thudded through him, for his father was grinning broadly, his bright blue eyes sparkling, his teeth white against the leathery tan of his complexion, which was in startling contrast to his only vanity—the thick silver hair he always wore uncovered, despite the sun's fiery rays—and bushy mutton-chop whiskers. However, the words Jacob Kane was bellowing were, fortunately for Gideon, snatched away by the wind. His son could honestly not have made them out, even had he wanted to!

Lifting his hand in a cursory wave, as if he hadn't realized his father was gesturing him to come, he rode from the shallows and cantered Akamai along the narrow strip of sand, in the opposite direction. Tarnation! Did it have to arrive so soon? But, judging by his father's broad grin, the news he'd been dreading all summer had come indeed, carried all the way from distant Boston to these far-flung Pacific isles. Pity it hadn't been lost at sea in the process!

"Uncle Kimo?" he asked softly as he rode alongside the ranch *luna,* or foreman, Kimo Pakele, a tall, stocky Hawaiian cowboy astride a chestnut horse. Side-eyeing his father, Gideon pretended he still hadn't seen the man furiously beckoning.

"What is it, Mo'o?" Kimo asked affectionately, grimacing sympathetically as he followed Gideon's gaze and saw the missive *Makua* Kane was brandishing.

Gideon wetted his lips, his dark-blue eyes troubled as he toyed with his mount's coarse mane. "The letter's come, Uncle. And right now, feeling the way I do, there's nothing I could say to Father that wouldn't anger him. I need a little time alone, to accept it . . . ?"

Kimo nodded in understanding. "I understand. And you've worked hard ever since you came home from Honolulu, eh? Done more than your share, the way I saw it. Sooo, get out of here! Me an' the boys, we finish up. Go! Take all the time you need—but no tell *Makua* Kane I went give you leave! He find out, he come wild like hell!"

"My word on it," Gideon agreed, grinning as the foreman rolled his eyes. *"Mahalo! Mahalo nui loa!* Thank you! I'll be home by supper tomorrow, I promise."

"For my sake, see that you are, Mo'o. You know your father's rules about going off alone. Be careful!"

With a nod, Gideon turned Akamai's head and rode away from the dusty scene at the landing, his departure remarked by none of the busy cowboys. By a stroke of good fortune, even his father's attention was momentarily diverted by one of the new Spanish *paniolos*—an exceptional young *vaquero* from Texas named Felipe—who was having trouble subduing a wild-eyed, black bull which had decided to fight his rope. With every eye on Felipe, Gideon was able to make his escape before his father noticed his disappearance.

Within minutes, he'd left the pens of lowing cattle far behind, and was heading swiftly up-country, northeast, toward home, following the old saddle road inland. It was by far the fastest way, if not the easiest on a horse.

Back at the landing, the air had been very still and hot, reeking of cattle, dust, dung, and the acrid sweat of both weary horses and hard-working men. The few native huts, fashioned of grass—or *hale pili,* as they were known—were clustered along the narrow shore beside a half-dozen or so New England-style buildings, and the wooden two-room hut in which the Chinaman, Ah Woo, ran his general store. Above the coastal village loomed Pu'u Kohola, the ominous, lava-rock ruins of an ancient *heiau,* or Hawaiian temple, both village and temple parched and baking beneath the hammered silver of a cloudless sky. The dwellings seemed to dance, seen through a heat-haze that shimmied like a liquid curtain over the hard land. Vegetation had been sparse back there, too—no more than a brace of straggly coconut palms, spindly creations with ragged tops, and a mesquite bush or two. What grass there'd been had seemed to explode from the hard ground in stiff white-bleached tufts, in sharp contrast to the scattered black rocks of the lava beds that reached for miles in every direction. Prickly-pear cactus with its luscious fruit sprouted everywhere, along with tangles of *kiawe*—the twisted, low-growing trees the Spanish *paniolos,* called mesquite—but not a blade of green was to be found for as far as the eye could see.

Yet within an hour's hard riding, another world entirely unfolded all about him; a world where lush, rolling green hills collided with rain-forested valleys, guarded by the looming, snowcapped giant, Mauna Kea, whose hoary head was ofttimes hidden beneath drifting banks of woolly cloud. Farther up-country, soft misty showers cooled the blood and soothed the angry spirit, and glorious golden light poured like a blessing from the gods over the land each afternoon and imbued everything with magic, heightening color, texture and form. The grass became dense and emerald underhoof there, starred with wildflowers and thick as any eastern carpet, while the rain forests were dense and glorious, green with young ferns and alive with the call of hidden birds, glimpsed now and then as flashes of brilliant color amongst the leaves. Their voices vied to be heard over the chuckling song of silvery waterfalls. *Ohia lehua* trees, their blossoms softly feminine scarlet pompoms, their trunks hard and masculine, grew everywhere. Vivid blue morning glories spilled down mossy rock banks like flights of butterflies, while sprays of tiny wild purple, white, or yellow orchids festooned the trees. About their roots, bristly wild boars rooted for grubs, snuffling snouts pressed to the spongy forest floor.

At such elevations, the air was cool and damp by day, the nights chill. Wisps of mist drifted between the trees like wandering phantoms, while in the lower valleys, the fine rain that his part-Hawaiian mother called the " *'ua ki pu'u pu'u,"* the "rain that brings gooseflesh," fell each afternoon. In winter, restless winds sang mournful *olis,* or chants, among the mulberry trees, and they were integral ingredients of the sights and sounds and smells he loved, too; ones he knew he could experience nowhere else in the whole wide world, no matter his level of education.

The stone in his chest expanded until it hurt to breathe, almost. Tears he refused to cry because he was a man and because men did not give vent to such feelings of weakness scalded behind his eyes. This was his *aina,* his land! It was part and parcel of the man he'd become; his love of it, the birthright bequeathed him by his mother's blood, the legacy of his ancestor. It was a beautiful, beautiful land, too! How could his parents demand that he leave it, even for a day? And how in the world would he ever bring himself to go—as go he must, sooner or later, he acknowledged miserably, partly resigned to it, for despite everything, he loved his parents and would obey their wishes because of that love.

He rode on and on, deep in thought, at some point turning Akamai away from home, and heading once again for the sea. Tears blinded him to the taro patches he passed, their heart-shaped leaves nodding sedately in the wind, and to the smiling brown skinned, beautiful people who harvested the leaves, standing knee-deep in the mud and waving and calling *"Aloooha!"* in greeting as he passed. He did not see the tiny white wooden church with its spire pointing skyward toward heaven like a sharpened pencil lead, nestled snugly against the emerald hills, nor the tiny graveyard where the babes his *makuahine* had lost before his safe arrival had been laid to rest, nor the village of native grass huts scattered about it. Nor—or did he purposely ignore it?—did he glimpse, on the hillside far above the village in the valley, his home, Hui Aloha, Gathering Place of Love, just a tiny whitewashed dollhouse from this distance, surrounded by rail-fenced breeding pens or paddocks with low walls of native volcanic rock, where cows frolicked, or corrals where captured wild horses called Mauna Kea broncos were saddle-broken to supply the strings the ranch's cowboys used for cattle-herding.

Although he considered himself a man already, able to work

a grown man's backbreaking day for a grown man's pay, his throat nevertheless constricted like a mewling infant's at the thought of leaving all this beauty behind him. And for what, he thought scornfully? So that he could listen to the droning voices of boring teachers in their dusty robes day in and day out, instead of the wind soughing in the trees, or the lovely native *meles,* songs, sung by men and women he considered his family and friends, clothed in fresh, fragrant lengths of native *tapa*, instead of stifling wool and linen? Why should he willingly condemn himself to reading page after page of dusty textbooks, when he could stay here and listen to Old Moki recite the genealogies of his ancestors in musical Hawaiian, reaching as far back as the old one's great-grandfather had been able to recall, to an almost forgotten time when the first intrepid voyagers—the ones who had been his Polynesian ancestors—had left their native Tahiti in search of new lands to conquer? Could he settle down to lectures in airless halls, when from birth he'd been used to the open air, to the cool sweet winds of the mountains, to the balmy trades, and the fresh, salty gusts off the Pacific? Could he learn to sleep each night in a stuffy chamber, when he was more accustomed to a sleeping mat unrolled on an open veranda when the weather proved too warm for a bed, or a bedroll on a hillside under the stars and the tropical moon? What did he want with all-night study sessions, poring over books by candlelight? Or with endless examinations? Or with blotters and inkwells and ink-stained fingers? With cold and gloomy Boston, in all its shades of gray, instead of the warm, bright sunshine, the vivid colors, the perfumed breezes of the islands? Devil take America! Devil take life as a freshman and Old Campus, too! To Hades with Harvard College itself. Goddamn and blast them all to hell and back! Such an existence was as far removed from his beloved Sandwich Isles as the moon was distant from the sun—and he would have no part of it, he vowed!

Hurling another ripe curse that smacked of the Honolulu wharves at a startled steer, which had emerged from a tangle of *ohia lehua* trees and was thoughtfully chewing its cud until his explosive yell sent it careening away, he kicked poor Akamai into a gallop, not reining him in until they'd reached a small yet perfect bay.

Riding down the narrow, rock-strewn path to the beach proper, he tethered his horse in the shade and dismounted.

A breeze off the ocean fanned the reek of cattle, horses, leather, sweat, and dust to his nose. He sniffed his armpit in disgust. He was the culprit. His shirt was filthy, as well as sweat-soaked, he realized belatedly. The garment had dried and stiffened on the trip there. He tugged off the offending garment, and flung it from his body. His boots, belt, and breeches followed. Standing naked as a young god in the bright sunlight that beat down upon his tanned shoulders, torso, and legs, he gathered up his soiled clothing and strode down to the sparkling water with it.

He let the sea's arms take him; let her cool caresses salve his wounded spirit momentarily in a welcoming embrace, before turning onto his belly to swim. With powerful arms cutting the waves, he moved through the water like a predatory yet graceful shark. Savage, powerful, his strong, angry young body cleaved the glassy water like a deadly fin as he pushed himself to the very limit, ignoring muscles that screamed from fighting the pull of terrified steers since dawn and thighs that throbbed from struggling to stay astride a horse, hoping he could rid himself of the seething rebellion in his heart by hard physical exertion.

But when, much later, he staggered back up the beach, exhausted, nothing had changed. Damn it, he was a fool to think it would have! Well, he'd done more than enough mewling about if-onlys and what-might-have-beens. He could either put a good face on it, and make the very best of his four years in Boston, then return to the life he loved. Or, he could keep complaining bitterly, determined to hate every minute, and have four years of hell. He sighed. Since complaining was alien to his nature, he might as well accept whatever—

The rest of the thought eluded him as Akamai whickered a greeting to another horse. The sound froze him in place on the sand. Should he dive for cover or remain put? Dark-blue eyes narrowed against the dazzling sunlight, he saw the rider following the zigzagging path down the cliff to the sandy cove. It was a woman, her crimson-red skirts billowing around her as she rode!

Remembering belatedly that he was quite naked, he clapped his dripping garments over his groin and dived for cover.

Two

Trying frantically to fit his wet body back into his dripping corduroy breeches—which seemed smaller, somehow, since he'd doused them in the sea—he rolled onto his belly, then wriggled forward on his elbows and knees to peer between the low-hanging, leafy branches of the stunted sea-grape tree under which he'd hidden, trying to see what the wretched woman who'd interrupted his solitude was up to.

He sucked in a startled breath as she slithered from her horse's back about fifteen yards from his hiding place, looped the reins about a handy *akoa* bush, then ran down to the water, cutting loose with an unladylike, joyous whoop as if, much to his relief, she believed herself alone.

Twirling around, she tugged off her woven hat, revealing her face, and Gideon's heart skipped a beat. He could tell straightway by her lovely, beige satin complexion that, like him, the girl was *hapa-haole*—of both Hawaiian and white blood—and quite the loveliest creature he'd ever seen! As he gaped openmouthed at her, a practiced flick of her wrist sent her hat sailing across the sand, then she groaned loudly, plucked pins from her hair, and loosened a glossy, inky waterfall that fell to her hips.

Dry-mouthed, Gideon wondered belatedly if she'd seen him before he dived for cover? Surely she must have! Or at very least, should have seen his horse, and wondered about another rider? Then again, maybe not, he considered hopefully. From her angle, Akamai was probably hidden among the ironwood rees. He frowned. What should he do? Show himself, bid her cordial good day, then leave? He scowled. That was the obvious ourse, but . . . what a damned fool he'd look crawling out from under the low sea-grape tree with his wet breeches twisted about his backside and legs, and sand plastered to his bare chest! Still, he alternative—to remain hidden and risk being mistaken for a 'eeping Tom later—was far from appea—

He sucked in a shocked breath as—clearly believing herself lone, as he'd thought—the lovely stranger suddenly lifted her hapeless crimson, ruffled *muumuu* over her head, and hurled it fter her hat! Wearing only a skimpy lace-trimmed bodice and nee-length drawers—the latter sewn from what looked like leached rice sacks trimmed with eyelets, he noticed, hiding a rin—she suddenly arched forward, plunging into the surf, leav- ng him with a tantalizing view of bare golden calves and small ink-soled feet. She began swimming strongly toward a pair of ocks that jutted up from the bay the very moment the frothy urquoise water surrounded her.

Not till she was several yards off-shore did Gideon release he breath he'd been holding in a shaky *Whoo-eee! Lord Al- ighty!* His broad shoulders slumped as he leaned back against he sea grape's gnarled trunk and closed his eyes, staring up rough the tree's leafy canopy but still seeing the *hapa*-girl in is mind's eye as she'd looked for one titillating second, with er wet undergarments plastered against her lissome body. *Who as she? And how was it possible such an angel could exist on he same island as him, without him knowing of it?*

Ducking back under the sea-grape tree, he decided to wait a while and see what she would do next. After all, he told himself, he couldn't fail to see his horse if he rode off now, and if she id, she'd surely think he'd been spying on her. He certainly idn't want that.

Closing his eyes, he tried to forget the way her tiny nipples ad showed as darker peaks, puckering up the gauzy cloth of her bodice, and the way her hair fanned out behind her like an ebony mantle when she swam . . .

Turning onto her back and floating, the "angel" in question turned her head to sneak a look at the boy on shore—a young man, really—who crouched uncomfortably beneath the sea grape tree farthest from the path she'd ridden down. She giggled. What a silly boy he was, skulking there with his long legs folded up before him so that his knees were on a level with his chin, just as if he were a . . . a grasshopper or some other small animal that could easily hide itself among the low, leafy boughs of the sea-grape tree.

Perhaps, like an ostrich, he believed if he hid his head and couldn't see her, then *she* wouldn't be able to see *him?* The very idea struck her as amusing, and made her giggle merrily again, for had he but known it, she'd seen a great deal more of him as she rode down the zigzagging path to the beach than he knew. Enough to know that his face was very handsome and pleasing to her eyes from a distance, and that *his* eyes were dark, though of what color, she'd been unable to tell. His hair was black, that she knew—as black as the lava her island people called *pahoe hoe,* which cooled into sparkling ebony whorls and thick, glossy waves, while his shoulders, arms, and chest were almost as fair skinned as her own, though tanned darker by the sun than hers were, and far more powerfully muscled. His back was broad as any mountain, his rump flat and tightly muscled, if paler than the rest of him—and his *ule* seemed very large!

She clapped her hand over her mouth to keep from laughing out loud, afraid he would hear her from shore. Judging by the horrified way he'd spotted her, then suddenly clutched his garments over his privates and scuttled frantically beneath the tree like a very large crab—pointing his naked *okole* in her direction!—he must have hoped to hide his man's root from her eyes. She frowned thoughtfully, thinking that the strange youth's modesty was a far cry from the olden days, when Hawaiian chieftains had given their *ules* special names, and revered them as the procreative parts of their bodies. Why, the people had even praised their chief's virility and his physical endowments by singing sacred *meles,* or songs, in praise of his *ule!* What would that shy boy have called his *ule* a hundred years ago? she wondered. Fertile Sea Cucumber? Mighty Spear? Great Toothless Eel? No, no, none of those—not this morning, at least, she amended. She had a much better name: Shrinking Giant!

Deciding she'd best swim, or else run the risk of him hearing her gales of helpless laughter, she turned smoothly onto her belly and struck out toward the twin rocks that gave the cove its name, wondering if he'd pluck up the courage to speak to her when she waded out—or if she would have to speak first.

Shaking his head beneath the sea-grape tree, Gideon thought ruefully, *Tarnation! What that* wahine *does to me! And, if today's like the last three afternoons I've been coming here to spy on her, she won't come out for a good hour, maybe longer!* He sighed heavily. This was the third day since leaving the cattle lading that he'd ridden down to Twin Rocks Cove in hope of seeing the *hapa*-girl again. And, to his delight, his wish had been granted both days, but surely his luck couldn't hold forever? Now, it was up to him. By his reckoning, he had about sixty minutes left in which to decide whether to remain a sneaky Peeping Tom for a fourth day, or be a man and introduce himself to the loveliest girl he'd ever seen. It was now, or never, after all.

Just as he'd feared, the letter his father expected had been delivered the other morning by the *Mariposa*'s captain was the one he'd been dreading since the New Year. He'd been accepted as a freshman student at Harvard College and would be entering in the fall. By this time next month, the ship *Galileo* would have carried him far across the ocean to distant Boston, where four years of stuffy Congregationalist aunts and uncles, a college education, and a (hopefully) brief apprenticeship with the Kane ship-building company and whaling fleet awaited him.

Hell and Damnation! Relishing the taste of the forbidden cuss words on his tongue, he scowled darkly. The prospect of leaving his beloved islands for any length of time was still not one he welcomed, however enthusiastically Father and Makuahine might recommend the experience as "beneficial to the youthful character." Hell, no. He had everything he could ever want right here; fast horses, the dangerous, exciting work of a *paniolo,* and above all, this land—this beautiful, beautiful land!—on which to nourish his soul.

There were literally thousands of acres of Hui Aloha Ranch land, land as diverse as the men who lived and toiled upon it. The terrain varied from slopes littered with jagged black lava rock, hollowed lava tubes surrounded by lush ferns and creepers, to the snowcapped mountain peaks of Mauna Kea; from plunging valleys threaded with sparkling waterfalls, to lush green plateaus. And for as far as the eye could see, Kane cattle grazed and grew fat on the range beneath a vault of glorious tropical-blue sky. His fierce scowl deepened. Only a fool would willingly abandon this Paradise on earth for stuffy old Bean Town, snow cold weather, and gray faces—and he was no fool.

Gideon shaded his eyes against the brilliant light as the girl's slim gold arm crested the waves and a seal-dark head rose above the whitecaps. Damn, but she was a beauty! Distracted, distant Boston and college once again receded into memory, paling alongside the far more pleasing pastime of watching the *hapa-* girl swimming. When she waded back up the beach, her skimpy bodice would be clinging to her curves, her small breasts making darker peaks against the almost transparent wet cloth, and the prospect made him scowl in self-disgust. Just watching her made his loins ache unbearably, but—for reasons he didn't understand—his youthful, lusty responses angered him, too; filled him with a shame and confusion he'd never felt before.

Despite his youth, and despite being the grandson of stout

Congregationalist missionary stock, Gideon was far from innocent. He knew what went on between a man and a woman first-hand, for his father's younger brother, Uncle Sheldon—surely the only black sheep of the Kane family—had seen to that facet of his education two years ago, during one of the rare summers when he'd stayed on the island of Oahu with his aunt and uncle, instead of coming home to the Big Island when the school year ended.

"Let my brother worry about your college applications. It's time we saw to your education in—um . . . other directions, my boy," Uncle Sheldon had promised with a rascally wink. Taking him by the elbow, he'd led Gideon through the warren of narrow streets down by the wharves of Honolulu; streets whose Hawaiian names meant Fragrant Breast Street, or Heavenly Kisses Street—names, he was soon to discover, that aptly extolled the wares to be found in the bawdy houses there!

Gideon's eyes had widened at the lovely native, Oriental, and white beauties he saw lolling indolently in the doorways, their hair falling loose about their dusky shoulders. Wearing only lengths of flower-printed calico wound about their nubile brown-, white-, or gold-skinned bodies, they'd beckoned to the passersby, inviting the men to join them in their sultry, singsong voices.

"You numbah-one handsome boy!" one woman—younger than the others—had squealed in delight on spying Gideon. "Come to Kolina, yeh, *ku'uipo?* She make you plenty happy tonight!"

To Gideon's amazement, his uncle Sheldon had winked and handed him over to the smiling *wahine* with a sharp nudge in the small of his back, leaving instructions to "knock all o' that stuffed-shirt, missionary nonsense out of him, eh, sweetie?" At which Kolina had giggled and promised with a flutter of dark lashes, "For you, I try my bes', Mistah Kane," as she slipped his uncle's money down her dusky cleavage.

And Gideon had to admit that, by the time dawn had broken, Lina had earned her fee—and royally.

Since then, he'd found one or two willing native girls with whom to practice his lovemaking skills, but . . . what he felt for this *hapa*-girl was something different entirely.

From the moment he'd first seen her, he'd been unable to sleep at night. Indeed, he'd been so preoccupied with thinking about her, his reaction to his father's announcement that the letter from Harvard had arrived had been curiously remote, causing his parents to exchange fond yet puzzled glances over the supper table.

That night, tossing and turning under the shrouds of mosquito netting that curtained his bed, he'd thought about the girl with a single-minded intensity he'd never felt before, finally rising from his bed to go downstairs and wander outside in the cool moonlit night.

He'd strolled the gardens deep in silent thought until exhaustion had finally driven him back to his bed shortly before dawn. The same thing had happened the following night, after he'd seen her again.

"Your *makua,* she is concerned about you, my nephew," Old Moki—the old Hawaiian man who'd come to Waimea with his mother years ago, upon her marriage to his father—had told him this morning as he sat in the gazebo, watching a fine rainshower watering his mother's rose and herb gardens, and idly enjoying the antics of a family of sparrows bathing in a puddle by the sundial. "You sleep poorly. You eat but little. You have dark shadows beneath your eyes and your belly grows thin. You talk very little—and laugh not at all. Why is this, my nephew? Is your spirit sick?"

"Perhaps I have nothing to laugh about, Uncle," Gideon said with a heavy sigh.

Moki nodded his white head sagely. "A wise man might wonder if you are sick with love for a *wahine a ka po,*" he observed with deceptive casualness that made Gideon want to smile, though of course he did not, out of respect for the old man's age and wisdom.

A *wahine a ka po* was, in its literal translation, a night woman;

beautiful female spirit that came to a man's bed by night—
perhaps rising from the sea, or even leaving the cool dark depths
of a mountain stream—to become his lover. Such visitations
could prove so pleasing, a man would grow enamored of his
night mistress, and want always to sleep, just to be near her. He
would forget to eat or drink, and to fish or hunt, for love of her.
And, eventually, the spirit woman would persuade the mortal
man's spirit to stay in the spirit world with her, and his body
would sicken and die.

"What!" Gideon exclaimed.

"What else is your mother to believe, my nephew? For many
days, you have been behaving strangely, and Haunani is worried
about you." Haunani, Dew of Heaven, was his mother's Hawaiian name. "And if it is not a night woman, then it must be the
news from America that has made you this way. She knows you
are heartsick because you do not want to leave here, although
you seek to hide this from your father. You will tell me the truth.
Is it so?" Moki asked sternly. Since Gideon was an infant, the
old Hawaiian man—who was reputedly a *kahuna,* or native
priest, and gifted in many arts—had appointed himself Gideon's
guardian, keeping Haunani and Jacob Kane's long and dearly
awaited *hiapo*—firstborn—and those the child loved, safe from
harm, caring for him as solicitously as any mother hen might
cosset her favorite chick.

It was Old Moki who'd been trusted with Gideon's *piko,* his
navel cord, by the midwives following his birth, carefully
wrapped in a piece of soft *tapa* cloth, so that Moki might hide
it in the niche of a rock known only to him, safe from evil spirits
and sorcerers, according to the old Hawaiian way. It was Old
Moki who cut Gideon's hair whenever it was necessary, too, and
he who buried the dark trimmings in the ground to keep them
out of the reach of those evil ones who might seek to do him
harm.

Though Gideon questioned the old superstitions, he loved and
respected his mother and the old man, and would never offend

them, nor hurt their feelings by saying so. Accordingly, he smiled and ruefully shook his head in answer to Old Moki's question. "There is *no wahine a ka po,* my uncle, but rather a very beautiful, very *real* flesh-and-blood *wahine* who has stolen my heart. It is thoughts of her beauty that disturb my sleep and make me restless."

"*He! He!* And are you sure it is your heart she has stolen, my nephew?" the old rogue asked slyly, and, bloodshot eyes twinkling, he winked and grinned broadly at Gideon, showing the gap where his incisors had been dashed out years before, an action to show his sorrow at losing his wife.

The young man returned his grin and nodded. "Alas, yes."

"Aah. So that is the way the wind blows! And will you speak to your parents of this maiden? Will you ask them to go to the house of her parents?" That had been the way of things in Moki's time, when a young man's heart had chosen a certain *wahine* and no other would do. The young man's family went to speak with the girl's family, and if all agreed, then the young people would become man and wife.

"In time, perhaps, Uncle. For now, I know only that I cannot bear to think of leaving her—although she does not even know that I exist!"

Offering a polite excuse, he escaped to the corrals and roped the young bronco he'd started breaking the previous week, before Moki could press him for details about the girl's family, her bloodlines, her virtue, and her character he could not possibly supply, in his ignorance. He strongly suspected anything he ever said would fall far short of Moki's standards. After all, his mother, Miriam Haunani Kane—half Hawaiian on her mother's side—was a descendant of the great Hawaiian king, Kamehameha. Her father had likewise been a man of considerable breeding; a British Naval captain, Sir Thaddeus Gideon, who'd retired to the Sandwich Isles, and for whom Gideon had been named. Time enough later to discuss pedigrees, he thought ruefully. For now, it was enough that he find the courage to wish the girl a good day!

Over the past three days he'd spent watching her, he'd come to the conclusion it must be more than lust he was feeling for the elusive water sprite. He wanted . . . he wanted to *talk* to her, to learn her feelings and opinions on anything and everything under the sun. To whisper his dreams, hopes and ambitions in her shell-like ears, knowing—in some mysterious way!—that she would laugh neither at them nor at what he had to say. He wanted to take her little hand in his and wander with her along the moonlit sands, lost in silent communion. Or else to see her lovely lips part in a smile, to hear her silvery laughter like the song of a waterfall, and know he'd been the one to make her smile, that it was his teasing that had made her laugh.

He grunted, disgusted with himself. He wanted . . . he wanted, and yet, he was too damned yellow to even show himself, let alone ask her name, damn it! Well, enough was enough! Either he would make some move to introduce himself today, or else he'd—

"Didn't you hear me? I asked, What's—up—there?" an impatient female voice suddenly inquired, yelling the words as if his hearing was severely impaired. *"I've craned my neck till I'm blue in the face, but I can't see a thing. Is it a bat? A bird? A lizard?"*

Three

Gideon's head snapped around so sharply, he could hear the bones in his neck crack, loud as popping corn.

She—*the girl!*—was standing only a few feet from him! Her hair streamed over her golden shoulders in dripping black arabesques, while her wet chemise clung to her body, gloriously outlining its budding curves. He gallantly went through the motions of averting his eyes, but she, rather than appearing embarrassed, smiled back at him with no trace of maidenly modesty whatsoever. Rather, her dark eyes sparkled mischievously as she crossed her arms over her breasts and looked boldly down at him.

"Well?" she challenged when, tonguetied, Gideon still said nothing. "What's wrong, *hapa-haole* boy? Cat got your tongue?"

"No! No, I . . . er . . . !" he began, jumping to his feet and dusting the sand from the seat of his breeches. "I was just . . . daydreaming, I suppose you'd say," he explained lamely, and could have kicked himself for sounding such a priggish fool.

"Daydreaming. Hmm," she said, gravely nodding, the corners of her mouth twitching impishly. "Daydreaming, was it? Then I suppose you must do a great deal of *daydreaming*, must you not?"

He stiffened. "I beg your pardon?"

"I said, you must daydream a great deal, because I've seen you here before, sitting in this very same spot. In fact, you've been here every day this week."

"Just the last three days, actually," he blurted out, and felt his ears grow red with embarrassment as he did so.

"Yes. It must be about that long," she agreed, casting him a disconcerting, level look from a pair of wide violet eyes.

They were, he noticed, dry-mouthed, very lovely eyes, too: large, dark, and thickly fringed with long, curling lashes the color of lamp-blacking. The amethyst-colored irises were flecked with tiny motes of gold. Aah, yes, they were beautiful, haunting eyes, eyes with a hint of some secret sadness in their depths that her smiling lips denied.

"Be honest. Is that *really* what you were doing—daydreaming?"

He shook his head and grinned, a trifle sheepish. "Not really, no. After the—er, after the first day, I've been coming here just to—just to see you." There. The truth was out. The loveliest *wahine* he'd ever seen, and he'd made a perfect jackass of himself. He couldn't blame her if she jumped back on her horse and rode off without giving him a backward glance.

"Really? So have I! I've been coming here to see *you!*" she confessed to his utter amazement and delight. "And since I'd quite given up on you ever speaking to me, I decided I'd have to speak to you!" She smiled again, more shyly this time, risking a peek at him from beneath her sooty curtain of lashes. "You don't mind, do you? You don't think it's terribly forward of me?"

"You mean, you knew I was here all the while?"

"The whole time, silly!" she admitted. "You're hardly invisible, after all, Gideon Kane. I mean, how *could* you be, a big old thing like you, even if you *did* hide beneath that silly little tree like an ostrich with its head in the sand."

"You know my name!"

"Oh, yes." He caught a flash of pretty white teeth as she smiled mysteriously, and swept her wet hair back, over her golden shoulders. Her lustrous lashes swept down again, seductive fans that made his groin tighten unbearably as she explained, "After the first time I saw you, I made it my business to find out. I asked about you at the saddler's, and at the church—everywhere."

He didn't ask why. Strangely, there was no need to ask! Their eyes met and—a thrill running down his spine—he knew instinctively that she felt just as he did: as if they'd known each forever, and all of a sudden, he felt peculiarly light, weightless, as if he could rise up, off the ground, with as little effort as a French balloon, and float away.

"You're lovely," he blurted out, wanting to bite his tongue the instant the words popped out.

"Am I really?" she asked, sounding as if she was truly interested in his answer, rather than trying to wring another compliment from him.

Dry-mouthed still, he nodded.

"Then *mahalo nui loa!* Thank you very much! Guess what?"

He shrugged.

"So are you!" she came back cheekily, her velvety pansy eyes shining, the sadness in their depths quite gone. "Now that that's all over with, come on! Come swimming with me! The water's lovely and warm—and I've wasted three whole days, waiting to share it with you," she reminded him, pouting delightfully.

He needed no further invitation. Dragging the shirt Auntie Leolani had starched and ironed so carefully that morning over his head, he dropped it to the sand as if it were a rag mop; kicked off his brown leather riding boots, and shucked off his cord breeches, clumsy in his haste. Finally, wearing only his cotton drawers, his bare torso sparsely sprinkled with hair yet deeply tanned from countless skinny-dipping excursions, he held out his hand to her in invitation.

"What? You're not going to take those off today?" she teased, nodding at his unmentionables and quite unable to keep the laughter from her voice. "As I recall, you weren't wearing quite as many clothes the first time I saw you, Mister Kane."

So, she had seen him, as he'd feared, the minx! "Will you take yours off?" he challenged, nodding at her bodice and pantalets as if he could see straight through them. When she said nothing but simply stood there, her eyes downcast, a warm blush filling her cheeks, he grinned in triumph and offered her his hand again.

To his delight, her blush deepened but she took it nonetheless, slipping a slender hand with a *hula* dancer's long, tapering fingers into his as she murmured naughtily, "Later, perhaps . . ."

He grinned. "Then so will I."

Together, laughing, they ran headlong into the surf, Boston and Harvard forgotten.

For two golden hours, Gideon and the girl swam in the warm waters of the Pacific, frolicking like porpoises, diving like young seals, delighting in each other's company until daylight suddenly faded into the flamingo pinks, flames, sulphurs, and charcoal of a glorious tropical sunset.

The sun had set, then vanished completely over the rim of the horizon, and a foamy full moon was fully risen when they at last emerged from the water. Hand in hand, they followed the curve of the bay, walking along the warm, wet sand to dry off just as he'd imagined walking with her from the first day he'd seen her. She was all Gideon had dreamed she'd be, and more.

"Would you meet me here again tomorrow?" he asked, trying to disguise his eagerness. He didn't want to leave her. Couldn't bring himself to say goodbye. What the devil would he do if she said no, she wouldn't see him again? It was, suddenly, the most important thing in the world that she say "yes."

She shrugged her slender shoulders expressively. "I don't know if I can . . ." she began, and his heart dropped to the pit of his belly like a stone.

"But why not? You have to try!" he insisted fervently, and quite forgetting propriety, he touched her cheek. Catching himself a second too late, he drew his hand away as if scalded, keenly aware of how petal-soft her skin had felt against his fingertips in that single, fleeting moment. "Say you will! For me?"

"It's not that I don't want to. It's just that . . . Oh, all right. I'll try." She bit her lower lip and looked down at her bare, sandy feet, scuffing one against the other to dislodge the powdery grains. "But . . . I can't promise."

"Why ever not?" he blurted out. "Is something wrong?"

"Yes. Very. It's my *makuahine,* my mother," she murmured, her voice sounding choked with tears. "She's very ill. She has *ma'i a'ai,* and she only has me to care for her. My . . . my father is often away, you see?"

So that explained it! It wasn't that she didn't want to see him again, but that her *makuahine* had cancer, and she was taking care of her on her own. His heart going out to her, he nodded in sympathy and understanding. A sick heaviness filled his chest just thinking of his own mother being similarly stricken. How could she bear it, his poor, brave little love? he wondered. But to her he only murmured, "That's awful. I'm really sorry."

"So am I," she admitted with a sigh. "At first, the *kahunas,* the priests and healers, said they could help her. They believed the sickness had come because she'd displeased an *aumakua,* a household god, in some way, or else was being prayed to death by someone. So, we made offerings as the *kahunas* told us, and many prayers were said, yet nothing worked, so last month, I sent the *kahunas* away and had Doctor Forrester come and examine her, instead. He diagnosed her illness very quickly. There's very little he can do, except give her medicines to make her comfortable."

"Is she going to—?" He swallowed, unable to say the word.

"Die?" she finished for him. "We really don't know. Doctor Forrester couldn't say, so we try to enjoy each new day that dawns as a gift from God, whether she's with me for weeks, or months, or even years. Anyway, *Makua* takes laudanum most afternoons so that she can rest for a little while. And when she's sleeping, it's all right if I'm gone for an hour or two. So you see, whether I can come here or not depends on how she's feeling. I'm sorry I can't promise you."

She smiled up at him, and his heart skipped a beat. There was such sweetness, such innocent vulnerability and *goodness* radiating from her, she made him feel clumsy and black with sin, all at once. There was something about her . . . some elusive quality that drew him like a reckless moth to a dazzling flame. She made him want to protect her, cherish her; to spare her the ugliness of life—though why that strangely disturbing thought should pop into his head in that moment, he did not know, unless it was because they'd been talking about her mother's dreadful illness.

"Yes, please try. If you're late, it doesn't matter. I'll still be here. I'll wait, no matter how late you might be. Just . . . just come, if not tomorrow, then the next day, or the next."

"All right." With a quick smile, she retrieved her hat and *muu-muu* from the sand, dressed, and walked slowly back to the horse she'd left tethered beneath the ironwoods. She cast him several shy yet lingering looks over her shoulder as she went, then looked quickly away—though not before he'd seen the telltale blush that filled her cheeks, and the tiny hint of a smile that tugged at the corners of her mouth. He was almost certain that she liked him, too, and felt as if he were walking on air!

He followed her, taking quick, long strides up the beach, wanting to touch her, however briefly, in his reluctance to let her go; looking for any excuse, however small, however contrived, to make her stay even a moment longer.

"Aloha oe, Gideon Kane!" she told him softly, leaning down from the saddle to catch his hand in her own. She drew it to her lips and kissed his broad, calloused knuckles in farewell, loving the leathery masculinity and huge size of his hands.

The contact stunned him, for it was as if a bolt of lightning had moved from her body through his in that charged second before she drew her hand away.

Smiling shyly and seeming quite unaware of the chaos she'd created in his heart, she turned her horse's head inland, toward the Kohala foothills.

"Wait!" Gideon cried, reaching for her horse's cheek strap as it leaped forward. "Your name! Fool! What can I have been thinking of?" he berated himself, slapping a palm to his forehead. "I don't even know your name!"

She laughed. "It's Emma Jordan. Emma Kaleilani Jordan," she called over her shoulder.

"Emma," he repeated. "Lovely Emma!" For one delirious moment, he thought she might lean down and kiss his cheek, but then she was gone in a rush of flowing black hair and billowing dark-red skirts, leaving his hand still tingling where her lips had pressed it.

Four

Gideon's happiness knew no bounds when Emma returned to Twin Rocks Cove the following day, although a little later than she'd arrived the other afternoons.

"You came!" he exclaimed, knowing how inane he sounded even as he said it.

"Yes! Sorry I'm late."

"Never mind that. Better late than never!" he reminded her as he came to meet her. His dark-blue eyes were sparkling with pleasure in his tanned, handsome face as he reached up to lift her down from her horse. Long after her feet had safely touched the ground, he continued to stand there with his hands spanning her tiny waist. What a slender slip of a girl she was, he thought fondly, for the top of her head reached only an inch or two above his shoulders.

"I would have been here sooner, but my father came home just as I was leaving," she explained, seeming nervous somehow as she slipped from his hold.

"Your father! Won't he be angry that you've left your *makuahine* alone to be with me?"

"He'll probably be angry that I'm gone, yes—though not for the reasons you imagine. But don't worry. He won't find out I'm with you." She scowled, then shrugged her shoulders as if the matter of her father was unimportant. Looping Makani's reins about a bush, she smiled at Gideon. "Come on. Let's swim!"

"All right. But first, please answer my question, Emma. I don't want to get you into trouble with your parents. Would your father be angry?"

She glared at him. "You won't get me into trouble, silly. My *makuahine* knows all about you."

"She does? And she doesn't mind you coming here?"

Emma shook her dark head so that her inky ringlets jiggled about like springs. "Not a bit. If you want to know, she thinks you sound very handsome." A mischievous grin made her eyes sparkle wickedly. "Naturally, I exaggerated your good points when I described you to her."

"Oh, naturally." He flashed her a rueful grin that quickly faded. "But, getting back to what you were saying. You feel your father would mind you being with me, if he knew? Is that it?"

"Yes! Are you satisfied now? Is that what you wanted me to say? Now, that's enough about my father! I don't want to talk about him, thank you—and that's an end to it!"

Gideon's lips thinned. *Where was his head? Of course her father would mind! Any father worthy of the name would be livid if he discovered his lovely young daughter was meeting with a boy—any boy, not just him!—without benefit of a chaperon! And it was probably Emma's guilt that was making her so waspish.* "Then perhaps I should meet with your father face-to-face, and introduce myself? I'm sure it would help if I explained my intentions toward you?"

His suggestion occasioned an unladylike snort from Emma. "Oh, come, come! Even *you* wouldn't dare do that, Gideon Kane!" she scoffed. "Jack'd shoot your head off with his bullock gun as soon as look at you if you even hinted at your *true* intentions toward me!"

Gideon knew she was referring to his wandering hands the evening before, and had the grace to look shamefaced. "On second thought, maybe the truth wouldn't be such a good idea!" he agreed ruefully. "What if I just asked his permission to court you, instead?"

"No!" she insisted hotly, her violet eyes flashing. "No, no, no, to all of it! My mother knows about us, and that's enough. If you try to meet with my father or come anywhere near our *hale pili,* our grass shacks, I'll never, ever speak to you again, Gideon Kane, I swear it, understand? *Never, do you hear me?"*

He threw up his hands in surrender, surprised and taken aback by her vehemence. Well! Well! When angered, his sweet, gentle little Emma could turn like a cornered cat and become a veritable spitfire! He couldn't help but wonder what it was she was so anxious to hide. "I hear you, loud and clear! If you don't want me to talk to your father, then I won't, I promise. You don't have to get so *hu'hu* about it!" he shot back at her.

After a moment's hesitation, she nodded. Her shoulders sagged and she seemed to calm down. "All right, then." In a smaller voice she added, "Gideon—?"

"What?" Hands balled at his sides, he did not turn to look at her.

"I'm sorry I yelled at you. Forgive me?" she asked his stiff back.

"Maybe I will."

"Just maybe?" she coaxed. "Oh, please say you will! I couldn't bear it if you were mean to me."

Her pleading tone melted his hard heart. "Weeell, if you make it worth my while, I might consider it."

"Very well. Name your price, sir," she agreed readily, a coy smile dimpling her cheeks. "Anything!"

"Anything?

"Yes!"

"A kiss, then."

"You're much too easily pleased!" she crowed, going up on tiptoe and kissing him quickly, lightly, on the cheek while he leaned against the trunk of a coconut palm, his muscular arms crossed over his broad chest while he tried to look bored and unimpressed by her efforts.

"Hey, not so fast, brat!" he drawled when she drew back,

tweaking a length of her long black hair. "When I said I wanted a kiss, I meant a real one, right here," he said sternly, pointing to his lips. "Not some hasty little peck on the cheek."

Rolling her eyes in exasperation, Emma again went up on tiptoe, puckered her lips, and chastely pressed them to Gideon's. She would have quickly moved away afterward had Gideon not caught her around the neck and held her head firmly in one place so that her mouth was pressed to his. Her eyes closed as he kissed her long and hard, her lashes quivering like ebony moths upon her cheeks.

A throaty chuckle escaped him when he finally released her, for those lashes came up like a pair of flirtatious fans and her beautiful eyes widened in breathless surprise, the irises a dazzling, liquid shade of amethyst in the sunlight as she exclaimed, "Oh!"

"There! Consider yourself well and truly forgiven, Miss Jordan! Shall we swim now?" he asked huskily.

Unable to speak, she nodded.

As they had on the days before, they swam lazily in the warm ocean together, then dried off by riding their horses along the sandy beach that followed the curve of the little bay.

"I know. Let's race! Last one to the lovers' rocks loses!" Emma cried, her earlier outburst apparently forgotten. Before Gideon could either accept or refuse her challenge, she'd dug her heels into her mare's sides. The horse suddenly streaked forward, like an arrow shot from a bow.

"Hey! No fair, brat!" Gideon roared. "I wasn't ready!" He kicked his mount after hers, his gray stallion soon catching up with the smaller yet game little horse.

Neck and neck the pair raced, manes and tails flying, hooves scattering clods of wet sand in their wake as they galloped around the bay to the farthest point, where the crescent of sand gave way to natural breakwaters of rock.

"I win!" Emma's sweet voice was breathless. Reining in her mare level with the dark rock formation she'd chosen as their finishing post—a prominent landmark that rose above the sparkling waters of the bay—she dismounted and flopped down on the sand.

"I'm not surprised you won. You had a head start," he accused, grinning.

"I did, didn't I?" she admitted naughtily, smiling a smug smile and sticking out her small pink tongue. "And what shall you do about it, sir?"

"Oh, boil you in oil, maybe? Or sell you to Arab slave traders? Then again, I could always . . ." He paused, lips pursed as if considering a strong possibility.

"Could always what?" she asked warily as he circled her slowly, like a stalking cat.

"Ohhh, I could always . . . pick you up—" he dived for her suddenly, arms locking about her waist, "—like this, and dump you in the ocean! Maybe a second dunking would shrink that swelled head of yours and cool that temper!"

So saying, he swung her up into the air and tossed her carelessly into the ocean, ignoring her shrieks of pretended terror.

"You'd best be careful, Gideon Kane," she warned, trying to look cross but failing miserably as she waded, soaked again, from the water. "This beach is a part of my mother's land. It reaches from the sea, clear up into the Kohalas! Lay a hand on me, and the gods will turn you into stone, just like them!" She pointed toward the two tall rocks that jutted up out of the water, side by side.

"Them?" He grinned.

She made a horrible face at him. "Uh huh. *Them.* Oh, go ahead, laugh all you want, but they weren't always just rocks, as you see them now, you know. Long ago, they were sweethearts. Like us," she added pointedly, pleased when he did not correct her.

"Sweethearts, you say?" he echoed.

She nodded. "The young man was a commoner, while the woman was a beautiful princess of royal blood. She was also the *wahine kapu*—the virgin daughter—of a high chieftain, and had been promised from her birth as the bride of yet another important chieftain. Their marriage was to have formed an alliance for her father."

"And? What happened to turn them into stone?" he asked, curious despite himself. According to Old Moki, every rock, spring, plant, and land area in the islands had a legend behind it, and he enjoyed hearing how one spot or another had come by its name. He propped himself up on one elbow to listen, while she sat demurely, slender legs tucked to one side, upon a flat shelf of rock, her damp hair falling in inky seaweed strands about her heart-shaped face.

"They made the mistake of falling in love with each other," she explained simply, "despite their differences. And, for a little while, everything was perfect between them. They met in secret, sometimes by a hidden mountain pool, other times at this very cove, and soon became lovers. But before too long, the princess's father found out about their affair, and sent his warriors to slay his daughter's lover! She begged him to flee south to Honaunau, and the ancient place of refuge there—a place where he would be given sanctuary and pardoned of any wrongdoing—while there was still time. But he refused to leave her to face her father's anger alone. If they could not be together in life, he and the princess decided they would be joined in death, instead. Hand in hand, they waded into the water, letting the fierce currents beyond the reef take them. But the gods took pity on them, and turned them into standing stones, as you see them there. Side by side, hand in hand, they will remain that way forever. Together throughout eternity."

She chanced to look up in that moment, and saw the way he was looking at her; the heat that smoldered in his dark-blue eyes. The intensity and hunger of his expression made her flustered and weak, and stirred gooseflesh in prickly waves down her arms, like the fine, chill rain that fell in the upland valleys.

Afraid he would read an answering heat in her own eyes, she looked quickly away, wondering what on earth had come over her since meeting him? Why did she feel that strange quiver in the pit of her belly and between her thighs whenever he was close to her or kissed her or touched her? And where did that husky little catch in her throat come from, making her tongue-tied and silent when she wanted to say something wicked, something clever and bold that would impress him, and make the silly, fluttery feeling go away?

Whenever she was with him, she felt giddy and confused, happy and sad, all at once! And she behaved like someone else, too, she knew it—someone she hardly knew, nor wanted to know. What in the world had she been thinking of earlier, to snap at him one minute, then challenge him to a race and charge off before he was ready in the next? Just thinking about the way she'd shrieked with childish laughter made her squirm with embarrassment. He must think her *lolo*—a foolish, stupid creature—a mere *child,* when she'd been trying so hard to impress him, to make him see her as older than her years, as a grown woman, instead of some silly schoolgirl.

But, "If you ask me," he only said softly, his eyes caressing and not a trace of scorn in his tone, "the princess must have been a woman worth dying for."

The following afternoon they met again, and explored the tidepools together, finding a huge, ugly black eel with twin rows of sharp teeth caught in one, and tiny brightly colored fish left high and dry by the ebbing tide in others. Gideon chased her with a small crab cupped in his hands that he threatened to drop down the neckline of her bodice, his feet leaving a trail of deep prints in the damp, unmarked sands. She ran from him, screaming once again in mock terror, though no island-born *wahine* would truly fear such a tiny sea creature. Noo, it was the stranger inside her again, acting foolishly.

As afternoon wore on to evening, Gideon gathered shells for her, presenting her with them as if they were priceless pearls, and she, *ali'i nui*, a high chieftess. With a regal incline of her head, she thanked him gravely and accepted his offering, murmuring, "And now, in return for your peerless gifts, Sir Knight, I likewise have a gift for thee!" With that, she brandished the swollen sea cucumber she'd hidden behind her back, and squirted it at him, shrieking with laughter once again as, taken unawares, he leaped backward from the spray as if scalded.

"That's it!" Gideon roared. "You've done it now! If it's war you want, my lady, then 'tis war ye'll have! Beware, great Mo'o, the dragon of the deep—!"

He ducked down behind a rock, then sprang out from behind it with a ghastly roar, ribbons of black or dark-red or green seaweed dangling over his face and festooning his broad shoulders like some horrible sea monster. Hands raised, fingers curved like claws before him, he swayed from side to side. "Come to me, my beauty!" he commanded in a deep, snarling voice, and made a sudden lunge at her. "Let us go down to my kingdom, many fathoms beneath the sea!"

"Oooh! Get away, you horrid boy!" she cried, and fled down the beach with Gideon—armed to the teeth with still more seaweed mops—bounding after her, roaring threats and hurling the mops at her one after the other, with deadly accuracy.

When they were exhausted by their seaweed battle, they gathered a pile of driftwood and Gideon built them a huge, crackling fire, for the breeze off the ocean had grown markedly chill and damp.

Flopping down beneath the sea-grape tree to enjoy its warmth, they "talked-story," as the island people called it, while they enjoyed the cheery blaze, and the way showers of orange sparks whipped up by the wind whirled away into the gathering dusk.

Shyly at first, then with mounting ease, they held hands and traded dreams and ambitions, then swapped spooky legends they'd learned at their mothers' knees until the light faded and night had truly fallen.

Nestled arm in arm now, they shared myths about the Hawaiian demigod, Maui, who'd tried to harness the mighty Sun in his daily ride across the sky so that his mother's *tapa* cloth would dry more slowly. Other such myths told of the volcano goddess, Pele, who appeared to mere mortals either as a frightening, wrinkled old crone or as a beautiful maiden with flowing red hair. According to legend, the goddess could—when angered, or ignored, or refused help or food in any of her guises—cause rivers of molten lava to spew over the island, unless she was first properly placated with offerings and prayers.

"I know a *hula* in honor of the goddess Pele," Emma murmured after Gideon had finished his story. "Would you like me to dance it for you?" she offered shyly.

He almost groaned aloud. Would he like her to dance the forbidden *hula* for him? Hah! Was the grass green? The sky blue? He nodded, trying not to look as eager as he felt. "I would, very much. That is, if you'd like to dance for me?"

She smiled and stood, and then, still clad in only her clinging damp bodice and damp eyelet-trimmed pantalets, she took up her position and began to dance, her bare feet tapping the rhythm, her lovely hands describing with fluid, graceful motions how the fire goddess, Pele, had desired the handsome, flashing-eyed Kamapua'a, a demigod who was part wild boar, part mortal, and had wanted to mate with him. Kamapua'a had desired the beautiful, fiery-haired goddess, too, but they were always fighting and quarreling and trying to outdo each other, rather than admitting their true feelings for each other. The graceful motions of Emma's *hula* explained that indeed, the fierceness of their battles was equaled only by the intensity of their inevitable matings. Lusty Kamapua'a would pursue Pele, but each time he came close to catching her, she would hurl hot boulders at him and rain showers of molten lava over his head while roaring at him to go away and leave her be. Kamapua'a would then retaliate with rainstorms, until he'd finally overpowered lovely Pele by almost dousing her fire. Only then could he force her to submit to his attentions and make passionate love to her! There were many sites in the islands where—or so the legends claimed—their fierce, lusty matings had occurred: areas where it appeared a great struggle had taken place.

Another verse of the dance told how Pele, jealous of her beautiful sister Hi'iaka's graceful *hula* dancing, had transformed poor Hi'iaka into a balancing stone, forcing her to rock gently to and fro until the end of time.

The languid sway of Emma's hips against the moonwashed ocean as she mimicked Hi'iaka's rocking motions mesmerized Gideon. The delicate gestures of her long, slender fingers bewitched him. With her drying hair transformed into a glowing reddish, nimbus of curls and wisps by the roaring driftwood fire at her back, it seemed she did not merely dance a *hula* sacred to Pele, but, for a short time, she *became* Pele.

Time stood still. Reality receded. In Emma's movements, Gideon could see Kamapua'a's fierce attempts to woo the goddess to his forest bower, or her sister, poor Hi'iaka's wonderful dancing. The liquid undulations of her hips became the fluid dance of angry Pele's fiery rivers of lava as they flowed down the sides of her mountain home on their headlong rush to the sea.

On still another, earthier level, he saw the way her eyes seemed to soften and burn with desire when she looked down at him. He noted the moistness of her slightly parted lips, the way her breasts rubbed against the damp cloth of her bodice, how her hair swirled about her in a heavy cloud as she turned to and fro, the gentle roll of her buttocks, the flash of bared golden thigh or shapely ankle, and grew hard as the standing stones. Even the lust of Kamapua'a for his Pele paled beside the lust of Gideon Kane for his Emma! His mouth felt dry. His treacherous manhood hardened and rose hugely in response to her female charms, until it seemed she must surely notice.

"Who—er—taught you the *hula?*" he asked huskily, hoping to divert his thoughts in boring small talk.

"I learned how to dance at the convent of the Sacred Cross in Honolulu," she supplied with just the tiniest twitch of merriment at the corners of her delectable mouth. If she noticed he was behaving strangely, she gave no sign of it. "I attended the orphanage school there until last month, when my mother fell sick and they sent for me to come home. In just a few more months, I would have received my teaching certificate." There was regret in her tone.

"The Catholic sisters taught you the *hula?*" Gideon exclaimed in disbelief. The lovely yet sensual native dance—considered lascivious by the strict missionary fathers—had been banned in the islands for several years, though he knew the art had continued to flourish in secret. In such a fashion, his own *makua* had learned to dance the lovely *hula* as a little girl, and had never forgotten her *kumu hula's* teachings, he knew. "You learned at a *convent?*"

"In a manner of speaking, yes," she confirmed impishly. "You see, whenever I was naughty, Sister Mary Angela used to banish me to the convent gardens. She'd set me to weeding or hoeing the vegetable patches there, in punishment for my sins. And— since I sinned rather frequently—I spent many hours there! Often, when I was supposed to be dutifully weeding, I'd hear the throb of the gourd drums or the click of the bamboo sticks and know that the King's Court *hula halau,* hula troupe, was practicing in the garden next door to the convent, where their *kumu hula,* their hula teacher, lived! I used to climb up onto the wall between the two gardens and sit there for ages. Then, after I'd watched them and learned the steps and the hand movements, I'd practice what I saw. So there you have it!"

"Well, it worked. You dance like an angel," he murmured, his voice husky, his gentian eyes still dark and stormy with desire.

She grinned. "If I don't, then I certainly should. I was very naughty, you see, so I had lots of opportunities for practice! I'm—er—also very good at weeding," she added with a giggle.

When they returned to the place where their clothing lay forgotten, the air between them had grown thick with tension. Neither of them could look at each other, let alone speak.

"Emma?" he whispered.

"Yes?" she answered without turning to look at him. She did not trust herself to do so.

"Oh, Emma . . . Emma!" Unable to hold back any longer, Gideon turned her to face him, pressed her roughly back against the trunk of a coconut palm and, without another word, took her in his arms and held her for the very first time, inhaling the herb-and-white ginger fragrance of her hair, the musk of her salty skin. Meeting no resistance, he tilted her chin up and kissed her hungrily, cradling her damp head in both hands as he crushed his mouth over hers.

The sweetness of her yielding lips, the eager press of her ripening body against his own hard angles and planes, the innocent warmth of her tentative responses, were almost more than he could bear! And yet, he told himself he would not take her; swore he would not follow his body's slavish urging through to their logical conclusion. She was not generous with her favors, like the other girls he'd bedded; girls who didn't give a jot who they coupled with, or if they bore a *keiki a pueo,* an owl's child, as illegitimate children were called. What was more, it would be unfair for him to take Emma as his woman, when he'd soon be leaving for Boston, he reminded himself unhappily, recalling for the first time since he'd met her that his time was running out and that Harvard College awaited.

His throat ached of a sudden, and the burning sensation was back, behind his eyes. How would he find the words to tell her he was leaving, after all they'd shared this week? More importantly, how ever would he endure the next four years without her? It had been a nightmare imagining himself leaving these beloved islands. How much worse it would be now that he must leave his darling Emma, too!

A tremor ran through him as he cupped his hand over the small, firm mound of her breast. The tiny nipple at its peak stirred and grew hard as a little whorled shell in response to the brush of his thumb. Trustingly, she let him caress her breasts as he chose, uttering only a small, contented sigh—like a kitten's purr—to show her pleasure.

He closed his eyes, overcome by emotion and hard with youthful lust as he tentatively ran his hand down over her sleek, damp body to her flat belly and from there to the little shield-shaped mound above the joining of her thighs. His heart thumping like a gourd drum in his ears, he touched her there, above her pantalets. Holy Moses, he could feel the heat of her, even through the wet cloth; could feel, too, her breath fanning his cheek as she gasped. Emboldened, he slipped his hand lower, until it was firmly lodged between her thighs, then stayed very still, scarce breathing, his blood roaring like a whirlwind in his ears and throbbing in his aching *ule*.

She began to tremble then, but made no move to push his hand away. He waited for what seemed an eternity before daring to continue, slipping his hand slowly, oh, so slowly, up the leg of her pantalets below the knee, gliding up over the sleek length of a thigh until he found the warm folds of silky flesh between them. *Oh, Lord, she felt so wonderful!* He would have tried an even more intimate caress, had her hand not firmly covered his in that moment.

"No!" she whispered hoarsely.

To her relief, he drew his hand away without protest, sliding his arms about her waist instead and drawing her against his chest. Holding her so tightly, she feared her ribs would snap, he buried his face in her hair and murmured, "I'm sorry. It won't happen again, I swear it. It's just that . . . God, you're so lovely, Emma, you make me crazy! Forgive me?"

"Hush, hush. There's nothing to forgive," she assured him,

her own voice husky with desire. "Can't you tell that I want you, too? That it took all of my willpower to say no?"

A shudder ran through him. *She wanted him, and the good Lord knew he wanted her!* He ached to press her down to the ground and cover her throat and breasts with kisses; to lodge himself between her silky thighs, sheath himself deep in her sweetness and put an end to his torture. And yet, he could not. Or rather, *would* not, he amended. He was a man, not some rutting lecher, while she . . . she was a lovely young woman, a treasure to be cherished, wooed and won with a wedding ring; not some painted doxy to be used then carelessly discarded without second thought, as the sailors used the native women. "I should leave."

"You're angry that I refused you. I knew you would be!"

"It's not that at all. Don't even think it. It's just that I can't bear being here with you like this, without wanting to . . ." He shook his head. "This is impossible. Perhaps I'd better go home and cool off, before I—we!—yield to temptation? For tonight, anyway?" So saying, he ducked his head and kissed her full on the mouth.

It was a long, passionate kiss—one that more than settled her doubts. Surely he wouldn't kiss her so ardently if he were truly angry? And when he tried to part her lips with his tongue, instead of turning her head away, she opened her mouth beneath his like a flower unfolding its petals to the sun. He felt her breathing quicken, felt her breasts rising and falling rapidly against his chest, and an answering shudder moved through him.

"You're right. I think it's best you leave," she whispered, for it was as if she was drunk on the night, on his kisses and her need for him.

"Yes," he agreed, nuzzling her earlobes, torching a path of tiny, searing kisses down her slender throat to the fragrant hollows at its base, where her pulse throbbed wildly. "We should both go." Setting his jaw, he firmly put her from him. "It's dark, and your *makua* will be wondering where you are, my love. Go on home. I'll see to dousing the fire."

She nodded, gathering up her things. "All right. And you?"

"I think I'll take one last swim before I head home," he ground out, thrusting his hands deep into his pockets and shifting his stance to hide his arousal from her eyes. He didn't explain why he desperately needed that chilly swim. A *wahine* wouldn't understand such things.

"Be careful, then, and I'll . . . Oh, I almost forgot! I have a surprise for you!"

He tried to look interested, though in that moment all his thoughts seemed to have coalesced in his groin. Lord, he hoped and prayed her surprise was a speedy one! Gritting his teeth, he murmured, "Really?"

She nodded. "My aunt is coming up from Waimea village to spend a day or two at our *hale,* our house, with her sister, my *makuahine*. Mama thinks I need a respite from tending to her, so it's all been arranged without any help from me. I'm to ride to Laupahoehoe to visit our 'calabash'—honorary—auntie there tomorrow, then come back home in a day or two, but I was hoping . . . ?" She blushed, thinking how forward she must sound. "That is, if you wanted to, and could get away . . . ?"

". . . that we could spend the time together, instead?" Gideon exclaimed, unable to believe his luck. Two, possibly three days together? It would be heaven on earth!

"What else?" she agreed, laughing at his foolish grin. "But only if you want to," she repeated, shy all over again. "Do you? Want to?"

"What do you think?" he challenged, but his broad, wicked grin was answer enough.

Five

The sky was red enough to serve as warning to an armada of sailors the following morning, yet Gideon and Emma were too excited by the prospect of two whole days—and nights—together to notice it, or if they did, too sensible to set much store in silly superstitions.

They met at sunrise near Waikaloa, where the dirt saddle road took a southeasterly turn, their destination, the volcano Kilauea, atop mighty Mauna Loa!

Gideon had brought a packmule with him, Emma saw, as well as his big gray horse, Akamai. Her brows rose in surprise, for the mule was loaded with blankets, heavy woolen ponchos, food supplies, canteens, firewood, extra clothing, a lantern, and a canvas-and-rope bundle that looked like a rolled-up tent.

"A tent? Blankets? Where on earth are we going, Gideon?" she exclaimed. "To the volcano, or on an African safari?"

"You'll be surprised at how cold it can get up in the mountain at this time of year. There'll be snow at those altitudes, or frost, at the very least. You'll be glad of all this gear tomorrow night! Here," he added, tossing her a poncho, a pair of men's thick corduroy breeches, heavy knitted stockings, and some leather riding boots. "Haven't you been up to the crater before?"

"No, but I've always wanted to."

"Then you're about to get your wish," he promised with a broad grin, pleased that he would be the one to show her the volcano's grandeur. "We'll take the saddle road south, and head for the foothills of Mauna Loa today, camp there overnight, then make an early start for the crater first thing tomorrow morning! After the first hour or two, it's a long, hard ride up to the crater. We'll need to rest up."

They passed that day riding side by side for miles and miles along the old saddle road that skirted the flanks of Mauna Kea. The mountain's snow-covered peaks were hidden today beneath thick gray cloud cover that reminded Emma of the woolly sheep grazing its emerald slopes, herded by Hui Aloha ranch hands, who waved to Gideon in greeting as they passed.

They ate their midday meal of bread, cold quail, and peeled mangoes that Emma had packed for them as they rode along, laughing and talking companionably about whatever pleased them. And when, by chance, they stumbled upon carefully heaped mounds of stones, or bundles of sacred *ti* leaves, left as offerings in some sacred place, they murmured their apologies to the unseen spirits they'd disturbed for breaking the *kapu,* or taboo placed upon that holy spot, before riding on through the rainforest.

Here and there, they glimpsed bristly wild boars—a sow and some piglets—foraging amongst the trees, or goats that quickly scampered away when they approached. Among the *'ohia lehua* and pandanus trees grew a few sandalwoods that had survived the islands' sandalwood trade with China the century before. Around their trunks twined fragrant *maile* vines, the plant sacred to the hula goddess, Laka, and one much loved by the Hawaiians for making *leis,* because of its sweet-smelling leaves. In other places, sprays of orchids bloomed from rotted logs, or red, white, and yellow "torches" showed where sweet-smelling ginger grew. Midafternoon, they stopped to water the horses at a crystalline pool beneath a sparkling waterfall, its cascades fed by icy mountain streams. Nearby, Emma found a huge lava tube, like an enormous, crooked cavern that reached for almost fifty feet. Ferns, tangled vines, and roots almost hid its entrance, while its walls were etched with petroglyphs—stone drawings of fishermen and warriors, or of women giving birth, made by the ancient ones who had lived in these islands many years before the coming of the white men.

Before Emma mounted again, she plucked a length of *maile* vine and draped it about Gideon's neck, leaving the leafy ends trailing, then tucked a creamy ginger blossom behind her own ear. "There!" she declared, pleased with her efforts, for he looked very handsome wearing a collarless white linen shirt with her deep-green garland about his neck. "Now we look properly festive for our holiday!"

Gideon smiled. Perhaps *he* looked festive, but with her hair swept up beneath a pert woven hat and saucily tilted forward and adorned with a purple-pansy-and-fern *lei,* her trim figure encased in a lace-edged, leg-o'-mutton-sleeved shirtwaist that buttoned primly to the neck, and a divided riding skirt of plum velvet—why, *she* looked beautiful!

That night, Gideon pitched their tent close by another waterfall that spilled sparkling cascades into a rocky pool surrounded by ferns and other lush plants far below. Worn out by a whole day spent in the saddle, they ate the supper Gideon's housekeeper, Auntie Leolani, had prepared, and crawled into the tent, both falling asleep almost immediately.

They awoke just as a gold-and-rose dawn was breaking to a noisy morning chorus of sparrows and raucous, squabbling mynah birds. Gideon loaded their goods onto the mule while she washed herself and braided her hair, and then they were off again, riding up into the sparkling morning air.

Gideon was true to his word. For the first two hours that day, their trail was relatively easy. It snaked lazily back and forth between tall grasses, bushes, an occasional straggly sandalwood, and many low-lying *koa* trees, which were bearded with the trailing grayish moss that the natives called Pele's Hair.

Soon after, they reached the treeline, and the difficult ascent began in earnest. The trail was almost nonexistent now; the going—an upward climb through several thousand feet of hard ridges, rifts, and crevasses, all sculptured by winking black *pahoehoe* lava flows—proved hard on the hooves of both their horses and the hardy mule.

Gazing about her in amazement, Emma found it hard to believe that the lush green hills and plains she loved could still exist only a day's ride away. Here, everything was desert—a dead black wasteland as far as the eye could see, where only the exotic silversword could find foothold and flourish, and the only living creatures save themselves were the elegant beige-and-brown *nene* geese, with their smocked throat feathers, that waddled alongside their trail.

The billowing gray clouds lay below, rather than above them now, while the sun was very bright and hot on their heads, and Emma was glad of her hat. In the distance, the ocean showed as a dull sapphire blur encircling the curving coastline of the island itself for as far as the eye could see. The altitude made her feel a little light-headed and lethargic. Darting a glance at Gideon, who seemed disgustingly unaffected, she found herself wondering if this was how the Orientals back in Honolulu's Chinatown felt when they smoked opium.

It was late afternoon and daylight was fast fading when they reached the summit. A great pall of fog lay ahead of them, like a mantle of gray moss, its gloomy folds stained a brilliant crimson from what must be the seething firepit of the crater itself far below.

They were forced to go very slowly on account of the dangerous footing hereabouts, Gideon warned, letting the horses and the surer-footed mule pick the path over the lava, although they sometimes gained only a single yard at a time, for wide crevasses and deep shelves filled with sparkling snow had to be clambered over or around.

Off in the distance, Emma saw faint wisps of smoke and great billowing blasts of steam rising from the sulphur banks, while a strange, faintly rotten-egg odor overlaid the already smoky-smelling air. From time to time, she jumped at what sounded like explosions—similar to gunfire, only much, much louder. The sounds were made by rocks exploding and becoming liquid under the force of pressure changes occurring deep within the volcano, Gideon explained, and Emma felt a stirring of excitement, coupled with a few twinges of honest fear—fear at the dangers of being so close to an active volcano, but also excitement at being able to witness great Pele's wonders with her own eyes! How Makua would enjoy hearing about the sights she'd seen when she went home, she thought happily, flashing Gideon a nervous smile.

Soon after, he raised his hand, signaling her to halt. Straightaway, she reined in her poor, frightened little Makani and turned in the saddle to look where he was pointing, struck dumb with awe and amazement as she saw that, even from such a distance, Gideon's face had been turned ruddy by the reflected light—as, no doubt, had her own. Could such breathtaking beauty, such unbelievable magnificence, possibly be real? But real it was!

Some distance below them, a curtain of fire rose from the center of a vast, lakelike crater scooped from the mountain proper; several towering fountains of liquid-gold lava jetting hundreds of feet up, into the darkening sky, rising side by side from a bubbling, seething lake of shimmering white-hot or blood-red molten lava. The brilliance of those fiery jets far outshone the glorious orange-and-gold flamboyance of the sunset above them, lovely though it was, since the lava cascades lit the sky for a good mile around like great magnesium torches, sending everything beyond their radiance into gloom. Their reflected light drenched the grayish lava with magic, imbuing the lifeless, stark terrain with marvelous shades of rose or ruby or amber color, revealing an otherworldly beauty unseen by the naked eye, till now. Beyond the lake's farthest banks, glimpsed through fissures in the black crust, they could see a river of scarlet—like a raw, bloody wound seeping beneath a gaping slash of black-charred flesh—moving sluggishly beneath the crust. And, when they dismounted, they could feel the ground vibrating beneath their booted feet, hear the volcano's muted roar—like the boom of the surf against the cliffs—though they were yet a half-mile's distance away.

"Holy Moses!" Gideon breathed. "I've never seen it this beautiful! It looks—it looks like the pit of Hades itself!"

Awestruck, bedazzled, mesmerized, she could not look away, but only nodded her fervent agreement. Instinctively, he reached for her hand, found it, and squeezed.

The strange and incredibly beautiful sights and sounds all around her made Emma think of some enormous, fettered dragon, a fire-breathing gold-and-crimson creature that had smoke pouring from its nostrils, kept chained in the very bowels of the mountain—perhaps by the goddess Madame Pele herself!—now straining to tear free again. What was to keep it from doing just that, right here, right now? she wondered, a little shiver running down her spine. After all, just four years ago, in '55, the mountainside had opened up under the strain of the enormous pressure building from within, and lava had burst forth in an eruption that had lasted over a year, and destroyed everything in its path for an area of close to three hundred square miles!

"I think we'll camp over that side, closer to the fern jungle," Gideon observed.

"There's a grass hut up there, by the path. Look!"

"I know, but there are already some people staying there for the night. I saw their horses earlier. I think it best we go around. If we pitched our tent this close to the crater, we'd have a better view of things but might not be safe. Some of this lava looks solid enough, but it's really just a brittle shell with a crevasse beneath. We'd run the risk of our campsite caving in while we slept, if there was even a small shock."

"Sh-shock?"

"A small earthquake," he explained airily. "They're quite frequent in these parts."

"Ah. Then your fern jungle will do very nicely," she agreed hastily, before he could change his mind and ride closer to the crater.

There was a dull throbbing in her head now that promised to worsen, though she made no mention of her discomfort to Gideon as they rode on, following the curve of the crater to its far side. She couldn't bear to spoil his obvious enjoyment at being her guide.

Their tent was erected with little difficulty by jamming its poles firmly into small fissures in the rock, then weighing down its folds with sturdy rocks to keep them firmly anchored in place. It was a fine campsite, shielded from the wind a little by the lush ferns, low trees, and vegetation, yet the endless music of running water and the dampness of the area made it seem miserably cold.

Indeed, the already chilly nip in the air grew markedly colder as the last of the sunlight faded, though it was still unnaturally light as day everywhere, thanks to the towering torches of lava shooting up into the night like giant Roman candles. When the new moon rose at last, she appeared a pale, insignificant thing, compared to the gloriously bright lava jets and the shimmering lake of rose-and-ruby fire from which they fountained.

Noticing that Emma was shivering, Gideon draped a blanket about her shoulders, then unloaded the mule. He unsaddled their mounts, threw horse blankets over all three animals, then spread others in layers across the smooth lava rock that formed the floor of their tent, trying to soften its unyielding hardness a little. Their saddles would be used as pillows, *paniolo*-style, as they had the night before.

In just a few moments more, he had a fire going, kindled with the wooden tree stumps he'd brought along, and a small iron pot of coffee heating over it.

"Look at those idiots!" he exclaimed, straightening up and

pointing to where three men—just tiny black stick figures that looked for all the world like lantern slides at this distance—were trying to get closer to the crater. "They're asking for *pilikia*—trouble!"

Emma's dull headache had progressed to a constant, throbbing pain. Her teeth were chattering uncontrollably, and the tips of her nose and her fingers had grown quite numb. Struggling to keep awake, despite her mounting lethargy and her pounding head, Emma pulled on all of the extra clothes Gideon had brought along for her, in her effort to get warm. Feeling quite ill, she hunkered down beside him, knowing by his grin that she must look a sight in the voluminous poncho and baggy breeches, his muffler wound twice about her head to keep her ears warm, but she felt too nauseated and uncomfortable to care. Having no gloves, she held her freezing hands out to the fire's heat to warm them.

"I've never been this cold before in my life!" she muttered, hunching her shoulders and thinking with longing of the warm, sultry days and the hot, humid nights she'd always taken quite for granted back on the other side of the island till now.

"Here, drink this. You look blue, love! Some coffee will warm you up a little."

He vigorously rubbed her back, then wrapped his arms around her and pulled her against him. Huddled in the crook of his arm, she gratefully sipped the mug of scalding coffee he'd thrust into her hands, thinking—despite feeling so ill—how very handsome he looked, dressed as he was, like a handsome Mexican *bandito* in a romantic ballad! He wore his hat jammed snugly down on his head, while his striped woolen poncho was pulled snugly about his shoulders. His midnight hair spilled in unruly commas about his brow and collar. Why, he only needed a mustache, a smoldering cigarillo, and a guitar to complete the picture! While she . . . ! She grimaced, thinking she'd never looked *less* like the romantic heroine of some novelette or ballad than she did right now! Worse, the painful pounding in her head made her feel sick to her stomach.

Mistaking her silent perusal of him for contented musing, Gideon raised his tin mug to her in gallant salute. "Your very good health, my lady!" he declared, and drained its dark, bitter dregs. "Will you have another mug?" he offered, his gentian eyes twinkling in the flickering light.

"No, I still have some, thank you. Perhaps—perhaps a little later." What a dear he was, she thought guiltily, always so kind to her. All the way here, he'd seen to her every comfort as tenderly as any lover, although she'd behaved awfully to him at the beach the other day, and certainly didn't merit such tender care.

She thought of the long night that yet lay ahead, and how very cold it would surely become in the wee hours. They would be forced to sleep very close to each other in order to keep warm, and a delicious thrill of anticipation ran down her spine. She wasn't at all sure she'd be able to refuse Gideon's ardent advances the next time—and there *would* be a next time. The fire in his eyes told her so.

Side by side, they huddled together in the opening of their tent, hugging the warmth of their fire as they watched the glorious display of pyrotechnics that Madame Pele had generously staged for their delight.

The night air held a frosty bite even colder than Emma had imagined. Though she'd laughed earlier at the novelty of being able to see her breath condensing in the air, and at the way the tip of her nose had turned first red, then blue with cold, the plummeting temperatures were not nearly so amusing now— though being here, sheltered by the tent's thick canvas walls, was far better than being outside proper. Surely the heat of their bodies, pressed closely together beneath the thick woolen blankets, would make them warm?

"I love you, Emma," Gideon suddenly whispered. He turned

oward her, his handsome face bathed in ruby light so that he ooked like a god of fire, and cupped her cheek and jaw in his and. "I love you so much!" he repeated, tilting her face up to is and kissing her chill lips. "Shall we—shall we turn in for he night?"

Unable to speak, she nodded.

"I'll make sure the horses are all right, then I'll join you." Though his words of themselves were innocuous enough, the usky tone in which he said them promised all manner of de-ights to come!

Breathing shallowly, she crawled into the low tent, dragging he blankets after her. Pulling them up to her chin, she lay on er back, thinking ruefully that Gideon's layer of horse blankets ad done very little to soften the rock below. Her head propped n her saddle, she gazed up at the canvas walls of the tent.

With the volcano's brilliant light outside making everything right as day, and the loud explosions of detonating rocks crack-ng and booming at regular intervals, she fancied it must be like amping in the midst of a battlefield. Ohhh, if only this wretched eadache would go away, so she might enjoy it all!

Moments later, Gideon crawled inside the tent after her. He ied the flaps securely behind him, cocooning them in a blood-ed gloom that was peculiarly erotic. Straightway, he slid under he scratchy blankets alongside her, drew her into his arms, and overed her lips with his own.

"I've been waiting all day to hold you like this."

"Me, too. I'm sorry I fell asleep so quickly last night."

"We both did. We were worn out," he murmured, burrowing eneath the layer of blankets, then clothing, until he found the em of her poncho. He lifted it aside, then fumbled briefly with he tiny buttons that closed the fronts of her blouse beneath it, efore he drew them apart. The narrow ribbon ties of her bodice roke under his clumsy efforts to untie their bows, but that limsy undergarment soon followed the shirtwaist, falling open

to bare her breasts, which were firm, almost opalescent globe
in the tent's ruddy confines.

She gasped at the sensation of cold air upon her bared breasts
for it made her nipples pucker with cold.

"I'll soon remedy that," Gideon promised. Ducking his head
he took the peak of one breast in his warm mouth, drawing on
the small nipple gently at first, then more deeply, until the peak
swelled and hardened between his lips, making her moan with
delight. His suckling grew more ardent as his lust grew, until
he seemed determined to devour her. She shivered with pleasure
for the damp friction of his lips and the slight graze of his teeth
upon her breasts made her giddy with excitement. Uttering a
small cry, she moved against him, not truly knowing what it was
she sought, but instinctively seeking his closeness.

"Yes, oh, yes, my love," he murmured raggedly, sensing her
arousal. Tearing his mouth from her breasts, he kissed her lips
instead, his kisses harder than before. Touching his tongue to
hers, he warred with it until she tentatively did likewise, then
pressed his knee to her mound of Venus.

Cocooned in warmth beneath the tickly blankets, with
Gideon's mouth hot, moist, and hard on hers, his hand cupping
the fullness of her breasts, his heavy knee creating delicious
tickly pressures in her loins, combined to fill her with unbear
able pleasure. "I love you, too, Gideon," she cried softly, curl
ing her arms about his neck and offering him her moist lips

Taking her in his arms, he thrust her thighs apart with his
knee and slid on top of her, kissing her again and again as he
whispered her name like a prayer.

Urgently, they moved against each other, but it was only a
cruel pantomime of the proper lovemaking they both craved, for
the thick barriers of their clothing kept them chastely apart
Though he ached to feel the silk of her flesh rising to meet his
and though she ached to feel his hard body pressing down upon
her, filling her, he had given his word, and would not take her

he knew. To him, a man's word and honor were as inviolable
as law.

Her hands slipped under the layers of his garments, finding
his bare shoulders and his back. She followed the hunched line
of his spine as he moved against her, her fingertips like the
whispering glide of raw silk against his flesh, arousing every
sense and nerve ending he possessed until he came perilously
close to exploding: could not stand to hold and touch her as he
was doing now, to move against her, yet go no further. Rolling
from her, he took her hand in his and guided it to the hard ridge
of flesh that strained against the heavy cord of his breeches.
"Here," he whispered. "For the love of God, touch me."

She did as asked, then took his hand and placed it over the
mound of her *pua* with a whispered, "Only if you'll touch me,
too? Teach me how to give you pleasure. Please?" she implored,
then drew his dark head down to hers.

Their feverish caresses and whispered endearments took on
the unreal quality of a dream thereafter, an erotic dream from
which he hoped never to awaken. Drawing aside her garments,
he kissed her everywhere, nuzzling the scented hollows of her
throat, tracing the valley between her hard little breasts, laving
the sleek flatness of her rib cage and belly, where he dipped his
tongue into the tiny well of her *piko,* her navel, so that she giggled and shrank away from his teasing tongue. But when, breathing heavily, he trailed his tongue over the dark triangle of her
mons, she stiffened and whispered, "No, don't! You must not!"
and pressed her thighs tightly together.

"Why?" he murmured, his breath a warm, tickly feather
against her thigh. "Tell me why not?"

"Because it's . . . it's wicked."

He laughed softly, feeling far older, more worldly, than his
darling in that moment. "No more wicked than anything else
we might do together, my love . . ."

Very gently, he caressed her, kissed her, building her hunger
with every tender caress, every teasing kiss, until she could not

help but open herself to him. She trembled uncontrollably and her breasts rose and fell rapidly as he ducked his dark head and took her to the very heights of desire.

"Oh! Oh!" she gasped just moments later. Starbursts exploded to fill her vision, and she clawed at the blankets beneath them, her slender body arching like a drawn bow beneath his mouth as wave after wave of incredible pleasure rippled through her. "Oh, Gideon, my love—!"

"Halooo, there! You in the tent—hellooo!"

Startled, he clapped a hand gently over her mouth to hush her outcry. "Shh, darling. Someone's out there. *Yes? What is it?"* he called back.

"I'm terribly sorry to bother you at this hour, sir," the speaker, who sounded British, painfully precise, and much closer to their tent now, continued. "But my brother Charles has taken a rather nasty fall into one of the crevasses. He's back there a short distance, and seems to be in considerable pain. I rather believe his leg is broken. I need someone to help myself and our native guide lift him out. Would you be so kind?"

"Of course, sir. One moment," Gideon called back. To Emma, he whispered. "Stay here. I'll help them, and be back as soon as I can."

She nodded. "All right. But . . . be careful."

He straightened his rumpled clothing, then leaned down and kissed her cheek. There was laughter in his voice as he promised, "Ooh, I will."

After he'd gone off with the British fellow, Emma made her way outside, found the tin basin and washrag she'd brought with her, then washed herself as best she could in the tent, dressed, and crawled from the tent.

Her headache was somewhat improved, yet the nausea and shortness of breath she'd experienced earlier still lingered. Noticing that their campfire had burned down, she tossed another of the dried stumps onto its glowing orange heart, then sat down with a blanket drawn over her shoulders to watch the fountaining lava until Gideon returned.

She'd not been alone long before she heard the horses whickering shrilly and stamping their hooves nervously. In the same moment sensing someone at her back, Emma turned and saw an old woman standing some feet away among the ferns, watching her.

"Why, Grandmother, I didn't hear you coming!" she exclaimed politely. *"He mai!* Welcome! Please, won't you eat with us and share our fire? It is so cold tonight, you must be freezing!"

Tall and handsomely built, the regal old lady wore her long white hair flowing loose over her shoulders and down her back, adorned with a beautifully woven head garland of scarlet *lehua* pompoms and red *ohelo* berries. Despite the cold, she wore only a dark-red length of cloth wound about her body, and her shoulders and feet were quite bare as she walked gracefully across the lava to sit by Emma's fire. Surely she must be from hereabouts, Emma decided, to be so immune to the cold? Or, she amended, perhaps the old woman had no warm coverings to put on?

Crouching down, she reached into the tent and withdrew a blanket, which she draped around the woman's shoulders. "There. A cup of coffee will soon warm you, *Tutu,* Grandmother. It won't take but a minute or two to boil. The beans were grown over on the Kona side of our island. They taste delicious!"

The dried tree stump quickly caught, and the water—still warm from earlier—was reheated in no time, just as she'd promised. Emma moved about the camp, filling a tin mug and placing it before the old woman, fixing a platter of cold quail and cold baked taro root, which she placed beside her.

"It would be well if you left this place with the first light of morning, Kaleilani, my daughter," the old woman murmured suddenly. Looking up at Emma, her piercing amber eyes blazed into the young woman's. "There will be danger to those who stay, mark my words . . ."

"I've come back!" Gideon called out as he strode up the well-defined trail that skirted the fern jungle to their camp.

Emma hastened to meet him, relieved that he had returned unharmed. "Was the man badly injured?"

"A badly broken leg, as his brother feared. Those idiots were trying to get closer to the farthest fire lake when the lava crust gave way and he fell in. Luckily, we managed to get him out without even burning the soles of our boots! They had a Hilo man guiding them, and together we were able to rig up a litter and lift him back up to the top. They've had enough sightseeing, though. At daybreak, they'll be heading back down—and so will we."

She nodded approval. "I think we should go. *Tutu* tells me it could be dangerous up here tomorrow. Oh, I'm sorry, you two haven't been introduced! Grandmother, I'd like you to meet my friend, Gideon Kane . . ." As she spoke, she turned, intending to introduce Gideon to the little old lady, but to her surprise, there was no one there. The blanket she'd draped around the old woman's shoulders lay in a crumpled heap beside the fire. The tin mug and the plate were where she'd left them, their contents untouched, but the old woman was gone.

"Where did she go?" Emma exclaimed, spinning about. "Did she pass you on the way back up the trail?"

"Did who pass me?"

"The old woman. The one who was sitting right there, by the fire. You must have seen her just now?"

He frowned. "I didn't see anyone but you."

"But you *must* have! She had long white hair and she was wearing a red wraparound, and a head *lei* of lehua blossoms. You must have seen her . . . *Oh! Lehua* blossoms—?" She broke off, clapping her hand over her mouth, for the feathery red flowers and the *ohelo* berries were both sacred to the goddess of volcanos. The blood drained from Emma's face in the golden light. "Dear Lord, she knew my name, Gideon! Can it—do you think it could have been—?"

"Madame Pele?" Gideon shrugged. "Who knows? All I can say is, no one passed me on my way back here—and there was no one sitting by the fire but you . . ."

Six

"I'm going now, *Makua*."

From the sleeping mat upon which she lay, the Hawaiian woman nodded and smiled as her daughter hesitated in the doorway of the grass hut, her hat in her hand, a doubtful, troubled expression in her violet eyes. Reaching out, Malia Jordan caught Emma's hand in her own and drew it to her pale lips. "No look at your *makua* that way, darling girl. I be all right, I promise. Go, now. Go have little bit fun with that sweetheart of yours!"

Emma frowned. "But I left you alone yesterday, and the day before . . . I hate to leave you so often, especially when *he's* here and drin—"

"I not alone yesterday. Yesterday, your auntie come. We washed *hala* leaves for weaving and talked story. We had nice time. Jack sleeping now, my little *keikimahine*—and he goin' stay asleep until the rum wear off." Malia clicked her teeth and shook her head in disgust. "Auwe! Him no better than one whaler! Go now. Go quickly, 'fore he wake up."

Her daughter sighed. "You promised, *makua*. You said Uncle had seen to everything. You swore Da—Jack—wouldn't come here. I would never have stayed on the Big Island if I'd known! I'd have taken you back to Honolulu with me, instead, and finished my schooling there. Then next year, I could have sat the examinations for my teaching certificate. On a schoolteacher's salary, I could take proper care of you," she added wistfully, biting her lower lip.

"Don't look so sad, my little Emma Kaleilani. You take plenty good care of Mama as it is. I such a wicked woman, I don't deserve my good daughter! Every day I say my prayers, thank the blessed Lord in heaven I have you!"

"And Jack?" Emma asked sharply. As much as she loved her mother, she was also realistic. Malia was inclined to gloss over her own weaknesses, the things that were wrong with her life, and pretend they didn't exist, rather than go to the trouble of dealing with them. She'd never overcome that failing, although her inability to leave her husband was one of the reasons Emma had been taken from her as a little child and sent away to the convent orphanage in Honolulu.

"*Auwe*—! *Jack this*—! *Jack that*—!" Every time that no-good *haole* give me hard time! Why he come back heah, eh? Kaleilani, sweetheart, I know Mama promise you," her mother began with a teary quaver in her voice that brought tears to Emma's eyes—almost. "But I think—I *truly* believe!—that this time, Jack be too scared for come back our place, or for make trouble! But—!" she sighed heavily, "you know how he act when he drinkin'"—that man not to be trusted! The grog an' rotgut, they geeve him false courage. He talk big, he say he 'no' afraid of your uncle"—that Jack Jordan 'big mans, no' afraid anybody, Devil take 'em all!' He say he goin' geeve 'em all dirty licking, teach 'em for respect him! But . . . I'll tell him go 'way when he come sober, promise. He won't like it, but . . . he scared your uncle. I goin' give him little bit moneys. I t'ink he go this time, he know what's good for him."

"He'd better," Emma conceded, reluctant to upset the sick woman any further by demanding more than she'd already promised. Besides, there was only so much her mother could do. Jack Jordan was a law unto himself. "If you're sure you won't need me this afternoon, I'll be off."

Malia shook her head. "No, girlie. The laudanum make me little bit sleepy already. You, you go along now . . ."

Emma bent down and kissed her mother's cheek. Was it just

wishful thinking, or did her color look a little better this afternoon? She brushed the heavy dark hair, threaded liberally with
silver, back from her mother's brow. Plaited into a single, heavy
braid, her hair reached past her waist, an inch or so longer than
Emma's own. There were still traces of Malia's former beauty
in her gaunt face. Her light-brown eyes were lively and clear
today, though shadowed, and she seemed a little stronger than
when Emma had first come back from Honolulu to take care of
her, she thought. *Dear God, let it be so!* she prayed silently. *Let
her get well! She's not had much of a life, Lord, and we've had
so little time together!* But to her mother she only murmured,
"Sweet dreams, then . . ."

Settling her hat upon her head, Emma slipped from the hut,
giving the spot where her father sprawled beneath a breadfruit
tree, a stoneware jug of rum cradled to his chest like a baby,
wide berth.

As she passed the pen, some distance from the grass houses,
she tossed their only sow and her litter of squealing piglets a
handful of vegetable peelings before she moved on, giving the
spring-fed taro patches a cursory yet satisfied glance.

When she'd returned to the Kohala foothills at the beginning
of summer, her mother's vegetable patches had been overgrown
with weeds, the taro plants sickly things with puny corms and
yellow-spotted, tattered leaves. Now, after hours of backbreaking
labor, the results of her hard work were obvious in the deep-
green, flourishing taro plants, the leafy sweet-potato vines spilling down their neat rows of hills, the corn rows heavy with a
fine crop of ears that would quickly ripen in the sunshine. Ah,
yes! Now that it was carefully tended, her mother's land could
provide more than enough to feed the two of them, and they'd
still have enough vegetables left over for her to sell in the village
of Waimea or at Kawaihae on the coast, so she could buy the
things they lacked—such as fresh fish and a little meat and fowl
from time to time, or flour for bread, perhaps some eggs and
milk—foods that Doctor Forrester had said would build up her

mother's constitution and make her strong enough to fight the sickness in her blood.

Makani, her mother's sweet mare, was grazing the lush emerald grass in the paddock behind their *hale pili,* grass huts. The horse came at Emma's low call, arching her sleek bay neck over the rail fence to gently nuzzle her pocket in search of treats. Emma fed her a carrot, then quickly slipped a bridle over the mare's head while she was munching on it. Blackie, her father's poor old horse, came trotting up to the rail, whickering and nibbling expectantly at Emma's pockets for a treat of his own. Laughing, she gave him the last carrot, then grasped Makani's mane and swung herself up onto the mare's bare back.

Her heart gave an excited little flutter as she turned the horse's head in the direction of Twin Rocks Cove and touched her heels to its sides. No matter how many times she might see Gideon, each day was like the very first all over again! Anticipation filled her with a warm glow, a bubbling eagerness to be with him, and she knew that she was falling in love with him—*had* fallen in love with him, if she were honest with herself, at first sight, though everyone claimed that such things happened only in fairy tales. She was smiling dreamily as she leaned down from Makani's back to swing the paddock gate shut, not really concentrating on what she was doing. These last halcyon days of summer had been like some beautiful dream from which she never wanted to wake, except that she'd been *living* her dreams, playing a part in a real-life fairy tale in which Gideon was her Prince Charming! Surely he was handsome enough to be the hero of any girl's fairy tales, with his strong, striking features and those magnificent, glittery deep-blue eyes that were the exact shade of the deepest ocean water and always made her feel as if she were melting inside.

After she'd reached home yesterday evening, she'd had to sidestep countless questions about her supposed visit made to Laupahoehoe, over on the Hamakua coast of the island, and wait until her auntie left before she could tell her mother all about the wonderful sights she'd really seen: the lake of molten lava in the crater, the jetting golden fountains, the bursts of steam rising from the vents, the sad footprints left in the lava centuries before by warriors killed by a rain of suffocating ash and poisonous gases before they could escape. She'd told her, too, about the eerie disappearance of the old lady, and her dire warnings . . .

"And then, as we were riding back down the mountain to the saddle road again," she'd told her mother, "we met someone who Gideon knew who'd come from Hilo—and something terrible had happened that very morning, just as the *kupuna,* the old one, had promised!"

"What?" Malia had asked, wide-eyed.

"You remember the two Englishmen I told you about—the one with the broken leg, Charles, and his brother?"

"I remember." The older woman nodded.

"Well, Mister Bainbridge was understandably anxious to get his brother to Doctor Judson in Hilo as soon as possible. He insisted their guide take them down the mountain by the shortest route possible. When the poor man quite sensibly told Mister Bainbridge that the shortcut was now unsafe because of the volcanic conditions, Mister Bainbridge became irate and dismissed the guide completely. Of course, the poor fellow felt responsible for them, and was loath to leave either the injured man or his brother, but when Mister Bainbridge insisted—in no uncertain tones!—he had no choice. Shortly after they parted ways, their horses fell through the crumbling lava crust, in the very area the guide had warned them about."

"And?"

"Unhappily, both were killed."

"Auwe! God rest their souls."

They'd talked long into the night, for Malia had insisted her daughter describe everything she'd seen, down to the smallest detail, no matter how insignificant it seemed, for in this fashion, it was as if she had seen everything with her own eyes. Consequently, it had been very late before they fell asleep, and her mother had let her sleep long past her usual hour this morning. Jack had been there for some time when she awakened, looking a little furtive and sly, she fancied. Emma suspected he'd been trying to wheedle coin for a bottle of illegal liquor or a jug of grog from her mother, and the knowledge had infuriated her, for her *makua* had little enough to live on, as it was. Still, she knew from bitter experience that Malia Jordan would give him whatever she had, and she'd learned it was of little use to rail at her about it. Still, it went against Emma's far stronger nature to pander to the man's fondness for liquor, or to let him get away with such low behavior. He might be her father, but she knew him too well to feel anything but loathing for him.

So preoccupied was she by her thoughts of the man that she did not notice him standing by the gate as she trotted Makani through it.

Like a flash, his hand came out and caught the little mare's cheek strap. "Whoa, gal!" he roared as the horse, obviously afraid of him, half-reared up, whickering nervously.

"Let go of my horse!" Emma snapped, jerked back to reality with a painful wrench.

Jack shoved back the battered *pandanus* hat he always wore, with the beautiful *lei* of iridescent golden-pheasant feathers that Emma's Hawaiian grandfather had made many years ago, before his death. "Tsk. Tsk. That in't no way t' talk t' yer da, Emmie," Jack Jordan scolded with a sly grin. "A little respect, gel, if you please," he demanded, his words slurred with liquor.

"If you want me to respect you, Father, you'll have to earn it," Emma said.

"Now, you listen here, an' you listen good, Little Miss High and Mighty! I don't have t' prove nothin' t' you, d' you hear me, my gel? Nothin'!" Jack growled, releasing Makani's bridle to waggle an admonishing finger in her face. "You think you're better than yer old da, don't yer, with your pretty convent airs and graces, but I know what you're really like! I knows what you bin up to gel. Aye, that right, I do!"

Her face paled. Had he been following her? Did he know about her meeting Gideon at the cove all these afternoons?

"Aye, that's it!" He confirmed her fears with a leering smile, his blue eyes kindling. He wetted his lips. "Like yer bleedin' ma, you are, gel—turned out no better than a dockside trull, did ye, opening yer legs t' any Tom, Dick, or Harry—or should I say, any *Kane?*"

"Get out of my way."

"Not likely, luv. You need a father's firm hand, you do. Discipline t' set you straight. I've been remiss in my dooties as yer da, I see it now," he said piously. "All that's about t' change!" Suddenly reaching out a wiry arm, he wound his fist in her flowing hair and pulled her by it from her horse's back.

"Take your hands off me!" she cried, flailing at him even as she tumbled to the grass. But before she could hit the ground, he lifted her up, stubby fingers clamped about her upper arms, his face thrust into her own.

The gorge rose up her throat in an acid flood as she saw him duck his dirty-blond head, for she knew what would come next. Closing her eyes to blot him out, she screamed, "Nooo!" and thrust at his chest with all her might.

The force of her surprise attack tipped her off balance and threw him backward, to the grass. Rolling onto her knees, the full folds of her long, loose dress tangled about her legs, she tried to scramble to standing, but Jack had beaten her to it. As, sobbing, she heaved herself upright, he clamped his hands about her waist and twisted her smoothly to face him. "That's my gel! Good try, ducks!" he crowed, his eyes dancing with malicious enjoyment. "Not good enough t' best yer ole da, though! Now, come 'ere . . ."

"Let her go!"

At the sound of that imperious voice, Jack stiffened. Still keeping his grip on one of Emma's wrists, he turned to see an old Hawaiian man standing beneath the mulberry trees. His long hair was white and flowed loose to his shoulders, while his bony chest was quite bare. He wore a white loincloth wrapped around his scrawny flanks, and cut such an unprepossessing figure, Jack snorted with laughter. "And who's goin' ter make me? You, you scraggy old git?"

"Let the girl go. She is not for you."

"She needs discipline, she do," Jack protested. "It's my place, as her father."

"I know who you are, Jack Jordan—even as I know what foulness lies in your heart. I will ask only one more time. *Release her!*" As Jack, half mesmerized by them, gazed deeper into the old native's eyes, they seemed to glow with an unnatural power, almost amber rather than brown, those strange irises set amidst bloodshot whites.

Bloodshot eyes—the mark of a true *kahuna,* Jack thought. Everyone knew that the native medicine men chewed the sap of the *awa* plant, a mild stimulant. It reddened the eyes, but it also gave them magical powers—powers that no sane man would scoff at—and Jack's cocksure expression faltered. Again, he wetted his lips, and his grip on Emma's wrist slackened considerably. *She's back t' stay. There'll be other times,* he told himself. *Times when the old* kanaka *int sniffin' around.* "All right, then, Grandad. No need t' get yer hackles up!" he declared loudly. In a lower, raspy voice that was laden with menace, he looked his daughter up and down so that her flesh crawled as he murmured, "There'll be another reckoning, my gel. You mark my words! Now, go on—scarper!"

Emma needed no second urging. Picking up the skirts of her long shapeless dress, she ran after Makani, who was cropping the grass by the fence, only a few feet away. Clambering up onto the fence, Emma mounted the mare and gathered the reins in her fist. After a respectful nod of thanks to the old man, she shot her father a withering glare, and rode quickly toward the coast.

Jack watched her ride away, staring after her trim figure until both horse and rider had blended into the distance. Turning, he opened his mouth to hurl a curse at the interfering old man beneath the mulberry trees, but there was no one there.

Shrugging off the uneasy shudder that ran down his spine, Jack set about catching Blackie, jingling in his pocket the coins his useless slut of a wife had given him earlier that morning. Perhaps he'd ride down t' Kawaihae, see if that yeller-skinned, slant-eyed storekeeper—was his name Ah Wong? Or was it Ah Woo?—would slip him a bottle o' rotgut, under the counter?

Gideon was already waiting when Emma rode up. The very moment Makani's hooves touched the sands, she slipped from the animal's back and ran to him, falling into his arms. He held her close and kissed her long and hard, aware that she was trembling inside, though she gave no explanation for her upset.

"Is everything all right? Your *makua* isn't worse? Your parents weren't angry that you were late home yesterday?" he asked as his gentian eyes lovingly searched her face.

"Yes, no, and no! There! That's all your questions answered!" she declared, almost too brightly. "Let's swim! I can't wait to get in the water!" So saying, she lifted her muumuu over her head and flung it aside, her violet eyes sparkling as she saw his mouth drop open in shock.

"Holy Moses. You're—!"

"Naked?" She grinned cheekily. "What a clever boy you are, Mister Kane—and so very observant, too. Come on!"

With that, she scampered away, running barefoot across the sand. Moments later, her golden buttocks twinkled at him as she arched forward, arms extended, head down, diving into the turquoise water with the lithe grace of a dark-haired mermaid. Shrugging, Gideon grinned, peeled off his own clothes and followed suit.

He had never known her as abandoned as she was that day. No sooner had he swum alongside her than she took his hand in hers and placed it over her breasts, shooting him a smoldering

look that demanded he caress her, fondle her. Her unusual for-
wardness acted like a spark upon the dry kindling of his own
desires. With her first touch upon him, he burst into lusty fire,
kissing her hungrily, gently drawing her lower lip between his
teeth, touching his tongue to hers as she treaded water before
him. Without a single word passing between them, he swung
her up into his arms and carried her from the water, laying her
down on the sand within the low-hanging branches of the sea
grape's leafy bower. The sand held the day's warmth, yet it felt
cool compared to the burning heat of their bodies as they
stretched out, side by side.

Her eyes like dark stars, she cupped his jaw and turned his
head to face her. "Gideon? Make love to me."

Her words went through him like a lightning bolt that found
its target in his loins. And, despite his sternest intentions, he
hardened. "No, Emma. You don't mean that."

"If you loved me—as you say—you'd make love to me."

"Wrong, little girl," he countered softly, his voice husky with
lust, his eyes dark with desire. "It's *because* I love you that I
won't."

"But why? Don't you desire me?"

*Oh, Lord, how could she even think such a thing? Had she
no idea of the agony his denial had cost him these past weeks?*
"You know better than that, minx." He rolled onto his back and
pulled his shirt over the swelling at his flanks. Lying there, he
stared up at the bright blue sky between the dark filigree of tree
branches, wondering if she was truly as naive as her years, or
but playing a wicked game of her own devising. A small green-
ish lizard was stretched out on one of the branches. It stared
back at him unblinkingly, as if mocking his predicament.

Emma leaned up on one elbow and idly ran her fingernail
down the middle of his chest to where the straight hairs grew
thick about his navel. His hand came out to trap her fragile wrist
before she could venture lower. "Don't—"

"Then answer me. Why won't you?"

"Because you're too young, Emma. Too young, too decent—and because we're not married, nor even formally promised to each other. What would your family say if they found out you'd given yourself to me?"

She scowled at him, her full lower lip jutting mutinously, her violet eyes banking purple fire. "I don't care. And God knows, *they* wouldn't care. Besides, doesn't what *I* want matter? Doesn't what's important to me count for anything? I love you, Gideon. I love you . . . I love you . . ."

She flung off his restraining hand and lowered her lips to his sparsely furred chest, dropping light, quick kisses on his firm, salty skin.

When he would have stood and walked away from her, too aroused for her good, she took her hand in his and placed it over her breast with a whispered, "No, I won't let you stop, not this time. I'm begging you, Gideon. Make love to me. Please?" she urged, and drew his dark head back down to hers, placed his hand over the swell of her *pua* and whispered, "Please, oh, please, oh, please . . ."

All at once he felt as if he was drowning, drowning in a warm sea of sensation, and he didn't care anymore if the water came up over his head, or if it drove the breath from his lungs.

Her skin tasted of warm sunshine and salty sea, and although they'd been swimming, somehow the fragrance of white ginger still perfumed her damp hair as he nuzzled her throat, her ears, the downy nape of her neck. The subtle scents of her body were erotic aphrodisiacs that aroused him, pushed him to the brink of madness. It no longer mattered what vows he'd made himself, what promises he'd sworn her. Nothing mattered anymore but that he have her; that he rid his body of this aching fire.

His eyes devoured her for, naked, she curled upon the white-gold sand beside him, her hair making a dark silken pillow beneath her head. Stray midnight skeins spilled across the beige satin of her shoulders, while her arms were raised above her head in languid abandon, a carelessly provocative pose that invited him to touch her where he would. Her eyes were closed, and he saw that her teeth had trapped her lower lip, yet by the way her small, hard breasts were rising and falling shallowly, he knew that she was not asleep. She was fully awake, and but awaiting his caresses.

With exquisite gentleness, tenderness, he rubbed her flat, silky belly with his palm, uttering a stream of endearments as he caressed her.

"Ah, little kitten, how soft . . . how soft and silky. Yes, oh yes, darling girl, how wonderful you feel. Look at your nipples, Ka-leilani—see, my love? How they've hardened . . . like little pink shells." So saying, he mouthed her breast, swirled the hardened nipple with his tongue, and straightway felt the fire leap from himself to her as a rosy warmth fanned outward beneath his hand, infusing her silky body with heat.

With a sigh, she arched backward, like a kitten stretching herself, offering herself to her master's hand, and he took the breast she offered between his hands and grazed his teeth across the swollen nipple.

"Oh!" she cried, and, giggling, rolled over, onto her belly. She was shivering as Gideon lifted her hair aside and kissed and nipped at her downy nape, not stopping until goose bumps broke along her arms, then squirming anew as he made his tongue dance down the line of her spine to her bottom. She sighed, a long, drawn-out sigh of contentment. Grinning, he ducked his head and took a playful bite from one delectable, saucy cheek.

"You *kalohe!* You rogue!" she accused, rolling over so that she was facing him again, laughter dancing like stars in her eyes.

Leaning back against the sea-grape tree, he drew her onto his lap. Slipping a hand between her thighs, he hungrily kissed her, exploring every trembling inch of the lovely body part draped across his knees, part cradled in his arms. When his fingertips brushed the soft dark hair between her legs, he whispered, "Open, my dearest love. Let me touch you. Let me feel how very much you want me . . ." When he plundered the hidden flower of her sex, delicately caressing the tiny bud hidden within its petals, her eyes suddenly darkened, turned deepest indigo. Her fingers tightened like talons over his upper arms. Whispering his name, she clung to him, pleading with her eyes for him to take her, to make love to her and end her torment.

Lord in heaven, she was so lovely, so perfectly fashioned, so intensely feminine—and yet for all that, he sensed that there was a brittle fragility beneath her carefree veneer, a deep and abiding sadness somewhere in her past that had deeply wounded her; a pain that her eyes had hinted at more times than he cared to recall. In truth, she was as fragile as the tiny porcelain doll that twirled in dainty circles upon his mother's musical box. Dare he take her at her word? Dare he treat her as the desirable, lovely woman his body craved, and make love to her as she demanded? Or would his lovemaking push her over the edge— make her shatter into a thousand crystal shards at his slightest touch?

Whispering her name like a prayer, he turned her smoothly beneath him and parted her thighs with his knee. She saw him glance down, and her face burned with shame that she should lie before him, so exposed, so open, and yet still want him. He must think her a shameless wanton . . . a half-white, wharfside doxy of the lowest order.

Braced upon his elbows, he loomed over her. "Say it again, my little love. Tell me! Tell me that you want me."

"Yes, oh, yes, yes," she whispered throatily. "Don't stop . . . not now—I couldn't bear it!"

He could feel his thundering heart slamming against his ribs in that moment as he looked down at her pale oval face, so trusting in the full moonlight. Her head was thrown back, the pale, fluid elegance of her throat exposed and vulnerable. Her dark eyes were closed, the fans of her thick, sooty lashes quivering ever so faintly upon her cheeks in a way that made him think of lovely dark moths, hovering there. His treacherous limbs quaked as if it was his first time with a woman as he lowered himself, covering her golden female body with his own darker, hairier one, fitting the swollen head of his hard, hot flesh to her softness and pressing between them.

With a glad cry, she parted her thighs even wider to take him. Pressing between them, he tried to ease the head of his *ule* into her heat. But although she was ready and moist for him, he found he could not enter her. She was too small, somehow, unlike the other women he'd bedded. What was more, a barrier impeded his entry.

Sweat standing out upon his brow and his upper lip, he eased forward once again, but it was still there. And when he pushed harder between her thighs, her eyes flew open and she uttered a short, piercing cry that cut him to the quick and froze him into stillness upon her.

"What is it? Oh, God, my sweet, have I hurt you?" It was unthinkable that he had. He would never forgive himself.

"Just . . . just a little," she whispered, her gaze sliding away from his. Yet he could see that her cheeks were glistening with crystal tears in the sunlight, and his guilt and shame knew no bounds as he remembered, too late, some of the other facts of life his uncle Sheldon had taught him that never-to-be forgotten summer in Honolulu Town.

"God, Emma, please don't cry," he implored her, gathering her into his arms and kissing her cheeks, her mouth, and tasting the salt of her tears on his lips. "I didn't realize—I never meant to hurt you, honestly. I just . . . I didn't think you'd be . . . But of course you are . . . would be! Emma, speak to me! Say something! Say you'll forgive me?" he ended lamely, mortified that in his raging lust to have her, he'd acted like a green boy, and made no distinction between a decent girl like Emma—a *wahine kapu,* a virgin—and one of his uncle Sheldon's ladies of the night.

He made as if to stand up, filled with self-loathing.

"No! No, you mustn't . . . you mustn't stop. *Please!* I don't want you to stop, truly I don't," she whispered urgently. Tugging him down beside her again, she rained kisses over his face and pressed her delectable self against him.

His blasted manhood recovered and responded hugely in response to her charms, predictable as ever. "Emma, darling Emma, don't! Don't make me hurt you!" he implored, but she was ready for him, wanted him—and he was ready and wanted her—and between the wanting and the readiness, denial was akin to trying to hold back raging wildfire! Her small, knowing hands were suddenly everywhere, stroking him, caressing him, inflaming his lust, building the torment. His mouth was on her breasts, his teeth tugging at her swollen nipples, his tongue dancing over her flat belly, his hands molding the firm little globes of her bottom—until in the end, desire won out over all else; triumphed even over the solemn vows he'd sworn himself.

This time, when he lay upon her, she arched forward and took him deep inside her before he could rear back, gritting her teeth against the sudden, sharp pain that shot through her as she held him fast, the sudden hot rush of her virgin blood as it ran down her thigh.

"Oh, God! Oh, God—!" he groaned, and shuddered, thrilling to the exquisite sensation of being sheathed to the hilt in the delicious heat of her body; sheathed more tightly, more deliciously than he'd ever known.

"Don't be sorry. It's done now," she whispered, running her fingers through his dark hair, and down, over the broad muscular width of his shoulders. "It's over, and I'm yours forevermore! Love me now, Gideon Kane. Just . . . just love me!"

With a shudder, he began to move upon her, slowly, tenderly at first, every thrust deepening his entry until he was lodged fully in the sweet, tight warmth of her untried, innocent body. *Dear Lord!* he thought blasphemously, closing his eyes and poised above her on his elbows. *If there is truly a paradise on earth, as the ministers claim, then surely it is here, being joined with her this way!* He gently kissed her eyelids and the crushed flower of her mouth as he slowly withdrew, leaving only the tip of himself lodged within her, before he thrust deeply forward again.

"Gideon! Oh, my love—!" To his delight, she drew a deep, shuddering breath and arched against him, matching her rhythm to his own. They moved together, their movements growing faster, harder, more intense as their passion mounted, their breathing becoming low, guttural grunts and groans until he felt her suddenly stiffen beneath him. For a second, she was perfectly still, and then a throbbing, a pulse, rippled through her body. Like a whirlpool, it drew him ever deeper into her as she found her release. In the same instant, he felt the sensual storm of his climax building, gathering momentum within him.

He rode the storm's crest to its tumultuous end, at the last pulling himself from her and spending his seed in the sand. His chest heaved, and to his ears, his hard, raspy breaths sounded embarrassingly like those of an animal on the cove's hush, for the only other sound was the splashing refrain of the waves against the shore.

Afterward, they held each other, breathing heavily, exchanging the quick, hard kisses and possessive little caresses of lovers, until sleep claimed them.

To Gideon's surprise, several hours had passed when they awoke in a tangle of limbs. He shivered and drew Emma closer, for as they slept, the day had vanished, leaving only the silver splendor of the evening in her wake. The night wind felt chill upon their cooled bodies.

When Gideon took her in his arms, Emma suddenly burst into tears. She buried her hot, damp face against his chest and sobbed, her slender shoulders heaving. "I love you, Gideon," she whispered brokenly in his ear.

"Then why are you crying, silly little girl?" he demanded, brushing the tears from her cheek with the ball of his thumb.

"Did I hurt you? Is that it? Or are you sorry about . . . you know! Sorry we did it?"

"No, silly. That's not why I'm crying, not at all," she insisted, though her eyes were still huge and shiny in the light of the full moon. "I'm crying because I love you so much!" she said illogically, "I'll always belong to you now, won't I? No one can change that. Ever!" she added in a fierce tone, like a little tigress, for all the world as if he argued the matter with her. "We'll be together always, won't we?"

Guilt turned in Gideon's belly like the twist of a naked blade. Reaching for his clothes, he began dressing, realizing, with a sinking feeling in his gut, that there was no putting it off any longer. He must tell her that he was leaving the islands right now—as he should have told her long before it had come to this pass, he thought guiltily. It would be even worse if he waited till the last moment.

"Emma, there's something—there's something I have to tell you," he began.

Smiling mysteriously, she sat up, brushing the sand from her body as she reached for her *muumuu*. "I already know!" she declared.

His brows rose in surprise. "You do?"

"Of course." She smiled. "My *makua* told me about it."

"Your *mother?* How does she know about it?"

Misunderstanding, she stuck her tongue out at him. "Not about tonight, silly. It happened at the beginning of summer, before I met you. *Makua* was telling me about men and women, and about . . . all about life, oh, and mating, and how babies are really made, because, you see, I thought they came from kissing. Isn't that silly?" She grinned mischievously, but instead of laughing, he urged her, "Go on."

"Well, *Makua* said that the nuns at the convent are all married to Christ, and that they remain *wahine kapu*—virgins—until the day they die, so they know very little about women and men. My mother believes that no girl should be kept in ignorance about her body, or about the powerful stirring of desire. *Makua* thinks girls should be told everything there is to know by the time they're fourteen—and I was fourteen in August."

"Fourteen!" The blood drained from his tanned face, leaving him ashen.

She nodded, blissfully unaware of his shocked expression, or of the chaos into which her casual announcement had thrown his thoughts. Dear Lord, she was a girl—little more than a child!—while he'd thought her a young woman, or at very least, far closer to his own age!

"Makua said it was . . . safer, you know, for a girl to know about such things than to be ignorant so that she could be careful. So, you see, I know I could have a baby because you made love to me, Gideon, but I-I don't care!" she said defiantly. Her face darkened. Her eyes took on a distant, remembering sort of light and burned fiercely. "I'd rather have your baby than . . . than anyone's, really I would."

He gaped at her in disbelief for several seconds before he recovered his wits and, with them, his voice. "Emma, don't! You don't have to fret about having a baby, not from what we did today, I promise." He squirmed like a schoolboy in the shadows as he gingerly explained, "I . . . er . . . pulled myself . . . my . . . er . . . *ule*—out. You know, before I . . . er . . . spent? So you don't need to worry. You can't have a baby. But, that's not what I've been trying to tell you."

"Oh?"

"No. Emma, I know you'll be upset, maybe angry, to hear this, but I have to say it anyway. I have to go away!" The words, so long withheld, so dreaded, came out in a rush. To his ears, they sounded callous, unfeeling, almost brutal, and yet he was not sure there was a gentle way to break the news.

For a moment, she was silent, her expression tranquil, impassive, unchanged. Her lovely features betrayed none of the sudden frightened churning in her breast, the sudden wild flutter of panic in her heart. "Where to?" she whispered. "Honolulu?"

Surely he meant Honolulu, and she could go with him, she told herself. *Makua* would understand that she couldn't bear to be parted from him—or maybe she'd come, too? Malia was not so desperately ill she couldn't travel on the steamer to Oahu.

"It's much farther than that, I'm afraid. To Boston, and school there at Harvard College."

"Noooo!" she cried, unable to hold back.

Her anguished cry was like that of a small, wounded animal having a lead ball slammed into its tiny body. It made the fine hairs stand up his nape. He sighed heavily. "I'm afraid it's true. I sail for Honolulu on the first of next month," he told her unhappily.

"Next month! But—that's just next week!"

"Yes," he admitted heavily.

"And how long have you—I mean, did you know this before . . . when we first met?"

Feeling sick to his stomach, he nodded, forcing himself to meet her eyes. The radiant glow she'd worn but moments before had faded from her lovely face, he saw. In the stark blue-white moonlight, she looked close to tears, drawn and pale, and he was filled with guilt and pain as he reached out and touched her quivering mouth with his finger, then muttered, "Oh, damn it!" and drew her fiercely into his arms, hugging her as if he'd never let her go as he stroked her midnight hair. If only they'd met sooner! he told himself. He would have married her, taken her to America with him—done *something* to keep them together. "I know it hurts, *ku'uipo,* sweetheart," he murmured. "It hurts me, too."

"If you mean that, then stay here! Refuse to go!"

"I can't, don't you see? I don't like the idea any more than you do. I even argued with my father till I was blue in the face, but his mind's made up that I should see the world—and when my father's decided on something, that's that. Emma, please try to understand. I'm eighteen, and I love my parents. They expect me to go to school in Boston, and I can't disappoint them. I just can't."

She wriggled herself from his arms and pulled her *muumuu* over her head, smoothing down its folds over and over again, as if her very life depended on ridding the garment of every tiny wrinkle. When she was done, she sat there, her hands clasped primly in her lap, her back to him so that he could not see her face. Never had she looked smaller, more vulnerable to him than she did in that moment.

He swallowed. The silence seemed to expand, to become a gaping void between them. Desperate to fill it, he began, "From Honolulu, I'm to board the *Galileo,* bound for Boston, on the eighth of next month. It's all settled."

"Boston!" she repeated, as if what he'd said had only just sunk in. "So soon? Oh, Gideon, noo! Tell me it's a game? Tell me it's not true—I can't bear it!" Bowing her head, she bit her lip and tightly closed her eyes, yet fat, shiny tears trickled from beneath her lashes nevertheless, and slipped down her cheeks to drip onto the ruffled bodice of her dark-blue *muumuu.* In the bright light of the lovely full moon, the damp splotches looked like spilled India ink on the cloth. "Boston is so very, very far away—the other side of the world! H-how long must you be gone?" she whispered, but her haunting violet eyes were already brimming again. Another second, and her voice broke. More tears ran down her cheeks as she tremulously asked, "M-months?"

There was a deafening silence. "Worse. *Years,*" he managed to choke out, his own deep voice sounding strangled. "Four years, at very least." That it could take even longer was a very real possibility he suddenly found unbearable to contemplate.

"Four years! Oh, my dearest love, a lifetime!" she cried softly.

Her words cut him to the quick; each one stabbing like a thorn into his heart. "I know. Damn it, I know!" He hesitated, then drew her stiff body against his chest again. Holding her, he stroked her dark head in a boyish attempt to comfort her, while her tears fell like scalding rain upon his bare chest. "Emma, I know I have no right to ask you this, but I have to. Emma, may I presume upon your affections, and ask if you would do me the great honor of—"

"—waiting for you?" she finished for him.

Swallowing the painful lump in his throat, he nodded.

She looked him full in the eye, her fingertips resting lightly on his upper arms. "I'll wait," she vowed. "Forever, if need be, because I love you, Gideon Kane. Come what may, I'll always love you! I swear it on these, my grandfather's bones." So saying, she drew something from the pocket of her dress and pressed it into his palm.

Uncurling his fingers, Gideon saw she'd given him the good-luck charm she sometimes wore; a fishhook carved from human bone. The large, elegant hook was shaped like a thick, upside-down question mark, and had been strung on a cord of sennit fiber through a hole at the top. He gaped at her in disbelief, for he knew from old Moki's teachings that this was a very special gift, one that possessed the great *mana,* or spiritual power and essence, of the man from whose thigh bone it had been carved.

He swallowed, moved beyond words. "I shall wear it always, *me ke aloha,* my beloved," he promised hoarsely. "Here, close to my heart. If only I had something to give you, in return!"

"Hush, hush. You've already given me something wonderful to treasure—a keepsake more precious than any gift," she whispered. "For I have your love, and my memories of the special times we've shared this summer." The haunting sadness was there again in her eyes as she added, "No one can ever change that, *or* make . . . or make what we've had ugly or shameful, can they, Gideon?" She blinked back her tears and smiled up at him.

"No. Never!" he swore, and gathered her into his arms and held her tightly. "When I come home, we'll be married immediately," he vowed. "We'll live with my parents for the first few months, until I've built us a fine, new house of our own, hewn of the best *koa* wood in the mountains. It'll be a house with a long veranda from which we can look out across the plains to this very beach, and remember the night we first made love by the light of the full moon."

"Oh, yes!" she exclaimed softly, her violet eyes shining. "And I'll carry you always in my heart, Gideon Kane, till you come back to me. You *will* come back to me?"

"I'll always come back to you, love," he vowed. "But until then, we'll write to each other, every week. Until I send you my address, you can post your letters to me in care of the Abraham Kane & Sons, Shipping and Chandler's Emporium of Boston, Massachusetts." He smiled. "And where shall I write to you?"

"You can send my letters in care of Ah Woo's store in Kawaiihae. I can pick them up from him."

He nodded and they kissed. "Will you come again tomorrow?"

She nodded, her expression wistful. "We don't have many days left us, do we? We must make the most of those remaining. I'll try to come a little earlier. Can you?"

He nodded. "I can come at dawn, if you can get away. My father's *luna* has given me leave to enjoy myself until I sail." He shrugged, embarrassed. "I suppose there are certain advantages to being Makua Kane's son."

"I'm sure." She brightened. "I know, let's go on a picnic tomorrow!"

"All right." He grinned. "Where shall we go?"

"To the falls. I want to gather some herbs for drying. There are plants the old ones use to increase the appetite."

"Ah. For your *makua?*"

She nodded. "Until then?"

"Until then. *Aloha nui loa,* my love, And Emma—?"

"Yes?" She looked back at him over her shoulder.

"We'll weather this separation somehow, Emma. You must believe that. One day, we'll be together again."

She nodded, and was gone.

* * *

The next morning—and every morning and afternoon for the next week—Gideon came to the cove and waited for Emma beneath the sea-grape tree, pacing back and forth, back and forth, growing frantic with worry; then furiously angry by turns. But Emma never returned following that last evening, and nor did she send him any word to reassure him that she was well.

There were times, in the lonely, empty week that followed, when he began to wonder if she'd truly been real, or just one of the *wahine a ka po,* or night-women, that Old Moki had warned him about. Could she have been just a lovely figment of his imagination?

But then the bone fishhook would burn like a brand against his chest and his aching heart would remind him all over again that she had been all too real.

Seven

The first day of September dawned bright and clear, the dour rainclouds of the past week having chosen just that morning to disperse. The hills of Waimea and the Kohala foothills beyond were just as lush and green as he had ever seen them, broken only by the dark blots that were his father's longhorns, and his heart ached to think he was leaving all this beauty behind him.

Here and there, wisps of mist drifted like silent ghosts among the mulberry trees. Vivid blue morning glories tumbled in giddy profusion over the low, dark walls of native moss rock that defined Hui Aloha's holding corrals, and in the distance Mauna Kea, the White Mountain, loomed as guardian over all, her snowcapped peaks clearly visible this morning—a rare display intended, his mother laughingly declared, to honor his departure.

Standing on the veranda of the ranch house, Miriam Kane clinging to his elbow, Gideon made his farewells to the *paniolos,* the cowboys, ranch hands, serving men and women, and neighbors from other ranches who'd congregated on the lawns to wish him a fond goodbye and a bon voyage.

He moved among them, shaking hands, slapping backs, receiving many farewell punches and more farewell *leis,* feeling very self-conscious in his brand-new frockcoat and breeches, his neck already chafing against the stiffly starched wing collar, and the hated dark cravat fastened about his throat like a garrote.

"Did you contrive this torture to remind me of you when I'm long gone, eh, Auntie?" he demanded, grinning down at his honorary auntie—the woman who kept house for his mother, Miriam Kane.

"Of course!" Auntie Leolani sniffed. "I wen' put fresh *poi* in that collar, 'stead of *pia* starch, and just look at you! You plenty handsome, Mister Gideon Kane!" she exclaimed, framing his face between her plump palms and soundly bussing both of his cheeks and his lips before she released him. "Come, now, honey-boy. Your turn for kiss Auntie bye-bye! Right heah!" She pointed to her plump cheek, still flushed with the heat of the fire on which she'd cooked him an enormous farewell breakfast.

Bending a little, he hugged the enormous Hawaiian woman who had loved him only a little less fiercely than his mother ever since the day he'd been born. Only when he had hugged and kissed Leolani Pakele until she squealed in protest did he dare move on to say his goodbyes to the others, several of whom were crying openly, for it was not the island way to hide one's feelings. Emotions flowed as openly and freely as running water.

"If we're to reach the Landing before dark, we should be on our way shortly, Son," Jacob Kane, Gideon's father, reminded him.

"Yes, sir," Gideon promised. "I'll be right there," he added over his shoulder as he came at last to Old Moki.

"Well, here I am," he said huskily. *"Aloha,* Uncle! I shall miss your wise counsel while I'm away," he murmured, bending down to embrace the old fellow. "Four years is a long time to be gone."

"Auwe! It is long indeed, my nephew! But . . . four years will yet find *you* far from these islands, Mo'o," the old man murmured. "Far from the islands you call home, and from those you love, and who love you."

Gideon stiffened. Wetting his suddenly dry lips and mouth, he swallowed, for everyone knew that the old *kahuna's* prophecies, though rare as hen's teeth, could invariably be depended upon. "Why in the world would I stay any longer than I must in America?"

The old man's light-brown, almost amber, eyes took on a faraway, dreaming light. "The choice will not be yours, my nephew. The god of war, Kukailimoku, will demand that you serve him! Only when you have done so shall you return to these islands."

"And the girl, Uncle?" he asked in a lower, urgent voice intended for his mentor's ears alone. "I have not seen her in over a week—not once! What of the *wahine* I love? Will she be faithful? Will she wait for me till I return? Does she . . . does she truly love me, as she swore she did?"

"Auwe! You ask me of her loyalty, when it is *your* heart you must search, my nephew. It is *your* loyalty that will be questioned, rather than hers," Old Moki replied enigmatically. And, despite Gideon's coaxing, he could not be persuaded to say more.

Feeling disturbed and disgruntled by the old man's unwelcome predictions, Gideon was scowling as he swung himself astride his horse for the last time, and rode down from his home on the slopes of the mountain to the landing at Kawaiihae.

It was late afternoon before they reached the landing, yet the steamer, *Hoku* had delayed its departure, pending his arrival, and still rocked at anchor offshore.

Gideon watched as some of the hands loaded his two small trunks and a duffle bag aboard a waiting outrigger manned by three native men, then turned to embrace his parents one last time.

"Aloha, Father," he said thickly, wrapping his arms around the older man's burly shoulders. "I'll miss you. Take care of yourself, and of Mother."

"And you, my son. May the good Lord watch over you and keep you safe till that time you come back to us," Jacob returned, his blue eyes misting over with emotion.

"Farewell, my little *makuahine!"* Gideon murmured, taking his mother in his arms and pretending he did not notice her anguished expression. "Now, now, you promised, *Makua,* no tears—you swore it!" he scolded, hugging her so tightly, her feet left the ground. Yet despite her towering young son's scolding,

Miriam Haunani Kane was weeping openly when he set her down, though trying gamely to smile through her tears.

"Be a good boy, Gideon. Make us proud of you, and never, ever forget that we love you. God Bless you, my *hiapo,* my firstborn! *Aloooha, my son! Aloha nui loa!"*

Turning from his parents, Gideon looked up, then down the narrow beach, squinting against the sunlight. To those watching, it seemed he was committing the landing and the arid country beyond to memory, before he took his last leave of the island, yet it was not so. He was looking for his darling Emma, hoping and praying for one last glimpse of her before he left, yearning for a final, radiant smile to take with him over the miles to eradicate his last image of her lovely face, streaked with tears.

But she was not there, and, with a sigh, he turned away.

"The captain's anxious to lift anchor, my boy," Jacob Kane reminded him. "Best do it fast, and get it over with."

"Yes, sir," Gideon agreed, extending his arm. The two men clasped hands, then Gideon turned and strode to the waiting canoe, taking his seat without looking back. Even when the steamship *Hoku* pulled away from the reef and headed for the open sea, Gideon stood with his legs braced on the deck by the for'ard taffrail, his eyes steadfastly on the distant horizon, and with it, the future that lay ahead. He did not look back, not even once.

A small lifetime would come and go before he again set foot on his beloved Sandwich Isles. Yet in all those years, Gideon would never forget his Emma's haunting violet eyes, would never forget her sad, sweet smile or the fragrance of the white-ginger blossoms she'd worn in her hair.

And neither time nor distance nor the horrors of civil war would ever diminish his love for her.

Eight

1866

Nuuanu Valley, Honolulu, The Island of Oahu,
The Sandwich Isles

"How lovely to have you with us again this morning, Gideon—and how very unexpected, too! After being away for so long, we didn't think you'd stay on Oahu a moment longer than it took to board a steamer for Kawaihae, did we, children?" Sophie Kane observed, spreading a snowy napkin across her lap.

She smiled across the table at Elizabeth, her eldest child, and beside her, at Thomas—two years Elizabeth's junior—and beside him, at her youngest, Jeremiah, who at the tender age of twelve nevertheless towered over his petite mother. The next chair had been left vacant. Sophie's second daughter, Moriah, had married a Congregationalist minister four years before, and had sailed with him to the Marquesas islands, there to devote her life to converting the heathen savages, as had her grandparents before her. Accordingly, Moriah and her husband, the Reverend Mister Micah Trace, were duly remembered in family prayers each evening.

A diminutive woman with a spine as unbending as her morals, Sophie Sheldon wore gold-rimmed pince-nez spectacles perched on the very end of her nose. The thick glass lenses magnified her round, watery blue eyes so hugely, his aunt always reminded Gideon of a little owl dressed in prim lace caps and serviceable pastel gowns.

Peering at him over the rims of her spectacles, she added, "Surely you must be eager to get home, dear boy?"

"I certainly am, Aunt Sophie. Most eager," Gideon confirmed with an engaging smile, one guaranteed to melt the heart of the most hard-hearted spinster or prudish aunt. He drew a gold pocket watch on a long gold chain from his inner pocket and, raising the heavily engraved lid, checked the time. A few tinkling bars of "Greensleeves" played before he closed it with a snap and continued, "However, since I had some pressing business to discuss with Alexander McHenry, I decided it might be simpler—and far more pleasant!—were I to get the matter concluded before going on to the Big Island, and home." He deftly flipped the timepiece back into his pocket by the chain alone, the smooth little trick eliciting a broad and admiring grin from young Jeremiah as the timepiece plopped smartly into Gideon's pocket with a solid-sounding thunk. "It's not inconvenient for me to stay, I trust, Aunt? If so, I can certainly find lodging elsewhere?"

"Silly boy, of course it's not inconvenient—not in the *least,*" Sophie scolded, clearly distressed that her nephew had imagined himself unwelcome. "In fact, I wouldn't hear of you leaving us—what would your dear mother say? Why, we're always happy to have you with us, aren't we, Mister Kane? Children?"

"Indeed, yes. Delighted, Gideon, old man," Gideon's uncle confirmed warmly, glancing up from the sheaf of correspondence a Chinese houseboy, clad in baggy navy-blue pajamas and a small black skullcap, had brought in on a silver tray. "Stay as long as you like. You're always welcome, my boy. You know that." He winked and grinned at his nephew.

Gideon grinned back. Spearing a piece of sausage on his fork, he saluted his uncle with it, then popped it into his mouth and chewed with the gusto of a man long removed from the simple delights of home. "Hmm, Auntie Abigail's *linguisa!*" he exclaimed appreciatively. "Hotter than Hades, just the way we like 'em, eh, Thomas? There's nothing like it back in Boston!"

"Speaking of Boston, dear, how was Great-Aunt Arabella Kane when you left?" Sophie inquired, pouring breakfast tea for herself and Elizabeth from a willow-patterned china teapot.

"Amazingly well for one of her advanced years, Aunt Sophie. She sent you her warmest regards, as did Great-Uncle William, and asked to be remembered to you both," Gideon returned, accepting a slice of toast from the rack Thomas offered him. He slathered it generously with fresh butter and marmalade. "Oh, I almost forgot, Uncle William sent a barrel of apples and pears from his orchard, and there are some jars of Aunt Bella's gooseberry preserves and green-tomato chutney, Aunt. I'll bring them in from the stable presently. Some toast for you, Missus Lennox?" he cordially offered his aunt's guest, smiling at the attractive fair-haired young woman seated on his right. She was dressed in the severe black of heavy mourning, which flattered rather than overwhelmed her coloring.

"No, really, I couldn't eat another bite, thank you," Julia Lennox demurred with a graceful flutter of an elegant, long-fingered hand. "The lappered milk and pureed banana was more than sufficient. I'm afraid my poor constitution's been somewhat delicate since I arrived in the islands. A result of the excessive heat and humidity, I do believe," she added, favoring Gideon with an apologetic smile and fanning herself with a tiny handkerchief.

Ignoring the sharp kick Thomas dealt his ankle beneath the table, Gideon made appropriately sympathetic clucking noises. "My condolences, Missus Lennox. But I'm sure that, given time, you'll become used to our tropical climate."

"There you go again! 'Missus Lennox,' indeed," Julia scolded, resting her slim fingers on Gideon's forearm. Her deep-gray eyes were admonishing beneath delicately arched, pale-blond brows the same shade as her upswept hair as she chided, "We're second cousins by marriage, after all, *Cousin* Gideon, not quite strangers. Please, call me Julia, do."

"Very well, *Julia*," Gideon concurred, his smile freezing as he felt the faint pressure of a second hand—this against his trousered thigh—beneath the folds of the tablecloth. Gritting his teeth, he shot Thomas a murderous scowl—one that his cousin blithely ignored. In as level a voice as he could muster, he continued, "I'm sure the climate you're accustomed to must be very different to that of our little island chain?"

"Ah, yes, indeed! The Sandwich Isles do tend to be rather *steamy*, am I right, eh, *Cousin* Gideon? Or should I say, hot and—er—umm—devilishly *humid?*" Thomas gushed, studiously ignoring both Gideon's ferocious scowl and his father's hastily smothered laughter from the head of the table, which he followed by a violent fit of coughing. Sophie Kane was forced to summon the houseboy, Wong Lee, to bring the cane planter some water.

"Humid, ahh, yes, quite so," Julia agreed, dabbing delicately at her brow, upper lip, and swanlike throat with the same tiny, black lace handkerchief, though Gideon could see no trace of moisture upon the widow's porcelain skin and the paddle fan was whirring monotonously overhead, wafting cool currents over their heads. "Being close to the Atlantic," she added, answering Gideon's question, "Baltimore has a most agreeably temperate clime—it's never too hot nor too cold for comfort. And, I am happy to say, it is even more agreeably *civilized* there." She smiled.

"Ah. So you're from Baltimore! I should have guessed," Gideon observed gallantly. "Maryland's a charming state."

"You know it?" Julia exclaimed, a faint blush tingeing her cheeks following his compliment.

"Indeed I do, though I regret not near as well as I would have liked. I was billeted near Sharpsburg briefly, during the war years." A shadow seemed to cross Gideon's handsome face. "I fought under McClellan at the Battle of Antietam in '62, you see."

"Antietam! Why, Gideon, then I'm doubly fortunate! You're not only my own dear cousin, but a true war hero, in the flesh!" she declared, her gray eyes shining. "Tell me, Coz, have you made the military your career?" She eyed his broad shoulders, as if mentally fitting him for a dashing officer's uniform, one trimmed with lashings of gold braid.

"No, not at all, ma'am. To be frank, the War Between the States was more than enough soldiering for my liking." His serious expression brightened as he added, "I'm delighted to be back in the islands. Perhaps they aren't civilized by American standards, but they're my home. Besides, my mother is *hapa* herself."

"Ha-pa?"

"It literally means half—in this case, half Hawaiian, half American. Island blood runs in my veins. I belong here!"

"Oh, yes, of course. Truly, I meant no disrespect by my comparison. These islands are truly a Garden of Eden! And the people are so happy, always smiling! But, what will you do with your life, now that you're back? Forgive me for being forward, but you seem such a . . . well, such a dynamic—even ambitious—man! Surely there's little excitement in these sleepy islands, however charming, to hold your interest for long?"

"On the contrary, I expect to have my work more than cut out for me here." He smiled and took a long swig of scalding coffee from the dainty porcelain cup—its willow pattern matching that of the teapot—that was dwarfed by the tanned fingers clamped about it.

"Indeed? May I ask in what fashion?"

"You may. My father has asked me to take over the running of our family's cattle ranch."

"Surely you can't mean to become a rancher?" Her tone and the disgusted way she wrinkled her nose spoke volumes.

"Not just any rancher, nor just any ranch, Cousin Julia.

Gideon's far too modest to brag," Elizabeth, Thomas's older sister, added from her seat on Julia's right, "but the Kane Ranch is one of *the* largest cattle ranches in the entire world, and by far one of the two most successful in all the islands—perhaps anywhere! There are simply *millions* of Kane cattle. Why, the ranch takes up almost half the Big Island, doesn't it, Gideon?"

"Allowing for a slight exaggeration on your part, Lizzy my pet, yes. I'd say that's a fair enough description."

"Big Island?"

"That's what we islanders call the island of Hawaii. It's the largest in the chain, you see? Pass the bacon, would you, Jerry?"

"Gideon, you horrid wretch, you called me Lizzy! I told you, you are *not* to call me Lizzy!" Elizabeth hissed at him, color filling her fair cheeks and staining her neck bright crimson above the high neck of her prim dark gown. "Eliza or Beth are quite acceptable, but you know very well I won't abide being called Lizzy now that I'm grown up."

"Sorry . . . Lizzy, old girl," Gideon apologized with a wicked grin, wiping his mouth before tossing his rumpled napkin to the table. Winking at a grinning Jeremiah, whose pudgy red cheeks were bulging like a squirrel's filled with food, he pushed back his chair and stood. His striking dark good looks, his height, and the breadth of his shoulders were incongruous in the long, narrow dining room with its fussy furnishings, lace draperies, and elegant crystal chandeliers. "Aunt Sophie, Uncle, everyone, please, finish your breakfasts. I'm afraid I must excuse myself and rush off. I've an early appointment at McHenry's offices and I really should get going."

"Take the covered carriage into town, Gideon," Sheldon urged, glancing up at him over the pages of the *Honolulu Gazette*. "Unless I'm way off the mark, it'll be raining cats and dogs well before noon. This time of year, the streets'll be a quagmire."

"If you're sure you won't be needing it?"

"Quite sure, my boy. Be my guest."

"Wait up, Gideon old man. There was something I wanted to ask you before you left," Thomas exclaimed, springing up to follow Gideon from the dining room.

"Well?" Gideon asked Thomas moments later as he waited on the *lanai,* or porch, steps for the Kanes' Portuguese groom, Luis, to back the horse into the shafts of the carriage.

"Well what?" Thomas came back, grinning.

"What was so blasted important that you couldn't wait to ask me?"

"Oh, that!" He laughed, brushing a cowlick of fair hair from his eyes. "Just a harmless ruse. A means of escape, so to speak."

"Escape?" Gideon snorted. "From what? Or should I say, from whom?"

"As if you didn't know! The Black Widow was at her spinning rather early this morning, else I'm a Dutchman! Do you feel the sticky strands of her web about your throat, old man? If not, you should—because they're there!"

"The devil, you say! It's you Julia Lennox is after, Tom, old man—your little trick with the hand on my knee notwithstanding."

"*My* hand on *your* knee?" Thomas snorted, and managed to appear amazingly innocent. "Sorry, Gid. Not guilty—at least not of that! If there *was* a hand on your knee, it was the fair Julia's hot little palm, not mine."

"Aw, come off it. You know damned well you did it. And quite frankly, I'm a bit disappointed in you, Tom. A joke's one thing, but to say things like that about poor Julia! She's your own mama's cousin by marriage, for pity's sake—hardly the sort of woman to indulge in under-the-tablecloth fumblings!" He winked.

"You'd think so, wouldn't you? But, 'that sort' or no, it wasn't my hand on your knee, Gideon, old man—I swear it. And let's face it, it *was* your blue eyes she was gazing into over her coddled eggs and milk toast. I saw that oh-so-casual brush of her fingers against your arm, you lil' old 'hero-in-the-flesh' you! Yikes! All that simpering and cooing was enough to make a grown man lose his breakfast." Thomas grinned and shuddered, looking very much like his father as he added, "Speaking of flesh—and the sins thereof!—I'd bet ten silver dollars you could have Julia in your bed by the Sabbath, if you only crooked your little finger. What do you say? Is it a bet?"

"I'll pass."

"You'll *pass?* Is this the cousin I—at the tender age of fifteen years!—tomcatted the Honolulu bawdy houses with? The same Gideon who was the wicked darling of the Alakea Street Playhouse? Gideon, tell me the truth, man to man. Those Johnny Rebs didn't shoot off anything—er—vital in the war, did they?" Tom asked, all false concern.

Gideon swung a playful punch at his cousin's shoulder. "No, damn you, you young rogue. I'm just not interested. Not in your fair Julia, anyway. So, the field's clear, brat. And with a war hero like me out of the running, hey, you might actually have a slim chance with the Black Widow—*if* you work at it."

"Me? Hmm, no, thanks," Tom declined with a shudder. "Icy blondes festooned in black crepe give me the willies. I'd rather cuddle up to a golden skinned *wahine* any night. What've you got planned after your meeting with McHenry?"

"Nothing pressing. I thought I might go to the races for the afternoon. There were some horses from Kentucky on the ship I arrived on. Beautiful animals! Fast, too, I'd say."

Tom nodded. "I'll meet you at the track, then, if I may?"

"By all means. I'll look forward to it. And, after we've lost our respective shirts, perhaps you'd come with me to the jeweler's. I thought Van Meek's, perhaps, or that Chinaman's—what was his name? The one who used to be on Merchant Street?"

"Yee. If it's jade or pearls or Hong Kong gold you're after, Yee's your man. Anything else—diamonds, rubies, whatever— I'd try the Dutchman."

Gideon nodded. "Van Meek's it'll be, then. I'd welcome your opinion on a purchase I plan to make there, all going well."

"Really? Then I'd be happy to offer it," Thomas agreed as Gideon swung up into the carriage. He'd been hoping his cousin would elaborate; at least drop a hint or two about the expensive bauble he planned to buy—and, more importantly, which little beauty he planned to give it to. But Gideon was being his usual closemouthed self this morning, and so Tom shrugged. No matter. He'd find out the details soon enough. "Kapiolani Racecourse at, say, two o'clock?"

"Two it is."

"Whoa there!" Gideon's mood was distracted as he drew the matched pair to a halt before the offices of McHenry, Brooker, and Fitch on Merchant Street.

He sat there, deaf to the steady drumming of the rain on the carriage's raised leather hood, blind to the sudden, roaring downpour that was quickly turning the hard-packed dirt of the Honolulu street before him into a muddy quagmire, as his uncle had predicted. Nor did he notice the lowering skies that hung over the town, festooning the landmark ridge of Diamond Head like the sagging gray folds of an old circus tent, for as he turned his head, something white had caught his eye in the doorway of one of the fine brick buildings. Surprised, he poked his head from beneath the carriage's hood, ignoring the rain in order to get a better look, for he was almost certain he'd glimpsed Old Moki standing in a shadowed doorway across the street, staring at him with an eerie intensity that made the fine hairs on his neck rise in response. Gideon frowned. Moki, here? Impossible! To his knowledge, the frail old fellow had never left his beloved Big Island! So, what in the world would the old Hawaiian be doing here, in Honolulu? He told himself he'd been mistaken, yet it had certainly looked like Moki, dressed in the flowing white *tapa* wraparound he'd always favored, his white hair and long white beard lifting wildly about his shoulders in the wind.

But, by the time Gideon had slowed the horses and tried to

peer through the sheeting rain for a closer look at the fellow, there was no one there. Moreover, a quick glance to left and right showed a deserted street, quite emptied by the downpour. Had Moki ducked inside one of the office buildings—or had he simply imagined him standing there?

A prickly sensation of foreboding washed over him, bringing with it the unshakeable, skin-tingling conviction that some kind of *pilikia,* trouble, lay ahead, though why he felt that way and from what direction that trouble might come, he could not say.

Lord, don't let anything have happened to Emma! he prayed, silently and fervently. If he closed his eyes, he could see her as clearly as if it were yesterday, rather than seven years ago, that he'd seen her last: her pansy eyes, her rosy lips, her coal-black hair—the beautiful, laughing island *wahine* who'd haunted his dreams and made the nightmare days of the war endurable!

Although *he* was convinced it'd been a true and enduring love that had flared up so suddenly between them, what if he'd been wrong all these years? What if he'd just imagined something that, like a mirage, or the glint of fool's gold in a miner's pan, had never really existed, except in his dreams? And what if—unlike his own steadfast love—Emma's feelings had changed?

He had cause to worry, for she'd never answered any of the dozen or so letters he'd sent her in care of the Chinaman Ah Woo's store in Kawaiiahae, as agreed. Nor had she written him back—at least, not that he knew of. In the end, he'd stopped writing, telling himself she'd been too busy caring for her sick mother to write. But what if she hadn't written back because she was sick—or worse?

The nibbling mouse of foreboding in the pit of his belly had become a roaring tiger of doubt now. Why the devil was he putting off going home, dilly-dallying in Honolulu, when he could be on the last leg of his journey to the Big Island? He *had* to see her again, *had* to talk with her, as soon as possible! He needed to know she still felt the same after all the years they'd spent apart. Only then would the nibbling mouse in his gut be dispersed, the tiger silenced. He didn't have to see McHenry right now. He'd handle the transaction by post, instead.

"Gideon? Is it you, mon, after all these years?"

He glanced up to see the lawyer, Alexander McHenry—a little older, a little more bent than he remembered—staring up at him from beneath the spokes of a battered black umbrella, off which a deluge of warm rain was pouring in silver sheets. The voluminous folds of a raincape swathed the lawyer from his chin to the toes of his stout boots.

"It is indeed, Mister McHenry. It's good to see you again, sir! I was waiting for it to stop raining."

"I dinna blame ye. But it's easing off a wee bit now, I ken. Come along wi' ye, laddie!" the Scot urged. "Let's make a run fer it!"

"Weell, now. And here we are. A spot o' something to drive the damp from your bones and welcome ye home, Captain Kane?" McHenry offered moments later in his offices, where they were ensconced in comfortable wing chairs. The spacious rooms had been done up in gleaming leather and polished *koa*-wood furnishings, with brass fittings winking here and there at inkstand, candlestick, and picture frame. The man, with dual profession of lawyer and accountant held up a decanter of Scottish whiskey. "Or t' toast the North's victory, mayhap?"

Gideon declined the offer with a wry smile. "Thank you, but no, sir. To be honest, it's a little early for me, homecoming or no."

"As ye will, laddie. Ye won't mind if I indulge mysel' before we get down t' business? I know the damned authorities cast a dismal eye on liquor in these islands, but by my reckoning, a wee dram t' celebrate your safe return canna hurt, hmm?"

"By all means, sir. Go right ahead."

McHenry poured himself a generous two fingers of Scotch and drained it in a single swallow. "Ah, that's better. Nothing like a drop o' guid whiskey for taking the rheumaticks and the cursed damp from a mon's body. Now, let's have a look at these wee pieces o' property ye're interested in."

McHenry lit a hanging lantern to dispel the gloom of the dour afternoon, and the two men, heads bent, studied the maps the lawyer had spread across his desk.

"These few acres are the ones, sir, right here," Gideon murmured after a lengthy silence, stabbing his index finger at a marked area on a map of the biggest island in the Sandwich Isles, the island of Hawaii, better known as the Big Island. "Did you make inquiries, as I instructed in my letter?"

"Aye, laddie, I did."

"And? You're not smiling, sir. Is it bad news then?"

The Scot pursed his lips. "That depends. What was it ye had in mind for the smaller parcel?"

"I intended to build a house there. Or should I say, a home. A fine one of *koa* and stone for myself and my bride, and, God willing, for any children we may be fortunate enough to have someday."

"Och, so you're to marry! I should have guessed!" He beamed. "My felicitations, Gideon."

"Thank you, sir, but I'm afraid your good wishes are a little premature." He grinned ruefully. "I have yet to formally ask the young lady in question for her hand."

"Ah. A mere formality, I'm sure," Alexander reassured him, clasping his shoulder warmly.

"I hope with all my heart you're right, sir."

"An island bride?"

"Would I take any other, sir?"

Chuckling, McHenry nodded. "Indeed. Now, getting back t' business, laddie. As your letter instructed, I researched the title t' that particular wee parcel on the ridge—one with a bonny view of the distant Pacific, I might add—and discovered it is held by one Ah Woo."

"The storekeeper at Kawaihae?"

"The same."

"Hmm. Any luck with the purchase?"

"Aye, laddie. I've already approached Woo by letter on your behalf, as you requested, and was given a prompt reply. Mister Woo would be more than willing to sell, if the price is right. It appears his attempts to grow sugarcane there have proven successful, but insufficiently profitable for his liking. He's eager to invest his *cash* elsewhere." The Scot grinned and nudged him. "Well? Have ye nothing t' say? Congratulations, laddie! It looks like ye'll have the bonny wee spot ye've been wantin' t' build yer nest! But you'd best listen t' me. It's a verra serious matter, marriage. Serious, terrible serious. Are ye sure ye won't have that wee dram o' whiskey after all?"

"Thank you, sir, but the answer's still no. Now, what about that other piece of land?" he pressed, impatient for an answer. "The one that borders the ranch's eastern boundaries?"

"Ah. That one. Might I ask why it is ye want it? Is it the water?"

Gideon nodded. "In his last letter to reach me before I sailed from Boston Harbor, Father mentioned last year's terrible drought, and how hundreds of head had dropped dead in their tracks because of it. As it stands, some of our herds had almost twenty miles to walk to water! That's too damned far. As I recall, there's a stream running through that piece of land? One that doesn't dry up in the scorching summer months."

"Aye, there is."

"Our herds need that water desperately when our cisterns and pipes run low—especially if we're to keep on expanding those herds and fattening our stock, as I've planned. If we could buy that piece of land, many of our water problems would be solved. We could divert the stream's flow to our pastures, and save hundreds of beeves each year."

McHenry frowned, sad-eyed as a bloodhound. "Och, laddie, did ye think your father hadna considered doing just that for himself?"

"My father tried to buy it? Then what went wrong? The owner won't sell, is that what you're saying?"

McHenry sighed. "I don't know, because I've never asked. I must tell ye what I told your father. I canna represent the Kane Ranch in this purchase."

"What?"

"Ye heard me t' rights."

"Why the devil not?" Gideon exclaimed.

"It'd be a conflict of interest, laddie. Ye ken, the owner's another o' my clients. It'd be improper for me to undertake the purchase on your behalf."

Gideon sighed and leaned back in the chair. "Then can you at least tell me who owns it?"

"A young woman of mixed blood. She inherited it from her mother, a Hawaiian woman, upon her death a short while ago. Her grandfather received it from the first King Kamehameha, in return for some good deed or other."

"I see. And does this woman have a name?" Gideon asked him curtly.

"It's Emma . . ."

"What?" His dark head shot up. His deep-blue eyes blazed.

". . . Wallace

He looked blank. "Never heard of her."

"No? Her auntie's yer own Leolani Pakele."

"Auntie Leo? Kimo's wife?" Gideon's brows rose in surprise.

"The same, laddie, the same."

"But . . . how is it you represent the Pakeles' niece? I thought we were your only clients at Hui Aloha?"

"Weell, it's a long story. To make it short and sweet, before my dear wife Katherine passed on, we had two Christian Hawaiian lassies t' tend t' the running of our house in Nuuanu. They were the Kahikina sisters—Leolani and Malia—and a bonnier pair ye never set eyes on!"

Gideon grinned. "If my memory serves, they don't come any bonnier—or much bigger!—than our 'Auntie' Leo, bless her!"

Though no more than a "calabash," or honorary, aunt, the Hawaiian woman who was his mother's housekeeper had as good as raised him, while her husband, Kimo, had taught him to sit a horse and how to hold a lariat before he could even walk. Along with old Moki, he remembered.

"Bigger indeed, ye young pup. But Mistress Leolani was as slender as a bamboo in those days. Aye, and just as pretty as a picture, too. Ye should have seen the pair of them dance the *hula!* Anyway, they cared for me and my puir, crippled wee Katherine as if we were their kin. Why, our home shone like a brand-new pin from roof t' floor. And the food . . . !" He rolled his eyes. "But, after my Katherine passed on, I had no need of such a big empty house, nor of servants t' run it. Nevertheless, I was reluctant t' see the lassies lose their livelihoods, and so I—"

"Forgive me for interrupting you, sir, but I fail to see how any of this concerns me or the land?"

"Ah, but you will, laddie, you will. Just bear with me . . . Now, where was I? Ah, yes. I was about to say that this happened when your father was building Hui Aloha. He needed lassies to help Miriam with the running of it, what with her losing babe after babe as she did. I told Jacob I had just the pair! Leolani and Malia were happy to be going home to the island where they'd been born, and where their father still farmed his taro and sweet potato patches, so it proved a fine solution all around.

"The oldest girl, Leolani, met your father's young *luna,* ranch foreman, Kimo Pakele, soon after, and wed him, whereas little Malia . . ." His chiseled features softened. "Well, our Malia didna fare s' well, the puir wee lamb. She got in wi' a bad lot—a Botany Bay man named Jack Jordan—an' lost her heart t' him. Within months, she'd left Hui Aloha to be his woman and had birthed his bairn. The puir lassie suffered for it till her dyin' day. He's a bad lot."

"*Jordan?* A Botany Bay man, you say?" Gideon exclaimed, his mind racing to piece together what McHenry had told him. The blood drained from his face. *The woman, Malia and a run-*

*away convict named Jack Jordan had had a baby daughter they'd
called Emma—surely the same Emma Jordan he'd met all those
years ago on a deserted beach—and never stopped loving?*
"Correct me if I'm wrong, sir, but you said the landowner's
name was Emma *Wallace?*" He had to ask the question, though
he was praying McHenry's answer would not be the one he
dreaded.

"Aye, I did. Do ye know the lassie after all, then?"

"I believe I do, yes," Gideon mumbled, his stunned mind refusing to digest what the Scot was saying. "But, are you quite
certain you have the boundaries correct? The parcel of land we're
interested in is clear over here . . ." He gestured at the map,
pointing to an area much farther north than the spot where
McHenry had stabbed his finger earlier.

"Malia Kahikina Jordan's land reaches from high in the
mountains. Here . . . across this area. Here . . . then down to the
beach fronting Twin Rocks cove, which is right about here. That
wee spot is but a small part o' the whole parcel. By rights, I
shouldna be telling ye this, Gideon, but I trust ye t' keep a silent
tongue in your head."

Woodenly, Gideon nodded.

"Just last Christmas, while I was on the Big Island, seeing
to your father's business, Malia Jordan sent her daughter to
Kawaiahae t' fetch me. Mistress Jordan had been ill for some
years—*ma'i a'ai*—and she feared the end was finally drawing
near for her. Accordingly, she sent for me to draw up her will.
In it, she left her land to her daughter, Emma Kaleilani Jordan,
and—in the event of the lassie's death—to her betrothed, Charles Keali'i Wallace. Malia wanted to take no chances the land
would fall t' Jack Jordan when she was dead and gone, ye
ken? She hated the mon wi' a passion!"

Gideon's head came up so sharply, he could hear the bones
in his neck creak in protest as he echoed, "Emma was betrothed,
you said?"

"Aye. Wallace is a fine young *hapa* man who hails from Kamuela, as I recall. He's a schoolteacher, too. The School Board in Honolulu had just appointed him inspector for the Big Island, when I met him," McHenry supplied casually, obviously noticing nothing untoward, though Gideon's deeply tanned face had paled and his knuckles were white where he gripped the curved arms of the chair. McHenry chuckled. "No doubt the lovebirds have been wed long since, for Malia was pressing them t' name the day before she drew her last breath, and Wallace was powerful eager t' make the lassie his bride." He chuckled. "So ye see, laddie, ye' ll have to hire yersel' another lawyer to approach Mistress Wallace and her husb—*Gideon?* Are ye listening, mon? Have ye heard a word I've said?"

Gideon nodded curtly, but in all truth, his chaotic thoughts were elsewhere. McHenry's words still boomed in his mind like the thunder of a cannon: *The lovebirds! Betrothed! Wed! Married! Powerful eager. Husband!* while his poor heart roared, *"Nooo—!"*

Suddenly, he sprang to his feet, toppling the chair to the floorboards without even noticing. "If you'll forgive me, Mister McHenry, I've just remembered a pressing engagement elsewhere," he ground out, and was striding for the door even as he spoke, moving as woodenly as a marionette.

"Whist! Are ye ill, mon?" McHenry asked, his weatherbeaten face concerned. "Dear God, ye're pale as a shroud!"

"It's nothing. Good day, sir."

With that abrupt farewell, Gideon left.

McHenry shrugged and went to the window, drawing aside the lace curtains to look out onto the street below.

Rain was still pelting down from a dour sky, and the dirt street, lined with wooden boardwalks, was awash with puddles the size of small lakes through which small, brown-skinned children were splashing and playing, shrieking with delight.

Ignoring their antics, Gideon Kane leaped aboard the covered carriage and slapped the reins across the horses' backs with unusual force. The startled beasts shot forward, dragging the vehicle behind them, its churning wheels throwing great waves of water across the boardwalks as, turning dangerously close to the children, the carriage rumbled from view.

With a shrug, McHenry returned to his desk and thoughtfully poured himself another dram. What in the world had he said to upset the laddie? he wondered ruefully as he sipped, his eyes—the color of peat bogs and Highland heather—shadowed with concern. Or had the infernal War Between the States shattered the puir laddie's nerves? He shrugged. There was naught he could do about it now.

Raising his whiskey glass to the light, he murmured, "God bless ye, Katherine, my love. And may ye rest in peace, Malia, my wee lass. Ah, but ye were such bonny wee things, once upon a time. Aye, lassies, that ye were."

Nine

Where the devil was he headed?
It didn't matter.
And why the hell was he going there, wherever there was?
Damned if he knew!

Where and why or even with whom, or how—damn it, nothing mattered anymore, now that Emma was lost to him. His sweet, faithless Emma, who'd vowed to wait for him, if only he would promise to return, had married another. His lovely, lying Emma who'd given him her innocence as easily as she'd given him her promises—though neither her kisses nor her promises had proven worth a damn—was Missus Charlie Wallace now, devil take her!

Weaving unsteadily, he staggered down the narrow dirt street that ran parallel to the Honolulu Harbor, careless of the rain puddles through which he splashed, of the mud that splattered his trouser cuffs and city boots, or of the wilted blossoms, squashed mangoes, and papayas that lay crushed in the gutters, cast off by the native greeters who'd thronged the wharves earlier that day to meet the steamer passengers arriving from America, the Orient, or one of the other Hawaiian islands with *leis* of exotic flowers and fruits.

He could remember nothing since leaving McHenry's offices that morning in the middle of the worst downpour of the rainy season—or at least, that was what the first saloonkeeper had told him. Where he'd been since then, where his uncle's carriage and pair might be, and how he'd come here—wherever "here" was!—he couldn't say, but now, the sky was dark, the streets were shadowed and deserted save for a solitary scrawny cat slinking through the narrow alleys.

"Aloha, mistah. You come upstairs, Lily show you numbah-one good time, yeh?" a rum-voiced siren called from one of these open doorways. "You get money, I give you plenty sweet *honi honi!"* She puckered up her lush lips and blew him a kiss.

Bleary-eyed, Gideon raised his head and managed to focus on the speaker—a Hawaiian-Chinese beauty wrapped in a blue-flowered sarong with a scarlet hibiscus tucked behind one ear. Her hair was black as the night—like Emma's. Her eyes were almond-shaped, but dark and seductive—also like Emma's. *Paggh,* too, too damn much like Emma's for comfort!

With a curse, he reeled away and took another swig from the half-empty bottle in his fist. "No thanks, sweetheart," he refused the woman's offer, trying for a lecherous wink and failing miserably before lurching on down the street.

Earlier—how much earlier, Gideon had long since lost track—he'd followed a golden-skinned, almond-eyed Oriental lovely up a steep flight of stairs to her pitiful lodgings in a Chinatown whorehouse, and discovered too late that her slender charms were no antidote to the poison that filled him. Indeed, to his chagrin, he'd proven unable to do the poor little love justice, what with so many slugs of whiskey under his belt and that gaping hole where his heart used to be. Shamefaced and babbling his apologies, he'd paid the China doll and left, growing maudlin and sorry for himself by turns as the liquor gradually took over and blessed numbness finally began to set in.

What the devil had the blasted war done to him? he wondered bleakly. He'd taken only minor wounds—a scratch here, a powder burn there—no injury that would account for the driving need in him to find a peace of mind that seemed always to elude him, a peace of mind and spirit that being reunited with Emma had promised to provide.

Surely he'd been a starry-eyed fool to think a fourteen-year-old girl would keep her adolescent promise to wait for him. Indeed, what grown man in his right mind would have *expected* her to keep it? She'd been little more than a child back then, for pity's sake, scarce out of the schoolroom, while he'd been eighteen when he'd seduced her and made his vow to come back to her—old enough to go thousands of miles from home to college, more than old enough to spend a year at sea on a Kane whaler and become a man, and to fight in the goddamned Army, by God!

Yessiree, he thought, tightening his jaw, he'd been a damned Yankee Billy Boy, old enough to see lads younger than himself torn apart by cannon fire, or to watch helpless as they lay in a muddy ditch with their legs shot off and their guts pouring from them, screaming for their mamas till death granted them blessed release. Certainly old enough to know what he wanted—and, God help him, what he'd wanted throughout those seven long years was Emma. Only Emma. Nothing more.

Oh, there'd been other women, lovely women, many of them, women who'd shared his bed briefly for a price and, in their fashion, taken his mind off the fighting and the bloodshed with a few blessed moments of pleasure. Or a merry war widow here and there with a penchant for beardless young lads he'd been too exhausted and heartsick to withstand. Never once had there been anyone he'd ever considered marrying or spending the rest of his life with. No one he'd have chosen to mother the children he hoped to have someday. No one he'd loved like Emma.

When the Menie balls had been falling thick and fast, the Johnny Rebs yelling for Union blood on all three sides, and his men sitting their horses restlessly behind him, their sabres drawn as they nervously awaited his order to charge, Emma's face had come to him amidst the smoke of battle or in the white-bright flare of magnesium like a vision, smiling and promising she'd wait for him, just as she had that golden evening on the beach when she'd promised she'd wait forever. And, with her beauty and goodness imprinted on his mind and her name on his lips like some battle cry of old, he'd led his men into the thick of the fighting time and time again.

A fierce, wild joy had radiated from him in those stirring moments, for with Emma waiting for him, her love watching over him, he'd felt invincible, inviolate, as if he carried his own guardian angel on his shoulder!

If he'd once doubted the veracity of Emma's promise, would the outcome of those glorious, victorious charges have been any different? he'd often wondered since. Would he even now be dead, buried in a hero's grave somewhere, or lost forever beneath the brambles of some muddy ditch, unmourned and unsung like so many others? Had he clung to the memory of that romantic interlude—his unrealistic *ideal* of Emma, rather than the young girl she'd really been? Had he hung on because he'd *had* to, in order to keep his sanity intact amidst all the madness that was war? Or did he truly love her?

He thought, he truly believed, that he loved her, and would always love her, but it was a question that would remain forever unanswered, now that she'd become another man's wife.

"Gideon! Damn it, Gideon, wait up, man!" he dimly heard Thomas calling after him. Halting, he swung about, trying to focus bloodshot, smarting eyes as his younger cousin loped down the rain-washed muddy street after him.

"Good God, Gideon! I've been all over town looking for you! What the devil's gotten into you? You look like death warmed over!" Thomas exclaimed, shocked by his cousin's appearance. Gideon's clothes were disheveled, his vest askew, the buttons of his coat incorrectly fastened, his stock missing. Worse, his eyes held a wildness that was frightening to him, a person who'd always looked up to the older Gideon as his hero.

"What's wrong? Women—that's what's wrong, Tom, my lad," Gideon declared bitterly, weaving a little as he tried to waggle his index finger in Thomas's face. "You think—think they're as constant as the damned stars. You set the course of your life by them—steer by their promises and their whims, but they're fickle, Tom lad. Fickle as the wind that blows where she will! She was what got me through the war—did I tell you that, Tommy boy? That stupid, bloody senseless war! Thinking of Emma, of the life we'd have together someday, if only I could survive that hell—it was all that kept me sane and whole. It's all fallen apart now. All of it. All of me. Nothing matters anymore"

"The deuce it doesn't, you damned fool. It's the liquor talking. Whatever's happened, it's just a temporary hitch, you'll see," Thomas countered valiantly, steering his cousin to the nearest street corner and propping him up against the gray brick wall of a chandler's emporium while he flagged down a passing hack.

A fine yet soaking rain had begun falling again—the tail end of the vicious winter storm that had lashed the island chain for the past two days and nights—and they were both getting soaked. The sooner he had Gideon home and safely abed, the better he'd feel. And perhaps in the morning, with his cousin sober and rested, he would find out what the devil Gideon'd been talking about.

"Temporary hitch, my ass!" Gideon growled in an ugly tone, sounding as if he were spoiling for a fight and none too picky about whom he fought with. "My Emma's married someone else, damn it! *My Emma!* You know how news travels in the islands, Tommy lad! She must have known I'd be coming back—must have! But she couldn't wait a few months to tell me. She just had to marry her precious *Charles,* didn't she? Or maybe she was just too damned scared to face me, and decided to go ahead and get it over with? A fait accompli I couldn't argue with. Ye think that's it, Tom? Answer me!" he bellowed, trying to shrug Thomas's hand from his elbow.

"Pipe down, for God's sake, Gideon, before someone calls the police!" Thomas snapped, forcefully hoisting Gideon up the steps of a hired hack and pushing him down onto the leather seat opposite him. Leaning over his cousin to keep him there, he rapped on the hack's roof to instruct the cabby where to proceed. "You're as drunk as the proverbial skunk! Let's go now, so you can sleep it off, old man. Come morning, things will look better, you'll see. Your . . . Emma, is it?—she's not the only bloody girl in the world."

The Sheldon Kane house with its white walls and green-tiled roof was dark and silent when the hack rolled to a halt before its wrought-iron gateway. A low wall of off-white coral blocks surrounded lush tropical gardens and sweeping lawns where peacocks called during the daylight hours. The two-story house was flanked by lofty royal palms that tossed ragged heads in the wind and rain, and by frangipani trees, whose bridal bouquets of white blossoms secreted a sweet, pungent perfume on the damp night air.

With the cabby's help, Thomas managed to heft Gideon down from the conveyance and paid the man. As the coach turned and the horse clipclopped back toward Honolulu, Thomas hooked one of Gideon's arms over his shoulder and half walked, half dragged him down the curving driveway and around to the rear of the house.

He managed to get him inside the back door with little difficulty, then guided him through the kitchen and scullery, down the narrow pitch-black hall. From there, he helped him to navigate the perilous obstacle course of the parlor's fussy bric-a-brac and heavily carved furniture to the main hallway, and thence to the sweeping staircase that led up to the second story.

"For God's sake, sit down here for a minute. My back's breaking," Thomas grumbled, pushing Gideon down onto the lowest tread. His cousin obediently sat there, his knees apart, his dark head and slack arms dangling limply between them like a puppet with its strings severed. "Wait here, and I'll see if there's any coffee left over from supper."

Thomas glanced warily over his shoulder as he slipped back

down the hallway to the kitchens, half expecting to find his dear mama behind him with her candlestick in one hand and her Bible in the other, ready to deliver a thumping sermon on the vile sins of drunkenness and carousing. Ruefully, Thomas shook his head. Father would have chuckled, winked, and looked the other way if he'd caught them, murmuring that, "Boys will be boys, eh, you young rogues?" But not so his prim mama who, like Joshua and Sheldon Kane, had been the offspring of missionary parents, but who had absorbed their teachings far more thoroughly than had either of the two men!

But to his relief, he was not apprehended, and found a half pot of coffee left simmering over the banked kitchen fire. It looked strong enough to grow hairs on one's chest! Setting both the pot and a sturdy earthenware mug upon a tray, along with a half loaf of bread to sop up the liquor in his cousin's belly, which was undoubtedly empty, he returned to the stairs. He'd chivvy Gideon up to his room, then see what he could do about sobering his cousin up and getting him undressed, before turning in himself. He shook his head. Gideon and he had always been close, despite the infrequent visits exchanged between the two families on account of the distance between the islands of Oahu and Hawaii.

Thomas had known from childhood that he would someday follow his father in the running of the Kane sugar plantation, while Gideon would eventually follow in *his* father's footsteps and take over the running of the Kane Ranch when Uncle Jacob became too old or infirm to carry on.

Consequently, Thomas had not been surprised by Gideon's declaration that he was home to stay. He sensed, however, that Gid had changed in many ways since he'd left the islands, and suspected from the few bitter comments he'd let drop and from things his cousin *hadn't* spoken of at all that it was the war in which he'd fought—the terrifying things he'd seen, perhaps been forced to do—that had caused these changes. He had never once suspected, however, that Gideon had ever been in love, truly in love.

Who was she, this faithless chit named Emma? he wondered, curious. Some fickle miss poor Gideon had met and lost his heart to in Boston? Some shameless hussy?

Thomas pulled up short and frowned as he reached the bottom of the stairs. Gideon was gone! And, as he stood there wondering how the devil his sotted cousin had managed to climb the long, winding staircase unaided to his room, he heard the soft click of a door being closed on the upper landing.

"Well, you son of a gun, good for you!" Thomas chuckled to himself, shrugging. "I'd have bet hard money you couldn't climb these bloody stairs alone!"

With that, he returned the coffeepot to the kitchen and climbed the stairs to his own bed.

Ten

Gideon woke with a groan, opening throbbing eyes to brilliant, blinding daylight and the warbling song of a veritable choir of blasted cardinals and squawking mynahs in the tree below the window, raucous sounds that did nothing to ease the pounding in his skull.

White lace curtains billowed into the room like snapping sails, bellied by a breeze coming through the open casement. For a fleeting moment, he thought himself back aboard the whaler, *Arabella Kane,* and wondered why the musky fragrance of a woman's perfume rather than the stench of the rending pots filled his nostrils.

A cock crowed somewhere in the valley. Realizing it must still be early, certain he could have slept only an hour or two at most, Gideon groaned again and rolled over, burying his aching head beneath a goosedown pillow. It was not until he bent his elbows to cradle his throbbing head that he discovered he was not alone in the hand-carved tester bed. No, indeed. A woman lay beside him!

She was quite naked, he saw, raising one leaden eyelid a fraction of an inch to inspect her. One pale arm was flung above her head, one full, firm breast was exposed, while her body lay loose and warm beside his in intimate abandon. And, although he'd brushed her shoulder, she remained deeply asleep, her fair hair spread across the snowy lace-edged pillow next to his, her breathing slow and regular as a sleeping child's.

Moving away from her as hastily as if he'd discovered a scorpion shared his sheets, through bloodshot, gritty eyes Gideon gaped at her in bleary disbelief, unable, in his foggy condition, to put a name to that elegantly beautiful face. Who the devil was she? And what, for God's sake, was she doing in his bed, as naked as Eve?

He tried, despite the hammering in his skull, to put order to his thoughts, to think!—*Goddamnit, Gideon, think!* And, after some time and no little effort, he found he could vaguely remember following a swaying-hipped, golden-skinned Oriental girl with a waterfall of inky hair up a steep flight of stairs the evening before; even that she'd pouted and sulked when he'd mistakenly called her Emma in the heat of the moment . . . An Oriental beauty, yes, but a willowy, fair-skinned *blonde?*

He frowned, kneading his temples, trying to recapture memories that were suddenly as elusive as will-o'-the-wisps. He was almost certain that, at some point during the wee hours before dawn, his good ole cousin Thomas had appeared from nowhere and insisted he "call it a night, Gid, there's a good fellow!" But after that, everything was a blur. He recalled nothing of his homecoming whatsoever. Indeed, he hadn't so much as a clue as to how he'd gotten back to the Nuuanu Valley from the saloons and whorehouses along the wharves of Honolulu, nor how he'd ended up back here in the guest room of his uncle's house, bucknaked and in his own bed, let alone who the deuce the pretty doxy beside him might be!

And then . . . a name to match that face and long golden hair suddenly surfaced out of the blue, a name and a face that only increased his anxiety. Jesus Christ Almighty, what in *hell* had he done? *Julia, the widow from Baltimore.* He was in bed with Julia Everson Lennox of the black silk gown and the cool, slim hands—the woman Thomas had slyly called "Black Widow" Lennox, joking that, like the spider, she'd probably killed her first husband, once they'd mated, if the predatory glint he swore he'd seen in her eye was anything to go by!

Oh, Sweet Lord in the morning, his naked bedmate was none other than his aunt Sophie's distant cousin by marriage! He groaned silently. What the devil had he been thinking of last night, drunk or no, to take one of his pious aunt's kin to bed? And, now that she was there, how the devil was he going to get rid of her gracefully? Scoundrel he might be, womanizer he had certainly been on occasion, but he was not a cruel man by nature. He had no wish to callously admit he remembered nothing of what had clearly transpired between them, nor how she'd ended up in his bed, and by so doing, destroy the poor woman's pride.

But . . . *had* he bedded her? Had he kissed that somewhat thin-lipped, patrician mouth? Had he wound his hands through her pale-golden curls? Caressed and fondled, even suckled, the surprisingly voluptuous breast he glimpsed now, peeping out from beneath the corner of a bedsheet? He wracked his brain for some telltale memory—a vague, remembered sensation of touch, a fleeting scent, an endearment exchanged—but found none.

Cursing, he flung the tangled sheet that covered them both aside and sprang from the bed, groaning anew at the pain such sudden movement sent ricocheting through his skull—and by the realization that this was not, after all, his room, but hers! That was clearly evidenced by the yards of snowy lace and feminine fol de rols everywhere!

Cursing a blue streak, he staggered about the room in a frantic search for his trousers, far from reassured to find the floorboards littered with an array of frothy female underthings, along with his own mud-spattered garments, all of which appeared to have been shed in some urgency and with no little lusty abandon.

His black scowl deepened as he finally found and drew on his wrinkled trousers. Things were looking worse by the minute, damn it. He supposed he *must* have bedded the wretched woman—all evidence screamed that he had, and in some haste, too!—though he'd be damned if he could remember so much as exchanging civilities with her last night, let alone anything more intimate!

Right now, he decided, he needed to beat a speedy retreat, to go downstairs and help himself to a stiff bourbon from the bottle hidden in his uncle's study. Perhaps a shot of the hair-of-the-dog, followed by several cups of Wong's strong black coffee, would help him to remember. Or at least, to think things through and formulate an appropriate reaction.

The mirror over the dresser threw back the reflection of a scowling, disheveled, wild-eyed stranger. A quarter-inch of prickly black stubble darkened his cheeks and jaw. His black hair was rumpled. The whites of his eyes were the unappetizing color of ripe guavas, while the irises were muddy as bruises.

Muttering a curse, he yanked his wrinkled shirt from where it was draped across the dresser, jolting the blue-flowered porcelain ewer and basin atop it so that they clattered noisily. Both would have toppled to the floor had he not dashed forward and righted them in the nick of time with a swift rugby "save" that further pained his throbbing head, and wrung from him a colorful stream of curses he could not muffle, despite his sternest efforts.

With the commotion, the woman stirred and stretched. Her eyelids fluttered open. Yawning sleepily, she covered her mouth with the back of her dainty fist and rolled over onto her side to see him standing there, staring at her, with his shirt half on and half off, and a guilty expression on his face.

She smiled demurely and averted her eyes.

"Why, Mister Kane—er, Cousin Gideon. Um—good morning," she murmured, sitting up and modestly drawing the sheet up to cover her breasts. Her ivory cheeks filled with color "It—er—it *is* morning, isn't it?"

Gideon opened his mouth to make some response. Exactly what he might have said he was never to discover, for before he could speak, a light tapping sounded at the door, and he heard his aunt's sweet voice calling, "Julia? Cousin Julia? Are you awake, my dear?"

Gideon stiffened as, without further ado, the door swung inward and Sophie Kane tripped into the room, bearing a small tray on which reposed a dainty china cup and saucer. Smiling, she stood primly at the side of the bed, looking down at her cousin-in-law with obvious concern. Her back was to Gideon, who'd frozen in place where he stood.

"And how are you this morning, Julia my dear? Recovered from your little indisposition yesterday evening, I trust? I thought perhaps a cup of hot, weak tea and an arrowroot biscuit or two might be welcome on an empty stomach, since you declined supper last night?"

"Why, yes, indeed. Er—thank you, Cousin Sophie," Julia whispered, looking anywhere but at Gideon. "It's—very thoughtful of you."

Sophie smiled. "Not at all, dear girl. Now. It's almost seven. We'll be leaving for morning service directly after breakfast. I thought you might like to accompany us, if you're feeling bet—" Her cheerful voice died away. Her watery, round eyes narrowed behind her thick lenses as, sensing another's presence, she suddenly flung about.

As her gaze fell upon the half-dressed man, frozen in place in the farthest corner of the room, his coat and shirt in hand, the blood drained from her already pale cheeks, and her mouth dropped open.

"Gideon?" she cried in disbelief and shock.

"Er—yes, Aunt Sophie. I'm rather afraid it is," Gideon admitted.

Julia promptly burst into tears and covered her face with her hands, crying, "Oh, Cousin Sophie, please, you must let me explain—! It's not how it seems! You mustn't think for a moment that Gideon and I—that we—that anything *improper* occurred here last night, despite appearances!"

"That is quite enough, Julia. Indeed, it is more than enough."

Pale-faced and trembling with shock, Sophie Kane set the cup and saucer down upon the nightstand with a rattle of china. Drawing herself up, she clasped her hands primly over her flat bosom and fixed a stern, baleful eye upon her ne'er-do-well nephew, who—grown man that he was—nevertheless seemed to be praying the floorboards would open up and swallow him like lucky Jonah had been devoured by the proverbial whale.

"My—disappointment—in—you—knows—no—bounds, Gideon," she whispered, spitting the words out with obvious difficulty and quite unable to look him in the eye. "My poor, dear Miriam! And Jacob, too! Oh, to think that you, of all men— my own nephew, no less!—would conceive of such . . . such immorality and wickedness, and while a guest under my roof, too! To say that I am deeply shocked does not begin to describe my feelings at this moment."

Resisting the urge to consign his little aunt and her narrow Congregationalist morals to hell, Gideon ground out, "Aunt Sophie, please, be reasonable. As Julia said, there's—"

"Enough, Gideon. Say no more." She covered her ears with her hands. "I believe this distressing matter is one your uncle is best fitted to deal with, as a man of the world, rather than myself," she continued, her lips tightly pursed, though her normally watery eyes now swam with tears. "I—I shall inform Mister Kane of what has occurred here straightway. I will also tell him to expect you in his study within the quarter hour."

"And I shall most certainly be there, ma'am," Gideon gritted, bowing stiffly as his aunt, her crisply starched blue skirts rustling noisily, turned and marched from the room, closing the door none too quietly behind her.

Julia sniffed back her tears. 'Oh, my Lord," she whispered, gray eyes lifting to a scowling Gideon's blazing blue ones in mute appeal. "Whatever are we to do? You promised . . . last night, remember, my darling? When you sweet-talked me into letting you in here? You promised no one would know! That Aunt Sophie would never find out. You swore it would be our secret, if only I would . . . !" She swallowed and looked away, blinking rapidly, her pale, thin-lipped mouth quivering in a tremulous, little-girl fashion that flayed his conscience with whips of guilt.

"What can I say?" he ground out, his fists clenched at his sides. "I was reeling drunk! Damn it, er—Juliet—if I reneged on any promises, I'm . . . sorry." Though not half as sorry as he was about getting caught.

"Sorry? Sorry! Is that all you can do?" she flared, her gray eyes ablaze now. "Stand there like a fool and insist that you're sorry? Ha! My good name and my reputation have been ruined, sir—destroyed! My late husband's memory has—has been utterly besmirched. And while you insist that you're *sorry,* you can't even get my n-name r-right! It's *Julia,* you—you scoundrel, not Ju-Ju-Juli*et!*"

She flung herself face down on the bed and sobbed, her slender shoulders shaking. "Oh, how could I have been so weak and foolish?" she wailed, her voice muffled, though each word was like a thorn in Gideon's conscience. "How could I have succumbed to your drunken flattery? I'd never have done so, but for the things you said! You quite swept me off my feet, you were so . . . so very ardent and charming, while I . . . ! I was unforgivably weak, and far too easily won!" A shudder ran through her as she dragged herself upright, the sheets twisted around her, and beseeched him through brimming, reddened eyes, "I swear, upon my beloved late husband's grave, that I am not a l-loose woman by nature, sir. M-my only excuse for my wanton behavior is that I was unwell last night, and so not at all myself." She dabbed at her tears with a corner of the bedsheet. "I've felt so—so very *alone* since David . . . went away, you see. And you seemed so kind. You said you'd lost someone you loved quite recently, and so I thought—I thought you understood how it is, you see?"

"I do see, Missus Lennox," Gideon said stiffly, not seeing at all, but giving up on all attempts at trying to remember the events of the night before. Had he truly been "ardent," as she claimed? Had he, in his drunken state, seemed "kind." Had he told her about Emma—oh, God, Emma!—and shared her bed in order to exorcise his grief? His jaw tightened. Self-contempt filled him. Apparently, he'd done all of these things, and more.

He squared his shoulders. Well. So be it. He'd had his fun, damn it. Now it was time to pay the piper his due, to make reparations for his "sins," not catalog them! A man was less than a man if he shirked his duties or turned his back on honor and responsibility.

"You needn't worry about your reputation, ma'am. Naturally, I shall do the proper thing by you."

"You mean, you would marry me, Mister Kane?" she asked in patent disbelief.

His jaw hardened. "Indeed, yes. In fact, I believe my uncle will insist upon it, Missus Lennox," Gideon answered heavily, feeling as if his every word were but another nail being hammered into his coffin. "And even should he not, I see no other alternative to remedy this matter satisfactorily, do you? To undo the damage that has been done you. Only by my marriage to you can we restore your good name."

"But surely Cousin Sophie would never breathe a word!"

"My aunt, no, of course not. She would prove the soul of discretion. The servants, however, are a different story. They enjoy nothing better than salacious gossip. Rest assured, last night's events will be the talk of Honolulu drawing rooms and parlors long before luncheon."

Color seeped into her cheeks like red ink spreading across a blotter. "Nevertheless, Mister Kane, I could never marry you under these strained conditions. I may have little else, sir, since my dear David left me all alone, but I still have my pride. No," she repeated firmly, bravely, lifting her head a little higher. "I could never marry a man I did not love. Nor one who merely felt honor-bound to make me his bride."

"I respect your feelings, Missus Lennox, but . . . there could be a child," he heard himself say, and wished with all his heart and soul he'd bitten off his tongue the moment he'd said it. *Oh, Christ. What was he doing here? Why the devil was he saying these things? And why, for the love of God, had he proposed marriage to a woman he scarce knew—nor, to be honest, wanted to know better—and felt nothing for, besides? And why was he urging her to consider the possibility that they'd created a child in a moment of lust that he—its father, goddamnit!—couldn't even recall? Did he want to punish himself, was that it? To wear a hair shirt, to make himself a whipping boy, because he was feeling sorry for himself and still angry about Emma? None of this was happening, that was it! This was all a repugnant dream—a nightmare from which he'd soon awaken.*

Julia, he saw, had paled in the wake of his words. Her slender, beringed fingers flew to her throat. "A child?" she echoed in a whisper. "Why, yes. Yes, of course. You're quite right, Mister Kane. There could very well be a child." She sighed heavily, and her blue eyes filled with tears. "I confess, in my shame and confusion, I'd not considered that dreadful possibility. A child! Oh, dear Lord! It would be ironic, would it not, were I to find myself carrying your child, when I could not give David the son and heir he wanted!"

"When will you know?" Gideon forced himself to ask, already heartily sick of David, dead or nay.

Julia blushed at his reference to such delicate female matters. "Not for another whole month, I'm afraid," she whispered, bowing her golden head. The red ink was back, seeping into the alabaster pallor of her cheeks to stain them with hectic color. "You see, I was . . . unwell just this past week."

He coughed and nodded brusquely to show that he understood, gallantly sparing her the embarrassment of any farther explanations. "I see. Well. As you heard, my uncle's no doubt waiting to speak with me downstairs. I'll—er—leave you to your morning toilette for the time being, but I feel we should discuss this—er—matter at greater length very soon."

"Oh, yes, most assuredly. Perhaps after luncheon?"

"Very well. Would you meet me in the Japanese garden, Missus Lennox?" he asked with stiff formality.

"I'll be there, Mister Kane."

With a half-bow, he strode toward the door, fully dressed but looking like hell warmed over.

"Oh, Mister Kane, before you go . . . ?"

His hand on the doorknob, he halted. "Yes?"

"I think, under the circumstances, it'd be appropriate if you called me 'Julia,' as I asked, don't you?"

"Very well, Julia." With a curt nod, he left the room, slowly closing the door behind him with the uncanny sensation that he was also closing a door on the life he'd known. That nothing would ever be the same again.

When he'd gone, Julia lay back upon the feather pillows. Smiling, she stretched as languorously as any well-fed cat in the tropical sunshine that fell through the windows across her body.

"Missus Gideon Kane. Missus Julia Everson Lennox Kane, mistress of the Kane Ranch." Her smile deepened. "It has a real nice ring, Julia, you clever girl," she told the empty room. "Almost as purty as the big gold one you'll soon be wearing on your finger."

Eleven

"For God's sake, be sensible, Gideon!" Sheldon Kane remonstrated. "There's still time to back out if you've reservations about this marriage. Or about the Lennox woman, come to that."

"The 'Lennox woman,' as you persist in calling my bride, Uncle, has already left for the church," Gideon observed with a faint, sardonic smile. "It's a little late to think of jilting the poor woman at the altar, wouldn't you say?"

His uncle snorted. " 'Poor woman,' indeed! Frankly, I'd sooner you did just that, rather than 'wed her in haste, and repent at leisure' as the old saying goes! There's something about the woman I can't put my finger on, something that's not quite . . ."

". . . genuine?" Thomas supplied, leaning back in his chair with his heels propped on his father's desk, a snifter of fine brandy in one hand, a smoldering Cuban cigar in the other, the sight of either of which would have sent his mother into a swoon.

"Genuine's as good a word as any, I suppose," his father acknowledged doubtfully. He frowned. "After all, what do we know about the Le—about her, really? Only that she's the widow of David Lennox of the Baltimore Lennoxes, and therefore my Sophie's cousin by marriage on her mother's side. Hrrumph. And it's not as if your aunt was all that well acquainted with dear Cousin David himself, for that matter! From what Sophie's told me, they met on only a half-dozen occasions in Lennox's lifetime—and most of those times were meetings at family gatherings when they were just children. She hasn't heard anything *of* him, let alone *from* him, for years! I might say, it came as quite a surprise when Julia's letter arrived out of the blue, bearing the news of David's death and asking if she might spend her six months of mourning with us. But . . ." he shrugged expressively, "your dear aunt was eager for visitors from 'home,' as always, bless her, and I could not deny her in so small a matter."

Thomas hid a grin, thinking *"dare* not deny her" would have been a more appropriate turn of phrase. Though not above an extramarital dalliance here and there, or an occasional visit to one of the bawdy houses down by the harbor, Thomas knew his father went to great lengths to keep his amorous forays a secret from his mother—and assuaged his guilt by indulging her every whim. Though he did not approve of his father's shenanigans, Thomas understood them, for he and his father were alike in many ways, sensual men who adored women. More than once he'd wondered what Divine Providence could have been thinking of, to yoke a fun-loving libertine like his father—fresh from the bosom of his own strict Congregationalist family, and raring for a taste of sin—into marriage with a prim and proper missionary's daughter! He'd not make the same mistake when he chose himself a bride, he vowed, tipping his glass.

Gideon scowled, glaring at the emptied shot glass in his hand as if it was to blame for the fix he was in now. "I believe Missus Lennox's past is irrelevant at this point, sir. What's done is done. I'd as soon we left for the church and got it over with."

"That's all well and good, but frankly, Gideon, I'd still feel better if you waited—gave me a month or two, say, to look into your—er—future bride's past? I have an old acquaintance, a fellow named Pinkerton, who's done just that sort of thing ever since the war ended."

"Father's right, Gid. Take off that damned hairshirt you're wearing and tell the Black Widow you've opted to wait a while. Or better yet, hop a slow boat to China—and don't look back!"

"I can't do that. Or I won't, if you prefer. I gave Julia my word, and that's that. If a—if a child should result from that night, I'd as soon not have people counting on their fingers and coming up short."

Sheldon sighed heavily. "Very well. It's your choice, Gideon. As your family, we'll support your decision in any way we can." Brother Jacob had raised himself a fine son, Sheldon reflected as he firmly clasped his nephew's hand. Despite his own reservations about Lennox's widow, he respected Gideon for opting to do "the right thing" by the wretched woman rather than as that rascal Tom had jokingly suggested—running out on her with no regards for the consequences.

Retrieving his black stove-pipe hat and silk gloves from a small side table by the door, he urged, "Come along, then, gentlemen. And let's step on it, there's good lads! The carriage is waiting, and I have a bride to give away before I can dispense with this blasted cravat."

"Coming, Tom?" Gideon asked, his expression that of a man about to go before a firing squad rather than one in any way eager to be married.

"Of course. Where else would I be going? I'm the best man, after all." Thomas grinned, flicked the blond cowlick from his eyes, and clapped his cousin across the back. "Lead the way, bridegroom!"

Twelve

"Is there no other way to land?" Julia Kane asked five days almost to the hour later, her expression apprehensive as she eyed the bobbing canoe far below the schooner's gently rocking sides and the distant, unprepossessing shore.

"None whatsoever, I'm afraid. Come. I'll carry you down to the canoe. There's nothing to worry about. The water's deep here, true, but I shan't let you fall." He wondered, fleetingly, if she could swim, and what would happen if—perish the thought!—he should drop her, then caught himself and immediately felt guilty for his homicidal turn of mind. He forced a smile by way of atonement.

To his surprise, his breezy grin seemed to reassure her somewhat. She drew a deep breath. "Very well. If you promise not to let me fall."

"I not only promise, my dear. I swear," he vowed, placing his hand upon his heart and mustering a sincere expression.

True to his word, Gideon swung over the taffrail and lifted Julia down the rope-ladder after him, slung over his shoulder like a sack of rice. As he clambered down, he called greetings to the Hawaiians who waited below.

The men and boys had paddled out to greet the arriving vessel in a slim-nosed wooden outrigger canoe that had been decked out with brilliant flower garlands in honor of their island son's return. The *leis* added their intoxicating perfume to the kelp-and-brine-scented air.

He saw the Hawaiians' dark eyes flicker to the white woman slung over his shoulder, noted the quick, knowing grins they exchanged amongst themselves, and knew that within the hour, word would have mysteriously circled the island via the "jungle telegraph" that Jacob Kane's son had returned from America with a woman in tow. And by this evening, the entire island would know that, after being gone for seven years, he'd brought back a bride—though, alas, not the bride he'd always imagined taking, he thought with a pang, filled once again with the hollow feeling that surfaced each time he thought about Emma, and of the glorious woman she had surely become.

"Mo'o, aloooha! Welcome home!" they cried, looking up at him, their brown faces wreathed in expectant smiles as Julia gingerly took her seat on the crosspiece beside her rancher husband.

"Mahalo, mahalo nui loa, " Gideon thanked them, drawing Julia's clammy hand between his. "And what about my bride, boys? Do you have a warm welcome for Missus Julia Kane, too?"

For *Missus* Kane? They certainly did! The grins broadened. Handsome brown eyes sparkled. Elbows slyly nudged brown ribs as if to say, "See! I told you so!"

"Mo'o's bride very welcome. *Aloha! Aloooha,* Missus Mo'o!"

Gideon chuckled, looking relaxed and casual without his coat, and undeniably handsome with his wavy, glossy black hair ruffled by the faintest of sea breezes. His wing collar and rolled-up sleeves seemed dazzling against his tanned face and forearms as, cocking his head to one side, he shot his wife an amused glance.

"And why, pray, are you grinning at me?"

"Because they called you Missus Mo'o," Gideon told her, his smile broadening.

"Mo'o? And what's that?"

"My old nickname. I was skinny and kind of active as a boy, so the people named me *'mo'o'*—lizard! And now, for obvious reasons, they've decided to call you Missus Lizard." Brows arched, he waited, expecting some waspish comment from Julia in return. Tact, he'd already learned, was not his wife's strong suit when she was out of sorts; nor was silent forbearance. In fact, in the five days since they'd been married, she sometimes seemed like two totally different people.

"How very quaint," she muttered absently, more concerned with whether this glorified floating flower arrangement could possibly make the shore safely than what a handful of ignorant heathens chose to call her.

"You gonna be numbah-one *haole wahine* dis island, Missus Kane. Very much happy. Very much *honi-honi,* kissy-kissy, very much *aloha!* I t'ink you and Mo'o make plenty babies, by an' by! Six . . . seven . . . some more, maybe!" Alika, one of Gideon's childhood playmates, assured the pale-complected woman with a cheeky wink and a grin before he bent to his paddle.

Julia—tight-lipped—shot the native's broad back a withering glare, but made no further response, although she'd caught the drift of his highly exaggerated, singsong pidgin well enough. Let these ignorant *kanakas* think what they would. She'd be damned if she intended to be bred each year for their young master's pleasure, like a milk cow in need of freshening Or, come to that, like her own worn-down, dried-up momma, or her fool sisters, with their litters of snot-nosed, sniveling brats clinging to their grubby skirts. No, sirree. She didn't reckon on swellin' up like a brood sow each long, hot summer!

Years ago, she'd set her sights on living the sweet life of the idle rich: on hitchin' up with a wealthy planter, and havin' him set her up for life in a pretty little house. Nothin' but good times, pretty clothes, and fun for lil' Miz Julie from here on, she'd promised herself! David Lennox . . . Well, Davie'd seemed the answer to her prayers for a while, but then he'd gone and chosen the wrong side in that dumb old war, and spoiled everythin' she'd been working for!

She gave a mental shrug and hardened her jaw. To hell with Davie! Davie didn't matter anymore. Heck, no, not anymore! She was Missus Gideon Kane now, and she'd learned a heap from her stupid mistakes.

The native men bent their backs to their paddles, and soon the sleek, carved canoe was skimming over the crystaline turquoise water toward shore and the small village of Kawaihae, like a slender bird winging home to its nest.

Whether she'd understood his friend or had simply chosen to ignore that teasing rascal Alika, Gideon could not say, for Julia was staring at the cluster of clapboard houses and native grass huts with dawning horror in her eyes.

Gideon sprang ashore and thanked his smiling landing party of bare-chested Hawaiians with a warm, *"Mahalo, Kamuela! Keoni, Alika, mahalo, mahalo nui loa!"* before lifting his bride into his arms and wading through the shallows onto the beach.

"Is . . . is that it?" she whispered, her expression aghast as he set her down on the sand. "Gideon? Is that it, I said?"

Gideon shaded his deep-blue eyes against the blinding sunbursts that reflected off the glassy water, Julia and her shrill questions quite unheard as a delighted smile tugged at the corners of his mouth. Raising his free hand in farewell salute to the *Lydia*'s captain, who'd watched their landing from the schooner's starboard taffrail, he turned back toward the small port of Kawaihae proper and sighed with pleasure.

To all appearances, little had changed since he left. The air was as dry and breezeless as he remembered. Prim, whitewashed houses, reminiscent of a New England fishing village, still baked in the shimmering waves of heat, towering over the squat, native *pili*-grass huts that clustered about the shore. Looming above the village, silhouetted atop the ridge that backed the port, were the ominous rock walls of a huge abandoned *heiau,* an ancient heathen temple where human sacrifices had once been

offered up, abandoned and desolate since the coming of the
Christian missionaries some forty years before.

His gaze moved beyond the village. On this side of the island,
the coastline was dry and barren for close to ten miles inland,
entirely without shade except to the south curve of the bay, where
a few spindly coconut trees broke the monotony with ragged
green heads. The arid red-brown slopes that rose behind the
sleepy little port gave the newcomer, or *malihini,* no hint that at
higher elevations, there were snow-covered slopes and lush rain
forests; green and grassy plains where daily rainclouds scudded
overhead like stately Spanish galleons. There were, too, thriving
native villages of grass huts set amidst lush tropical vegetation
where several thousand Hawaiians grew taro, sweet potatoes,
and other vegetables, kept pigs and chickens, horses and dogs,
and exotic blossoms rambled in bright profusion.

His heart seemed to swell with joy. After an absence of seven
long years, he was back in the Sandwich Isles at last, by God—
the land he loved as no other place on God's good earth!

Dropping his bulging duffle bag to the sand, he had to fight
the ridiculous but compelling urge to kneel and kiss the soil of
his homeland. Instead, inhaling, he hungrily filled his nostrils
with its scents, half convinced he could smell the fragrant jasmine his mother always wore in her hair, its perfume carried on
misty breezes over jagged lava wastes, down sheer mountain
slopes and across rain-dampened green plateaus, from the lush
valley of his birth . . .

"Gideon, answer me! I said, is . . . is this it? Is this all of it?"
Julia demanded shrilly again, plucking at his sleeve.

He turned to her with a vague expression of surprise, as if
he'd forgotten her very existence. "Hui Aloha, you mean? Good
Lord, no! This is just Kawaihae, where the ships drop anchor to
take on our beef steers for transport to Oahu. We round them
up in the hills, then . . ." His voice died away as he realized her
face wore a blank, disinterested expression. Clearing his throat,
he amended, "I'm sorry, my dear, I forgot myself. Er—no, this

is not it at all. Hui Aloha's a good day's ride from here. It's a beautiful house—one that forms the heart of a beautiful land—about as close to Paradise as a man can get, this side of heaven!" His gentian eyes took on a fond, distant light.

"A *day's* ride, you said?" she exclaimed, cutting him off as if she'd heard nothing else he'd said since then. "But where is the town proper? And where are all the people? Surely there must be hotels and restaurants and . . . and shops—dressmakers and milliners and such? Civilized buildings other than these native . . . hovels?"

Gideon bit back a curt response, stung by the disdainful edge to her voice. He must be patient with her, he told himself, not for the first time. The five-day ocean voyage from Oahu to the Big Island had been a rough and unpleasant one. His bride had spent much of the time in the dark, evil-smelling, and cramped space below deck, sick to her stomach and wailing that she was dying. She was probably still feeling out of sorts but would surely be her usual charming self once she'd rested. And if she wasn't, he thought heavily, what then? What if this complaining shrew was the real Julia—the woman he had pledged to spend his life with? He set his jaw, for there wasn't a damned thing he could do about it. He was bound to her till death did them part . . .

"Gideon, you young rascal! You're home!" bellowed a hearty voice.

"Father!"

The two men hurried across the sand to greet each other and embraced warmly.

There were tears in Jacob Kane's eyes as he stepped back to search his son's face for traces of the youth he remembered. They were gone, long gone! A boy had left these islands. A grown man had returned, a strikingly handsome man with an erect, military bearing who, at six feet two inches, towered over his graying father by a span or more!

"It's truly good to see you, my son. I thank the Lord for bringing you safely home to your mother and me! When we heard you'd joined the Union cavalry, the strength of our faith was sorely tested. There were days when Mother Kane despaired of ever seeing you again." He shrugged ruefully and sighed. "And between the two of us, so did I. It was then we had to pray the hardest—both for you, and for ourselves!"

Gideon's grin deepened, his gentian eyes bright with pleasure at his father's unreservedly warm welcome, for Jacob Kane— God-fearing, decent man that he was—was unlike his brother Sheldon and rarely given to such open, even boisterous, expressions of emotion. "Boston's seen the last of me, Father. The cavalry, too. If you'll have me, I'm home to stay."

"For good? You're sure?" Jacob murmured, carefully guarding a beaming smile of relief until Gideon had nodded and firmly answered, "I am, indeed."

"And what about taking over the ranch? Have you given the matter any thought?"

Gideon sidestepped with another question. "That hip's no better?"

Jacob grimaced, and Gideon noticed for the first time the lines that increasing age and—perhaps—constant pain had etched in his father's leathery face. "Weell, I have good days and bad days, son. Alas, the bad seem to come around far more often the older I get."

"That's to be expected." Gideon shook his head. "You're lucky to be alive, the way I heard it. Before I left, I warned you to shoot that crazy horse—!"

"And I remembered your sound advice—after it fell on me," Jacob Kane recalled with a rueful chuckle, slapping his thigh. "You could have . . . Why, now! And who might this be?" he exclaimed suddenly, as the young woman squinting at him from over his son's broad shoulders caught up with the two men.

Jacob saw a young woman whose fair hair was beginning to escape its elegant knot. The light-blue-and-gray tartan gown she was wearing had a faintly bedraggled look. Her face was sweaty-looking and, he decided, even a trifle grubby, while the narrow bridge of her nose was beginning to redden and freckle from sunburn. Add to that the way the corners of her mouth turned down and her eyes screwed up against the light and she cut a sorry figure indeed.

"Oh, Lord! Forgive me, Julia," Gideon apologized hastily, taking his wife by the elbow and leading her to his father. "Julia, I'm proud to introduce my father, Jacob Elias Kane. Father, this is my bride, Julia Lennox Kane."

"Your *wife!*" Jacob exclaimed.

"She is indeed, sir. We were married five days ago, at the Kawaiahao Church in Honolulu. Uncle Sheldon gave the bride away in her own father's absence." He endeavored to appear pleased, but succeeded only in looking grim.

"Well, then, my congratulations to both of you, children! It's an honor and a privilege to welcome you to our island, my dear, er—"

"Her name is Julia, Father."

"Er—yes, of course, Julia, my dear girl—to welcome you, both to our family and to our humble home here on the Big Island. And, I pray, if the good Lord blesses it—to a long and fruitful union with my son, who I . . . Gracious! What can you be thinking of, Gideon, allowing your poor wife to stand in the full sun for so blessed long, and her so fair-skinned! Have you no sun bonnet or parasol with which to shade yourself, my dear?" Jacob inquired.

"Both, Mister Kane. But I'm afraid they were left in my steamer trunk on the canoe."

"Ah. Then we'll have to find you something else for the time being. I'll have Kimo whip you up a coconut-frond hat—one with a large, shady brim. We can't have that delicate skin burning, can we now, my dear? This way, children," he declared, clapping his son companionably across the back with one hand and tucking his new daughter-in-law's hand through his other elbow with a smiling look and a fond pat to her hand. To Julia's surprise, she found herself warming to the older man.

"Do you feel up to going on to your new home today, Daughter? Gideon?" Jacob asked as he shepherded the newlyweds toward the wooden boardwalk that fronted a handful of clapboard stores.

A full day's hard riding across rugged country and a night camped in the open air yet lay ahead of them before they reached Hui Aloha—the lovely, European-style home that Jacob had built himself. Gideon had been at sea for many weeks on the notoriously long and uncomfortable voyage from Boston. As Jacob had cautioned his excited wife, Miriam, when they'd received the letter Gideon had forwarded via steamer upon his arrival in Honolulu, there was every possibility their son might wish to rest and refresh himself for a day or two, before continuing on to Hui Aloha. That possibility was even greater, Jacob was sure, now that they had the comfort of Gideon's bride to consider.

"There's nothing I'd enjoy more, sir," Gideon confessed. "However, I think it's only fair that Julia should decide. Which shall it be, my dear? Set out for Hui Aloha immediately, or rest here for the night?"

Julia hesitated, casting a quick glance at Gideon's face. Although he'd gallantly offered to let her decide, his choice was in his eyes. "I'd just as soon go on, I do believe, Gideon," she said brightly. "I'm eager to meet Mother Kane and to see the house where you were born as soon as may be."

She was rewarded by a surprised and pleased smile from her new husband. "Splendid! Shall we have a litter prepared, or can you ride horseback?"

"Can I?" She laughed, her gray eyes sparkling. "I'll have you know, Mister Gideon Kane, that I could ride almost as soon as I could walk!"

"Could you, indeed! Then you have that in common with almost everyone on the island—including myself!" he acknowledged, his smile deepening. Color filled her cheeks as his gaze lingered thoughtfully on her face, as if she knew, somehow, that he was thinking about their wedding night, and the narrow bunk he'd been unable to share with her on account of both her biliousness and the schooner's overcrowding. His expression suggested he intended to correct that omission in the near future.

She was still blushing when they reached the group of native and Mexican ranch hands smoking slim black cheroots, cigars, or pipes as they lounged in the shade of Ah Woo's storefront.

The Chinaman, Ah Woo himself—resplendent in baggy black pajamas, shaved head, and a long, glossy black pigtail growing from the crown—was doing a brisk trade serving the ranch hands little cups of fragrant Hawaiian-grown coffee, or refreshing guava juice, or steaming green tea with much respectful bowing, while his diminutive wife, dressed as was he, save for a very large dish-shaped coolie hat, scuttled about with bowls of hot peanuts, boiled in their shells, or little white balls of steamed dough stamped with a red flower and stuffed with a fragrant ground pork-and-vegetable filling, which the men seemed to regard as a great treat.

To a man, the ranch hands sported broad-brimmed, low-crowned hats made either of felt or of woven pandanus fiber that the Hawaiians called *lauhala*. Their cowboy garments made them look almost Spanish. Brilliant silk or patterned calico bandanas were knotted loosely about their throats, while their colorful cotton shirts were long-sleeved and tucked into broad leather belts. Their legs, grown bowed from many years spent astride a horse, day in and day out, were hidden beneath sturdy denim or corduroy work breeches that buttoned on the side from knee to ankle to allow room for the boot legs. Over the breeches flapped bat-wing chaps of cowhide, so only the toes of their low-heeled Spanish boots showed beneath the chaps. Indeed, except for the exotic surroundings and their broad Polynesian features, they could have stepped from one of Remington's paintings of the hard-riding cowboys, or *vaqueros,* of the western frontier, Gideon thought as memories of growing up around these courageous, hard-working, tough men came flooding back.

As the three of them approached, one of the men exclaimed in the singsong pidgin of the islands, *"Alooo-ha!* Welcome home, Mo'o!"

"Long time we nevah see you!" declared another.

"You wen' grow little bit, yeh?"

"You're right there. I have grown an inch or two, Uncle Kimo, you old rascal!" Gideon agreed warmly as the old Hawaiian *paniolo,* came forward to embrace him. The Hawaiian tossed a rosebud-and-fern *lei,* around his neck, hugging him in welcome. "And I think it's time you boys quit calling me Mo'o," he added in a stern voice that his grin belied, "and call me Bossman instead—since I'll be running the Kane Ranch before year's end."

His eyes met his father's over Kimo's gray head and Alika's curly black one, and he saw the other man's fill with tears of relief as his secret fears were laid to rest. The Kane Ranch would go on, as he'd always intended it should; prospering, expanding, improving . . .

"And while I'm running the ranch," Gideon continued, "I'd like you to welcome the boss lady who'll be running *me!* Boys, I'd like you to meet my bride, Missus Julia Lennox Kane."

Gideon's announcement was met with whoops of approval and hearty congratulations from the ranch hands. More flower garlands followed the first, fragrant *leis* reaching up to, and then past, his and Julia's ears as the other *paniolos* welcomed him and his bride home with more hand-shaking, back-slapping, and cries of *"Alooo-ha!"*

After a brief discussion, one of the cowboys led three saddled mounts forward. After Gideon had lifted Julia up into the saddle of an even-tempered brown mare, another ranch hand tossed him a battered yet familiar *lauhala* hat. Its woven fibers had been weathered to a deep tan hue by time, weather, and wear so that it now resembled a western-styled felt Stetson but for the band of exotic mauve orchids, ferns, and sweet-smelling *maile* vines that someone had fastened about its low crown. With a sheepish smile, the Mexican cowboy murmured, "I found this in the bunkhouse, Señor Boss. I figured you might be needing it, now that you're home to stay, *sí?"*

Gideon's grin was answer enough.

He'd already removed his dark frockcoat. Now he yanked the stifling cravat from the wing-collared shirt he'd worn beneath it and sent it flying carelessly off into some bushes. Bare-throated now, his sleeves rolled up, he set the hat at a rakish angle and hooked his left foot into the *tapadero,* the hooded stirrup, before swinging his lean frame up and into the high wood-and-leather Spanish saddle. Stroking his stallion's neck, he murmured, "It's been too damned long, Akamai, old fellow. Let's see what you and I remember, huh? Git up there!"

Thirteen

They followed the old man-made trail that Kuakini, the former governor of the island of Hawaii, had ordered built to improve transportation from arid Kawaihae to the lush plains of Waimea, where the governor had loved to hunt wild boar, heading steadily up country to the lovely region of half-hidden valleys and gentle rains.

The first ten miles of the trail were miserably barren. They slipped and scrambled their way over rocky stretches that offered little by way of purchase, the going difficult despite the wiry Mauna Kea' horses they rode, hardy little beasts that had been born and raised high in the rugged mountains of the island. Nevertheless, the new trail was a considerable improvement over the old one, which had woven in and out of the rugged rocks or squeezed its narrow way past plunging cliff walls to the booming sea far below.

It had been that same Hawaiian king, King Kamehameha the Great, conqueror of all the islands, who had made Jacob Kane's father, Elias Kane, his *konohiki,* his favorite among the handful of white men living on the Big Island. In recognition of Kane's love for the land and her people, and in gratitude for the young man's wise advice in many matters, Kamehameha had given Gideon's grandfather the small tract of land that had been the beginning of the Kane Ranch, Gideon reflected as they rode.

One of the only two surviving sons born to the very first Boston missionary couple to settle on the Big Island, Kane's eldest son, Jacob, had, in his twenty-fifth year, married Miriam Haunani "Dew of Heaven" Gideon—the lovely half-Hawaiian daughter of Kamehameha's cousin and British-born naval captain, Sir Thaddeus Gideon, whose surname they'd eventually given their first and only surviving child. It was by marriage to Miriam that Jacob Kane had acquired the extensive acreage to expand the small but flourishing ranch his father had begun, lands that would one day become pasturage for the vastly improved herds he planned to cultivate.

With the lucrative sandalwood trade with the Orient exhausted, the forests denuded of their sweet-smelling timber, Jacob Kane had shrewdly seen that the Big Island's economy was in serious jeopardy. He and a handful of others, including Jacob's most successful rival and longtime friend, Sam Parker, had believed that one answer to the problem lay in the thousands of wild long-horned cattle that had been allowed to roam the island unchecked, and the idea for both the Kane and the Parker ranches had been born.

The British sea captain, Vancouver had brought the first cows and bulls to the islands from California in the late 1700's as a gift for King Kamehameha I. However, the long sea voyage and miserable conditions had killed off all but a handful of the beasts. King Kamehameha had ordered that the survivors be set free to roam the island at will. He had also placed a royal *kapu*—taboo—upon the animals, to ensure they would not be hunted or harmed.

As a result of this taboo, the handful of sickly creatures had recovered and reproduced over and over again, adapting so successfully to their new environment that their descendants were deemed wilder and hardier and meaner than any longhorn to be found in Texas. So wild, indeed, that some of the vicious beasts had gored humans without provocation, persuading Kamehameha to have stone walls built around the native villages for his people's protection.

Elias Kane had reasoned that if these hardy animals could be

herded up and interbred with prime stock brought from Europe
and America to improve their quality and weight, they could
provide the thousands of pounds of badly needed, prime quality
beef for the multitude of trading or whaling ships that took on
provisions or anchored in island harbors each year.

At first singlehanded, then later with the help of his growing
son, the foreman Kimo and other native herders, Eli Kane had
begun to put his plan into action. And, in due course, his son
Jacob had taken over. The ranch had prospered and flourished
under their care. Fine-blooded bulls, cows, horses, and sheep
arrived now at frequent intervals, prime breeding stock pur-
chased and sent from Kentucky, Texas, New Mexico, and as far
away as the Highlands of Scotland, animals whose bloodlines
had been selected with a careful eye toward improving the ex-
isting herds and flocks. The result had been huge herds of hardy,
healthy animals that bore little resemblance to the captured wild
mavericks from which they were descended.

Eli and later Jacob Kane had also sent to America for skilled
vaqueros to instruct their men in cattle-herding. These cowboys
had called themselves *españoles*. Consequently, over the years,
the shortened word *paniolo* had become the Hawaiian name for
these cowboys, and for the native Hawaiian men who had learned
from them their matchless riding and roping skills, and likewise
their colorful working costume of spurs, chaps and bandannas.

Over the years, the Kane Ranch had expanded and prospered,
eventually becoming one of the largest ranches in the islands.
Now, forty years later and no longer young, Jacob Kane was a
successful, wealthy man. As a result of the fall from his horse
six years before, he was frequently in pain and was ready now
to relinquish the reins and hand the daily running of the ranch
over to his son.

"How's Makuahine?" Gideon asked as they rode along a
shady trail where lavender and blue morning-glory vines rambled in colorful profusion. "In good health, I trust?"

"Indeed, yes. Since you wrote to tell us you were homeward

bound, my girl's had such a glow about her!" He chuckled. "And once she's seen you and heard your happy news, she'll be doubly thrilled, my boy!" He smiled across at Julia, perturbed to see that his daughter-in-law was gazing bleakly ahead apparently lost in silent misery, although the barren trail had fallen away behind them, giving way to lush, tropical vegetation, tender ferns, banana trees, breadfruits, flowering hibiscus, candlenut, and lianas on every side in breathtaking profusion. Jacob clucked his tongue in understanding. "Aaah, poor child. She's feeling homesick for her family, no doubt," Jacob murmured softly to Gideon, nodding in Julia's direction, "Patience and understanding on your part will take care of that. And—in due time—children of her own."

"No doubt," Gideon agreed, grunting noncommittally. He made no effort to explain that it was the attractions of big-city life his bride mourned, rather than her absent relatives. His father must assume what he would from Julia's behavior, and his own, for that matter. He had no intention of describing the sorry chain of events that had led to their hasty marriage. "Does *Makuahine* still mourn the babe she lost after I left?"

Jacob sighed and nodded. "Perhaps even more so, now that she's past the age of childbearing, and knows there'll be no more babes for us. She wanted very badly to give me another son, you know."

"A grandchild would make her forget," Gideon observed, sitting tall and loose in the saddle, as if he'd never been away. His father's casual comment had reminded him that Julia could even now be carrying his child. His mother would be delighted, if so. "You may rest assured we'll do our utmost to provide you with a few as soon as possible," he promised with a grin that made his deep-blue eyes glint like *popolo* berries in the bright light slanting through the trees.

Jacob caught the wicked twinkle in Gideon's eyes and shook his head. "You may be a head taller than when you left, but you're still a young rogue! Sometimes I fear you take after my reprobate brother more than you do me!" Jacob shook his gray head. "God rest their souls, your grandfather and mother had despaired of keeping him on the straight and narrow long before he'd reached your age! By the way, how are he and dear Sophie and the children keeping?"

"Much the same as ever. Uncle's the very picture of the prosperous sugar planter, overseeing his cane fields from the comfort of his Nuuanu mansion. Of late, he's taken to surf-riding with the king—who has a beach house nearby—and his entourage off Waikiki swamps. I should imagine he cuts quite a dash!" Gideon grinned, for Thomas's description of his portly, bewhiskered uncle riding the surf wearing a bathing costume and precariously balanced astride a giant *koa*-wood surfboard as he tried to outdo the fun-loving Hawaiian king, Kamehameha V, had been comical.

"Prosperous, surely, if he's built himself such a large residence—and in the Nuuanu Valley, too," Gideon's father observed. "It never ceases to amaze me that my younger brother can find ample time for a full social calendar, and turn a handsome profit, besides."

There was disapproval rather than envy in Jacob's tone. To Jacob, the worship of God came first in a man's life, followed by his devotion to parents, wife and family, and then to hard and unceasing, productive work. The pursuit of pleasure for pleasure's sake alone was beyond his understanding.

"Nonetheless, Uncle appears adept at doing both—and with considerable zeal! By the way, he sent you his fondest regards, as did Aunt Sophie."

"Poor, dear Sophie. Such a good, pious woman! She surely deserved a fitter helpmate than my brother."

"Amen to that!" Gideon agreed, thinking if one were to harness two similarly mismatched horses in the traces of the same cart, disaster would be inevitable.

"In Sophie's last letter to your mother, she mentioned that they were entertaining a guest in their home for a time—a Missus Lennox, I believe her name was? A widowed relative by marriage from back East, to all accounts"

"Indeed they were, sir. The lady in question is the one you have met, the one who is now my wife! You see, Julia was formerly Missus Julia Lennox, of Baltimore, Maryland—Aunt Sophie's late Cousin David Lennox's wife? She was widowed just last year, and had intended to spend her period of mourning with Sophie until . . ." He shrugged expressively. "Well, it was at Uncle's supper table that we first met."

"Indeed? Then your courtship must have been something of a whirlwind affair, must it not? Or . . . perhaps you'd met before, in America?"

"We hadn't, no. It was very . . . fast." He offered no more details, to his father's obvious frustration.

"Hmm. I see. But—I'd rather gathered the impression that Sophie was entertaining thoughts of marriage between the lady and young Thomas?"

"It's quite possible she had such hopes, but . . . !" Again, Gideon shrugged and allowed a faint smile to curl his lips. "Well, let's just say that a 'faint heart never won a fair lady.' Isn't that the way the saying goes, Father?" he came back curtly, flashing his father a darkling look and wishing fervently he'd change the subject.

So that's the way the wind had blown! Jacob thought, happily misreading his son's expression. Gideon and his cousin had obviously both been smitten, and become rivals for the young woman's affections! Perhaps they'd even had a falling-out over her that had come to blows? Either way, Gideon truly must have fallen head-over-heels with the girl at first sight, to have met, courted, and married her all in a fortnight!

His smile deepened as he imagined his beloved wife, Miriam, holding their first grandchild in her arms; himself dandling a laughing infant on his knee, the picture of a doting grandpapa. *Praise God two such fine young people have found each other!* he thought with a feeling of deep contentment and gratitude as they rode on. *Dear Lord, may they always love each other as deeply and fully as they do this day. I ask your blessing on their union, that they be fruitful and multiply. Amen.* Ah, yes, life was indeed good, and filled with the Lord's countless blessings!

Fourteen

"Mai! Mai! Welcome!" Miriam called as Emma rode up to Hale Koa the following morning. The rancher's wife was busily stringing *leis,* seated on a grand peacock chair like a queen upon a throne. At her feet was a woven basket filled with dewy jasmine blossoms, and another—this filled with lengths of fragrant green *maile* vine—had been placed on a small table before her. She held a long, metal *lei*-needle between slender fingers and a flower in the other but set her work aside and arose, smiling, to greet the rider, thinking what a charming picture the lovely *hapa* girl made as she slithered from her horse. A strand of jasmine blossoms crowned her flowing dark hair, while her slender body was gowned in a long, ruffled *muumuu.* The yoke was of deep violet cloth, almost the same color as her eyes, while the flowing folds were white, sprigged all over with lavender and violet flowers. She looked lovely—cool and fresh and elegant as any tropical queen—for all that her feet were quite bare, in the island fashion.

"No school today, Miss Jordan?" Miriam asked

"Good morning, Missus Kane. No, no school today," Emma confirmed, laughing. She dismounted and led her horse up to the veranda steps, wishing she didn't look so disheveled as she tried to neaten her appearance. "I . . . um . . . canceled it."

Her wretched hair was curling from the morning's misty rains and the cool damp air. First wisps, then strands had escaped the tidy single plait as she rode so that it was loose now, and refusing to stay neatly in place, while her second-best muslin *muumuu*—freshly laundered, then crisply starched and ironed before she set out—had grown horribly wrinkled. Worse, the ruffled hems were spattered with dried mud—hardly proper attire for a serious schoolmarm! She couldn't have made a worse impression on Gideon's mother had she tried.

"I see. Then what brings you all the way from the Waikalani Valley to Hale Koa?" Miriam asked, coming forward with the grace of a clipper ship in full sail to stand at the top of the veranda steps and look down at the young woman with dancing brown eyes and teasing smile curving her lips. "Could you have heard of the wonderful *luau* I have planned for tomorrow, hmm? It'll be the biggest feast this ranch—perhaps this island!—has ever seen, and all in honor of a certain very *special* someone's homecoming?"

"How excited you must be! I had no idea Master Gideon was coming home!" Emma exclaimed, trying very hard to look innocent but wanting badly to jump up and down—scream—do *something* to vent the excitement—and joy!—that was bubbling up inside her and threatening to explode.

"You hadn't heard? What a pity!" Miriam said with a sigh. "And after I'd asked your auntie to send word to you, too. You see, I was so hoping you'd dance the *hula* for us? Please say you will," Miriam implored the young woman.

Would she dance for her beloved's homecoming? What a question! "I was just teasing. Auntie Leolani sent word to the valley yesterday. And I'd be honored to dance for your son's homecoming, Missus Kane," she agreed, smiling broadly. "Thank you for asking me."

"No, no, *mahalo nui loa* to you, my dear," Miriam thanked her warmly. "How is it that you're here so bright and early?"

"Auntie asked me to come and help her and Pua and the others with the preparations."

"It's going to be wonderful!" Miriam exclaimed, her eyes shining with anticipation as she looked beyond Emma to the lawns, where the ranch hands were laughing and joking with each other as they built windbreaks of banana leaves and coconut fronds, or spread woven mats of *lauhala* fiber over the grass, on which would be placed the platters and gourds of food.

Looking at her, Emma sighed wistfully. Missus Kane always looked so cool, so composed and elegant—very much the mistress of Hui Aloha, Emma thought enviously, her tongue suddenly feeling too big for her mouth.

Try as she might, she'd never forgotten the first time she'd been inside Hui Aloha, for it was also the *only* time she'd been inside the ranch house. Nor, she fancied, squirming, had Miriam Kane ever forgotten that night, for there was—or at least, so she'd convinced herself—a look of pity in her gentle brown eyes that made Emma's cheeks burn with shame.

A dark-eyed, frightened little waif, that night she'd clung to her uncle Kimo as if her life depended upon it, and begged him not to send her away. Promising she'd be good, she'd hung on to his bat-wing chaps while he quietly asked his boss, Jacob Kane, for a week's leave from his job as the ranch's foreman.

"I must take the *keikiwahine,* little girl, to Honolulu, Makua Kane," he'd explained. It was best his niece should leave, he'd added, than stay with her drunkard father, and her mother, who feared her husband too much to keep her little daughter safe.

Jacob Kane had gravely agreed. While the two men had discussed her future, their deep voices droning on and on, she had fallen asleep, exhausted by her sobbing. By the time she'd awakened again, they'd been on a ship bound for Honolulu—

"Auntie Leolani's in the kitchen *hale,* I believe." Miriam's voice interrupted her remembering. "Just go on around to the back, my dear, and tell whoever's there that you're looking for her. One of the boys will water your horse for you." She smiled. "I'll look forward to seeing you dance tonight, my dear." With that, she returned to her *lei*-making, smiling to herself as Emma led her horse away. Her Gideon, married at last! And, God willing, a father before too long! Who would ever have thought it! At last, her prayers had been answered.

Her smile deepened with pleasure as she swept inside the double doors and across the polished *koa*-wood floors of the entryway, catching a glimpse of herself in one of the long mirrors there.

Patting her elegant coiffure—though not a hair was out of place—she considered her reflection, murmuring, *"Tutu* Haunani. *Tutu* Kane!" How wonderfully strange it sounded! How deliciously sweet the Hawaiian word for grandmama tasted on her tongue! Surely the smiling woman in the looking glass was far too young to be a grandmother, a *kupunawahine,* she thought, trying to frown, but she could not seem to maintain the dignified expression of a proper grandmother. Rather, she hugged herself about the arms, dimples deepening in her cheeks as she laughed out loud in a most unseemly, happy fashion.

She'd lost her fourth child, also a son, to stillbirth shortly after Gideon had left for Boston, and had been desolate when the midwife had told her she could have no others without risk to her own life. But now, all that was about to change! In a year— surely no more than two—her empty arms would be filled with the sweet-smelling warmth and weight of a baby, her ears filled with the laughter and cries of her grandchild: her dearest Gideon's little son or daughter!

She beamed back at her reflection and declared softly, "Yes, Haunani. You are quite old enough—and more than ready—for that happy day. Dearest Lord, let it be soon!"

Emma stalked around the sprawling ranch house to the separate kitchen building, leading the poor little mare behind her and inwardly fuming. She'd acted like a perfect ninny, and had arrived looking as if she'd ridden through a bush backward. Hardly a good impression to make on the woman she hoped to be calling Mother-in-law very soon, all going well!

Old Moki was sitting cross-legged on the ground by the doorway of the kitchen hut. He held a hefty stone *poi*-pounder in one fist, and had a wide, shallow, wooden board before him in which he was pounding freshly-boiled taro root, mashing it into the starchy *poi*-paste that, when mixed to a smooth mauve consistency with water in a large calabash, would form the island staple, *poi.* Glancing up from his rhythmic labor, Moki smiled to see Emma standing there, showing the gap in his front teeth. Emma had heard the story often of how the old fellow had knocked out his own incisors when his wife had died, to show his grief.

"Aloha, Kaleilani, my daughter! It has been too long since we last saw you," he greeted her.

"It has, my uncle," she returned politely. "I am happy to find you in good health. Is my auntie Leolani also well?"

"She is. And she will be happy to see you, little one. Go inside and surprise her. I will take your *lio,* your horse."

Auntie Leolani was an enormous woman of close to three hundred pounds. Clothed in a flowing calico *muumuu* of vivid reds and yellows, a white apron straining over her ample belly, she had her back turned to the door as she deftly stuffed broad *ti*-leaves with portions of boiled *luau* leaves, pieces of salted belly-pork, and butterfish. After wrapping and tying them, the leaf bundles would be either steamed over a pot of boiling water or cooked in an underground oven alongside the roasting pig, to make the savory Hawaiian delicacy known as *lau-lau.*

"Kaleilani!" Leolani exclaimed in surprise at seeing her niece in the doorway. Her handsome brown face wore a broad smile. "Wait, now. Let me wash my hands, child, so I can hug you! Nani, Pua, you be good girls an' finish dis *lau-laus* for Auntie, eh? Hurry now!"

Her hands rinsed, her tasks delegated, Leo mopped her perspiring face on a corner of her apron, then enfolded Emma in her plump arms and held her close to her heart. *"Auwe,* little pansy-eyes! Too much long time I nevah see you, sweetheart—

not since your *makua* passed on! How come you never bring
Mahealani to visit your poor uncle and auntie, eh, my *kalohe*
girl, my naughty one? We are all the *ohana,* the family, you have
left, no?" she chided softly, holding her niece at arm's length
and searching her face.

Emma bit her lip and looked down at her feet, ashamed. "I've
meant to bring her so many times—truly I have, Auntie. But
since . . . since Makuahine died, I've been very busy with everything. There's the school, you see. And the children keep me so
busy. And I have to plan my lessons for each day . . ."

"Hmmph." The grunt said Leolani wasn't impressed. "And
where is Mahealani today? Didn't she come with you?"

Emma shook her head and rolled her eyes. "That mischievous
one! She wanted to come, but she and your granddaughter dis-
obeyed Anela and ate a bowl of half-ripe wild plums. Naturally,
they have sore bellies today."

"Poor little *keikis!*" Leo laughed. "And what about that good-
for-nothing . . . ?" Leolani could not bring herself to refer to
Jack Jordan either by name or as Emma's father, she loathed
him so intensely. By her reckoning, the white man did not deserve to be called by any name.

"My father is . . . as always, Auntie—or at least, he is as far
as I know. I haven't seen him."

"Then there is nothing wrong?

"Nothing at all." Emma smiled to reassure her, grinning and
rolling her eyes. "I'm here, as you asked."

"How good, darling girl . . . and your uncle Kimo will be so
happy to see you, Kaleilani," she added in a lower voice. "Uncle
and I, we wanted so badly to raise you as our daughter all those
years ago, honey girl, but . . . !" Leolani shrugged and sighed,
"it could not be. If you'd stayed here, on the island, my foolish
sister would have taken you back to live with—him. For your
sake, you had to go. We could not let that happen, you understand, my little pansy-eyes?" She cupped Emma's face between
her plump hands, her dark eyes earnest.

Emma nodded and swallowed. A knot of tears filled her throat, for it was as if she was gazing into her mother's eyes as she looked at her aunt. "I understand. And there's nothing to forgive, truly. It all turned out for the best."

Leo smiled. "I'm glad to hear it, sweetheart. Tell me, were those years at the convent so very bad?"

"Not completely. In fact, I was happy there most of the time, though I missed Makuahine at first, of course."

Leolani nodded in understanding. "Of course. But the Catholic sisters gave you a fine education, did they not? If you'd not been so stubborn, Kaleilani, you could have taught at any school in the islands, instead of hiding yourself away in that remote little valley, cut off from everyone. I still believe you should have gone back to Oahu or married that school inspector—Keali'i Wallace—instead of staying here."

Emma shrugged. "Perhaps. But Mama was ill then, and she needed me so badly. Besides, it's too late to change the past, Auntie. And regretting what can't be changed is futile. We can only go on, learn from our mistakes, and change what we do in the future."

"I know, child, I know. You must forgive me. Auntie didn't mean to scold you. You were always such a good daughter to my sister, Kaleilani. Better, perhaps, than Malia ever deserved, for she was not always a wise mother to you." She sighed and shook her head. "Well, enough of the past for now, eh? As you said, it's too late to change any of it. You've had a long ride, and you must be tired and hungry. Young people are always hungry, eh?" she added, beaming. "Come, sit here at the table and Auntie will bring you some fish and *poi*. And then, if you still want to, you can help me. The men have the pigs roasting in the *imus,* the underground ovens, already, but there's still so much to do!"

Emma sat as bidden while her aunt bustled about, bringing a cloth-covered *poi*-bowl from the cool stone larder, along with some fish and a small dish of kelp mixed with spices that she took from a grilled meat safe. She chattered on while the serving girls, Nani and Pua, filled a steamer basket with the *lau-laus,* side-eyeing Emma and whispering behind their hands before a sharp look from Leolani sent them back to their work. By means of a stout pole slung through its metal handle, the young women hefted the heavy pot outside, to the vast cauldron of water bubbling over an open fire.

"Is Uncle Kimo here?" Emma asked when she and her aunt were alone once more.

Leolani shook her head. "Mister Kane asked him to go to Kawaihae Landing. But he should be back long before the feast begins. I t'ink half the island's invited!"

Emma smiled. "I know. And Missus Kane has asked me to dance the hula."

"The forbidden dance!"

"Yes."

"And?"

Emma shrugged. "I said I would!"

"You did? *Auwe!*" Leolani exclaimed, pretending dismay. "I hope the sheriff and his policemen don't see you!"

"They won't. But if they do, they'll be too busy enjoying your *lau-laus* to care, Auntie!" Emma teased. "Will you chant while I dance?"

Leolani nodded. "Of course, honey girl. By the way, did you hear the big news?"

"What could be bigger news than Gid—Mister Kane coming home?" Emma asked. Covering the *poi* bowl with a cloth, she rose, intending to return it to the safe.

"Oh, everyone knows that! I'm talking about the *rest* of it! The other news the island's buzzing with?

Emma frowned. "Then I suppose I haven't heard it."

"It's supposed to be a surprise, girlie, but Missus Kane got word from Kawaihae yesterday that Mister Gideon's brought back a bride—"

The basin slipped from Emma's hand and crashed to the flagstone floor, splattering sticky *poi* in all directions.

"The luau is to celebrate their *we—auwe!* Kaleilani, you've grown so pale! What is it, child? Dear Lord, tell Auntie what's wrong!"

Julia sucked in a gasp of delight the following morning as they neared the house where Gideon had been born—the house that Jacob Kane had proudly called the heart of his ranch and the land itself. Why, Hui Aloha looked even larger and finer than she'd ever imagined! she thought as she urged her mount after the others, gazing with undisguised pleasure at the stately little jewel of a mansion before her.

Long, elegant windows flanked a double-doored entryway; windows that would boast breathtaking views of snowcapped Mauna Kea in the distance. There were long, deep verandas on all sides of the house. Rattan peacock chairs were scattered about there so that one could sit in the shade and catch the coolest breezes. The house was bowered about by lofty coconut palms and some kind of low-spreading trees with deep-green, waxy leaves and abloom with huge posies of creamy white blossoms, as well as hibiscus bushes flaunting enormous crimson or pink trumpets. Sweeping manicured lawns bordered with neatly trimmed mock-orange hedges fronted the house, and peacocks—their iridescent blue-green or silvery-white tail feathers dragging like a train behind them on the grass—strutted here and there, uttering strange, harsh cries.

A number of outbuildings showed between the trees, all some distance from the main house, and she could see corrals and stables and carriage houses beyond those before the land spread away in all directions to meet the bright blue sky, as green and rolling as an emerald blanket.

"That's the dairy you see over there, closest to the house," Gideon supplied, guessing her thoughts as he rode up alongside her. "And over there, the stables, a few storehouses, a smoke house, a spring house, and so on. The *lunas*—the ranch foremen—have their own little houses where they live with their families—all within a mile or so of Hui Aloha—while the unmarried cowboys sleep over there, in the bunkhouse, like they do on an American ranch. There's nothing out of the ordinary."

Julia nodded, thinking, *Maybe it's ordinary to you, darlin', but it's a far cry from the dirt-floor cabin where I was raised up!*

"Let one of the men take your horse while we go inside. I know you can't see her from here, but I'd be willing to bet my mother's hovering by the window, as nervous as all get-up about meeting you."

"About meeting *me?* But—how would she even know about me?" Julia asked, startled.

"Jungle telegraph?" Gideon suggested with a rueful grin and a shrug. *"Kahuna* magic? Who knows how news travels around the island? All I know is that it does—and damn quickly, too! Word of my marriage will have reached here ages ago! By now, my mother knows I've brought home a bride, and she'll be primping and fretting, convinced you won't like her on the one hand, while on the other, she's probably arranged the biggest welcome-home *luau* this island's ever seen!"

"Do you really think sh—Oh, look! How pretty!" Julia exclaimed suddenly.

Glancing up, Gideon saw what she was exclaiming over: an *ohia lehua* tree in full bloom. The tree grew only at higher altitudes such as this, and was covered with vivid blossoms like delicate red sea anemones, or scarlet dandelion pompoms. Before he realized what she was going to do, Julia stood in her stirrups and broke off a low-hanging twig covered with flowers. Airily twirling it around between her fingers, she admired the exotic blossoms. "I've never seen anything so pretty!" Just then, she happened to glance up and caught Gideon frowning at her. The ranch foreman, sour-faced Kimo Pakele, wore a similarly disapproving expression, and be damned if she couldn't hear the other *paniolos* muttering *"Auwe!"* or *"Pilikia!"*— "Trouble!"—

under their breaths. In fact, they were all eyein' her like she'd been caught spittin' in chapel! "Did I do something wrong, gentlemen?"

"Really, it's not important, my dear. Just an old island superstition. You weren't to know," Gideon assured her, dismissing the matter as unimportant with a shrug.

"What did I do that was so wrong?"

"The Hawaiians believe that this tree is sacred to Pele, the goddess of the volcano, Doña Julia," José, a young Spanish ranch hand explained. "They believe that if you pick her sacred blossoms—as *you* have picked them, Doña Julia—the goddess will become very angry and she will make it rain."

"That's what they say nowadays, perhaps," Alika agreed, casting Julia Kane a dark look, his former merry expression gone. "But in the old days, the days before the *haoles*—the white men—come here, it mean big *pilikia,* trouble." He paused and nervously wetted his lips. "It mean 'blood be spilled,' by an' by!"

"Blood be spilled? Oh, what backwoods nonsense!" Julia declared scornfully. With a yell, she spurred her mount toward the house, letting the sprig of scarlet blossoms fall to the white coral chips of the driveway, where they were crushed beneath her horse's hooves.

Fifteen

Emma pressed her already weary horse to the limits, riding the twisting bridle path at breakneck speed until she reached Twin Rocks Cove, and the beach where she and Gideon had first met.

Slithering from the back of her horse, she ran down to the water's edge and waded into the shallows, not caring that the saltwater soaked the flowing folds of her *muumuu* or that tears streamed down her cheeks.

Why? she asked herself over and over as she stood thigh-deep in the gently lapping water, staring blindly at the distant horizon where vivid blue sea met vivid blue sky. Why, oh, *why* had Gideon betrayed her? Why had he forsaken her for another? Had he not thought her beautiful? Had he not whispered that he loved her as he could love no other when she lay in his arms beneath the sea-grape tree? What, then, had changed his heart since he left the islands? Was there a chance—however slim—that her father could have been right? He'd scoffed and said Gideon would never come back for her; or jeered that if he ever did, he might make her his mistress, but never his bride.

"You an' me, we int' good enough for his fancy sort, Em. He'll use yer, he will, then cast you orf and wed one of 'is own kind. Stay wiv your old da, Em. Old Jack loves his pretty little Emmie, you know that," he'd always said, but she'd never given his words much weight, till now.

Drained from her weeping yet still weak with shock, Emma

waded back out onto the sand. She sank to her knees beneath the sea-grape tree where Gideon had loved her, unable to shed another tear. She felt empty, as hollow as a gourd, and so very numb, she thought she'd never feel again. And nor did she want to, ever! Caring for someone hurt too much.

"I'll always come back to you . . ." he'd promised, his gentian eyes tender in the soft purple shadows and the silvery light of the moon, and she—the naive, trusting little fool—had believed his lies with all her heart.

Oh, to taste such sweetness, to feel such love—to nurture it day after day with hopes and dreams, watch it unfold like some glorious flower only to have that sweet blossom of love wither and die in the space of a heartbeat, a scattering of words: *"Gideon's brought back a bride!"*

Auwe! The pain was too great to be borne.

She could recall as if it were yesterday the summer she'd met Gideon and lost her heart. Each afternoon she'd come here, to the cove, to swim while her mother slept in the hottest hours of the day.

Uncle Kimo and Auntie Leo had tried to talk her into going back to Oahu after the summer holidays had ended, but she'd insisted on leaving the convent altogether, and on staying at home to care for her mother.

"Doctor Forrester says she's dying, Auntie," she'd murmured, tears brimming in her violet eyes. "But she's far too proud, too ashamed of the past, to ask you for help. She needs me, so I'll stay until she either gets well, or until she . . ."

There'd been no need to finish her thought. They'd all accepted that it was unlikely Malia Jordan would live out that summer. But they'd been wrong. Somehow, against all odds, she had survived, clinging desperately to life, first day by day, then week by week, then month by month and then, unbelievably, year by year, hanging on with a grim tenacity that was heart-rending to see. Emma believed her mother's failing strength had been bolstered by her fear of dying and leaving her daughter alone with Jack Jordan, the husband she'd grown to hate. And Mama, God bless her, had had good reason to hate Jack, as it'd turned out.

Remembering, Emma sighed. Dealing with da day in and day out that long, hot summer had been every bit as grueling as the constant nursing her mother had required. The cooler hours of late afternoon—when *Makua* had been able to sleep with the help of a little laudanum—had been her only time to herself, and, consequently, the hours when she was most vulnerable to Jack. She'd made it a point to be as far away from the *hales,* the grass shacks beneath the lehua trees, as she could get.

"I love ye, Em," Jack'd begin weepily those afternoons, already a little drunk from the day's grog and growing more and more maudlin by the minute. "Come on over here, and sit on yer daddy's lap, Em. He missed ye while you were away at that bleedin' convent, he did. Let's have a little welcome home cuddle, eh?"

"Later, Da. Mama needs me now," she'd protested.

"My arse! She don't need nothin', that one don't. Look at her! Nothin' but a bag of bones—not a bit o' flesh on her to warm her man's blood! She's as good as dead already, she is. But even half dead, she's as tough as bloody nails!" He'd snickered with laughter at his own hateful joke. "I'm not like her. I need ye, Emmie, luv," he'd gone on in a lower, wheedling voice, patting the woven mat beside him. "C'mon over here t' Daddy, ducks."

When he was like that, it was no use arguing. She'd simply thrust another jug into his hands—usually rotgut rum she'd bought in Waimea with the precious money she earned from her taro and sweet potato patches—and promise him, "Not now, Da. Have another drink."

Once Jack had safely drunk himself into yet another stupor, she would slip quietly away from their airy, native grass huts, riding Makani hell-bent-for-leather down to the beach. It was on one of those stolen afternoons that she'd first spotted

Gideon's big-boned gray horse tethered among the ironwoods. Casting about, she'd finally spied its rider, seated beneath a sea-grape tree that grew close to the water, deep in thought, to all appearances.

She sighed dreamily, remembering that, from the very first, she'd thought him handsome, with his crisp, wavy black hair, golden-tanned face, and unusual deep-blue eyes. Seeing the interest that had ignited in those eyes when he'd caught sight of her, she'd yielded to an unfamiliar naughty impulse and pretended *she* hadn't seen *him!* Discarding her muumuu, she'd plunged into the water to swim in only her underbodice and drawers, cavorting about and shrieking like a perfect ninny. Truth was, it had both pleased and excited her to know he was watching her, thinking himself hidden and quite unaware that she knew he was there!

The following day, she'd gone back to the beach at exactly the same time, hoping he'd be there—and he was! He'd also been there again the following day, and the next. In between those impatiently awaited afternoons, she'd gone to some trouble to ask questions in the village and discover his identity, and learned he was Gideon Kane, the eighteen-year-old son of the cattle baron and rancher, Jacob Kane, and his *hapa-haole,* half-white, wife, Miriam Haunani Kane. Gideon, it transpired, had recently returned to the Big Island after attending school at the Punahou College in Honolulu, on the island of Oahu.

How could it be she'd never seen him before, she'd wondered then on discovering he'd been born and raised here on the Big Island, as had she? Or, if she'd seen him before, that she would have completely forgotten anyone as handsome as him?

And then she'd remembered the summer before she was sent away to the convent. One sunny Sunday morning, she'd gone to the little white wooden church in the village of Waimea with Auntie Leo and Uncle Kimo. She had seen a boy of about eleven years old to her tender six years standing in the front pew. He'd been dressed in a stiff new wool coat with a silly white sailor collar and short trousers—and scowling as fiercely as if he was wearing a hair shirt! His unruly black Gypsy curls had been so firmly slicked down with smelly pomade that his head had reminded Emma of a polished *kukui,* or candlenut, and the comparison made her giggle!

Seated on either side of the boy had been stern-faced Jacob Kane and a beautiful, statuesque *hapa-haole* lady, dressed regally in a fitted *holoku* of lavender silk with a high, ruffled collar, leg-o'-mutton sleeves, and a small train that she swept behind her by means of a loop about her silk-gloved fingers. Exquisite lavender, gray, and purple feather *leis* had crowned her upswept hair and been draped about her shoulders.

"Is that the Queen, Auntie?" she'd whispered, wide-eyed with awe that the *ali'i*—Hawaiian royalty—would visit the little country church to worship. But to her disappointment, Auntie Leo had shushed her, shaking her head. "No, silly one," she'd chided Emma fondly, her pretty brown eyes twinkling. "The beautiful lady is Missus Miriam Kane, while the little boy is her son, Master Gideon. They own the big house where I'm housekeeper. Now, hush, do, child, and listen to *Makua* Lyons's sermon . . ."

That first glimpse of Gideon had been her last. The next month, Uncle Kimo had taken her to distant Honolulu, and left her there with the good sisters of the convent of the Sacred Cross for the next eight years. Remembering, her lower lip trembled. Uncle Kimo had gently tried to explain everything. He'd told her that she was dearly loved, and that everyone wanted what was best for her. Because they cared so much, she had to go away. Nevertheless, she'd wept and clung to him, shrieking that she didn't want them to love her anymore, begging him not to leave her, promising she'd be very very good—oh, so perfectly, wonderfully good!—if only he'd take her back with him. In the end, a mean-faced nun had picked her up and carried her bodily from the room, cruelly pinching Emma's cheek to silence her.

She'd been unable to comprehend why her beloved *makua*

and her uncle and her auntie had sent her so far, far away until she was much older. And even then, shame and a peculiar, nagging guilt had made her reject the logical reasons for them doing so, and wonder if she was not to blame, somehow.

Emma sighed, remembering the convent. Once her little girl's too-thin body had begun to mature and take on the rounded curves of a woman, the sisters had been zealous in their efforts to impress upon her the importance of chastity and virtue. At every turn, they'd reminded her that Hawaiian blood ran in her veins, and hinted that—because of her mixed bloods—she was more likely to fall victim to "the idleness and laxity to which the native or half-breed is too often prone." Or worse, to "immorality and the sinful ways of the flesh"—whatever they might be!

Over and over again, the nuns had drummed into her confused little head their conviction that, without the sternest discipline and many, many long hours spent on her knees in prayer, she would "come to a bad end." Bad end or nay, she'd yearned for nothing as dearly as she'd yearned to leave the convent and the drudgery of lessons, endless prayer, Bible-reading, scrubbing floors, pot-scouring, laundry scrubbing, and too few hours spent in sleep before it began all over again! She grimaced. She could still remember feeling *glad* when Uncle Kimo's letter had arrived, telling her that the mother she'd hardly remembered by then had fallen ill, for it had meant she would have to go home.

Later, as she'd stood at the rail of the brig that had carried her back to the Big Island, she'd seen the island rising up from the turquoise sea, green and lush and beautiful, and had sworn she'd never go back there—never, no matter what! Although her mother was sick, life here would surely be a vast improvement over her life at the convent!

She'd been wrong about that. In some ways, her life hadn't improved, for following the unforgettable evening when she and Gideon had made love beneath the sea-grape trees, her life had become a nightmare—one in which she'd been trapped like a helpless fly in a sticky web, for her father had surprised her as she was riding home through the dusk, Gideon's kisses still warm on her lips.

Stepping out into the path of her horse, he'd grabbed Makani's bridle and demanded to know how long she'd been meeting "the Kane boy" in secret? How many times had they met, un-chaperoned, he'd wanted to know? Eyes blazing, he'd accused her of all manner of hateful, wicked things.

"Did 'e touch you, girlie?" Jack Jordan had thundered, staring at her swollen lips. *"Did Kane have you? Did he, then? That son of a bitch, I'll kill 'im if he laid a hand on you, my girl!"* Grasping her by the elbow, he'd dragged her from her horse's back and roughly demanded, "Answer me, Emma? Are you still *wahine kapu?"*

"We only held hands. I swear it, Father!" she'd lied, desperate to protect Gideon from her father's wrath. Who was he, anyway, she'd thought bitterly, to appoint himself keeper of her virtue?

"You bloody little liar!" he'd raged, lifting his hand to strike her.

"No!" she'd denied, ducking to avoid the blow that never fell. "We just—we just walked along the beach together, I swear it. He held my hand. He—" she bowed her head, "he kissed me, but it's not what you think, I swear! He's leaving the islands to go to college soon, but he—he's promised he'll come back and marry me, just as soon as he—"

"And you believed him?" Jack Jordan sneered, shaking his narrow, foxy head in scorn as he ran nicotine-stained fingers through his dirty-blond hair. "Don't ye see, Em? The randy young cock's just usin' you! His kind want but one thing from your kind, luv—and it int marriage! Forget Kane, you hear me? Aye, and forget his bloody promises, too. Him and his lot mean nothing but trouble."

"I can't forget him. I love Gideon—and he loves me. I prom-ised to wait for him, and I will, even if it takes forever!" she'd whispered, flinging herself across her horse and riding quickly away.

Despite Jordan's efforts to make her forget Gideon, for seven long years she'd clung to her memories of those halcyon afternoons, and of the tender passion they'd shared. Those few stolen moments had become a precious lifeline to all that was good and sane and beautiful in the world, when living with her father had gone from bad to worse.

Seven years spent waiting—sometimes patiently, sometimes impatiently—had come and gone, somehow. Even when she'd been flung headfirst into disillusioned womanhood, she'd still waited for him, polishing the memories of Gideon that Jack Jordan had repeatedly tried to tarnish or dull.

She'd wasted countless days in loitering beneath the iron-woods near Kawaihae Landing like some shameless waterfront doxy whenever she could escape her father's eagle eye and get away. She'd tried to be there after each round-up, or whenever the *paniolos* drove the Kane herds down to the Landing for loading onto the vessels that waited beyond the reef, yet there'd never been a letter from him awaiting her at Ah Woo's store, not one single word to read and reread, to cherish and sigh over, in answer to the countless letters she'd written and given to the smiling pigtailed Chinaman to send in return.

Hungry for some word of her beloved, albeit second or third hand, she'd loitered about, hoping to overhear a tidbit of information from the ranch hands, or to garner some small crumb of news tossed out by stern-faced Jacob Kane as he eagerly opened and read the months-old letters that the brigs or the steamers from America delivered to him.

"Ah ha! You see, Kimo? I knew Gid had it in him! Our boy graduated from Harvard last summer, summa cum laude!" Or, "Praise God, Kimo, will you listen to this! Gideon's safely back in Boston. The war's over! The North's won!"

In this indirect fashion, she'd known when Gideon had finished his college education, and been proud of the honors her beloved had received; known the very month he'd signed on aboard a Kane whaler, and gone to sea; known the heart-stopping news that he'd mustered into the Union cavalry. The latter unwelcome tidbit had been followed by night after sleepless night spent worrying that he'd been killed in battle, and the deep, gnawing terror that if the worst happened, she'd never be told of his death, but would go on waiting for him forever.

Tears burned behind her eyes, but she swallowed and gamely refused to cry. Fresh resolve poured through her, and burning anger began to replace dangerous, strength-sapping misery. *No! She wouldn't let him off so easily!* If Gideon had stopped loving her and decided to marry another, then so be it. She couldn't change that. Such things happened, after all. But . . . he must tell her to her face that it was ended between them. He must meet her, like a man, and admit that he had owed her the courtesy of a letter, the consideration of an explanation . . . *something!* He owed her that much, surely?

She hardened her jaw, stiffened her spine. Nothing else would do. Only by hearing the words from his very own lips could she ever begin to accept that, after seven long years, it was truly over between them, that he no longer loved her.

Or, *was* it over? Had he truly ceased to love her? Surely she would know in her heart if that were so.

She set her jaw and scrambled to her feet, brushing the sand from her sodden skirts. There was but one way to find out!

Tomorrow evening, at the *luau* Miriam Kane had planned to welcome home her son and his bride, she would dance the forbidden hula, as Miriam Kane had requested—*aiee,* she would dance it more sensually, more provocatively, than she had ever danced it before! And as she danced, she would gaze deep into her faithless lover's eyes, and she would *know* . . .

Sixteen

"Your bride is very lovely, Gideon," Miriam Kane observed.

"Yes, quite lovely," Jacob agreed. "I only pray her constitution can adapt to our tropic climate. She seems so fragile."

"Julia's tougher than she looks," Gideon assured him, remembering how remarkably swiftly the new Mrs. Gideon Kane had recovered from the rough voyage between Honolulu and the Big Island, then spent close to ten hours in the saddle without a murmur of complaint. "You'll see. She'll flourish once she's settled in."

"I do hope you're right. I must admit, she's . . . well, she's not at all what I'd expected," Miriam ventured, choosing her words with care so as not to offend her son. "To be honest, I'd expected one of the planters' daughters would take your fancy one day—they're such lovely girls! Or perhaps one of your cousin Elizabeth's school friends. But a widow from America! Fancy that! There were no children from her first marriage?"

"None," Gideon confirmed, knowing very well what his mother was leading up to. "By all accounts, David Lennox was considerably older than his wife, and fell into poor health soon after their marriage. The illness lasted until his death last year. However, that Julia failed to give Lennox a child does not mean the poor girl's barren, *makuahine*."

"*Kalohe!* You young rascal! I never meant to imply anything of the sort!" his mother exclaimed, indignant as only the truly guilty can be. For emphasis, she rapped him on the shoulder with her *lauhala* fan, then continued to scold him in a torrent of Hawaiian that only served to make his grin broaden.

He let her rail on. Protest she might, but if she was honest, his mother would have to admit that she was far more interested in the prospect of having grandchildren than she was in her new daughter-in-law, however lovely the young woman might be.

"Be that as it may, *makuahine,* my wife will think you don't like her if you persist in interrogating me about her past at every turn."

"Interrogate you, indeed! *Auwe!* I've done no such thing. And besides, we were speaking in Hawaiian! How could she possibly know what we were—"

"Makua!" he warned, his expression stern, with no hint of merriment in its hard, handsome lines.

"Oh, very well! Anela, Pikaki, *aloha!* Kaleoki, Makanui, Kekaimalu, *aloha nui loa!* Come, sit here with us and eat. Everything tastes so *ono!* You must try the *lomi-lomi* salmon and the *kalua* pig. And our Auntie Leolani's outdone herself with these *lau-lau!"* she exclaimed, pointedly turning her back on her son to greet some late-arriving guests.

Gideon shrugged and shook his head. From the moment the two women had met, a silent war had been declared. His mother had appraised Julia with the shrewd glance of a horse-trader estimating the bloodlines of a potential brood mare. Those sharp brown eyes had noted the too-slender hips, the fragile bone structure of face and wrists, and she'd frowned, obviously disappointed in what she saw.

By the same token, he'd seen Julia—who'd likewise read her new mother-in-law's thoughts—shrink within Miriam Kane's welcoming, perfumed embrace and behave somewhat coolly toward her mother-in-law thereafter, although she'd laughed and chattered charmingly to Jacob without any reserve, and had clearly won his approval.

That had been yesterday, soon after their arrival and an emotional reunion with his mother. Now, the lavish homecoming feast he'd expected was well under way.

Since early this morning, guests had been arriving. Some came on horseback, or by mule, others on foot, while still others bowled up the coral-chip driveway in dog-carts or wagons or buggies. There were all kinds of people, drawn from all over the island, almost every one of them bearing fresh-caught fish, or *limu*, seaweed, or a coconut cake, or perhaps some *kulolo*, a delicious taro pudding to add to the largesse and be shared by all in the true spirit of *aloha*, love.

The weather had showed its approval of the goings on by remaining warm and dry. In fact, it was a perfect evening for a feast, the sky a velvety midnight-blue in which the moon floated serenely, attended by a scattering of frosty white stars. The palm trees swayed lazily overhead, fronds wafting to and fro like ostrich plumes in the faint breeze that pleasantly cooled the air. The night was scented with the perfume of the flowers everyone was wearing, and with the pleasant fragrance of coconut oil that the Hawaiian women used to soften their golden skin and add luster to their ebony hair.

Tall torches ringed the lawns at intervals, their flames roaring from time to time in a sudden gust of wind. The torches cast shifting light across the faces of the merrymakers so that they seemed to glow with ruby color, like the faces in a Rubens oil. The light also sparkled on the dewdrops that clung to the scattered blossoms—hibiscus, frangipani, ginger, and delicate fishtail ferns—used to decorate the beautifully woven matting which served as a table for the feasters, seated cross-legged on either side of it.

Several wild boars, for pork was the traditional dish served for such glad celebrations, had been butchered, skinned, thoroughly cleaned, then rubbed with sea salt and wrapped—still whole—in fresh green banana leaves. Heated lava rocks had then been heaped inside each pig's belly cavity before the Hawaiian ranch hands carefully lowered the pigs into the pits, covered them with still more leaves, and, finally, heaped a heavy layer of soil over them. The pigs had been roasting since the wee hours in the *imus,* or underground ovens, cooked by a combination of the heat from the lava rocks and by the steam given off by the banana leaves. After several hours, succulent shredded pork—known as *"kalua* pig"—would literally fall off the bones.

Calabashes of a heady pineapple "moonshine"—an illegal beverage called *okolehau* or "swipe," that was brewed by the Hawaiians—who, as natives, were prohibited by law from purchasing bottled spirits or any other type of liquor here, in their own islands—were surreptitiously passing jugs of it from hand to hand. Conversation and laughter flowed just as freely once the feast got under way. While the musicians began tuning up their guitars and ukuleles, everyone sat on the grass behind windbreaks of banana leaves and palm fronds and feasted on the delicious bounty before them.

The shredded *kalua* pig was tender and deliciously smoky-tasting; the *lomi lomi* salmon—finely chopped salted salmon combined with diced tomatoes, green onions, and a little chilled water—was likewise tangy and delicious. Tender chicken, simmered in coconut milk with long-rice noodles, made the mouth water for more, while the chopped squid, cooked with still more coconut milk then thickened with pureed *luau* leaves—a spinachlike vegetable—was even better than anyone's *tutu,* or grandmother, could make it—high praise indeed! There was sliced raw fish and cubed raw fish and still more squid—likewise raw!—served with delicate varieties of kelp, the latter Kimo Pakele's specialty, which everyone declared—with much lip-smacking!—was fit for the old gods themselves. There were platters of sliced sweet potatoes that had been roasted alongside the pigs, roasted taro roots, and of course, huge calabashes of two-day-old *poi,* tasting slightly fermented and deliciously tangy, to be dipped straight from the calabash with a flourish of the index-and-middle finger together, in true Hawaiian style, before popping into the mouth with an appreciative roll of the eyes.

Looking down the long row of happy, smiling feasters, all dressed in their best, all busily eating and talking on either side of the mats, it seemed to Gideon as if everyone he'd ever known—even those from distant Ka'u and Puna, on the farthest side of the island!—must be here tonight. The guests included cane and pineapple planters and their families, dressed in formal, high-necked shirts and frockcoats, their ladies in elegant gowns, as well as a giggling coterie of boisterous, plump Hawaiian "aunties" in bright red-and-yellow flowered *muumuus*. They wore flower *leis* upon their heads and more slung about their necks, and loudly claimed some slight but tenuous kinship to his mother to anyone who would listen. There were regal Portuguese grandmothers with snapping black eyes and pure white hair, dressed in their finest black silk *holokus* and long-fringed silk shawls embroidered with roses; slender island beauties wearing fragile orchids in their dark hair, Spanish and Mexican cowboys rigged out in their finest silk fiesta shirts, strutting on stilt-heeled boots with jingling silver bell spurs, Doc Forrester and his diminutive wife, Thalia, who walked with a cane; the ranch schoolmaster, Mister Whittacker, and his widowed mother, Miss Rebecca; Reverend Mr. Aaron Cornwell and Missus Cornwell and their brood; the priest from the Catholic church, Father Gonzalo, as well as Ah Woo from the Kawaihae store, along with his little wife, Jade Flower—dressed today in a vivid crimson cheongsam of pure Shanghai silk, instead of black cotton pajamas—as well as many, many others.

After the Reverend Mister Cornwell had blessed the newlyweds and offered thanks for the feast, Gideon stood and briefly thanked everyone for joining their celebration, both in English and fluent Hawaiian, expressing his appreciation for everyone's good wishes and for the many generous wedding gifts he and his bride had been given. He noticed as he looked down the rows of upturned faces that many had aged since he'd left, while others

were missing completely. He would probably never see them
again, or at least, not in this world. More than anything else to
date, those missing faces brought home how very long he'd been
away.

Excited cries broke into Gideon's reflections as the musicians
took their places, whooping and hollering as if they were calling
cattle. They were drawn from among his father's hands, dressed
today in their Sunday-best shirts, which had been neatly starched
and pressed, while the crowns of their hats and their necks were
wreathed with beautiful flower *leis* that their wives or sweethearts had strung for them. They were singing melodiously and
yodeling, cowboy-style, as they strummed their ukuleles and
guitars, their song describing the loneliness a *paniolo* feels at
night, watching over the herd far from home. And how, in the
middle of the night, when the snow-goddess Poli'hau's breath
blows chill from the white-blanketed peaks of Mauna Kea, a
cowboy begins to long for his sweetheart's sunny smile, for the
comforting *lei* of her loving arms about him—and for the
warmth of her ample curves to keep the chill from his bones!

Grinning at the risqué melodies, Gideon took his seat beside
Julia and nodded at the entertainers to continue. "I think you're
going to enjoy this, my dear," he murmured. "There's nothing
in Maryland like the music you'll hear tonight!

"Is this the *hula-hula?*" Julia asked, abandoning all attempts
at filling her growling stomach from the unappetizing array before her. Raw fish—and squid, indeed! Still, the *hula-hula*
sounded like fun! On the long sea voyage from San Francisco
to the Sandwich Isles, she'd heard the deckhands talking about
the scandalous *hula-hula* of the islands, Polynesian dancing so
lascivious, so suggestive, the missionary fathers had seen laws
passed to have it banned. "I'd love to see it!"

Highly amused—and surprised—by her unladylike enthusi-
asm for a "forbidden" dance, he chuckled. "I very much doubt
you'll be seeing any of our wicked *hula* here tonight, my dear.
But if we should return to Honolulu in the near future, I'll see

what I can do to—Well, well! Look at this! It seems I was wrong! Here's your *hula* dancer now, Mrs. Kane!"

The musicians had stepped back, relinquishing the torchlit grass before the gathering to Leolani Pakele. The spectators grew hushed as Leolani—her graying hair falling loose to the middle of her back—walked solemnly to the far side of the area, carrying a gourd drum decorated with feathers. Her enormous yet gracefully rounded body was robed in a *pa'u*, or sarong, of brown-patterned *tapa* cloth. After Leolani knelt on the grass, a graceful young woman ran from the shadows into a pool of torchlight, to take her place before the gathering.

Her head modestly bowed on her breast so that her face was hidden in shadow, she held her arms out straight before her with her right palm resting lightly on the back of the other hand. Though barefoot beneath her elegant *holoku* of violet silk, the dancer wore her ink-black hair in elegant braids that she'd wound about her head, and was crowned like an island princess with a woven circlet of purple pansies and curling green ferns. A strand of the same flowers was draped about her neck. The untied ends of the *lei* swung gently to and fro as she began to dance, raising her long-lashed violet eyes to Gideon's as she did so.

Sweet Christ! Emma!

The shock of seeing her again so unexpectedly after all this time struck him like a thunderbolt. And—though he'd imagined this moment a hundred thousand times before this—nothing had prepared him for the reality of it!

At fourteen, she'd been a lovely, vibrant girl. In seven years, she'd become a ravishing woman, a breathtaking beauty!

Without any conscious thought on his part, he rose to his feet and stood there, staring at her as if he'd seen a ghost. He watched, entranced—bedazzled—utterly bewitched—as she moved to and fro with a fluid, boneless grace that was mesmerizing. Her dark eyes followed the movement of her graceful arms and her slim, tapering fingers, while the effortless sway of her hips and the light tap of her feet in counterpoint upon the grass kept time with the measured heartbeat of the gourd drum that Leolani tapped with either her fingers or the heel of her hand.

The *hula* Emma had chosen to dance told a much-loved island legend. A thrill of recognition shimmied down Gideon's spine as she began to dance, for the tale was one he remembered all too well. It was the story she had told him; the romantic yet tragic tale of a forbidden love affair between a Hawaiian princess and her commoner lover.

By all accounts, it had happened in the days before the Englishman, Captain James Cook, had discovered the strand of little islands set like emeralds in the turquoise Pacific—or so the legend claimed. It had happened at a time when the ancient chieftains and their sacred *kahunas,* or priests, had held the power of life and death over the common people—and woe betide those who broke the sacred *kapus,* or taboos. Those taboos placed upon a *wahine kapu,* a virgin maiden who had been raised to become the bride of an important chieftain, were even stricter than any of the others.

In Emma's movements, Gideon saw the palm trees swaying in the sultry breeze. In her gently undulating hips was the rolling motion of the breakers that pounded the cove where the lovers had first met. With a flick of her fingertips to left and right, she scattered handfuls of tiny stars across the sweeping sky, while with but a sweeping gesture of her slender arms, she embraced the full, round circle of the shining moon, who had kept watch over the beautiful maiden and her handsome sweetheart while they made love on the warm sand.

Time turned back for Gideon in that moment. Seven years vanished as if they'd never been. He held his breath, transfixed, for it seemed as if Emma was telling the poignant story of their own first meeting with her dancing, as if she was describing the tender passion they'd shared beneath the sea-grape tree, only to be parted by distance, time, and the cruel whims of fate.

As her violet eyes lifted to his for a second time, a tremulously sweet smile curved her lips for an instant, then her sooty lashes dropped, and she quickly turned her head away. A thrill ran through him in that moment, for he knew that no matter what, she loved him still. Loved him . . . as, God help him, he loved her.

> *So great was the chieftain's anger,*
> *When he heard of her defiance.*
> *That his voice made mountains tremble.*
> *'Go!' he bade his warriors. 'Find her!*
> *Find the maid,* wahine kapu—
> *From her birth, pledged to another—*
> *Slay the one who dared defile her . . . !'*

The flaming torches writhed and flared up on the sudden chill current as Leolani's rich, vibrant voice rose and fell in the ancient tongue of the islands. At times it was full-throated, loud and commanding—almost frightening; at others, it was sobbing and plaintive, shifting registers in a way that made the hackles rise on Gideon's neck.

Others joined Leolani The gourds and the clicking bamboo sticks took up the throbbing pulse—the heartbeat of a dying race—the throb of the forbidden *hula*—as Emma danced, the story unfolding to its inevitable but tragic climax:

> *Soon, the maiden heard them coming,*
> *Knew that they would slay her loved one—*
> *'Go!' she pleaded. 'Quickly! Flee them!'*
> *But he would not leave the princess*
> *To endure her father's anger.*
> *'While I yet have breath within me*
> *I shall not be parted from thee.*
> *Let them come. Yes! let them take me*
> *Sweet one, I will not forsake thee!'*

> *As the warriors drew nearer*
> *Hand in hand, the lovers fled them,*

> *Running—not toward the mountains,*
> *Nor to the sacred place of refuge—*
> *But into the perilous currents*
> *Where the waters swirled and eddied.*
> *As the sun set, as the moon rose,*
> *Shared one last kiss of aloha.*
>
> *There it was her father found them,*
> *When the sun rose with the dawning.*
> *And his grief made mountains tremble*
> *For he knew he could not part them—*
> *Knew the gods had blessed the lovers—*
> *For twin rocks rose from the waters,*
> *Where no rocks had stood before then.*

As the chanter's last note resounded on the hush, Gideon discovered his mouth was parched, that his eyes burned from the smoky torchlight—and from completely forgetting to blink. Like a man in a dream, he stood and watched as Emma finished her *hula* with her dark head once again humbly bowed on her chest. Then all at once, she picked up her skirts and fled into the shadows.

Dimly, he realized that the dancing was over. Knew, on one level, that Julia and his parents must be watching him, wondering why he was standing there, staring. Logically, he knew that he should move—applaud—say or do *something—anything!*— but for some reason, he could not. He stood stiff-backed and rigid, his fists knotted at his sides, his jaw clenched so tight, it was nothing short of a miracle none of his teeth were crushed, no bones broken as he stared at the place where *she* had stood just moments before, unable to turn away.

It was as if her essence—her *akua,* or spirit—still lingered, dancing on the sultry night air, invisible to all eyes but his as it swayed and gestured for him alone, a *houri* dancing through the dreams of her Arab lord.

It took the prickly sensation of being watched to bring him back to the present and restore his shattered senses. Catching a movement from the corner of his eye, he saw that Julia had risen from her seat on the woven mats beside him, and was watching him with a furious expression and brimming eyes. So, in their turn, were his startled parents watching the newlyweds. Their expressions were confused, questioning, as they looked from him, then back to Julia.

Mercifully, the musicians broke into a boisterous, risqué cowboy song in honor of the newlyweds at that same moment—one accompanied yet again by much "yeehaa-ing" and raucous laughter—and so he used the noisy diversion of their opening guitar and ukulele chords to recover his composure. Flicking his head, he forced a smile and turned back to his wife. "So, Julia. What do you think of our infamous *hula?*"

"I really don't think you give a damn what I thought of it, Gideon. Now, if you'd excuse me, I'd like to get past you."

His mouth thinned. "Past me? Why? Where are you going?"

"To retire, Mister Kane," she came back frostily, not meeting his narrowed eyes. Two spots of crimson stained the pallor of her porcelain cheeks.

"So early, my dear? But the entertainment's just beginning," he managed to say, though the words sounded hollow and false even to his own ears, "Besides, the hands are singing this song in our honor. Won't you at least sit beside me till it's over? I'm sure you'd enjoy it."

"I might, at that," Julia agreed. Then her chin came up and she looked him full in the eyes and added, "However, I doubt I'd enjoy it half as much as you seemed to be enjoying the last performance."

"Indeed I did enjoy it. After all, it's not often we get treated to a *hula* anymore, and Kaleilani danced beautifully, didn't she?" Gideon observed, sensing his wife's hostility. The last thing he wanted was a scene.

"I'm so glad you enjoyed it," Miriam declared. "I asked her

to dance for us tonight myself. It's so rare that the *hula* is performed at all anymore, isn't it, Jacob? Why, in my time, Julia, we young girls were absolutely forbidden to dance it, the missionary fathers frowned upon it so. Even so, *we* managed to learn the motions in secret, rascals that we were!" She smiled uncertainly, for neither Gideon nor Julia appeared to be listening to what she was saying. "The—er—the *hula* was considered immoral, you see, and my papa was British and very proper. Why, he once threatened to—"

"Perhaps you can tell us what your pa threatened some other time, ma'am?" Julia cut her off impatiently. "See, it's been a real long day for me and I'm about dead on my feet. Sweet dreams, Father Kane. Good night, Mother Kane." With that, she pushed past Gideon, wove her way between the startled feasters—still seated cross-legged on the mats—and ran across the lawns, back to the lamplit house.

"Julia, wait!" Gideon called after her, seeing his mother's stricken face.

But if Julia heard him, she made no response.

"Auwe! Was it Kaleilani's *hula* that upset her? Did it shock her terribly, was that it? Say you'll forgive me, Gideon? I wouldn't have upset the poor girl, not for the world," Miriam exclaimed, totally bewildered yet contrite. "Should I go after her, do you think?"

Tight-lipped, Gideon shook his head. He bent down and kissed his mother's cheek. "No, *Makuahine,* I'll go. I have a feeling my little bride's angry at *me,* not *you.* Unfortunately, you stepped into the line of fire—and took the bullet meant for me, so to speak."

"You're certain . . . ?"

"I'm quite certain," he insisted. "Enjoy the feast. I'll be back shortly."

* * *

The night was cool and hushed as Gideon started up the veranda steps of Hui Aloha minutes later, resigned to soothing Julia's ruffled feathers. His hand had closed over the doorknob when he caught a glimpse of something pale moving about in the darkened gazebo, off to the left of the house. Needing little by way of distraction to make him forgo an unpleasant duty, he opted to investigate before tackling Julia. Robberies were virtually unheard of in the islands, but still, he was curious— and the opportunity to postpone an upsetting confrontation was irresistible.

Mahealani, the full moon, hung like a giant pearl in the indigo sky as he plunged between the bushes, weaving his way through the rear gardens, where the spicy scents of Makuahine's herbs and spices, and the heady perfumes of plumerias and night-blooming Cereus that rambled over the gazebo's white-latticed walls, rose sweetly on the air. Royal palms tossed their fronds high above and whispered secrets on the sultry nightwind as Gideon mounted the gazebo steps and peered into the shadows.

"Hello? Is anyone here?"

There was no answer but the night's balmy embrace about him, and the reedy trill of the crickets.

His heart was still heavy, his spirit badly in need of balm and solace since the moment when Aunt Sophie had walked into a room and torn his entire life asunder. Closing his eyes, he let the utter peace of the night wash over him, fill him, hoping against hope that somehow, it could drive the bitter anger and frustration from his mind, could—somehow!—lessen the torment of discovering Emma was lost to him.

A little less than a fortnight ago, he'd returned to the islands filled with hope, eager to begin his life anew in the tranquil paradise he loved, and to build a home and start a family with the woman he loved still more. How had his dreams turned to ashes, gone so very wrong so very quickly? But here he was, chained to a woman he felt nothing for, one who, moreover, felt absolutely nothing for him in return, unless he missed his mark.

Both of them were trapped in a loveless marriage with no one to blame for it but themselves.

He sighed heavily. He might try to tell himself that Julia was to blame, or that he'd been blind drunk and therefore unaccountable for his actions. He might even take the view that it was she who'd brought him to this pass by playing the wanton and taking him to her bed. But ultimately, he knew it was *he* who—wallowing in self-pity—had sought escape in the bottle that rainy night. He and no one else who'd agreed to wed the woman, despite his Uncle and Thomas's cautions about marrying in haste, only to repent at leisure. He shook his head. *Gideon, you damned fool! You threw it all away that night, and to what end?*

The sounds of the feast were muted here, but the chirping of the crickets sounded loud on the hush. In no hurry to confront Julia, he sat down on the padded storage seat inside the gazebo, his long legs stretched out before him, his arms folded across his chest, and gazed up at the night sky, seeing Emma in his imagination, her hips gently swaying, her graceful hands weaving dreams in the air.

Emma.

The secret sadness that had haunted her violet eyes all those years ago appeared to have deepened since he'd been gone, and he wondered ruefully how much of that very sadness he was directly responsible for. Yet, the look that had flashed between them like forked lightning had been enough for him to know the truth. They might both be married to others—he to Julia, Emma to her Charles Wallace—but Emma still loved him, even as he, God help him, still loved her . . .

Just then, he caught a furtive movement, a scuffling sound from behind him. Springing to his feet, he plunged into the shadows, waving his hands about. "Step into the light, where I can see you," he ordered. "Whoever you are!"

There was a sudden, frantic rustling of skirts in the shadows, and then someone tried to dash past him to gain the gardens.

Reaching blindly for the trespasser, his fingers trapped a slippery, silk-clad arm, then a wrist, and held on tight.

"Let go of me!" his prisoner demanded angrily, trying to squirm free.

"Emma?"

"As if you didn't know! Let me go, *Mister* Kane!"

Seventeen

His grip tightened. With a muffled curse, he jerked her toward him. His gentian eyes blazed down at her in the moonlight. "You and I are old friends—or so I thought. Why the haste, Missus Wallace? Afraid good old Charlie won't approve?"

His tone rather than his words registered as he towered over her, a hostile, broad-shouldered stranger with her Gideon's face, her Gideon's eyes. The lips she'd so loved to kiss were thinned and curled in anger now, the long fingers that had once caressed her so tenderly now encircled her wrists like fetters of steel. The shadows the moon cast through the lattices made his handsome features look harder, more chiseled than they'd seemed in the flaring light of the torches as she danced, and a shiver ran through her. What if he'd changed since she'd seen him last? What if this vengeful, bitter—possibly dangerous!—man had lost all resemblance to the gentle Gideon she'd known and loved?

"Let go of my wrists, sir," she insisted softly, despite the pounding of her heart, despite quaking knees that felt ready to buckle. "Let go this instant, or I'll scream!"

The violence suddenly drained from him in an outpouring tide. *Christ Almighty, what had come over him?* He could see damp trails on Emma's cheeks in the moonlight and he could feel her trembling, despite her outward bravado. *My poor Emma,* he thought, his anger and frustration replaced by tenderness. Had it all come down to this? Married woman or nay, he ached to take her in his arms, to say he was sorry he'd made her cry, to reassure her that his feelings had not changed—that nothing had, no matter what she'd said to the contrary—and devil take their marriages and their spouses!

Desire curled through him like tongues of flame, settling as a hot, leaden weight in his loins. His throat was dry. Her violet eyes met his in the shadows before she looked quickly away. Color seeped into the gold of her cheeks. *Sweet Blessed Christ, give him strength!* He had only to take her in his arms and kiss her, and she'd surrender—he knew it as surely as he knew his own name. And if he did? Aaah, there'd be no turning back then. No undoing what had been done . . .

"Don't, Gideon!" she implored, as if she'd read his thoughts. "Don't make it harder than it has to be."

"Why?" he demanded thickly, his breath hot in her ear. "Nothing's changed, admit it! You still love me, Emma. And God knows, I still love you! Must we live a lie?"

"But it *has* changed, don't you see?" she cried, searching his face. "Whether we still feel the same about each other counts for nothing now, because you're married to someone else! And, since we can't undo what's already been done, we have to learn to accept that. Perhaps—perhaps it's God's will you should belong to Julia, instead of me? Perhaps we were never meant to be together?" she whispered hoarsely.

His eyes darkened to indigo in his scorn, smoldering beneath lowering dark brows. "God's will?" he thundered. "You think it's *His* will we should suffer this way?" he ground out, his voice harsh. "His plan that I spend my whole life loving you, yet bound to someone I feel nothing for?" He suddenly reeled away and slammed his clenched fist against the nearest wooden post, relishing the ringing pain that shot up his arm as the gazebo shuddered with the impact. "Damn it, Emma, no! I can't accept that. *I love you!* Neither Charles Wallace nor God and His will could ever change that."

"Gideon, please don't say such things!"

The breathy way she whispered his name was like the subtle

musk of her body—arousing, alluring, potent aphrodisiacs he couldn't deny. Fight it he might, but desire was coiling through him in ever-tightening spirals, though only the slightest tic of a muscle at his temple betrayed the emotions seething beneath his skin, the nerves strung taut, like wire on a fencepost.

He wanted her—oh yes, oh yes! But in his life he had spent much time learning right from wrong, and he knew it was wrong to have her!

He turned back to face her, his handsome face filled with despair instead of rage, and with a soft, strangled sob, she flung herself into his arms, clung to him as if she'd never let go. He held her so fiercely, so deliciously tightly, she could hardly breathe—and yet she didn't ever want it to end!

"Emma, my love, my heart! It's been so blessed long," he whispered, his voice ragged. And then, dipping his dark head, he claimed the soft, sweet lips he'd dreamed of kissing for so very long in a forbidden kiss.

His kisses were like some glorious, bubbly wine, a sparkling shower of magical embers that rekindled feelings she'd had to bury for so long. His mouth—his hard, thrilling mouth!—fanned them into quivering life all over again.

Small, incoherent sounds broke from her as she strained against him, twining her arms about his throat, hungrily burying her fingers in the midnight silk of his hair, unable to get enough of the feel of his lean, virile body, the salty taste of his skin, or the masculine scent of him—a mixture of bay rum, citrus, and soap.

Hungrily, his tongue parted her lips, then delved into the velvet cache beyond like a hummingbird sipping nectar from the rose-pink throat of a rare orchid. Desire mounting, his tongue ravished her velvety mouth, probed between its moist, lush petals with short stabbing strokes that made her knees grow weak and her breasts heave with every shallow breath she drew. Yet, when he would have pulled away, she grasped him by both shoulders and clung to him, hungry for more.

With a husky chuckle, he took a step back, gently teasing her, his retreat forcing her to initiate their next kiss, to go after him and prove she wanted his kisses just as badly as he did. Whispering his name over and over, she framed his dark head between her hands, went up on tiptoe, then fitted her mouth to his for the long, deep kiss she craved, moaning deep in her throat and begging him not to deny her.

His salty lips parted beneath hers as he kissed her thoroughly, hungrily, sending pleasure raveling through her in snaky ribbons. She felt warm and sweet as molasses drizzled from a spoon. With a low cry, she abandoned all restraint and caressed him hungrily, running shaky, eager hands over his broad, well-muscled shoulders, savoring the width of his chest, wishing she could tug that infernal shirt free of his belt and explore the bare torso beneath it with her hands. As a youth, his chest had been golden-tanned, almost hairless. Was it still? she wondered. His arms and legs had been long and wiry. Now, muscles and cords shimmied and leaped beneath his shirtsleeves and the cloth of his snug breeches, and his thighs were the well-muscled thighs of a horseman. In midthought, she realized the direction in which her thoughts had turned, and she shivered again. A boy had left the islands. In his place, a dangerous, exciting man had returned—one to whom the woman she'd become longed to respond with every nerve and fiber of her being but could not!

Oh, Lord, what was she thinking! Had she become the loose, immoral creature the nuns had predicted after all? But—

—Oh, Lord! How she'd missed him! And oh, Lord, how she wanted him! Wrong or nay, she ached to be cradled in his powerful arms . . . yearned to be . . . to be joined with him as one, for them never to be parted again by so much as a heartbeat.

"Darling Emma," he murmured huskily, breaking their kiss to tilt her face up to his. He brushed a stray tear away from her cheek with the ball of his thumb. "I can't believe you're really here in my arms at last! God, you'll never know how I've wanted you, Emma!" His gentian eyes blazed with the dark fire of sapphires, mirroring the smoldering amethyst fires in her own. His body was hard, tense as a coiled spring as he suddenly drew her roughly against its length.

Her lashes swept down. Overcome by emotion, she swayed as he tilted her head back to press his mouth to the scented hollows of her throat, where the pulse fluttered madly, steadying herself with her fingertips braced against his chest as he dropped featherlight kisses on her eyelids, her cheeks, the tender skin behind her ears. A shower of ivory pins spilled to the boards as he reached up and plucked them, one by one, from her ebony hair. As its perfumed cascade tumbled down her back, he wound his fist in its length and tugged her to him.

She cried out, arching against him like a drawn bow, stunned by her body's headlong, rushing response to his kisses and caresses. Her nipples had tightened, becoming exquisitely sensitive to the slightest friction. A peculiar quiver of sexual excitement and fear shimmied through her, centering in the very pit of her belly as a tiny, throbbing pulse. Although she knew she should resist, insist that Gideon cease his advances, she could not bring herself to do so, could not bring herself to tell him no. Oh, what was wrong with her? Where was her willpower? Her pride? Her sense of decency? Gideon had made her promise to wait for him, then played her false and returned to the islands wed to another woman! She should run from him—and keep on running, mindful of her reputation and, worse, of her immortal soul. After all, adultery was a sin, was it not? And she was no longer the naive little fourteen-year-old just out of the convent who'd responded to his seduction with the innocent, eager sensuality of a very young girl, driven into his arms by the far more powerful threat posed by her father. Now she was no longer innocent, no longer a child, no longer threatened or driven. She had a woman's body, a woman's desires, and what she desired above everything in that moment was to give herself to her beloved, and in the giving—

Her beloved?

She grew suddenly very still as the cold, hard truth cut like steel through the sensual euphoria to which she'd almost abandoned herself. She might pretend all she wished, but the truth remained unchanged. *Gideon was not her beloved, not anymore. He was Julia Kane's husband!*

As he bent to kiss her again, she forced herself to draw back, summoned every ounce of willpower she possessed to turn her head aside and avoid his lips. "No," she cried. "Don't. It's wrong, no matter what we want. It's too late for us. We have to say goodbye!"

"I won't believe that—not till they bury me six feet under," he denied, his voice a rasp. "Remember the *mele* you danced tonight, Emma? *'While I yet have breath within me/I shall not be parted from thee!'* That's how I feel about you, my love. We belong together."

"Oh, my darling! I love you, too, with all my heart and soul. And I want you—surely you can tell how much?" she said fervently, caressing his cheek. "But not this way. Not if we must meet in secret, with lies and deceit."

As she looked up at him, there was a flicker of guilt in his expression that he quickly masked. Thank God, her pleas had reached him! Abruptly, he set her from him and took a step back, standing there with his fists clenched at his sides. "Yes, you're right," he admitted harshly, running an agitated hand through his hair as he stared out at the darkness of the herb gardens—at the distant foothills, now black mounds in the distance—at any place and at any thing but her. "Emma?"

"Yes, Gideon?"

She looked up at him questioningly, her dark hair falling loose about her shoulders, her eyes luminous with love in the starlight. Her loveliness made him want to weep—almost swayed him from the course he knew he *must* choose, however unwillingly. His knuckles were bloodless where he gripped the handrail as he urged huskily, "It would be best if you were to go now, Emma.

Go quickly, and don't look back!" A shudder moved through him as he added, "Because if you do, I'll never let you go!"

She'd been gone for several moments before he realized he'd been holding his breath.

Inhaling deeply, he flicked his head to clear it, then turned to leave the gazebo, his movements as heavy as a lead soldier's. His toe scuffed some small objects, scattering them across the whitewashed floorboards. They shone like bone in the moonlight. Bending, he retrieved the ivory hairpins he'd plucked from Emma's hair and his throat constricted. *Emma! Oh, Emma!*

Some time passed before he felt capable of going inside to placate Julia. As he headed toward the house, he recognized Kimo Pakele standing in the shadows by the stables.

"You left the *luau* early! Is something wrong?" he asked the man, forcing himself to sound casual.

Kimo shrugged, unsmiling. "I don't know, Mo'o. Why don't you tell me, eh? Is somethin' wrong?" the ranch foreman asked softly, flashing Gideon a look that somehow managed to be both hostile and deeply saddened at the same time.

Understanding dawned. Hell and damnation! Emma's uncle must have followed Emma—or himself—out to the gazebo for some reason, and had seen them together. Christ Almighty—had he also seen them kissing? He sighed. Oh, yes. Judging by Kimo's expression, he thought so. "Wrong? You mean, between your—er—niece and myself? I can assure you, there was nothing improper about our meeting in the gazebo. We exchanged a few words, then Emma left."

"Only words, Mo'o?"

Gideon's jaw tightened. Lying to Kimo Pakele was like lying to his father or his commanding officer—or God Himself. It went against the grain. But, for the sake of Emma's good name, he had little choice, "Sir, I know how it must've looked to you, but we didn't plan our meeting. I saw somebody in the gazebo. It seemed rather late, so I went to investigate and——"

"And you found Emma Kaleilani there."

"Well, yes. In a sense."

"You not only found her, Mo'o. You kissed her. I know this, because I saw you. *Auwe!* Is this what you learned at your fancy school in Boston? Is this what your father taught you, eh, Mo'o?"

A guilty flush darkened Gideon's throat. "Damn it, no. Of course not," he ground out. But the Hawaiian's expression remained implacable, his dark-brown eyes hard, his expression unconvinced. "For pity's sake, don't look at me like that, all right? If the truth's what you want, then you shall have it. I love Emma, Uncle Kimo," he admitted heavily, flinching under the man's accusatory glare. "I've loved her for seven years now. She was all that got me through the war."

Kimo's brows rose in surprise. "You knew Kaleilani before you went away? But how could that be? She was away at school, in Honolulu."

"We met at Twin Rocks Cove just before I sailed, and fell in love. Neither of us planned it, Uncle Kimo! She'd just come home from the convent to care for her sick mother, while I—— Well, I was preparing to leave for college and was quite upset about going. It just—happened." He shrugged.

"Then why did you marry the *haole wahine,* if you still love Kaleilani, eh? Surely you know that an affair with a married man will break her heart and bring her shame!"

Gideon's jaw hardened. "As I live and breathe, I love Emma, Uncle. And I would never do anything to hurt her, or make trouble for her. It's already agreed. We won't be meeting again."

"I believe you," Kimo said softly. "But don't forgot, Mo'o, you're a married man now, for bettah or for worse—that's the way it goes. Stay well away from Emma Kaleilani, eh? Don't put yourselves in temptation's path. You no make *pilikia,* trouble, for her—and you'll have no *pilikia* yourself."

Stunned, Gideon stared at the Hawaiian man as if a cuddly pup had suddenly changed into a snarling mad dog and torn out his throat. "Well, well. If I didn't know you better, I'd say that was a threat."

Kimo smiled thinly, but the smile never warmed his eyes. "No, my young fren'. Kimo nevah make threats. I just giving you some good advice. More better you take it, eh?" His expression was still wary, his eyes still alive with mistrust in the heavy shadow of his hat brim as, with a curt nod, he headed back through the herb gardens to the feast.

Eighteen

"What the devil are you doing here? You've got your nerve! Go away! Just—just get out!" Julia protested. Without bothering to knock, Gideon had flung open the door and strode into the bedroom. Crystal chimney lamps threw his giant shadow upon the far wall as, slamming the door in his wake, he stood there, his restless energy making the air crackle with expectancy.

Julia had already undressed and unpinned her hair for the night. He frowned. By the look of things, she'd been primping before her looking glass since she left the *luau* rather than sobbing her heart out, as might have been expected under the circumstances. In fact, she looked anything *but* the slighted bride he'd expected to find!

Her surprisingly lush curves were sheathed in a robe of blood-red Chinese silk, embroidered with writhing black-and-gold dragons. The wrapper clung like a slippery second skin to the damp body beneath it. His brows rose a fraction in surprise, for rather than the widow's weeds he'd expected, the gaudy kimono put him in mind of war-time bordellos, where the scent of cheap perfume and the promise of a brief respite from battle had hung on the sultry air like musk. To his chagrin, his surprise was edged with a raw excitement he neither welcomed nor understood, for his treacherous body—already primed from holding Emma in his arms again after so long without her—responded like a trail of gunpowder to a lit fuse as he stared at her.

Fair hair streamed about her shoulders like a sheaf of pale

wheat, while the high cheekbones that gave her triangular face its elegant, feline quality were flushed with hectic color. Her light-gray eyes were almost silver as she whirled to face him, yet for all their brilliance they somehow lacked fire and warmth, and were as passionless and glacial as ice. Her spine was braced against the heavy dressing table, her manicured fingers arched like talons over its beveled edges as she faced him.

"May I remind you that this is our room, Julia," he snapped, his lips thinned. "I will *not* get out." In a dangerously soft voice, he added, "Indeed, I have every right to be here, if I so choose."

" 'Every right,' indeed! How like a man to be bleating about his precious rights," Julia accused, her tone harder than he'd ever heard her use before. "Well, what about *my* rights as your wife, Gideon? Have I none? Am I not deserving of respect, at the very least? Of fidelity?"

Taken aback, he blinked. "On the contrary, you have been accorded the utmost respect by everyone here!"

"Ha! I beg to disagree, sir! I have been accorded respect by everyone but . . . yourself! Tonight, you made me a laughingstock in front of everyone at the feast!"

"Laughingstock? In what way?" he ground out, knowing all too well what her answer must be, but loath to admit it, even to himself, for he was far from proud of his behavior.

"Come, come. Don't act the innocent! That half-breed hussy had only to wiggle her hips, and you couldn't take your eyes off her, could you? And at our wedding feast, with everyone your family knows watching us, too! Oh, I know we didn't marry for the right reasons, and that love had no part in our agreement, but we—we exchanged vows! Vows I believed we both intended to keep. You had no right to look at that—that *hula-hula* dancer in such bold fashion. No right at all! Like it or not, I'm your wife, not that native woman!" She flung about, took a tortoiseshell brush from the dresser and began brushing her hair so violently, crackling spun-sugar strands rose all about her head like a halo.

Good Lord! She's jealous! he realized, suddenly convinced Julia's anger had more to it than wounded pride. Had she begun to care for him? Or was she just fiercely possessive of her belongings, her husband included?

Staring at the stiff back and squared shoulders she presented him, he ruefully shook his head. Clearly, making amends with his little bride was not to be the simple, briefly uncomfortable matter he'd anticipated. But if he honestly intended to do his utmost to make this marriage work and forget Emma, he had to try. Fists at his sides, he began, "See here, you have no cause to be jealous, my de—"

"Don't 'my dear' me! And the devil I don't have cause!" she exploded, hurling the brush at his head. The missile struck him in the mouth, dashing his lips against his teeth and drawing blood that he wiped away on his fist. "I'm not blind—and nor am I a blamed fool! It was her, wasn't it?" she hissed, eyes suddenly narrowing.

"Her?"

"That half-breed woman! She's the one you were ranting and raving about in Honolulu that night. Your 'faithless Emma,' you called her? It *was* her, wasn't it?" she pressed, triumphant in her certainty.

Caught off guard, he stammered, "I don't—"

"Aw, don't bother denyin' it, lover. Heck, your tongue was hangin' out so darned far, it was a miracle you didn't trip on it like a carpet runner!"

He flinched, still amazed by her violent outburst, her coarse, taunting tone. She was even angrier than he'd expected. "All right. Yes, it was her," he admitted.

"Ah ha! I knew it! And? Go on!"

"And for a moment . . . well, seeing Emma again after so many years, and so unexpectedly, I suppose it was something of a shock to me, and I forgot myself. I know I was staring at her, but I couldn't seem to help myself." An understatement, if ever he'd heard one! "If I embarrassed you tonight, my de—

Julia, I'm truly sorry." Ruefully, he shook his head. "We haven't gotten off to a very good start in this marriage, have we, despite my very best intentions to do the right thing by you?"

Already taken aback by the gentleness in his voice, Gideon's rueful question surprised Julia even more. Her rigid shoulders slumped. "Nooo, I don't suppose we have. Perhaps . . . perhaps it was a mistake for us to get married? Maybe I should just have sailed away somewhere, and never mind the wagging tongues, or the gossip that would no doubt have followed me. It's my life and my good name, after all, to do with as I see fit, now that David's gone." She sighed and cleared her throat. "I'm sure if I'd absolutely *refused* to let the gossip upset me, I could have lived down the scandal about us eventually, though of course, with my reputation in tatters, a second marriage would have been highly unlikely—unless of course, it was a love match. It does happen, they say." Her sudden quick, hopeful glance and the wistful edge to her voice further flayed his conscience.

"Yes. I'm—er—sure it does," he confirmed solemnly. Drawing a kerchief from his breeches' pocket, he dabbed at the trickle of blood seeping from the corner of his mouth.

"Oh, my stars, just look at that! Please say you'll forgive me, Gideon? I don't know what came over me. I should never have thrown the brush at you, for pity's sake. Why, I couldn't blame you if you sent me packing!"

"Don't be silly. I won't do anything of the kind. I promised to take care of you, Julia, and I shall," he said softly. "That you can depend upon. If nothing else, I'm a man of my word."

She sighed heavily. "You will care for me, but you cannot promise you'll ever love me—is that what you're trying to say?"

"Who knows what the future holds?" he hedged. "There's every chance my feelings will change, given time. You're a lovely woman. Any man would be proud to call you his own."

"Any man but you . . . because you don't believe things will change between us, do you?"

He hesitated, then decided honesty was the best policy. "No, Julia. I don't."

She released the breath she'd been holding, "Weell, then, that's that for now," she exclaimed softly. "At least I know where I stand. And I thank you for your honesty, painful as it may be. I'd sooner know the truth than make a darn fool of myself."

"A fool? I don't understand?"

"I was starting to fall in love with you, Gideon—couldn't you tell? Didn't you even guess? From the first moment I met you, I knew that with David gone, you were the only man for me. Oh, don't look so guilty, darlin'. I'm not blaming you for the way I feel. After all, you promised nothing more than to make an honest woman of me—which is more than I had any right to expect! Silly of me to want more, isn't it, but I guess at heart I'm a foolish romantic? You've been so very kind since we left Honolulu—indeed, ever since your aunt walked in on us! So sweet and kind that tonight, sitting beside you in the moonlight, with the perfume of the flowers all around us . . . well, I foolishly found myself hopin' you'd soon forget her—Emma—and fall in love wi— wi— Oh!" Without finishing what she was saying, she quickly turned away, scrubbing at her brimming eyes with her knuckles. Her lower lip was quivering uncontrollably when she turned back to face him. "I—I know this is your room, too, Gideon," she murmured huskily, "and that you have every right to share it with me but . . . but I'd like you to go now. I'd like to sleep here alone tonight, if I may? I—I just need another night or two to set my feelings in order before we share a marriage bed. You—you do understand?"

He nodded, secretly relieved, yet still feeling like the lowest of the low for the second time that night. "I do. And take all the time you need," he offered expansively. "There's no hurry."

She smiled, blinking through her tears. "You really are a dear, dear man. May I presume upon you just once more?"

Her answer was a charming, rueful grin. "Presume away, Missus Kane."

"Say you'll forgive my silly, jealous outburst at the feast? It won't happen again, truly it won't. And I promise I'll make my apologies to Mother Kane for my rudeness, first thing in the morning."

"Say no more. As far as I'm concerned, it's already forgotten."

"Thank you." She crossed the room, went up on tiptoe and dropped a kiss upon his cheek, her musky perfume filling his nostrils. "Fresh start?" she whispered, the silky wrapper baring her shoulder as she caressed his cheek. For a fleeting second, her breasts brushed against his chest and he could feel her nipples, hard as pebbles, beneath her wrapper.

He lifted her hand to his lips and kissed it, vaguely angered by his body's response to her charms as he echoed, "Yes. Fresh start."

Julia smiled, a tight, mirthless little smile that never quite reached her eyes as Gideon turned on his heels and left the room.

Closing the door, she leaned upon it, a low, throaty chuckle of delight escaping her as she made her way to the bed. "Wriggle your little hips all you want, Emma sugar, but this one's gonna be *mine,*" she told the empty room. "That poor fool just don't know it yet!"

Nineteen

Naively, Emma'd hoped that by cutting short her confrontation with Gideon, she could escape her heartache just as easily. She should have known better. That night, curled on a sleeping mat on her aunt Leolani's veranda, where it was cool, she tossed and turned, wrestling with her emotions.

Part of her wanted Gideon at any cost, no matter who'd be hurt by it, despite knowing what a scandalous affair with a married man—and especially one of Gideon's social standing in the island community!—would do to her already tarnished reputation and, quite possibly, the teaching position she loved. The other part of her just wanted to crawl away and lick her wounds in private, to try to forget Gideon and go on about building a new life for herself and Mahealani. She'd wasted— yes, wasted!—seven long years. Enough was enough. It was time now to move on.

If only her wretched heart understood that . . .

When dawn broke in pink and golden splendor, and the chirruping and warbling of noisy sparrows, cardinals, and mynah birds began heralding the morn, she rose, washed, and dressed. She felt bleary-eyed and headachy, quite unprepared to face the new day, let alone embark on a new life in which the man she'd loved for so long and waited for so patiently had no part. She'd grown accustomed to remembering him in her prayers each morning and evening, and asking God to watch over him and keep him safe. She'd divided her future into compartments, commencing all of her dreams with, "After Gideon comes home, we'll . . ." But Gideon wasn't going to be in her life anymore.

As she tugged a brush through her tangled waist-length hair, she found her thoughts turning longingly to the home she'd shared with her mother before her death, back to the years that, despite the sadness of her *makua's* illness, had held more than their share of happy memories, too.

Yes! she decided. She'd go back there, to her old home, just for a day or two, before returning to what was home for her now in the lush little valley of Waikalani, and the children and the school that had become the focus of her life. Perhaps in familiar solitude, surrounded once more by the green and growing things she'd loved and tended so carefully for so long, she'd be able to accept the prospect of a future in which Gideon had no part.

"Auwe, darling girl!" Auntie Leo exclaimed, ducking under the low doorway as she came out onto the veranda, still clad in a full, flowing nightgown that resembled a small circus tent. "I went hear you tossin' and turnin' all night, honey girl. Did those pesky mosquitos keep you awake, hmm?" Smiling, the handsome Hawaiian woman dropped a gentle kiss upon her brow, and enveloped her niece in her plump arms.

Emma rested her cheek upon her aunt's enormous bosom, savoring the fragrance off white ginger potpourri that clung to Leolani Pakele's clothing as she hugged her. *White ginger.* While Makua had loved the fragrance of tuberoses and Gideon's mother always wore jasmine, both she and her Auntie Leolani Pakele had loved white ginger for as long as they could remember . . . "No, Auntie, it wasn't the mosquitos." She sighed heavily. "I'm just feeling . . . cranky."

"Cranky? Oh, my. Won't you tell Auntie why?"

"I'd like to. But . . . I just can't explain it." Her auntie was a dear, but she was also a God-fearing, extremely moral woman. She would certainly never understand—let alone condone—how Emma felt about Gideon, a married man, and one who was, moreover, the descendant of an island chiefess who'd wed a noble English lord. That latter fact meant Gideon was, in the eyes of both cultures, suns and moons above lowly Emma Kaleilani Jordan, a *hapa-haole,* a half-breed nobody!

"Is it something I've done or said, Kaleilani? Is that why you're itching to leave us so soon?" her aunt pressed, her brown eyes troubled.

"Of course not, Auntie. You've been wonderful to me, as always. I just . . . well, let's just say I have something I need to think through for myself, and I've decided the only place to do it is at the old *hale.* That's why I'm leaving a day early. I was going to come and say my goodbyes to you when I'd finished brushing my hair, honestly I was."

Nodding, Leo tenderly brushed an inky curl from her niece's smooth, pale-gold cheek. Leaning over the veranda railing, she plucked a spray of the white ginger growing there, and tucked it behind Emma's ear. "You miss your *makua,* I think, yes, sweetheart?" she asked softly, tears sparkling in her own eyes.

Emma swallowed and nodded. "Very much, Auntie."

Leolani sighed. "So do I, *keiki* darling. So do I! Last night, when you were dancing, I could feel her spirit close by as I chanted. And once, when the breeze changed direction, I could smell the scent of the tuberoses she loved to wear, sweet and heady on the night air. She so loved to watch you dancing the old *hulas* for her. But more than anything else, girlie, she loved *you.* Never forget it. Perhaps she didn't always act wisely, but she tried. She tried very, very hard to give you a proper home and a family, one with a mother *and* a father." Leolani shook her head and pursed her lips. Until this very day, she could not comprehend her little sister's obsession with that ne'er-do-well Botany Bay man she'd married. Poor, gentle little Malia, whose lithe beauty, dusky grace, and sweet generosity of spirit had bewitched the men—Hawaiian, white, and Asian—of two islands. She could have taken any man she chose as her husband, and she'd married that—that *Englishman.*

"I know, Auntie. I know. And I don't blame her—not for anything." Their dark eyes met in silent communion and understanding.

Leolani gave a small nod, then pursed her lips, pretending to be stern. "If you truly mean that, then why—*why* must you go back there! Jordan might still be there, girlie—and you'd be so far away from help if he decided to cause trouble."

"He won't. I asked some of the *paniolos* about him last night. He hasn't been seen in that area for weeks. The boys think he might have gone up into the mountains to see what he can beg, borrow, or steal from the sheep herders there. Or he could be playing 'guide' for the sightseers going up to the volcano crater. They say some of those people do nothing but travel all over the world, and have more money than sense. Why, they'll pay a small fortune for a guide and the 'privilege' of witnessing one of Madam Pele's glorious eruptions—which are free to all who go there!"

"Hmmph. Perhaps these Americans enjoy being cheated out of their money!"

"Either way, there's no need for you to worry. I'll be fine."

Leolani sighed. "I can tell I'm just wasting my breath. I can't talk you out of going back there, can I?"

She shook her head. "No. I'm sorry, but . . . no."

"Auwe! You were always a hotheaded little *wahine.* Wait while I pack you something to eat. The patches are all overgrown by now—you won't get a decent meal off them. Will you be going back to the valley afterward?"

"Of course. By now, Mahealani should be recovered from her bellyache. She'll have missed me, bless her, and the other children need me almost as badly. They've already had to forgo too many days of school this spring, thanks to the heavy rains, and in a few weeks, the school year will be over for the summer. We have so much to do by then." And perhaps, by immersing herself in her teaching, she could gradually come to forget Gideon.

Leolani nodded in understanding. "Then you should be getting back. But . . . Emma?"

"Yes?"

"Be careful. The Waikalani valley has been flooded many times unexpectedly. The last time was almost twenty years ago, but it was deadly. Several *kupuna,* old ones, were drowned before they could climb to higher ground."

Emma nodded. "I know. But it hasn't been bad at all this year. Just enough rain to make my taro and sweet potatoes nice and plump, and to turn the floor of my schoolhouse into a muddy pig-wallow once in a while, to the *keikis'* delight!" She laughed softly, her lovely face glowing.

"Aah. The *keikis.* You love teaching very much, don't you?"

"How could I help it, Auntie? Seeing their little faces light up when sounds suddenly become words—why, there's nothing to compare with it!"

The huge woman grinned broadly. "Then you've never been in love, girlie!" she teased. "Speaking of which . . . Has Charles Wallace abandoned all hope?"

Emma giggled at her aunt's choice of words. *Abandoned all hope, indeed!* It made her sound like a lost cause. "Keali'i Wallace is very sweet, but I certainly don't love him. Did you know the School Board in Honolulu has promoted him to an inspector? Now he rides all over the island, traveling from school to school each month. While the Reverend Mister Cornwell dispenses Christian baptism and Bible tracts and morality sermons on his mule circuits, Keali'i distributes school supplies and slates and chalk, and talks about the benefits to be gained from an education. He brought us a globe last month—can you imagine that, Auntie? A real globe for Geography, in our tiny valley! And more primers, too . . ."

"Puanani?" Julia murmured without turning around, drawing aside the lace curtain to peer at the small house beyond the corral. *"Puanani!* Leave off making that damn bed and come on over here."

"Yes, Missus Julia," Puanani murmured, giggling and covering her mouth with her hand because the new *haole wahine,* white woman, *Makua* Gideon's wife, had said a curse word out loud.

"Who's that?" Julia asked. She nodded at the veranda of a small house, situated some distance from the main house between some trees, where a large native woman was hugging a young, golden-skinned woman who looked all too familiar. The girl had long black hair shot through with bluish highlights that fell almost to her waist in a rippling, shiny waterfall, and had a spray of white flowers tucked behind one ear. She was wearing one of those ugly, full *muumuus* that somehow hid everything— but hinted at a great deal.

"That's Auntie Leolani and her niece, Kaleilani, missus. Auntie do the cookin' for *Makua* Miriam, an' Kaleilani, she teach school in the valley now. She come too smart for Puanani 'dem." The serving girl sniffed and wrinkled up her flat little nose in a way that spoke volumes. Obviously Kaleilani was no favorite of the serving girl.

"Hmm. She looks like the same girl who danced the *hula-hula* at the feast last night."

"The *hula?* Yeh, she same one! Kaleilani, tha's her Hawaiian name. Emma's her *haole* name. I get one *haole* name, too. Mine's Ruth."

"So that fat woman, Leolani, is her aunt?"

Pua nodded. "Leolani very big woman. Big woman get much *mana*—spirit power."

"So that means Kimo Pakele, the ranch foreman, must be Emma Kaleilani's uncle, am I right?"

Puanani nodded, turning and expertly snapping a sheet into perfect position on the wide four-poster bed, her broad brown hands deft as she smoothed the lovely red-appliquéd quilt neatly across it. "Tha's right, missus. Now, more bettah I get back downstairs. I get plenty cows need milkin' before breakfast.

Chickens to feed, an' eggs to gather, too. S'pose they start moo-ing, Auntie Leo goin' get mad at Pua, by 'n by!"

The native girl scurried off, leaving Julia standing by the window, watching Emma and Leolani while she combed the tangles from her fair hair.

Gideon had knocked on her door shortly before dawn to tell her one of the cowboys had been injured in a roping accident the evening before. He was needed up-country, he'd explained, to help out with the roundup and calf branding, followed by the dusty cattle drive down to Kawaihae.

"I see. And how long will you be gone?" she'd asked.

"I'd say about two weeks."

"Two weeks!"

He'd looked decidedly guilty, so she'd laughed and told him to go on, she'd be perfectly all right, and she'd see him whenever he got back. Moments later, he'd ridden off with Kimo Pakele.

Remembering, she wrinkled her nose at the thought of the older Hawaiian man. Though everyone else seemed to like and respect Kimo, and he seemed to like everyone in return, she had a feeling he disliked her from the moment he'd laid eyes on her. She frowned. The heck she cared. The feeling was mutual! There was something about those puppy-dog brown eyes that seemed to see right through a body. She grimaced. If there was trouble headed her way, as that boy—Alika?—had promised, she had a notion he'd be right at the bottom of it, one way or another.

Meanwhile, she couldn't help wondering why Gideon had looked so blamed guilty about leaving her to see to his herds. Was he secretly planning to meet his sweet little Emma while he was at it—did that explain the flicker in his eyes? She frowned. She had a hunch he meant to do exactly that . . .

Emma left Hui Aloha soon after her conversation with her aunt, taking with her Leolani's hugs and kisses of farewell, and leaving behind her promises to come and visit Uncle Kimo and her again, very soon. By late afternoon she was riding toward the hazy blue-and-green Kohalas, the mountains that loomed like ancient gods from the flat grasslands as they faced their distant sisters—lofty snowcapped Mauna Kea and Mount Hualalei—across the plains of tall, rustling grass.

From here, she could see the moving dark mass of the Kane herds in the distance, attended by an ever-present dust cloud. On its current, the wind carried the lowing and bellowing of the steers and the yip-yipping and yee-haaing of the *paniolos* who herded them. From time to time, she saw a rider break away from the moving mass to knee his sturdy Mauna Kea bronco— hardy horses little less wild than the longhorns they herded— after a stray steer, and wondered idly if Gideon was among them?

When she'd gone to the stables to saddle Makani that morning, she'd heard from old Moki that Gideon had left Hui Aloha at daybreak, headed "up-country," to where the *paniolos* were branding the yearlings and preparing for the year's first roundup.

Gideon.

She'd forgotten how very striking he was until last night, when she'd found herself drowning in long, sooty-lashed eyes the dreamy, bottomless blue of the deepest ocean water, exactly as she'd remembered them.

His skin had been tanned a lighter gold than she remembered, though, a striking contrast to his loosely curling, inky-black hair, so like her own. He wore it a trifle longer than was fashionable now, so that unruly waves tumbled over his stiffly-starched wing collar.

Tall for his age when they'd first met, he'd been wiry but leggy as an unbroken colt, though he'd possessed a pantherlike grace his height had belied. Now, his youthful wiriness had been translated into raw physical power and hard male strength, while his height—a legacy of his royal Hawaiian blood—had been complemented by muscle and breadth, his clumsy legginess replaced by the sinewy grace of his warrior ancestors. Even his gentleness had changed, becoming a breathtaking sensuality, a tenderness that had seared even as it excited.

Remembering, she shivered. They'd been little more than curious children back then, but she still remembered how his body had felt, throbbing against her own as they'd made love. Even now, the precious moments they'd shared were crystal clear, as if they'd happened just yesterday, instead of a lifetime ago. *Oh, yes!* Time and distance might dull some memories, but the beauty of their lovemaking beneath the sea-grape trees would never age. It would endure forever in her heart.

She'd never know, she thought sadly, what it would be like to make love with the *man* Gideon had become.

By late afternoon, she was letting Makani pick her path through the Kohala foothills. The lush emerald, grassy slopes were broken in some places by deep rifts, cluttered with huge, pitted black lava rocks in others. Over these boulders rushed swift red streams, adding their endless, noisy songs to the music of a distant waterfall and the mournful sighing of the constant wind.

As afternoon wore on to evening, a fine, misty rain began falling from the masses of billowing gray cloud that rested upon the mountains' shoulders like shawls of grubby kapok. Throwing a poncho about her shoulders, Emma quickly headed Makani toward a small hut used by the Kane *paniolos* as a line camp during round-up or branding. With its sturdy stone walls, grass-thatching, and hard-packed earthen floor, it would serve well enough for the night's shelter, she decided, relieved to find it empty.

As night fell and the light vanished with the suddenness peculiar to tropical climes, she devoured the simple supper her aunt had packed: strips of jerked beef, some cold roasted sweet potatoes with a little Hawaiian salt, delicious bananas—a delicacy that had been forbidden island women by the *kapu* system less than a hundred years before. Gazing into the fire she'd built for comfort and warmth, she ate her fill.

Not far from here—in the same year that a great red comet had lit the skies all around the world—Kamehameha, the Great One, had been born. Shortly after his birth, he had been taken from his mother by the highest *kahunas,* or priests, and hidden deep in the cavernous depths of the lava tubes, where those who wished to slay the infant chief could not find him. There Kamehameha had remained, carefully tended by faithful retainers, until the enemy chiefs and their warriors had left the island. Years later, on this very plain, King Kamehameha—now a grown man and a formidable warrior, besides—had marshaled his armies and gone on to conquer all the other islands in the archipelago, slaying every one of their chieftains. He had not been daunted by the enormity of the task before him, nor retreated from it, but had boldly forged on until victory had been his.

As I, she told herself firmly, *will succeed in this, my own small battle.* Somehow, she'd find a way to forget Gideon Kane, to seal her heart against him and go on with her life, she told herself, swallowing over the achy knot of tears in her throat. She would ask the spirits of *po,* the Night, to grant her a dream that would make her forget him. Or at very least, one that would teach her how to live with all that remained of their love: her memories.

Twenty

The airy, native-style dwellings that Emma had once called home were tucked snugly beneath several *lehua* trees, their branches ablaze with countless red pompom blossoms. The two large grass huts beneath them—called *hale pili*—both had wooden doors, small wooden verandas, or *lanai*, in the European style, and wooden floors, all of which had been spread with beautifully woven, spotlessly clean *lauhala* matting when her mother was alive. As was the Hawaiian tradition, one hut was used for sleeping, the other, larger one for cooking and eating.

As Emma rode up to the grass huts, she was furious to see a lean, weatherbeaten white man sitting before the doorway of the largest hut—*her* hut! It was Jack Jordan. He was wearing a battered hat above sun-bleached, shaggy hair, and his deep-set eyes were light gray above craggy features and drooping, nicotine-stained blond moustaches.

He sat cross-legged upon a woven mat, braiding narrow strips of leather into a lariat as he whistled between his teeth. He paused at frequent intervals to take swigs of rum from the brown-rimmed earthenware jug set within reach, then wiped his mouth on the back of his hand.

Hearing her approach, one of the heavy yellow mongrels sprawled at his side leaped up and bounded forward, barking wildly and wagging its tail in greeting. Thank God, the dogs hadn't forgotten her, she thought, relieved. They could be vicious to strangers.

Setting aside his leatherwork, their master rose to his feet. Squinting against the bright sunlight, he saw Emma astride her horse, and his sullen expression changed to a sly grin. Snatching up the jug of grog, he took a deep swallow, then went to meet her, swatting the eager dogs away and ordering them down.

"Well, well! If it ain't my little Emmie! What brings you back here, lovie?" he asked, his accent coarse as ever. "Found out it int so easy to live on yer own, have yer? I allus knew you'd come runnin' back." He winked. "Missed yer old da, did ye—"

"Never mind that. Why are you still here?" Emma demanded sharply, her clipped questions cutting him off. Her violet eyes flashed in warning, her lush lips were a thin, angry line as she tossed her dark mane over her shoulders and glowered down at him, beautiful as the goddess Pele in her fiery indignation. "Didn't I make myself plain at *Makua*'s funeral? You're not wanted here anymore—not for any reason. This is my land—and I'll thank you to leave it, Jack Jordan!"

He grinned and shook his head. "Jack Jordan? Tch. Tch. Is that any way t' talk to your old da, Emmie, after all we've bin to each other? Come on, gal. Give over with yer nagging, do. Give us a little cuddle, luv, for ole times' sake."

He reached up, as if to pull her from her horse's back, but— whether sensing her animosity, or reacting to its own fear—the little mare whickered and shied smartly away from her former master.

Jordan's easy grin vanished as he was forced to step back to avoid the mare's hooves, and it took Emma several moments to bring Makani back under control,

"You see?" she murmured with a mocking half-smile when she held the reins securely once more. "Neither Makani nor I have forgotten you, Jack. Not by a long shot! Now, pack your things and leave, or so help me, I'll—"

"You'll what?" he jeered.

"Or I'll tell the authorities that you're an escaped convict, and exactly where the sheriff and his men can find you now!" she threatened. "And if that doesn't frighten you, weell, I have a few other choice tidbits I think they'd be *very* interested in hearing, don't you, *Papa . . . ?"*

His cocksure grin wavered. Of a sudden, there was a flicker of genuine fear in his light-gray eyes. "You little bitch! You wouldn't dare . . . ?"

"No? Then go ahead, Daddy. Try some of your old tricks," she challenged in a steely tone. Her amethyst eyes were cold now, her stare unflinching. Exultation—relief—sang through her. As she'd hoped, the frightened little girl she'd once been had vanished forever with her mother's last breath. She could see Jack now for what he really was, and she wasn't afraid of him anymore. And never would be again!

" 'Strewth, you've grown proper hard, you have," he accused, scowling up at her. "Hard as bleedin' nails."

"No, *Da,"* she scoffed. "There's a difference. I've grown *stronger,* not *harder.* Stronger and much, much wiser. Now, for the last time, *Get off my land!"*

With her soft-spoken yet somehow deadly command, the smile fled Jack's face like a chalkline wiped from a slate. "All bloody right. If that's the way you want it, Miss Hoity Toity, then I'll go. But one fine day, you'll regret this, Emmie—you and that brat both! Just see if you don't!"

Emma laughed harshly. "I doubt that somehow, Jacko."

"Ye reckon so? Well, happen you could be wrong again, eh, and I could be right—like I was about Kane's snot-nosed son, remember? He came back with a brand-new wife on his arm, didn't he? Forgot all about his little island piece, didn't he?"

Her cheeks flamed. "So what if he did?" she flared, hating herself for letting him get to her, hating that his words cut so very deep when she knew what Jordan was and should never have paid him any mind. "What happened between Gideon and me happened ages ago. It's over. Finished. Past history."

"The devil it is," he snickered. " *'My Dearest One,' "* he quoted from memory, as if reading something aloud, and Emma grew very still. " *'Although it's been several years since you left the islands, I still hold you in my heart as, I trust and pray, I am yet in yours? I greet each passing day with a glad smile, happy in the certainty that each glorious sun that rises brings me ever closer to the day when you'll return t' me . . .'* Sounds familiar, does it, Emmie? I'll give ye a clue. It int Shakespeare!" He grinned.

Her face had gone white. "Where did you read that?" she whispered hoarsely, for he'd quoted from her last letter to Gideon! "Answer me!"

His leering grin broadened. "Where do you think I read it, you stupid chit? Ah Woo, your precious little slant-eyes, has been giving me the pretty letters you wrote t' High and Mighty Mister Gideon Kane all along!" He laughed as she moaned, looking as if she'd been struck a mortal blow. *"Oi! Oi!* Wot's this, then? Shocked, are ye? Well, ye shouldn't be. A yellow devil like Ah Woo could never help a man's daughter to keep secrets from her old da, could he, now? Like a sensible bloke, he gave me all o' your letters, along wiv the ones that came from Kane's son, and I . . . disposed of 'em as I saw fit."

"Disposed?" she whispered.

"Burned 'em!" he crowed.

"Nooo!" The cry was torn from the very depths of her being. She knew if she hadn't been mounted, her legs would have given way and she would have fallen to her knees. Never in her life had she hated anyone as deeply as she hated Jack Jordan in that moment.

Jordan's eyes kindled as he saw the shattering effect his disclosure had on his daughter. There! That'd teach the little bitch, he thought, well satisfied. Right now, she looked as if she'd been trampled by a runaway herd. Later, when she'd recovered a bit, she wouldn't be so quick t' try to tell him what to do. He chuckled. He still knew a trick or two when it came to women, he did—and she'd best not forget it, neither—

"Geeet ooout . . ."

He frowned and raised an admonishing finger in her face, stabbing it in the air at her as he ground out, "Wotch your lip, gal. I'll be buggered if ye'll talk t' me that—"

"I said, get ooout!" she shrieked, crowding Makani toward him. The mare snickered and tossed her head, eyes rolling back in her head nervously.

Jordan threw up his hands in defeat and hastily stepped aside. "All right, all right. I'm goin'."

She remained stony-faced and silent while he fetched his belongings from the two huts, rolling a few items of clothing and a couple of worn blankets into a tinker's bundle that he tied with a rawhide cord before slinging his other possessions into a sack he slung over his back.

"Wait! Your bottle."

Casting her a murderous look and muttering under his breath, he retrieved the half-empty jug, whistled up his dogs, and started walking down the sloping hillside, back the way she'd come. The animals trotted reluctantly after their master, from time to time casting longing looks in her direction, the disloyal brutes!

"Good riddance to the lot of them, hmm, Makani?" she muttered, waiting to dismount until Jack and his hunting dogs had become tiny dark blobs that grew smaller and smaller as he trudged off into the distance. Only then did she give way to the flood of tears she'd been holding back.

Some while later, dry-eyed and shaky but composed again now, she turned Makani into the small, fenced corral the mare had once shared with her father's poor old horse, Blackie. Since Jack was on foot, the animal must either have died or been sold off since her mother's death last Christmas, she presumed.

Afterward, unable to bear the clamor of her own tumultuous thoughts and emotions in the solitude of the foothills, she changed into an old shirtwaist and a pair of baggy knee-length men's corduroy knickers, crammed on a battered woven hat, and went down the narrow dirt path that wound between bushes and trees to her old taro patches, which were dozing in the shade of two massive mango trees.

How overgrown everything was! Many of the huge leaves were past saving, long since become yellow and brown, while others tossed gently on their succulent stalks like giant, velvety-green elephants' ears, dreaming sleepily in scattered patches of golden sunshine. Iridescent purple-and-emerald-green-winged dragonflies dipped and flashed over the fresh water from which the taro grew. She frowned. That lazy wretch! No one had picked the heart-shaped *luau* leaves for several months, nor dug in the soft mud for the huge gnarled corms that could be boiled, then pounded into tasty, grayish-purple *poi* paste or baked in the hot embers of an *imu,* an underground oven, to make a delicious food. What a waste, when there were people starving in other lands!

Using her old knife and the sackcloth in which Auntie Leo had packed her provisions, she waded into the taro patch and, standing thigh-deep in the cool water, began cutting the velvety leaves from their thick, succulent stalks one by one and stuffing them into her bag.

All of her life, she'd been taught that it was a sin to squander the blessed bounties of the *aina,* the land, or to let these nourishing taro leaves wither and die, when she could easily pick them for food. The unvaried rhythm of her labor served two purposes. The first was obvious: she was picking the leaves for a good purpose. The second was because leaf-picking freed her mind for remembering as she bent, cut, bagged, bent, cut and bagged over and over again, her sharp little cutting knife flashing in the mellow afternoon sunlight like the pink-and-purple wings of the dragonflies as they skimmed over the surface of the water.

Despite her fear that the heavy rains and strong winds of winter might have damaged them, the huts had changed little in the few months since her mother's death. When she'd ducked beneath the doorway after Jack's departure, the familiar woven walls had seemed to echo still with her mother's presence. She'd thought, too, that the faint scent of tuberoses—Malia Jordan's favorite flower—still lingered on the air. Island superstition held that when one smelled the favorite perfume of a loved one who'd passed on, it was a warning of imminent danger to those they'd left behind. But in this instance, Emma fancied the huts had simply retained her mother's favorite fragrance in the fibers of their walls, the weaving of her mats, in the same fashion a fine linen kerchief might retain an oft-used scent. And how evocative that heady scent was! If she closed her eyes, it was as if she could still hear her *makua's* low voice:

"Kaleilani! Where are you, my darling girl? Did you leave already, sweetheart?"

"I am going now, *Makua*," she'd whispered one lazy fall afternoon, lovingly smoothing a lock of hair from her mother's clammy brow. "Your medicine is right here, beside you. And there's fresh *poi* in the calabash, and some soup on the fire, if you should need anyth—"

"Hush, Kaleilani. Just hush and go, child, go quickly, before he wakes up." Malia Jordan had smiled, and there'd been traces of her former beauty in her gaunt face as she squeezed her daughter's hand between her own bony ones and murmured, "I will pray for you, very hard. The blessed Lord knows, you deserve a little happiness in your life, my own good girl. *Auwe!* What would your *makua* do without her little pansy-eyes, hmm?"

Emma had forced a smile as she bent down to kiss her mother's pale lips in farewell, trying not to let her anxiety show. That day, she recalled, her *makuawahine's* golden-brown complexion had seemed even sallower than usual, her large brown eyes had been ringed with shadows as livid as bruises above hollowed cheeks. She'd looked so frail, so gaunt, Emma'd had to swallow over the knot of tears in her throat to continue.

For nearly seven years now her mother had battled this pitiless cancer of the blood with its debilitating night sweats, fever, weight loss, swollen glands, and almost constant pain, inter-

spersed with a few precious days when she'd felt strong enough
to leave her bed and pretend for a few hours that all was well.

"As long as you still need me, I'll be here, my darling daughter," she'd promised Emma. *"I'll never, ever let you down again."*
And against all odds, Malia kept her promise, surviving far beyond Doctor Forrester's most optimistic estimates. She'd been
kept alive, Emma suspected, by her grim determination not to
leave her daughter all alone in the world with Jack Jordan. But
how long could she go on this way? Emma had wondered, blinking back stinging tears and forcing a bright smile for her mother's
benefit.

Suddenly fearful that day, Emma'd knelt down, laying her
head upon her mother's lap and wrapping her arms about her
wasted body. Her voice hoarse with unshed tears, she'd whispered, "You're certain you'll be able to manage while I'm gone?
I can stay. It doesn't matter, really it doesn't."

"Am I a *keikiwahine,* a little girl, and you my mother now?"
Malia had chided fondly, stroking her daughter's luxuriant
black hair with a thin hand. "I will be fine. Stop fretting and
go, Kaleilani! Go quickly! And if your *kuuipo,* your sweetheart,
has sent a letter to Ah Woo's store at long last, promise you'll
hurry back to read it to me, yes?"

"I promise!" Blowing her mother a kiss, Emma'd slipped quietly from the hut, giving her father—sprawled in a drunken stupor in the shade of the tossing *lehua* trees outside—wide berth.

Within minutes, she'd ridden Makani past her carefully
tended, spring-fed taro patches, where huge, heart-shaped leaves
flapped in the wind: past rows of small earthen mounds where
she grew the sweet potatoes they ate with salted beef, or sometimes a little dried fish, and was riding down the lush foothills
to the vast plain below, headed for distant Kawaihae—a two-day
ride away—and Ah Woo's general store.

In her *lauhala* basket had been tucked yet another letter—the
last in a long series that she'd written Gideon in the years since
his departure, addressed to him in care of the whaling company

his family owned in far-off Boston. Instead of paying him in coin, she'd made a bargain with Ah Woo, the Chinese store-keeper. She'd traded the taro roots he loved in return for his ensuring that her letters were properly stamped and posted for her, via the clippers and schooners and brigs that dropped anchor off Kawaihae Landing. Ah Woo had also agreed to hold any letters that Gideon might send until she came to collect them. But, in seven years, not once had she received an answer from him.

Now, at long last, she knew why, she thought with a shuddery sigh, before gritting her teeth and resuming her back-breaking labor. Jack Jordan had stolen her letters!

Last summer, she reflected, the part-Hawaiian schoolmaster, handsome Charles Keali'i Wallace—a Boston-educated fellow himself—had suddenly taken to visiting Emma and her mother whenever he was in the area, and whenever her father happened to be conveniently absent. The last time he'd visited them here had been about a month before Christmas. Over tea, Mama had suddenly insisted that Emma ride to Hui Aloha and bring a Mister McHenry back with her.

"He's Jacob Kane's lawyer and accountant," her *makua* had explained impatiently in answer to her questions. "And I know he'll be there because he comes to stay at the ranch each year at this time, both to enjoy the Kanes' hospitality and to go over the ranch's accounting books."

"But . . . what if he won't come?" Emma had asked, fright-ened by her gentle mother's sudden determination and strength, and by the unnatural vitality burning like hot coals in her eyes.

"Just tell him Malia Kahikina, Leolani's little sister, needs him. He'll come."

Like many Hawaiians, her *makuahine* had somehow known that the end, so long postponed, was coming for her very soon, though, of course, Emma had not understood at the time.

To Emma's surprise, Alexander McHenry had readily agreed to accompany her the long distance to her home. Moreover, he'd greeted her mother as if she were an old and dear friend, besides. They'd spent ages talking together, Malia's shriveled hands clasped in his, the two of them arguing amicably back and forth for ages before everything was set down on paper to Mama's liking, with the exception of her last request. It had been then that her *makua* had asked Keali'i what his intentions were toward her daughter.

"Makua, don't—!" Emma had hissed, red with embarrassment that her mother should say such a thing.

"I would like very much to marry her, Missus Jordan," Keali'i had replied softly, casting stunned Emma a fond glance and blushing beneath his dusky complexion. He'd added, "If she'll have me, I mean."

"Ah, Keali'i, Kaleilani, my dearest children! To see my darling daughter married before I die would make me happier than anything," Malia had murmured wistfully. "But what of you, Kaleilani? Could you grow to love Keali'i?" *Should the one you love never return to you?* she knew her mother must have thought silently.

Her question had caught Emma unprepared. "I . . . like Keali'i very much, *Makua*," she'd murmured, shooting a grinning Keali'i a withering look.

"Enough to accept his marriage proposal, *keiki* dear?" her mother had pressed, her haunted dark eyes resting eagerly upon the two young people. There'd been such hope in her voice as she continued. "I could leave this world in peace if only I knew you'd be taken care of, my little pansy-eyes. This land is mine. It is all I have left to leave you now, except for my blessing."

"You need not concern yourself, ma'am," Keali'i had reassured Malia stiffly. "If—when—Kaleilani and I are married, I shall be more than able to provide a good living for a wife on my schoolmaster's salary. Give no thought to your daughter's future. The land will pass freely to your poor husband, as your rightful—"

"Never! This land shall never be his!" Malia had cried out

rising off the bed in her vehemence. "Makua McHenry, write, write quickly! Set down the words for me!" she added. "Say that the land must belong to my daughter and her betrothed, Charles Keali'i Wallace, and to their issue, if any, when I've passed . . ."

Moist-eyed, Keali'i had whispered in Emma's ear, "I can't bear to see your *makua* so distraught. For her peace of mind, tell her we'll do as she wishes and be married, my dear," he'd urged. "I swear, I shan't hold you to your promise later if she should die, and you should decide that marriage to me would not be to your liking . . ." He hadn't finished the sentence. He hadn't needed to. They'd both known Malia Jordan would not live to see another Christmas.

Reluctantly, Emma'd agreed to the small deception. And, until Gideon's return and his subsequent revelations, had never regretted doing so. It had seemed worth the telling of a few harmless white lies to see the joy and peace of mind their announcement had brought her mother. Except that, in the end, those lies hadn't been harmless at all. In a bizarre twist of fortune, those lies had also cost her Gideon.

When Alexander McHenry had concluded his business, he'd summoned two of the Kane *paniolos* to witness the official document. Then, as he prepared to ride back to Hui Aloha, he'd taken Emma's hand in his and murmured, "If you should ever need help, lassie—er, Miss Jordan—ye've only to contact your aunt and uncle at Hui Aloha. They told me t' tell ye they'll do whatever they can for Malia and you two lassies—as will I. Ye've only t' say the word, hinny."

But her pride had cringed beneath the pity she'd glimpsed in McHenry's kind eyes. Standing up straight and tall, she'd murmured, "Thank you, Mister McHenry, but we'll be fine."

He'd nodded sadly and ridden away.

And then, just a few days later, her mother had simply stopped breathing one afternoon while Emma was darning at her bedside, softly singing the island *meles* her mother had loved. She'd drifted from this world into the next as effortlessly as the frigate bird soars from one wind current to the other, but for as long as she lived, Emma would never forget the terrible uncertainty of waiting—waiting for her to take that next, soft-drawn breath, waiting for the tremulous gasp that would never, ever come again.

Remembering that day, Emma blinked rapidly and cut faster and faster, until her sack bulged with its burden of huge green leaves.

Her back was breaking and she was exhausted but all cried out by the time the sack was filled. *Only four months of teaching, and I've grown soft!* she chided herself as she staggered to where the spring bubbled up from the ground. *How Mahealani would giggle to see me now, groaning about the stiffness in my joints like a* kupuna, *an old one!* she thought, missing the little girl keenly as she soaped and rinsed the mud from her legs and hands, then drank deeply of the spring's icy flow.

She ate the rest of the jerky and sweet potatoes her aunt had packed for her supper. And afterward, she brewed a kettle of delicious, fragrant coffee from a small bag of roasted Kona beans that Jack Jordan had forgotten to take with him, toasting his departure with several steaming mugfuls.

Soon after, daylight suddenly faded into indigo evening. The foothills grew hushed as night pressed all about the huts. Before the sun had fully vanished below the west, the moon had risen as a slender crescent against the darkening sky, where billows of charcoal cloud vied with the last stains of crimson and flame. Within moments, the sky was spangled all over with tiny pinpricks of glittering white light, though the huts were dark and silent.

Having no whale or *kukui,* candlenut oil with which to fill lanterns and dispel the shadows so that she could read or write in her journal, she banked the fire, placed her cutting knife within easy reach beneath a corner of the sleeping mat, and rolled herself into her single blanket. She fell deeply asleep within moments.

She awoke several hours later, no longer alone. She stiffened, for there was raspy male breathing in her ear, like the panting of a caged animal. She could feel the heat, smell the sweaty odor given off by the bulk of another body stretched out alongside hers on the mat. Trying to stay calm, she forced herself to remain very still, aware now that a calloused hand lay heavily on her upper thigh, had squirmed its way beneath the voluminous folds of the flannel gown she'd donned to sleep, and her flesh crawled. Loathsome memories came crowding back. Shame and disgust rose up her throat, stinging like bile as those stubby fingers continued their idle stroking, slyly climbing higher and higher. Their owner's breathing thickened as they grew closer to their goal, and now he crooned under his breath as if she were a frightened horse, or a little baby to be gentled and quietened.

"Easy, my lovie. Easy now, me li'l Em. Aaah, baby, you're so soft. Da's pretty little girl's so blooming' soft, she is . . ."

That caressing, singsong voice brought the sky crashing down around her—along with oh so many awful memories! She was trembling violently as he cupped her cheek in his hand, but too ashamed, too frightened in her shock, to utter the scream of rage and protest perched on her tongue. Dear Lord, it was as if her tongue had swelled up to fill her mouth and keep her from speaking, from demanding that this—this *outrage* cease! That this animal leave her alone! And *why* could she neither move nor speak, when she'd lived this same horror so often before? Had sworn, after that last time, she would die before enduring it again either in silent shame, or with this meek acceptance? *No, by God, she would not let him get away with it! She owed it to Makuahine, to Mahealani . . . to herself. For their sakes, if not her own, she'd never play the helpless victim again!*

Fingers tightening about the string-wrapped handle of her cutting knife, she rolled sideways, batting away Jack's clawing fingers to scramble to her feet, her rusty blade raised to defend herself. She caught the evil glint of his pale eyes in the moonlight as she flung about to face him.

"I told you to get off my land, you bastard!" she cried, clutching the folds of her nightgown to her breast with her free hand, as if it were a shield. "I swore if you ever laid a hand on me again, I'd kill you—and I meant it!" she hissed, violet eyes blazing.

Jack Jordan lumbered to his feet and stood there, swaying in the meager light of the banked fire and the moonlight that fell through gaps in the grass thatching. "Come on, Emmie girl. You don't mean that. Don't take on so," he crooned, licking his lips so that they glistened wetly. "I've missed my little Emmie's kisses and cuddles. Give us a kiss, eh, Em? Just a . . . just a little kiss?"

He was drunk. Again. Her belly heaved in revulsion and disgust, but that was all. Armed with new knowledge, he no longer held the power to frighten her. The terrified little girl she'd once been had grown up somehow. She didn't have to play Jack's games, ever again.

Shaking her head, she drew herself up and gritted, "No, Jordan. Thank God, I'm not 'your little Emmie.' I have news for you—*I never was!* So, I don't have to kiss you, nor cook for you, nor wash your dirty linens, nor do anything else for you, ever again, unless I choose to. And I won't! Because you see, as far I'm concerned, you're nothing, Jordan. *Less* than nothing!"

His light-gray eyes narrowed with anger under pale, shaggy brows that looked silvery in the gloom. "What's this? Wot're you trying to say, gal?"

"The truth, Jordan. *Makua* told me a secret before she died. One she'd carried for close to twenty years. She told me about my *real* father. It was her parting gift to me—and the one I'll always cherish, even more than I cherish this land. *My* land! She tricked you into marrying her all those years ago, Jacko. I carry your name, right enough, but *you're not my father! There's not a drop of your blood in me!*"

"Wot's this?"

"You heard me. *Makua* was desperate. She didn't know what else to do, or who else to turn to. And so, she turned to you."

"Why, that whoring bitch!" Jack snarled, his expression ugly. "What white man's bastard are ye then, if not mine? Jacob Kane's half-breed get?"

Smiling broadly, her violet eyes shining with triumph, she told him.

Twenty-one

"Over there, *Señor Jefe!* I'll get him!"

Gideon shook his head. He quickly dismounted to cinch up his saddle girth. "Take a breather, Felipe. This old devil's mine," he vowed, grinning as he swung up into the saddle again.

Coiled lariat in hand, Gideon headed Akamai toward a half-dozen *pipi,* wild steers, beneath the *ohia* trees, singling out a scarred, mean-looking bull that pawed the ground at his approach.

As he rode closer, the agitated mavericks bellowed and milled about, then panicked and tried belatedly to run. Akamai nimbly nipped and tucked his way in and out of the galloping steers, responding to either his rider's slightest touch or to his own unerring instinct for the job at hand. Together, they cut the bull from the rest of the small herd, crowding it toward a *kapuka,* a small clearing uncluttered by trees that might hamper Gideon's lariat.

Dogging the bull's heels, Akamai thundered on as his rider whirled the lariat above his head and prepared to throw.

But as the noose snaked through the air, the bull skidded to a halt, skewed around and tossed its head defiantly. The *kaula ili* glanced harmlessly off its shoulder and fell to the grass. Head lowered, the *pipi* pawed the ground once again, its wickedly curved horns lowered as it prepared to charge the horse careening toward it.

Cursing a blue streak, Gideon turned Akamai in the nick of

time, thanking God for his old partner's unerring skill as the horse obediently nipped sideways. The bull's horns missed the little bronco's unprotected flanks by a fraction of an inch as they thundered past, hooves raising red dust in their wake.

Reining Akamai to a skidding halt, Gideon turned in the saddle to look back over his shoulder, just as Felipe's game little buckskin mare also came to a sudden halt. Its front legs were braced and stiff, its rump almost touching the ground as her rider executed a perfect throw that lassoed the *pipi* solidly about the horns.

Caught and unable to run, the frantic bull bellowed with rage, then bucked and twisted wildly to free itself, its massive spread of curving horns slicing the sultry, dust-laden air like scimitars. Straightway, the Mexican *vaquero* hitched the lariat several times about his *okuma,* saddle horn, to anchor it, then—crooning softly to his mount—he urged his pony backward, working the bull, foot by foot, toward a sturdy *koa* tree. Once there, he securely lashed the bull's head as close to the trunk as he could with another short rope, retrieved his lariat and remounted his horse, all in the space of a few minutes.

"Bravo!" Gideon applauded as Felipe, grinning broadly, rode up alongside him. He grimaced and indicated the braided leather lariat he was coiling about his saddle horn. "Damned if I'm not rustier than I thought!"

"Your old skill with *la riata* will return, Señor Gideon," Felipe reassured him, "for there will be many, many chances to try again! Today, we catch as many wild steers as we can, then tomorrow, Señor Kimo and the others will bring the tame bullocks up from the holding pens. They'll lash each bullock's horns to those of a crazy old *pipi* like this, then set the pair of them free. In a day, perhaps two, the tame bullocks will lead the *loco* steers to the main corral, as tame as lambs. From there, they'll be driven down to Kawaihae, as always, *no?*"

"Where our *paniolos* will swim the steers out to the ships."

"But of course! How else could it be done?"

"The same old way of doing things, hmm?" Gideon observed with satisfaction. "While America was being ravaged by the War Between the States, here it's as if time stood still. Nothing's changed here, has it, Felipe?"

Felipe shrugged. "There is nothing wrong with that, señor. If something works time and time again, why change it?"

"Why, indeed," Gideon agreed thoughtfully, ignoring the little voice nagging him that there must be change if there was to be progress. But damn change, and to hell with progress, if it meant war and bloodshed and upheaval.

For a fleeting moment, he was back there again. The war. He could hear the thunder of the cannons, the terrified screams of men and horses, the stirring roll of the drums, and the piping of the fifes that had spurred them into bloody battle.

Flicking his head to clear it, he swabbed his sweating face on the bandanna about his throat. In just a few hours of exposure to its fierce rays, the tropical sun had quickly restored his tan, erasing all traces of "shark-bait" pallor save for a paler band where his hat brim had shaded his brow from the sun.

"Felipe, how long have you been here?" he asked, pulling his bandanna up over his nose and mouth as they rode on across the plain.

At dawn, when they'd dragged themselves from their bedrolls to begin the long day, the morning air had been cold and crisp. But now, it was almost midday, and the sun beat down from a cloudless blue sky and the wind was strong, laden with a fine, stinging dust that made the eyes smart, the nose and throat raw.

"Me, señor? Six, almost seven years. Remember, señor? I arrived just before you went away."

Gideon nodded. "And before that?"

"I was a *vaquero* on the largest *rancheria* in Texas when I heard that Señor Kane was paying many dollars for the best cowboys to come to the Sandwich Isles. Like my father before me, and his father before him, I could ride before I could walk, señor." Felipe confided with an embarrassed shrug, "and rope anything that moved before I lost my first tooth!" He grinned, his gentle cinnamon brown eyes sparkling, his teeth very white against his olive complexion and drooping black mustache that seemed incongruous on such a youthful face.

Gideon nodded. "Well, it shows. You're one hell of a cowboy, Felipe. I've been watching you, and you know working cattle inside and out—better than any man here. When Uncle Kimo retires in the fall, I've decided to make you *luna* in his place."

"Foreman? Me? Aiee, señor, you do me great honor!" Felipe murmured, clearly astounded. "And I am flattered, truly, señor, but . . . are there not others who've been here far longer than I? Men who'll be angry that you have chosen me over them?"

"Are they as good as you?"

"No . . . but perhaps almost as good?" Felipe hedged modestly.

"Let me worry about them. And if they give you a hard time, let me know about that, too."

"Oh, no, señor! If I am truly to become *luna,* I must handle my men myself—and in my own way."

Smiling behind the bandanna, Gideon nodded agreement. "That's what I was hoping to hear. I'm going to need all the help I can get to turn this place around. Since his fall, my father hasn't been able to run the ranch the way he used to, and it shows," he observed with a rueful grimace. "I'm hoping once he realizes the ranch is in good hands, he'll get the rest he needs for that hip—maybe have an American specialist take a look at it."

The Mexican nodded soberly. "I remember the day of the accident very well. It happened about a year after I came here. *Gracias a Dios,* it was a miracle *Makua* Kane was not killed!" he recalled, crossing himself. "I've seen many such accidents in my lifetime, and when a horse falls upon a man, it is rare he lives to speak of it, let alone walk again."

"My father was lucky."

"*Sí.* He was very lucky, señor," Felipe agreed soberly as they rode toward a pond that shimmered beneath a haze of heat. It was a favorite watering place of the *pipi,* and he knew they would find other mavericks there.

Gideon nodded, gentian eyes narrowed, square jaw hard and set. "I mean to whip this ranch back into shape, the way my father always meant it to be. What do you say? Are you up to being my foreman—even if it means ruffling a few feathers?"

Felipe's broad grin and firm, *"Sí, señor!"* was answer enough.

Gideon was preoccupied as he gazed into the flames of their campfire that night, impervious to the chill winds that gusted through the Kohala foothills from the snowy peaks of Mauna Kea high above; unmoved by the harmonious singing and yodeling of his *paniolos* as they strummed their ukuleles or guitars and sang of their sweethearts and the islands they loved. He'd even managed to forget Julia and their marriage for the time being, his thoughts completely consumed with the future of the Kane Ranch.

As he'd mentioned to Felipe, the small signs of neglect were everywhere. During the coming months, he'd have to work day and night to rebuild the Kane empire, either riding herd with his father's *paniolos,* supervising the breeding pens or the calving and branding, or just plain practicing his rusty roping and horse-breaking talents long into the evening, in an effort to regain his former skills and, with them, the respect of his men. He'd also have to go over the accounts and allocate the funds needed to have the most urgent repairs carried out immediately, while earmarking other, less-urgent repairs for later attention.

Money was no problem, not yet. The biggest problem he foresaw would be the shortage of water in the summer months just ahead, especially with the herds growing daily. He'd lost count of the number of prime newborn calves that had been dropped since his return three days ago. The upcoming roundup and spring branding would give him a more accurate tally, but he was sure that if this summer proved yet another long, hot one, like the last two his father had described, there would be a drought before the next rainy season, with dead cattle to show for it. He frowned, undecided. Should he have someone approach Emma—or rather, Emma's husband, Charles Wallace—about buying the land along the ranch's farthest boundaries—and with it, the water rights they so desperately needed—or handle the transaction himself? He scowled. The accountant, Alexander McHenry, had made his position plain enough. He was on his own as far as this purchase was concerned. Disturbed, he ran his hand through his tousled black hair. He had to talk Emma into selling! Water meant life for their herds, and there was no other source to supply the eastern ranges. Tomorrow, he'd ride the length and breadth of the property and try to get an idea of a starting price.

"We've decided to make an offer for E— your niece's land," he confided to Kimo, who sat cross-legged nearby, weaving the young ferns and flowers he'd tucked into his saddlebags that afternoon into an intricate band for his hat. "I—er—wanted you to be the first to know, so there'd be no misunderstanding my motives for approaching Emma."

Discussing the land purchase was as good an opening gambit to a conversation as any others he could come up with. There had been an uneasy coolness between himself and Kimo Pakele since they'd ridden from Hui Aloha that morning. In the hours since, Felipe had worked him too damned hard to spare any time in which to eat humble pie and set things right with the ranch foreman. The sooner things were back to normal between them, the better he'd feel.

"Kaleilani's land?" Kimo echoed in answer to his announcement, one heavy eyelid lifting suspiciously. He set the unfinished hatband aside on the damp sackcloth before him. "For the water rights, huh?"

Gideon nodded, relieved the man had not read some ulterior motive into his words and reacted excessively. "Right."

"I get bad feelings about that place. More better you stay away from there."

By the campfire's flickering light, Kimo's wary expression and the urgency of his low response made Gideon's skin crawl with what Hawaiians termed "chicken skin" or gooseflesh. He frowned. What the devil was wrong with the man? What was he trying to say? He knew that Emma's land had once been the site of many bloody battles between warring native factions. Moreover, it was said that on certain nights, when the wind was in the right direction, you could hear the clash of phantom spears, the tramp of ghostly feet, and the cries of warriors calling upon Kukailimoku, the god of war, to make their spears and clubs invincible and slay their enemies, along with the mournful moan of conch-shell trumpets, echoing down through the canyons of time. Was this what Kimo was trying to warn him about? If so, he couldn't afford to let superstition sway his decision to purchase the land, watered by that all-important stream, which had its home high in the mountains.

Within the forests' emerald tangle of vines, ferns, and leafy trees, there was a hidden place, one that was *kapu,* forbidden, to all but the native *kahuna,* or priests, who tended it, for it was sacred to their ancient goddess, Laka. Woe betide the unwary who trespassed upon Laka's sacred ground and ignored the symbols of warning! Such a man might suddenly fall ill, or worse, learn he was being "prayed" to death. Was it this Kimo was warning him about?

Frightened by the spooky tales he'd heard as a child and still superstitious years later, as a youth, Gideon had always given the Kane land that bordered the area wide berth, believing the place quite uninhabited, unless one counted spirits as inhabitants. Involuntarily, he wetted his lips. Though a grown man who had traveled far and wide, a man who feared no living thing in the normal course of events, he was suddenly filled with a twinge of his old childhood misgiving. There was a chilly, prickling sensation on the back of his neck as he answered Kimo's warning with a hoarse, "Why? Is it haunted?"

A mirthless smile parted Kimo's lips. "Perhaps not in the way you are thinking of, my boy. It is just that . . . Kaleilani's father, Jack Jordan, lives there from time to time. And believe me, his spirit is truly evil—as black and evil as his heart," Kimo observed with a rueful grimace. "Better you stay away." He made an expression of disgust and dismissal with his hand.

"You're sure? That he still lives there, I mean?"

The Hawaiian nodded, his expression guarded. "He leaves, sometimes for several weeks, but he always comes back, even though he has no right to be there. The land belongs to his daughter now, who has asked him many times to leave it."

Gideon's brows rose. "Why would Emma evict her own father?"

"Because there is no *aloha,* no love, between them. There has never *been* love between them, although Jack would have outsiders believe otherwise."

"Poor Kaleilani. What a shame," he murmured, thinking, *What a miserable childhood my poor darling must have endured! A mother she'd hardly known until the woman was dying a slow, painful death, and a father she'd obviously felt nothing but dislike for.* "Still, I think I'll ride over there in the morning and take a look at the land and the stream," he decided, poking a stick into the crackling fire and watching sparks swirl about like orange fireflies, before extinguishing themselves in the damp night air.

Kimo shrugged. "If your mind is made up, then you must do as you think best. But remember, Mo'o, Jordan and your father are old enemies, and the *haole,* the white man, is unpredictable. Watch your back."

"Old enemies? That's news to me! What happened between them?"

With his question, it was as if a veil dropped down over Kimo's eyes. "Only that Jack Jordan has never meant anything

but *pilikia,* trouble, to anyone, and *Makua* Kane—your father—
does not like him."

"Why the devil not? Father usually gets along with everyone."
He'd never heard of Jack Jordan—or known of the Jordan family's existence, come to that—until the day he'd met Emma on
the beach. And here Kimo was, claiming that his father and
Emma's father were old enemies, simply because Gideon's father
did "not like him!" What had really happened between them?
And had their mysterious quarrel taken place before he'd gone
away to college, or after? And what had caused it? Had it had
anything to do with him and Emma?

Kimo still looked uncomfortable—and, Gideon decided, eva-
sive. "Some things are better not discussed, Mo'o. You know
this."

The shifty expression in the old rogue's eyes was all Gideon
needed to confirm that Kimo was hiding something, while trying
to shut *him* up by slyly alluding to what he'd witnessed in the
gazebo last night! "Some things are better not discussed indeed!" He'd be damned if he'd be put off that easily! "Tell me
anyway," he drawled, a small smile playing about his lips as he
leaned back on one elbow and drew deeply on a slim black
cigarillo. "I'm a man of the world," he added, blowing a perfect
smoke ring and grinning.

Kimo sighed and shrugged his shoulders. "All right. Jack
Jordan's a poacher. If that was all he did, well, *Makua* Kane
would probably turn a blind eye to it, if he didn't object to the
methods Jordan uses."

"What methods?" Gideon demanded. A little rustling to put
beef in some lazy rogue's larder was the big secret? After such
a build up, Kimo's recounting of Jordan's sins was something
of an anticlimax! Poaching, be damned! He'd expected the rogue
to be guilty of murder, at the very least!

"He does as the bullock hunters in the early days used to
do—digs himself a deep pit, then drives a frightened steer toward
it. When the *pipi* falls in and breaks its legs, he clubs it to death.

Or—if he owns a rifle or pistol—shoots it. Unfortunately, the lazy no-good never fills the pits afterward. And open pits are treacherous to our cowboys."

"Hmm. Have you tried talking to him about it?"

"I have. Six years ago, and countless times since."

Gideon's eyes narrowed in sudden understanding. "Aaah. So that's it. You think Jordan had something to do with Father's accident?"

"There was never any proof, but . . . !" Kimo shrugged eloquently.

"And Jordan?"

"He denies ever rustling so much as a single Kane steer, let alone digging any pits! So . . . be careful, Mo'o."

With a solemn nod, Gideon promised that he would. Gazing into the fire, he pondered everything his calabash uncle had told him, unable to discard the feeling that Kimo had told him only what he wanted to hear about Jordan. Then of a sudden, his frown became a broad grin. His gentian eyes glinted in the firelight. Twice, Kimo had called him by his old nickname. And he'd seemed concerned for his safety, too! Unless he missed the mark, the Hawaiian was well on the way to forgiving him.

"Tell me more about this Jordan," he urged, curious about what sort of childhood Emma could have had with such a father.

Kimo snorted. "Aw, he drink too much, that one. Grog mostly. Sometimes wine. When he used to drink before, he go crazy and beat Kaleilani's *makuahine,* her mother. Malia would bring her little girl to our house an' hide from him there until he come sober. But as soon as her bruises faded, she'd take Kaleilani and go back to that no-good, till the next time." He sighed heavily and picked up his unfinished flower hatband. "We never knew if it was Jack Malia refused to abandon, or her *ahupua'a,* her land," he observed, his brown fingers deftly moving among the small heap of dewy blossoms, ferns, and vines.

"Jordan sounds like a bad lot."

"Very bad. Kaleilani was lucky to escape him for so many

years." Kimo's good-natured expression hardened, as if he'd remembered something especially repugnant. He shook his head. "We should never have let her come back here, not for any reason!"

"By we, you mean yourself and Auntie Leo?"

He nodded. "When she was very small, Mak— my Leo and I sent Kaleilani to the Convent of the Sacred Cross, in Honolulu. And there she stayed, in care of the Catholic sisters, until Malia—she was my Leolani's younger sister—fell sick. We wrote to Kaleilani, and she insisted on coming home to care for her mother. That was the year you left for Boston. My niece was only fourteen then. In another year or two, she would have been given a fine teaching position at the Missionary School for Girls in Honolulu. But she loved her mother, and would not leave her when the summer ended. She nursed her until Malia passed away, just before Christmas. Fortunately, her schooling was not wasted," he added, brightening. "Since February, she has been teaching school to the children in the Waikalani valley. My wife tells me she is happy there," he added, almost defiantly. Or, perhaps, Gideon wondered, in warning?

"I'm glad. But . . . what's his name? Jack Jordan? He's something of a puzzle. What cesspit did he spring from? He doesn't sound like the other *haoles* who settle here?"

"He is not. Jordan's a Botany Bay man."

"Aaah." Gideon grunted in understanding. There was a handful of Botany Bay men scattered throughout the Sandwich Isles, if memory served him. Convicts who'd escaped from the Australian penal colonies to make the isolated regions of the islands their hideouts. While none of the fugitives had become upstanding pillars of the community exactly, they usually shunned making the sort of trouble that would draw the attention of the authorities and lead to their recapture and extradition. Jack Jordan, however, sounded like a law unto himself. "If your offer still stands, I'd welcome a strong right hand tomorrow—and any advice you might have to go with it?"

Kimo grinned as he fastened the finished hatband around the crown of his beautifully woven *lauhala* hat. "If you're still up to it come morning, you've got it, Mo'o!"

"Up to it?"

The Hawaiian waved a greeting to the *paniolo* silhouetted briefly against the lighter night sky as the man rode back toward the camp. "Look! Luis is coming in now. It's your watch, Mo'o!"

Twenty-two

It was in the wee hours of his watch that Gideon spotted a yellow flicker of firelight in the foothills. He decided to go investigate. It was probably just a weary traveler making a comforting fire by which to pass the night before journeying on to Waimea village. Or a lost sightseer, headed for Kilauea, there to witness the fire goddess Madame Pele's newest and most spectacular eruption. Either way, a fire had to be investigated. Telling Ramon where he was headed, he skirted the fringes of the quietly milling herd and headed Akamai up-country.

He soon realized that the small blaze was growing rapidly. It was not Kane land burning as he'd first thought, but the land beyond it—the same land he'd hoped to purchase! The fire had started about a quarter of a mile beyond the line of stunted trees whose tangled branches divided the two properties.

He'd just about given up trying to find an opening between them when the moon sailed out from behind a cloud like a ghostly galleon in full sail, spilling silvery light everywhere. With a grim smile, Gideon turned his stallion and set his head at the barrier.

"Yiihaaah! Let's go, boy!" Hindquarters pumping, the valiant old fellow took a short, powerful run and a flying leap over the low trees that was worthy of Pegasus, his master crouched low over his neck.

As Gideon galloped Akamai up the hillside toward the blaze, he spotted a woman, bucket in hand, silhouetted briefly against the roaring flames before she suddenly vanished from view. Recognition and alarm surged through him simultaneously.

"Emmaaa!" With a hoarse cry, he spilled from Akamai's back and raced on foot toward the blaze—a brace of burning huts—throwing up an arm to shield his face as a wave of heat billowed toward him, hurling his giant shadow across the firelit grass.

Christ Almighty! The woven walls of both huts had already been consumed! The smell of burning grass was pungent on the cool night air. Now, only the blackened frames of the dwellings remained, tongues of fire licking at the bony wooden carcasses left to them. In but minutes, they, too, would be gone, and only twin rectangles of scorched turf would remain to show where the neat, comfortable huts had once stood. But there was no sign of Emma anywhere. *Where the devil was she?*

"Emmaaa!" he roared again, looking around. Nothing. With a curse, he plunged between several *lehua* trees, then tore down a narrow dirt pathway bordered with bushes to the taro patch, in search of her. The sick dread in his belly was mounting. How could she have vanished so quickly? He'd seen her only a moment ago! God forbid, had she somehow fallen into the flames?

"Here! Gideon! I'm over here!"

Turning, he saw her standing knee-deep in the oily black, glinting waters of the taro patch, a wooden bucket dangling from her hands. Surrounded by a forest of huge, heart-shaped plants as tall as her shoulders, she made a forlorn, slender silhouette in the leaping light of the flames, with her loose hair swirling about her shoulders and her face lit by firelight—like an artist's rendering of Madame Pele, Gideon thought fleetingly.

As Emma clambered out onto the grassy banks, the drenched skirts of her *muumuu* were plastered to her legs. Her hair was fanned by the same wind that was even now fanning the dying flames into a grass fire that would spread rapidly and consume acre upon acre of lush grazing in a matter of hours if he didn't act soon!

In that moment, the frame of the second hut collapsed like

some prehistoric skeleton, toppling sideways in a great conflagration of whirling sparks and scattered embers, like a shower of golden stars.

Seeing another upturned bucket, Gideon filled both it and the one Emma was holding from the bubbling spring, then made several laborious trips with slopping buckets to douse the fire.

When every last spark had been safely extinguished, he flung both buckets aside and went to her, hauling her roughly into his arms. He was too shaken to give a tinker's cuss whether holding her was right or wrong, or to notice that she seemed quiet and badly shaken. For a few dreadful moments he'd never forget, he'd thought she'd been swallowed up by that roaring red monster! Now, he needed to hold her—and hold her damn close!—in order to convince himself she was unharmed.

"Are you hurt?" he demanded at length, anxiously searching her tear-streaked, grimy face.

She shook her head. "Only where your fingers are digging in. You're holding me too tightly."

"You should be thanking God I'm all that's hurting you," he growled, loosening his hold a fraction. "And then maybe you can explain what the devil happened here?"

She grimaced. *"I* happened," she admitted, eyes downcast. "I—er—set fire to the huts myself."

"You?" He saw, then, the bundle of belongings, stacked neatly on the grass some feet away, and her horse—the same horse she'd ridden to the beach all those years ago—with its reins looped about a bush, stamping nervously and clearly terrified of the fire. "In God's name, why? You could have burned every damned blade of grass for miles, you little fool! Or been killed yourself!"

"I realized that, once the fire got started. But at the time I lit the thatch, I was so bloody angry, I wasn't thinking," she protested defiantly. "I'm sorry." Catching his furious expression, she amended, "Oh, all right. *Very* sorry." But her expression was still defiant as she explained, "I came up here to be by myself—

to think about us, and everything that's happened. Anyway, when I got here, I saw he'd come back. Can you believe he was actually *living* here? And he——he told me——or should I say, he boasted?—— that he'd convinced Ah Wong into giving our letters to him!" Her lower lip trembled madly. Tears filled her eyes, threatened to brim over.

"Jesus Christ," he swore softly, his shoulders sagging. "So that explains it."

She nodded, her tears overflowing, trailing crystal snailtrails down her pale-gold cheeks. "Now do you understand why I was so angry? The hundreds of times I've written to you over the years, and not *one blessed letter* had ever been sent! He saw how hurt I was, and he——he laughed. He destroyed our lives, Gideon, but he was laughing!" she sobbed, unaware that Gideon's huge fingers were curling into massive fists at his sides. "All I could think of were the years I'd spent waiting for you, hoping for some word that you still loved me, never dreaming anyone could be so——so hopelessly *evil!* If we'd been able to correspond, you'd have had no reason to marry Julia. You'd have known long before you ever left Boston that I was counting the days, the hours, till you came home! Oh, God, I was so angry—*so very angry!* Firing the huts was the only way I could think of to get rid of him."

The color drained from Gideon's face as a thought occurred to him. "Sweet Christ, he wasn't . . ."

"Wasn't what?"

"In—in—"

"Inside them? No, of course not, silly," she protested, sniffing back her tears to cast Gideon a scathing glare from her remarkable violet eyes. "We quarreled, then he left. But he must have sneaked back after dark to try and . . ." That same remarkable gaze slid away from his now, as if a veil had come down to curtain her thoughts—just as Kimo's had become veiled earlier. Whatever she'd been about to reveal remained a secret. "Well, anyway," she continued, "after I'd considered everything, I decided I'd have to burn the huts down. It was the only way he'd ever get off my land. I know it was a stupid thing to do, but I never thought about the fire spreading, truly I didn't!"

"Luckily, there's no harm done, so long as the fire stays out. It would have been a different story in the summer, though."

She nodded mutely, biting her lower lip like a chastened little girl.

He swallowed. The air of vulnerability, of fragile beauty, about her all but overwhelmed him with the urge to take her in his arms and comfort her, to protect her from her ogre of a father and his vicious tricks. To keep from doing just that, he thrust his hands deep into his breeches' pockets, unaccountably angry. Hell and damnation! What was he coming to? His decision to make the best of his marriage was not even twenty-four hours in the making, and here he was, itching to take Emma in his arms and the devil take Julia!

He cleared his throat. "Your—er—father had been living here, you said?"

A strange little smile twisted her lovely lips but never reached her eyes. She seemed about to correct him, but then thought better of it and nodded. "Jack Jordan. Yes. This land belonged to my mother, though. When she died just before Christmas, she left it to me. He has no business here now."

"I was sorry to hear about your *makua*," he murmured, his handsome face grave in the glorious moonlight. "Uncle Kimo told me. I know how much you loved her."

"Don't be sorry," she said huskily, forcing a brave little smile that tore at his heart. "I'm not! She's at peace now, you see? Free from pain, and from him." She bit her lip and blinked rapidly. "One of her last wishes was that he should leave her land. And she made me promise that if I sold it, he'd not profit by so much as a penny." A ghost of a smile played about her lips. "I think tonight should make quite sure of that, don't you? Old Jacko will have to find himself another rock to crawl under now."

He flinched at the bitterness in her tone. Was this bitterness one of the ways in which she'd changed since he left? "He will, indeed, you bloodthirsty minx! But what about you, now that the *hales* are gone? Where will you live?"

"Me? Oh, I haven't lived here since Mama died. Don't worry. I'll be just fine," she insisted, trying to meet his eyes but not quite succeeding. "Besides, I have my—I have the children to keep me busy."

"Children?" he echoed woodenly, raven brows quirked. "Aah."

She nodded, but would still not meet his eyes. "They're such a comfort to me."

"I'm sure they are. And I expect your husband's an even greater one," he ground out. "I look forward to meeting the wonderful Charles Wallace someday."

Her hand flew up to cover her mouth as she suddenly realized why Gideon persisted in mentioning Charles Keali'i Wallace's name over and over again, with such an edge of dislike to his tone. "Oh, Gideon, you're wrong about Keali'i, terribly wrong. I don't know where you came by the idea, but he's not my husband—although it's true that we were betrothed briefly. He consented to a betrothal between us for Mama's sake, you see, but it was only on paper. She . . . well, she was worried about dying and leaving me alone. It was the only way we could think of to—to give her the peace of mind to let go. I'm not married, Gideon. I've never been married."

Her words seemed to echo over and over. He grasped her by the upper arms and shook her, and there was a sick heaviness in his gut, a terrible, cold feeling of hopelessness in his heart. "Jesus Christ, Emma, don't tell me that now! *I thought I'd lost you*, that you'd married Charles Wallace—that's why I married Julia, the *only* reason!"

"But reasons don't change anything. You're still married! You still belong to her!" Flinging off his hands, she picked up the skirts of her nightgown and began running headlong down the grassy slope, her dark hair streaming behind her in the moon-light.

With a curse, he headed after her, catching up with her at the bottom of the hill. Grabbing her wrist, he flung her around to face him. "Is it so damned easy for you, then?"

"What do you mean?"

"What I said. I asked if it's so damned easy for you? What did you do when you heard that I was married? Just shrug your damned shoulders, and forget about it?"

"Of course it wasn't easy for me, not at all!" she screamed at him, tears rolling down her cheeks. "But at least I'm *trying*. I'm trying very hard to put the love I thought we shared behind us, where it belongs. Th-that's what you should be doing. Not running around trying to blame every one else because you married Julia! Not blaming it all on stupid reasons!" But even as she said the words, her heart was breaking all over again.

"Do you think I haven't tried?" he growled. "Damn it all, woman, love isn't like a—a pump handle! You can't turn your feelings off and on with just a jerk or two! Or at least, *I* can't. Ever since I left you and sailed off to Boston, not a day's passed when you didn't fill my thoughts—and precious few nights, either. During the war, you were the best reason I had to stay alive. Just one more day . . . just one more . . . and maybe I could come back to you and never have to leave you again. That's what I kept telling myself, over and over, while we—"

"Gideon, don't!" she implored him, but he couldn't stop. His emotions, too long buried, had risen like boiling milk spilling over a pot.

"—while we lay in muddy ditches alongside corpses that were crawling with maggots and blow-flies," he continued passion-ately, his handsome face intense in his desperation to make her understand how terrible those times had been. His hands were almost cruel where they gripped her wrists. "I rode alongside boys who were years younger than me. But, by some miracle, I survived, while they were killed. I also managed, somehow, amidst all that madness, to keep my sanity. I came through for you, Emma. Because of *you!* You were my beacon in hell's darkness. My ray of hope. My promise of a better tomorrow. Damn Julia! Damn convention and propriety! *I love you!* I love you, and I'll never give you up!"

There was no boyish hesitancy in the powerful arms that dragged her to him, nor in those that swept her off the ground. There was no youthful clumsiness in the ardent lips that crushed her mouth beneath his, nor in the broad chest to which he held her. He was a man now, a virile, passionate, and—God, yes!—a furiously angry man. The woman in her could neither resist nor refuse him, let alone condemn him.

As he kissed her, he drew her down to the coarse turf beside him as if it were an ancient altar and she, his lovely sacrifice, a *wahine kapu* to be given to the gods of the stars and the moon. His hands shook as he thrust up the folds of her nightgown, drawing it off over her head, and flinging it aside. She was quite naked beneath it, her body slim and pale in the silvery light that drenched the grassy plain. Her face hidden by the glossy waterfall of her midnight hair, she lay in the circle of his arms, her face uplifted to his like a flower to the warmth of the sun.

Her skin glowed with desire. The delicate feminine musk of her arousal and the fragrance of the white ginger blossoms she'd tucked behind her ear were underscored by the faint, acrid smell of smoke. It was an exotic concoction that stirred his hungry senses. With a groan, he knelt beside her and hungrily cupped one pale-gold breast, taking the darker, pebbled peak deep into his mouth and drawing deeply upon it, while with his free hand he unfastened his belt.

"Yes, oh, yes, beloved! But hurry, please hurry," she whispered raggedly, tugging at the folds of his red calico shirt. Coconut shell buttons popped free and rolled away, unnoticed, as she bared his muscular shoulders. Leaning up, she showered his face and chest with kisses and feverish caresses. "Make love to me, please, oh, please!"

Whispering his name like a prayer, she reached for him, loosened the buttons of his breeches, then lay back upon the grass, panting with her need, eager to guide his manhood to her aching core.

Shaking his head, he drew back and looked down at her. His gentian eyes were smoldering with lust. His strong, handsome face was dark and stern with his burning need. Still unsmiling, he shook his head and closed his eyes. "Dear God, don't ask that of me, my darling! Tonight, I can take you, Emma. I can hold you, have you, pleasure you, but what I can give you—here and now—it won't be making love, my darling. Not feeling the way I feel."

"Then take me any way you want," she whispered, "because—oh, God!—I want you, too." She shivered and raised her hips, rubbing her belly voluptuously against his flanks, arching her head back as heat curled through her loins like flickering tongues of fire.

With a muffled curse, he cupped her chin in his fist and ravished her lips with a sweet savagery that brought her to the brink of that little death which is ecstasy. Like a man starved, he drank from her mouth like a hummingbird sipping nectar from the throat of a flower, savoring her sweetness, drawing her fragrant breath deeply inside him.

"Beloved," he groaned, tracing the shell-like whorls of her ear with his tongue-tip. "Open yourself to me, sweet Kaleilani, my Lei of Heaven. Let me touch your fire, little pansy-eyes." Drawing shallow, raspy breaths, he kissed her throat and the shadowed hollows at its base, feeling the shudder of response that rippled through her as his lips moved lower still. But then, all of a sudden, she whispered, "Wait! Stop!"

"You've changed your mind?"

Shyly, she shook her head. "I want to feel you, too. I need to!" she repeated huskily.

His dark eyes held hers captive in a lambent gaze for endless moments until, a smile curving his lips in the moonlight, he nodded. "As you will, my love."

There was no hesitancy in the hands that dragged his shirt down from his shoulders, no reluctance in those that tugged off his boots. Breathing shallowly, she quickly freed the cloth of his shirt from his belt, then the belt from its brass buckle, finally tugged down his whipcord breeches with an exultant, "Aaah!" as he stood, proud and naked as a young god, before her.

Pleased, she saw that he was as comfortable naked as fully clothed. Standing there with his handsome dark head cocked to one side, his muscular arms folded across his broad chest, he watched in amusement as she gobbled him up with her eyes, not shrinking with maidenly modesty from the very prominent proof of his arousal.

"Well, Miss Jordan? Is everything to your liking?" he drawled wickedly, his eyes gleaming in the shadows as he dropped to his knees alongside her.

"Very much so," she confirmed with a giggle. Trailing her fingers through his curling dark chest hair, where the gleaming bone fishhook she'd given him still hung from a sennit cord, she traced the beautifully delineated muscle of his abdomen and hard, flat belly down to the column of throbbing flesh that jutted proudly from the ebony thatch at his groin, like a spear, observing, "You've grown."

He chuckled at the double entendre, unable to smother the deep rumble of amusement that bubbled up from inside him. "And you, beloved Emma, are as naughty as ever. I thank God for that small mercy," he added as he dropped to his knees beside her. "And, my love, for you."

She moistened her lips and cast long-lashed eyes up to his as she took his *ule* in her hands. It was a miracle that anything so firm, so arrogantly erect, should be sheathed in skin as velvety as the softest moss—albeit moss that felt as fiery as the crater of Madame Pele's volcano! She shivered with delight, feeling her *pua,* her woman's flower, grow dewed with excitement as her fingers brushed the pendulant weightiness of his seed sacs, tousling the nest of hair that was like the silky tassels of the corn.

With a low moan of longing, she drew his hand from her breasts and placed it upon her mound instead. Uttering little whimpers, she rubbed herself against his palm before reaching up to curl her arms around his neck and draw his dark head down to hers. As she kissed him, she languidly raised her leg, bending her knee to straddle his thigh and press herself voluptuously against him. "Please . . ." she urged throatily between kisses. "Oh, please, let it be now." Her eyes glinted with violet fires, like shattered amethysts in the sparse light. Her lips glistened moistly as she ran her tongue over them.

"Oh, Lord," he breathed, knowing he was lost while also knowing he'd never forgive himself come morning. In another moment, he'd have reduced the solemn vows he'd made to so much smoke on the wind. He'd be casting honor and propriety aside—but he'd be damned if he cared about anything but having her!

Cradling her head in the crook of his elbow, he lowered her to the long grasses, kissing her slender throat, her swollen breasts, suckling greedily on both hardened peaks as he fondled the silky inner flesh of her thighs. Parting the dewy petals of her woman's flower, he stroked the tiny bud concealed within the velvet folds. How wet she was, how ready to take him! His throat constricted. His breathing thickened with lust and desire. The thunder of his heart was loud as the rolling surf of Laupahoehoe in his ears.

Drawing his dark head from her breasts, he kissed her rib cage, then circled the tiny well of her *piko,* her navel, with the tip of his tongue before tasting the sea-and-flowers nectar of her secret perfume on his tongue.

She stiffened, his erotic kisses igniting tiny explosions of delight throughout her body. As countless little aftershocks rippled through her, she moaned softly and tossed her dark head from side to side, undulating her hips against his mouth as she whispered brokenly, "Oh, Gideon, yes, ooh, yes!"

He became her world as he loomed over her, filling all of her senses. Dear Lord, could anything that felt so blessedly *right* be so utterly wrong?

Grasping her waist, he moved strongly upon her, flexing his hips to fill her and withdraw, fill her and withdraw, over and over again, until she gasped with delight. How darkly handsome he was in the scattered starlight as he loomed over her, she thought dreamily. And how powerful and perfect he felt—hard and smooth-skinned in some places, deliciously rough in others, with coarse, springy hair that prickled her soft skin like tiny spurs. He smelled exciting and very manly, too, a tantalizing mixture of leather and saddle soap, Cuban cigarillos, citrus, and campfire smoke.

Curling her arms about him, she drew him down full-length upon her, wrapped her legs about his waist and showered his face with kisses. Taking his lower lip between her teeth, she gnawed playfully upon it, until the rasp of his husky breathing filled the shadows and she knew he could delay his release no longer.

When his climax came, she raised her hips and he plunged deeper, harder into her fiery heat, surging into her like the mighty sea, ebbing and flowing like the tides, until rapture claimed them, flung them skyward together.

Uttering little cries, she clung to him, mindless with pleasure. The trail her lips had forged across his chest grew wet with the salt of her tears now as she broke down and wept.

"Oh, Gideon, I can't bear it," she sobbed. "I've tried—oh, I've tried so hard to lie, to pretend, but I can't bear it, can't stand knowing we can never be together. Oh, Gideon, Gideon, what shall we do? What *can* we do?"

Twenty-three

They lay side by side on the dew-soaked grass, facing each other. His chest still heaving, his throat aching with emotion, he softly kissed her and held her close, stroking her trembling shoulders. He was wracking his brain, trying to find some words to comfort her when there were none he could offer. There was only one way either of them would ever feel better, and that was if Julia were no longer his wife.

"Don't cry, darling girl," he murmured, caressing her dark hair, brushing a tear from her cheek with the ball of his thumb. "I know what I must do. There's no other way. I must ask Julia for a divorce."

"A divorce?" She leaned up to look at him. "But you can't! What about the scandal? And what about your parents? Oh, Gideon, they'd never forgive you."

"None of that matters. Besides, it's the only way we can be together. Julia and I haven't really been husband and wife, anyway, not in the true sense of the words. Christ, we haven't even shared the same bedroom yet, let alone consummated our marriage! I'll do anything I have to do, Emma—and the sooner the better. I swear it!"

She sighed. "I suppose you're right. There's no other way, is there?" she whispered, drawing a deep, trembly sigh as she hugged him to her.

"None," he acknowledged.

Emma bit her lip, plagued with doubts as she remembered

Julia Kane's hard, calculating expression as she watched Gideon at the *luau*. "And you really think she'll agree to a divorce? As simple as that?"

"Providing I offer her a generous settlement, I have a suspicion she might jump at the chance, yes. After all, it's not as if she ever loved me, is it? We were just . . . lonely that night, I suppose you could say. And one thing led to another. Besides, Julia seems a reasonable woman, from what I know of her. Something of a social butterfly, too. Who knows? She might be overjoyed to leave our sleepy little islands and head back to the bustling cities she loves?"

She frowned, wishing she felt as confident as Gideon seemed to feel. "When will you speak to her?"

He frowned. "In a week or so. I'd like to do it sooner, but I'm needed to take Domingo's place until after the roundup's over, I'm afraid. Poor devil! He lost two fingers in a roping accident the day before I arrived home."

"Yes, poor man. I heard them talking about it at the *luau*."

The life of a *paniolo* was a dangerous one, and such accidents were, regrettably, all too common.

"As soon as I've approached Julia, I'll write to Alexander McHenry and have him get the divorce proceedings under way. You realize it could take months before it ever becomes final? Perhaps . . . perhaps even years?" he warned her.

She nodded. "I don't care how long it takes, not if we can be together someday, as we planned."

"Nor I. We've waited this long. That we're here together now must mean that it was meant to be," he said with a fatalistic air. Then he smiled. "When I've spoken to Julia and set everything in motion with McHenry, I'll ride out to the Waikalani Valley and let you know what's going on."

She nodded, nestled drowsily in the crook of his arm, feeling more at peace than she had in seven long years.

Soon after, though, he tossed her nightgown over her head and carried her—protesting sleepily—back to his horse. He mounted behind her and, leading the mare laden with her belongings behind his horse, he rode with her to the nearest linecamp hut, one similar to that in which Emma had passed the previous night.

Unnoticed by either of them, a shadowy figure shrank back into the dense shadow cast by a clump of thorny brush and prickly-pear cactuses as they rode by.

"I have to be getting back to the herd," Gideon murmured, framing Emma's face between his palms for a lingering farewell kiss. "Stay here tonight. It's safe and dry, and no one will bother you."

"All right. Gideon . . . ?"

"Yes?"

"I love you."

He smiled. "No more than I love you, *ku'uipo.*"

"*Aloha,* my love," she whispered as he rode away.

Standing in the hut's low doorway, she waited until she could no longer hear the silvery jingle of his *kepa pele,* his bell spurs, ringing out sweetly on the stillness and shadows. Only then—starry-eyed as some silly, lovesick maiden—did she stretch out on a woven sleeping mat and gaze up at the sequined heavens framed by the open doorway, hoping with all her heart she'd spy a falling star to wish upon.

But as she star-gazed, a pale, feathered form drifted low over the range instead. Emma heard the piercing, *"Puwheeet! Puwheet!"* as an owl passed over the little hut, and her dreamy languor evaporated.

The *pueo* was the *aumakua,* or animal totem, of her mother's family, she remembered as the owl disappeared. She shivered. Surely its appearance must be a warning? An omen of some misfortune to come?

Twenty-four

"Julia?"

The look of surprise and pleasure that lit her face as he came up the veranda steps caught him unawares—and riddled him with guilt and foreboding. Christ Almighty! What he'd suspected before he left was true. Julia had begun to care for him in some small way. Her shining eyes, her glowing cheeks, her radiant smile as she hastened to meet him—they all said so.

"You're back!" she exclaimed breathlessly.

He nodded. "Can I take it that smile means you've forgiven me?"

"For what?"

"For the quarrel we had before I left, for one. Remember? And for being gone much longer than I'd planned, for another."

"Oh, that. Consider yourself forgiven, sir," she murmured with a pretty incline of her head that made her crystal earbobs sparkle in the lamplight. Casting a sharp glance at him, her smile wavered. She frowned. "Is everything all right, Gideon? You seem . . . edgy somehow. There's nothing the matter, is there?"

He shrugged and drew a cigarillo from his shirt pocket, startled that she'd sensed his true mood, despite his casual tone. She could read him far more easily than he'd thought. His hands shook as he struck the match, the flame shimmying in a sudden chill breeze. *Enough small talk! Tell her now and get it over with, man!* his conscience urged, and he knew it was right. He was only postponing the inevitable unpleasantness. But somehow, he couldn't find the words to say what he had to say, *if* there were any "right" words to ask one's wife for a divorce, which he doubted. "I'm just worn out, I guess—not used to a cowboy's tough day anymore. After the past three weeks, even the war seems like a quilting bee by comparison!" He grinned ruefully. "But never mind the ranch. How did you fare in my absence?"

"Very well, thank you, Gideon. Mother Kane and Auntie Leolani have been kindness itself. They've been showing me how things are done here in the islands, as well as teaching me a smattering of Hawaiian words. I must confess, despite my misgivings, I've quite enjoyed their company. To be honest, there was only one thing that spoiled the past two weeks for me . . ." She stopped short and lowered her eyes, as if embarrassed to continue. "Never mind. It isn't important."

"Well, if there's anything I can do to make amends, I'll do my best . . ." She seemed reluctant to confide in him, but why? Dare he hope, by some miracle, she'd realized their marriage was a mistake? he wondered guiltily. Could she be trying to tell him she wanted to leave him? Not likely! He'd as much chance of that happening as of a Kane steer jumping over the moon!

"I was going to say that I've . . . missed you, my dear," she murmured demurely, unable to meet his eyes. "Missed you very badly, in fact. But I'll have you all to myself for a while, shan't I? With the cattle drive over?"

Seeming embarrassed, she crossed the veranda to stand before him with her head bowed, then went up on tiptoe to shyly kiss his cheek. He smelled so fresh and virile, a tantalizing combination of sun-dried linens, soap, and citrus. His hair was still damp and tousled, inky waves clinging to his nape as if he'd bathed only moments before coming up to the house. "I've been giving our marriage a great deal of thought while you've been gone, darling. And I realize now how very foolish I was to be jealous of your past loves. You're a man, after all, and you have certain—certain desires that I have failed to satisfy as a proper wife should. I promise that will change, my dear. I'm ready now to be your wife, in every way." Her lashes fluttered up, then swept coyly down. "You were right that night, you know. We were little more than strangers when we exchanged our vows. But we must still try to make the very best of our partnership. That 'fresh start' we agreed upon before you left . . . ?"

Dry-mouthed and sick at heart, he tightened his jaw and nodded. "Yes?"

"I want it, too, my darling. *Very* much. If you agree, we could start tonight, by celebrating our . . . honeymoon?"

That look of breathless expectancy, her flushed face, the almost feverish glitter of her eyes, needed no translation. *She wanted him.* Her body echoed the invitation with a silent yet eloquent plea of its own. Her breasts rose and fell voluptuously against the gray silk of her gown. Her lips were slightly parted and moist, as if but awaiting his kisses. An odd thought struck him. Was this how she'd looked the night he'd staggered—roaring drunk—up the staircase of his uncle's house? Had she been waiting for him at the top of that steep staircase, her lips red and glistening, her eyes feverish and excited, her breasts heaving, as they were now? Damn it, she looked almost *predatory!*

He wracked his brain, but not so much as a shred of memory surfaced. Nor was there even the slightest stirring of sexual response in his loins. Perhaps he'd wanted her then, but all desire for her was gone now.

She read his indifferent expression, and her face burned. Damn him! Damn him to hell and back! Rather than taking her in his arms, kissing her, doing the things a new husband should want to do after such a titillating suggestion from his bride, Gideon did nothing, said nothing—and his total indifference was far worse than any outright rejection. Moreover, she saw a dark flush fill his face, and realized that he was not only unmoved, he was angry, so angry he could barely contain his displeasure.

"Julia, please, not now," he snapped, flayed with guilt and

furious at himself. "If there was ever a time for us—and to be frank, my dear, I doubt there ever was!—it's far too late now. To be honest, that's what I wanted to discuss with you tonight. Just . . . just sit down, would you? We have to talk, immediately. It can't wait another moment."

Alarmed by his ominous tone, she sat, choosing one of the rattan peacock chairs his mother favored. Perched on the edge like a flighty bird about to take wing, her narrow back ramrod straight, her hands clasped primly in her lap, she appeared outwardly composed, but inwardly, her thoughts seethed. Had he learned something? she wondered, uneasy tentacles of dread unraveling in her belly. Did he mean to confront her with what he'd found out, was that it? Nervously, she wetted her lips. Perhaps she'd been right in thinking Sheldon Kane had seen through her pose back in Honolulu? She searched her memory, trying to recall if any letters had arrived for her husband from Oahu? Maybe that old lecher of a sugar planter had been doin' some pokin' and pryin' into her past? Could be he'd written to tell Gideon what he'd found out? she fretted, trying to still the uncontrollable trembling in her knees and hoping against hope her husband couldn't hear her heart thumping.

He moved a matching chair directly in front of hers, and sat so that their knees were almost touching. Damn, but he was a handsome son of a bitch, she thought, with that inky black hair falling loose over his brow and wearin' that brooding, sulky expression. He was so darned big and dangerous and moody-looking, she felt a shivery quiver of response deep in her belly, like the flicker of summer lightnin'.

"Please, get this over with, darlin'! You're frightening me," she cried, her voice a little shrill. *Calm down, you danged fool!* she chided herself silently. Whatever Gideon might say or do, she still had a trump card left to play, an ace-in-the-hole that would serve her well, 'less she misplayed it.

His brows rose. He shot her an intent look. "Why the devil would you fear me?"

"Well, I—I don't, exactly," she covered. "It's more that—that I fear *losing* you, I suppose, because—because I have some news to tell you, too, Mister Kane, just as soon as you've told me yours."

"News?

She nodded and forced a brittle smile. "Good news, I hope."

"I see. Then perhaps you'd prefer to begin?" he offered gallantly.

She shook her head. "No. Please, go on."

"Very well." Although he'd been seated less than a minute, he sprang to his feet and restlessly paced the *lanai* like a jaguar pacing its cage, finally halting with his fingers hooked over the wooden railing. He gazed blindly up at the darkening mountains as he chose his words. Moonlight threaded his ebony hair with filaments of silver, and struck steely blue glints in the gentian depths of his thick-lashed eyes, she saw, and her heart ached. "I—er—I really don't know where best to begin, my dear, except to assure you that when I offered you marriage, I did so because for me, there *was* no other possible course to take, given the manner in which I was raised. In the years since leaving home, both as a college student and later, as an officer in the Union cavalry, I prided myself on being a man of integrity, of honor, principle and discipline . . ." He looked down at his feet, then swung about to face her as he added, "Till now."

It took a second or two for his meaning to sink in. When it had, her mouth twisted. Her eyes filled. "Aah. Then that explains it. I should have guessed, after the *luau*. You want to end our marriage, don't you, Gideon? It's her, isn't it—that's why you were gone so long? You've been meeting that—that *hula-hula* dancer."

Rather than sounding upset or accusing, she sounded peculiarly resigned and saddened, instead, he thought, and was at a loss to respond. It would have been easier if she'd flown into a rage, or wept and clawed at his face and hair. Violence he could have dealt with, but this crushed, *accepting* air was far, far worse.

"Emma had nothing to do with my absence, as such," he denied, feeling guilty as hell nonetheless. He avoided her eyes as he added, "As I told you, I had work to do, an injured ranch hand to replace." He drew a deep breath. "But you're right about Emma being the reason I needed to talk to you this evening. Now that it's out in the open, there's no sense in beating around the bush, so I'll come straight to the point. I'm still in love with Miss Jordan, Julia. I want a divorce."

She heard the words as if from far away, and was vaguely surprised by the conflict they provoked. Relief was uppermost, certainly. Relief that Gideon was clearly no wiser about her wicked past than he'd been before! The second emotion was totally unexpected, for it was the hollow, chilly feeling of . . . of rejection, of loss. And pain. Oh, yes! To hear him confirm that he didn't want her hurt far, far more than she'd ever dreamed it could, or would.

"No!" The single word leaped from her lips without conscious thought. She repeated more softly, "No."

His features hardened. "Julia, I know you're angry and hurt right now, and who could blame you? But perhaps a divorce would be best for both of us in the long run? It's not as if we've ever loved each other, after all. And you deserve far better from life than a husband like myself, who—through no fault of your own—cannot love you as you deserve to be loved."

"You want me to believe you give a tinker's cuss about what *I* deserve? Why, you patronizing son-of-a-bitch!" Her expression was scornful, withering, as she turned to look at him. "The hell you give a damn about my welfare!"

He flinched. A muscle twitched at his temple. The refined woman he'd married could sure cuss like a trooper! "Let's try to keep this amicable, shall we? I'll—er—provide the legal grounds you'll need in order to procure the divorce, naturally, but . . . I'm urging you to initiate the proceedings immediately."

"Are you, indeed? Well, that won't be necessary, *lover.* You see, there will be no divorce," she hissed. "Not . . . not now, not ever," she added in a low, despairing tone.

"Julia, be sensible," he barked. "Do as I ask and set us both free."

"And I told you, I can't!" she ground out hoarsely, springing to her feet and whirling on him with her gray eyes blazing, her fists knotted at her sides.

"You mean, you won't!" he bellowed.

"No. *I cannot*. It's impossible."

"You prefer being trapped in a loveless marriage to freedom? You'd rather spend the rest of your days bound to a husband you care nothing for, than be free?"

"No, I don't! But leaving you is an option that's no longer open to me, Gideon. Nor does the fact that I've grown to care for you have any bearing on this issue. The fact is, I have . . . the well-being of another to consider now."

"Another?" He stared at her, understanding slowly dawning. He could hear the rush and roar of his pulse in his ears; the slowed "thud-a-thud" of his heartbeat. And, as if from a great distance, he saw her nod.

"That's what I was going to tell you. My 'happy' news!" She smiled bitterly. "I'm carrying your baby, Gideon."

"I'm carrying your baby, Gideon." The words echoed over and over in his mind, combined with a peculiar sense of unreality, as if time itself was suddenly grinding to a halt.

She laughed at the expression on his face. "Such a murderous look from the expectant father?" she accused in a too-shrill, sarcastic tone. "Shame, shame, *Papa* Gideon!"

"Does *Makua* know?" he demanded hoarsely. It was all he could think of to say. Julia's announcement had winded him like a punch to the belly; taken him totally unawares, though why it should have, he really didn't know. He'd known there was a chance Julia could be *hapai*—carrying his child—from the first. Hell, it'd been the main reason he'd proposed marriage! Unfortunately, he'd chosen to forget that possibility after he and Emma had made love, and he'd sworn to end his marriage, once and for all.

"No, I haven't said a word yet. But I know both she and Father Kane will be delighted. I—I wanted you to be the first to know. Oh, Gideon, be as angry at me as you wish, but please, don't be angry about our baby!" She caught her lower lip between her teeth, and her eyes filled with tears. "That night we shared—the night our baby was created—was so wonderful! But I swear, I never intended that it should trap you like this! Oh, it's all gone wrong, hasn't it?" she cried. "It's all my fault!" She buried her face in her hands and wept noisily.

Guilt hit him like a fist to the gut. Her sobs flayed his conscience. "Julia, please don't cry," he gritted, drawing a large white kerchief from his breeches' pocket and thrusting it at her.

"I'm trying not to, but I can't . . . can't seem to help it lately." She sniffed, then dabbed at her eyes. "I've had so much time to think this past fortnight. I've been praying you'd be happy about the baby, despite everything. Hoping you were missing me a little—perhaps might have decided being married wasn't so very t-t-terrible, after all."

"I am happy about the baby, in many ways," he hedged uncomfortably, patting her shoulder. He couldn't bear the way her lower lip trembled, the way her brimming eyes reflected the chimney lantern's tiny flame.

"It was you who suggested a 'fresh start,' remember?" she reminded him. "I thought you'd forget that native girl, that everything would work out. Stupid little ole Julia! I really believed your empty promises . . ." Her voice trailed away in a gusty sigh, but her unspoken accusation hung on the hush like a foul miasma.

"Julia, what are you trying to say?"

"That I expect you to honor your wedding vows, sir, if nothing more!" she flared. "Perhaps it was naive of me, but I fell for the 'honor and decency' speech you made after your aunt . . . surprised . . . us together. Well, I don't intend to be naive or gullible any longer! I have a baby and its future to consider. Now, you may have your little half-breed slut, if that's what you want. But a divorce? Your freedom? Hell, no, sugar! You can go whistle for that!" Eyes blazing, she turned to go inside.

"Wait! Hear me out first."

"Go right ahead," she snapped without turning around, tapping her foot on the wooden boards.

"I'd be willing to make you a settlement, in return for an amicable divorce and the custody of our child. Ten thousand dollars, Julia. What do you say? Ten thousand, free and clear! At least consider it, won't you?"

He heard her draw a shaky breath—or was it a gasp?—and for a fleeting second, fancied he saw a glint of pure greed in her eyes as she turned back to face him. He hadn't misread the signs, then. The gut instincts that had served him so well during the war were still sound. Beneath Julia Lennox Kane's cool, ladylike exterior beat the greedy, gold-digging heart of a fortune hunter!

Julia mustered a scornful grin and tossed her fair head. "Now, why in the world would I accept a li'l old settlement like that, when this here ranch must be worth a hundred times that much? As your lawful wife *and* your baby's dotin' mama, I can live like a duchess for the rest of my life, sugar. I can have just about everything my li'l ole heart desires, can't I?"

"Anything but me, yes," he acknowledged curtly, his jaw hard, his lips compressed to a thin, straight line.

As she looked up into his stern, handsome face, she felt again that tingling heat in her belly—the intensely sexual hunger she'd felt when he climbed the stairs to her side earlier, and knew a sharp pang of regret before she thrust all notions of love aside. Who needed love, anyway? Love was for fools, like her ma, like the trusting little girl she'd once been. Her pappy'd always claimed he loved her more'n her sisters, and look at the misery his brand of "love" had caused her!

"Really, now?" she purred, her hands on her hips, her head cocked to one side. "But the way I see it, I already *have* you,

Mister High-and-Mighty Kane." She pouted. "Leastwise, all of you I'm ever likely to want! Let's see. I already have your name, don't I? And come year's end, I'll have your little baby, too, hmm? So, I reckon I'll have to say, Thank you, but your offer is declined."

Again, the nerve ticked at his temple. "Is that your final answer?" he rasped.

"I'm afraid it is. About as final as Judgment Day, sugar. Good night, now!"

She fluttered her fingers at him, then swept inside the house with a soft rustle of silk skirts, closing the door noiselessly behind her.

Twenty-five

Tipping back his *lauhala* hat with its band of velvety purple *po'okanaka,* or pansies, about the crown, Gideon mopped his sweating face and reined Akamai in for a brief respite.

They'd had a hot and hazardous ride down into the almost inaccessible Waikalani Valley. By his reckoning, they'd more than earned a rest. Drawing a slim black cigarillo from his hat band, he struck a match to the end and inhaled deeply, enjoying the smooth tobacco flavor on his tongue and the fragrant aroma of smoke in his nostrils while he gathered his thoughts.

Sitting there that way, enjoying a smoke and planning his next move, reminded him of the lull that came in the moments before a battle—and the "skirmish" ahead of him promised to be a fierce one, he thought heavily. He'd have preferred to make a judicious retreat, but flight wasn't an option he'd left himself. No, sir. He'd promised Emma he'd let her know the outcome of his talk with Julia, and—since he was a man of his word, if damned little else these days—here he was, just one week later, wishing to God he could be anywhere *but* here, bearing almost any news than the one he carried!

Shiiit! Scowling, he shook his head, feeling a little easier. Cussing never failed to lighten his mood or help him blow off steam. He supposed he had his stern missionary upbringing— and Auntie Leo's repeated mouth-washing with lye soap—to thank for the vicarious pleasure an occasional cussing bout always gave him. Uttering a few juicy, choice expletives under his breath, he crammed his hat back on his head and looked curiously around.

Though he'd lived most of his twenty-six years in the islands, he'd never ridden down into this remote little valley before.

At one end, he saw, Waikalani opened out to the sea, glimpsed as a slash of vivid turquoise ruffled with white surf between the two steep *palis,* or cliffs, that embraced it. It could be approached only from the seashore, or as Gideon had approached it—by means of perilously narrow, man-made tracks. Worn by time, weather, and countless hooves into jagged precipices, these were a scant two-horses'-widths across—little more than ledges that zigzagged crazily back and forth down the sheer valley walls.

It was a breathtaking descent at the best of times, he judged, even for those seasoned valley-dwellers who were accustomed to making the climb down to the floor way below, and had a head for heights, besides. In bad weather, when flash floods, mud, and rushing rivulets would make the going slippery, and treacherously loosen stones and crumbling earth that could give way and lead to falling, it would be suicidal even to attempt it.

At the valley's farthest end, a waterfall cascaded fifty or sixty feet down over huge black boulders to a broad, clear pool below, surrounded by delicate maiden-hair ferns and mosses. The valley proper was long, narrow, and picturesque, lush with papayas, palms, breadfruits, candlenuts, and many other varieties of trees. Creepers, ferns, and leafy bushes grew profusely between them, but even from this distance, Gideon could make out the schoolhouse Emma had described, rising from among the tangle of vegetation.

It stood out simply because it was more a pavilion than a true *hale,* or house, with a sturdy wooden post at each corner, but there were no walls between them. It was roofed with *pili*-grass thatching for shade and shelter. The airy, open design would take advantage of the slightest cooling breeze to be had in the hot and humid months of summer, yet protect against all but the heaviest winter downpours.

Squinting against the sun that slanted between the valley walls, he realized he could make out three or four low wooden benches and a teacher's desk arranged neatly beneath the thatching, as well as a globe and a blackboard set upon an easel.

As he clicked to Akamai to carry on, the schoolchildren—boys clad in an assortment of colorful shirts and cotton drawers, girls in long wraparounds of patterned calico or baggy chemises, and almost all, boys or girls alike, wearing flower *leis* about their necks—trouped back under the shelter and stood in a line, their hands clasped demurely before them.

With Emma's nod, they began singing a hymn in Hawaiian. Their sweet, high voices rose like a choir of angels on the morning air, filling the length and breadth of the valley with glorious song that harmonized with the tumultuous music of the falls.

Above the angelic chorus, he could hear the voice of *his* angel, dressed in a dark-blue, ruffled *muumuu* this morning, her glossy black hair swept up and adorned with a circlet of feathery crimson *ohia* blossoms. Her pure, liquid voice soared above the children's on the golden wings of the morning, a heavenly soprano that sent thrills down Gideon's spine and made his heavy heart feel fit to bursting with its burden of sorrow and guilt. *How can I tell her?* he wondered for the hundredth time.

Again, he slowed his weary old horse to a walk, then a standstill on the dirt path leading down into the valley proper. He leaned over his saddle horn, and surveyed the tranquil scene below him. *In God's name, how can I ever give her up?* he wondered.

Several neat little grass huts were scattered about the edges of the small clearing where the schoolhouse stood. Beyond them, he could see the dark green of *taro* patches and the low moss-rock walls that divided the planting areas from each other. Whitewashed wooden fences enclosed grassy paddocks where several glossy horses of various colors were grazing, lazily flicking their tails as they nipped at the long grass. Stubby banana trees grew alongside thickets of spindly bamboo, while spiky-leafed pandanus trees perched gingerly on tall aerial roots, masquerading as pineapples. Wild hibiscus shot crimson flames through the greenery, while an occasional rose-red *ohia* pompom, or the vivid blue of the morning glories, or else the pristine white of coffee or guava blossoms, flirted a rainbow of colors among the leaves.

If there was in truth an earthly Garden of Eden, Gideon fancied this little jewel of a valley was as close to it as any mortal man would ever come. And the predicament in which he found himself? Aah. It was a veritable hell—albeit one of his very own making . . .

"Aloooha! A glorious morning, is it not, sir?" a hearty voice rang out on the sultry air.

Startled from his misery, Gideon glanced up. Another rider had followed him down the narrow track, a tall, husky fellow astride a pretty chestnut mare.

"Glorious indeed, yes," he agreed with a curt nod of greeting, gaping at the newcomer's formal attire.

Although obviously part Hawaiian, the fellow had made no concession to the tropical heat, nor to the arduous descent he'd undertaken just moments before, nor to what must surely have been a lengthy ride even before that, given the valley's remote location! Rather, he wore a black wool frockcoat over a starched shirt with a winged collar, a perfectly knotted cravat at his throat, and wool trousers. Despite the stifling ensemble, however, not a drop of sweat stood out on the man's brow or upper lip, as one might have expected. Nor did he appear in any way overheated or uncomfortable. Indeed, he would have been perfectly at home in any proper Beacon Hill parlor, were it not for his *paniolo*-style boots! His own coral shirt and black breeches seemed suddenly uncouth, far too casual. "I don't believe I've had the pleasure, Mister—?"

"The name's Wallace, sir. Charles K. Wallace of Laupahoehoe, to be precise, at your service. And may I say what a pleasure it is to finally make your acquaintance, Mister Kane!" He kneed his mare alongside Gideon's horse, swept off his broad-brimmed felt hat and extended a firm hand to Gideon, which the latter gripped with rather more force than civility required.

But, to his chagrin, Wallace didn't so much as wince! Rather, he returned Gideon's handshake with a formidable grip of his own and continued effusively. "I'm with the Native Schooling Board, you know? A sort of roving headmaster, one might say! I make my rounds each month, offering guidance and leadership to our teachers in outlying schools. In many instances, those dedicated souls are virtually isolated from the community at large for months on end. It's my duty to remedy that isolation with my visits."

"Are schools so numerous in the islands?" Gideon asked, genuinely surprised. Before he'd left for Boston, there had been few schools for native children, except those of the *ali'i*, royal blood. The school his father had built at Hui Aloha for the children of his ranch hands had been an exception, rather than the rule.

"Indeed there are, I'm happy to say. It is the Native Schooling Board's solemn undertaking to ensure that every child in the Sandwich Islands be able to read, write, and speak the English language."

"The *English* language? To expect proficiency in a second language is an ambitious goal, surely?"

Wallace smiled. "Perhaps. But the children's families are required to refrain from using the Hawaiian tongue at home, and our teachers sternly chastise those children who transgress in their presence, of course."

"Oh, of course," Gideon agreed in a scathing tone, his approval of the schools rapidly dwindling. "And, if the Board has its way, no doubt in a generation or two, our island children will be quite unable to speak their own language?"

"You have it exactly, sir! We can only hope and pray we shall be that successful in our endeavors," Wallace agreed with a wistful smile.

Gideon smothered a snort of disgust thinking the man a pompous ass. Did Wallace take himself so damn seriously, he couldn't tell when his leg was being pulled, let alone see that, like the dodo, the Hawaiian culture they shared was destined for extinction, once the language was forever lost? "By the way, Wallace," he demanded, irritated, "how is it you know me, when we've never met before?"

Charles smiled. "The entire island's still abuzz with the news of your return, Mister Kane. At every stop I've made this month, I've been regaled with descriptions of your lovely bride and yourself. Come, come. Don't look so dumbfounded, sir! It's only to be expected. You're an island son, after all, and the people love you, just as they love your father and your charming mother. In fact, I'd determined to visit Hui Aloha for myself in the near future, both to pay my respects and to offer my congratulations on your marriage. Then I learned just yesterday that additional felicitations are in order, are they not, sir?"

"Additional felicitations?" Gideon scowled blankly at him.

For the first time, Charles Wallace appeared uncomfortable. He coughed, blushing beneath his dusky complexion. "Perhaps I am in error, then? I was told your lady wife is—hmmph—that is to say, that you and your dear lady are to be blessed with a—er—new arrival?"

"What? Oh! The child, yes! Er—thank you."

Charles Wallace beamed, and nodded vigorously. His broad, handsome face—reflecting the finest of both Hawaiian and white bloods—fairly radiated intelligence, good humor, congeniality. So why, Gideon wondered saltily, quirking a moody dark brow at the man, did he have the sudden, overwhelming urge to plant his knuckles square in Wallace's middle? Or better yet, in the perfect center of that smiling visage? *Ah, why, indeed!*

". . . coming down, or going up, Mister Kane?"

"Your pardon, sir?" he ground out. "You said . . . ?"

"I asked if you were just coming down into the valley, or on your way back out? If coming down, I urge you to accompany me to the schoolhouse. Miss Jordan, the new schoolteacher here in Waikalani, is a shining example of what an education can do for our island daughters. Indeed, I would not be prevaricating nor exaggerating were I to say that, in my earnest opinion, our dear Miss Jordan would not be found lacking in any American drawing room in the land. As well you know, sir, one's ability to converse intelligently with one's peers is the truest test of what an education can do for one. Not only does knowledge nurture the starving intellect, but the very possession of knowledge bolsters one's self-confidence immeasurably, and adds a certain quality of—oh, poise, polish and refinement to the character, that may be lent by nothing else. Indeed, I venture to . . ."

Gideon let the monotonous stream of conversation flow over him unheard. One could wish that Wordy Wallace, the human hot-air balloon, would just keep on talking until he floated up and over the valley walls, and thence out to sea, one could! A sudden nightmare vision of Emma—*his pansy-eyed, laughing Emma!*—tucked primly into a marriage bed with the verbose Charles Keali'i Wallace, assailed him. He groaned inwardly. Wallace's stuffy manner and proper expectations would stifle Emma's open, sensual nature, smother her natural charm and vivacity as effectively as he'd insist she hide the lush, ripe beauty of her golden body under yards of flannel and calico. An image of them entwined beneath a tangle of sheets rose up to taunt him. But, damn it, what business was it of his who Emma married anymore? He had no right to be thinking this way. And surely, if he loved her, *truly* loved her, he'd want what was best for her, if he couldn't claim her for himself? A happy life with a good man who would cherish and admire her . . . and Wallace certainly admired her. Ha! Who was he trying to fool? Wallace *loved* her!

". . . Mister Kane? Sir? Excuse me, sir?"

"Yes?" he barked, glaring at the man.

"Would you care to? Accompany me, that is? I'm sure you'd

enjoy hearing the *keikis*—er, the children—recite their times tables for you?"

"Perhaps another day, Wallace. One when I've more time to spare. I was—er—just leaving the valley, you see. Good day, sir." He tipped his hat.

Sweat dripped from Gideon's brow as he turned Akamai's head, touched heels to the horse's flanks and rode quickly away. More sweat greased his palms as he gave the stallion its head. He let the nimble Mauna Kea bronco pick its own way up the sheer *pali* walls, for he was in no condition to take charge, not feeling as he did. The sweating had nothing whatsoever to do with the height, nor the steep cliffs that dropped away behind his horse's hooves. *Hell, no!* Coward that he was, he was running from Emma. Running, because he couldn't find the courage to tell her, face-to-face, that Julia was carrying his child, and that because of his obligation to that innocent child, he would never be free.

A sudden gust of wind threatened to tug the hat from his head. Roughly cramming it down, Gideon kneed Akamai up a steep, rocky little slope. As he did so, a blustery breeze caught the fragile flower wreath about the hat's crown, lifting it as if it were some exotic, velvet-winged bird. It tumbled slowly, over and over, until it reached the sparkling stream way below. From there, the current carried it away.

"You compliment me with your proposal, Mister Wallace," Emma said stiffly, "However, I'm afraid my answer is unchanged. I cannot marry you."

Wallace's face dropped. "Emma, please! You really must reconsider. If not for your sake, then for Mahealani's."

"Mahealani's?" Emma's gaze narrowed.

Wallace nodded. "Your little sister needs a home, a settled, Christian home with a proper father and mother."

She bristled, but could not find it in her heart to be truly angry with Keali'i. He was always as pompous as a peacock. "My . . . Mahealani has a perfectly good mother, Keali'i. *Me!* And before me, she had my cousin Anela and her husband Kanekoa as her foster parents. Or did your fancy schooling in Boston teach you to despise our old custom of *hanai?*" she demanded a trifle sharply, challenging him. *Hanai* was the old Hawaiian custom of fostering children. It ensured that every child was raised by parents who wanted him. In this way, orphaned children were cared for and frequently, women who already had several children of their own would bear children for couples who were barren, handing the infants over to their new mothers soon after birth. Such children, like Mahealani, were dearly loved.

"There's no need for you to snap at me, Emma. I wasn't criticizing your care of the child. Quite the contrary, in fact. You've been a model mother—and schoolteacher—since your own mother's passing. But wouldn't you welcome having someone to take care of you, for once?" he coaxed, his resonant voice husky now. "Wouldn't you enjoy being a cherished wife and helpmate, an adoring mother to your own babes?"

For a moment, Emma saw herself in both roles only too well— but it was as Gideon's cherished wife, and as the mother of *his* babes she imagined herself, not Keali'i Wallace's. However worthy and decent Wallace might be—and he was, in all respects, a fine, decent man—Keali'i struck no sparks in her soul when he said her name, unleashed no rivers of fire to race through her veins like molten lava with a single glance. In fact, comparing the two men was like comparing lightning to a—match!

"Someday I'll marry," she answered his question in a gentler tone. "But not yet. Not now."

"And not me?" he added stiffly, unable to look her in the face.

"No. I'm afraid not." She touched his cheek, her violet eyes filled with pity.

Flinching, Keali'i turned his head from her. "I've always wondered . . . Is there someone else, Emma?"

Her lashes swept down like sooty fans to veil her thoughts, but she nodded.

"Ah. I see. And how long have you know him?"

"Years, Keali'i." She sighed. "Many, many years."

"Did you know him before you agreed to our betrothal?"

"Yes. Long before then. But I warned you the betrothal could be nothing more than a charade on my part, remember?" she reminded him. "It was for my mother's peace of mind, nothing more."

"I remember. You were always honest about it, I'll grant you that, dear girl," he acknowledged, to her relief. For a moment, she'd been afraid he was angry, and it had saddened her deeply to think she would lose his friendship. "I'm afraid the fault was in me, darling girl. You see, I was so certain I could make you love me, in time."

He sounded so forlorn, so bleak, her heart went out to him. "Thank you for your understanding. Kea . . . ?"

"Yes?"

"You've become my dearest friend. I wish with all my heart it could be otherwise between us." It was no lie. Her life would have been immeasurably simpler had she fallen for Keali'i Wallace rather than Gideon Kane!

"I met Gideon Kane riding down to the school."

With a gasp, her head came sharply about, as if jerked by a string. For a single, crazy second, she thought she'd actually said Gideon's name aloud. "Gi—Mister Kane?" she echoed.

"Yes, indeed," Keali'i confirmed, tightening a leather carrying strap around a half-dozen primers. The tight set to his lips betrayed that he was using idle conversation and excessive attention to small details as a means of hiding his disappointment over her refusal, recovering his composure. "One can't help but wonder what a busy rancher like Mister Kane would be doing way out here?"

She smothered the sudden, wild flutter in her breast and reached up to smooth her hair, aware as she did so that her hand was trembling, and praying Kea wouldn't notice. Was he just idly curious, or did he suspect there was something between them? "Mister Kane is here, in the valley?" she asked.

"Was," Kea acknowledged absently. "I happened to be riding down into the valley as he was heading back up. Rather an impatient fellow, I thought. Brusque almost to the point of being rude. But, I suppose war could do that to a man, I'm afraid I didn't like the fellow overmuch. Why, I barely had time to congratulate him before he thrust his way past me and rode off!"

She steeled herself not to run outside and scan the valley walls. "Congratulate him? Oh! On his marriage, you mean?"

"His marriage, certainly. And that he's to become a father for the first time in the New Year. Hadn't you heard? The first Kane grandchild is on its way! Needless to say, the Kanes are delighted."

She felt suddenly faint, dizzy. The Bible she was holding slipped from her nerveless fingers, landing with a noisy thud on the matting spread across the earthen floor, just inches from her bare toes.

Like a wooden puppet, she bent and retrieved the weighty volume before Keali'i could do so, just as Meahealani skipped into the schoolhouse, yelling her name and hopping from one foot to the other. "Yes? What is it, Mahealani?" she managed to say.

"Look what I found! It's a *lei po'okanaka,* Kaleilani—your favorite! It was just floating in the stream, so I caught it, just for you!" Carefully the little girl lifted the dripping flower garland over Emma's dark head, her small hands settling it prettily upon Emma's shoulders. The pansies' thoughtful little faces glowed velvety-gold and amethyst against the dark-blue of her *muumuu,* making a pretty frame for her long, curling dark hair and lovely, pale face.

"Maikai! Good!" Mahealani cried. Her dark eyes were shining, her pink lips curved in a delighted smile. "You look *sooo* pretty, Kalei!"

"In English, if you please, child," Charles K. Wallace scolded, waggling a stern finger at the child.

"It is lovely," Emma murmured, glowering up at Keali'i as she took the child in her arms and hugged her. She tried to smile for the little girl's sake, despite the band that was growing tight about her throat, the awful weight in her breast, but she failed miserably. There were tears stinging behind her eyes and she felt suddenly weak, faint and old, as if she'd been very, very ill for a long time. "Thank you, Lani. Thank you very much," she whispered. She hugged the little girl fiercely—far more fiercely than the gift of a *lei,* however beautiful, usually warranted.

Mahealani returned her embrace just as fiercely, to Emma's relief, for when the full import of Keali'i's casual remarks hit home, it was only the child's loving arms, wound tightly about her, that kept her from falling apart.

Twenty-six

Julia was scowling as she swept off the broad-brimmed hat Miriam Kane had loaned her to mop her perspiring face. Shading her eyes, she looked first to east then to west across the rolling plains that stretched, green and unbroken, to the distant mountains. Nothing but cattle and more damned cattle, mounted Kane *paniolos,* and the occasional wind-stunted tree from here to where the blue sky met the distant Pacific in a hazy band! It weren't exactly fox-huntin' country, but then, she weren't exactly a Baltimore belle!

A whole month had come and gone since Gideon had asked her for a divorce, but in those four weeks, something real peculiar had happened—something she surely hadn't bargained on happenin' in a month of Sundays. After twenty-three years of using her looks and her body—and her sharp wits, too—to get what she wanted out of life, she'd gone and fallen head over heels in love with her own husband—a man who, by his admission, wanted no part of her. It was darned near funny, 'cept it hurt too damn' bad t' laugh.

Over breakfast the morning following Gideon's return, his parents had mentioned that he'd gone back to the herd. Using the comment as her cue, she'd burst into tears, flung down her napkin, and escaped to her room. As she'd expected, Miriam Kane had followed her.

"May I come in?" she'd asked after tapping at her door. "I'd really like to help, my dear, if you feel a need to confide in someone?"

Her performance as the frightened, pregnant wife, forsaken by her uncaring husband in favor of his work, would have received encores in the San Francisco playhouses! As it was, poor, unsuspecting Miriam—thrilled at the prospect of becoming a grandmother—swallowed the whole sad story, hook, line, and sinker. And, in her gentle, proper way the part-Hawaiian woman tried to comfort her daughter-in-law without being disloyal to her only son.

"I agree that Gideon's behavior has been unforgivable, my dear girl, but try not to judge him too harshly. Some men have great difficulty in sharing their wives with anyone—even if that someone should be their own little child. Perhaps Gideon thinks you won't have time for him anymore, or that you'll lavish more affection on the baby than you will on him. It isn't that he doesn't love you anymore, Daughter, I'm sure. He's just . . . confused. And time will take care of that," she'd reassured Julia with a smile. "You'll see. The next time he comes home, he'll be tripping over himself, trying to show you how very sorry he is."

"Do you really think so?" she'd whispered tearfully, playing her role to the hilt.

"I *know* so. Now, come. Dry your eyes, *'ipo,* and we'll go back downstairs. You can tell Father Kane your wonderful news while you're finishing breakfast. After all, you're eating for two now, are you not?" she'd added, smiling in a joyful, irrepressible way that had tweaked Julia's conscience just a tad. "Look outside! It's such a glorious day! Tell me, do you enjoy riding?" she'd asked suddenly.

Julia nodded. "I've ridden since I was a child."

"Good! Then I'm sure a leisurely morning ride on a placid mount won't hurt you now, and besides, the fresh air will put the roses back in your cheeks. Come, girlie! After breakfast, I'll take you exploring!" She'd laughed with the infectious gaiety of a much younger woman, and to her surprise, Julia had found herself caught up in Miriam Kane's excitement.

"Weell, all right—if you're sure it won't affect my condition?" she'd inquired with just the right amount of doubt and hesitancy, though the notion of a day spent away from Bible readings, putting up guava and mango conserves, baking bread, or darning, was an appealing one.

"*Auwe!* You know how much I've looked forward to having my first grandchild, Julia! Would I let you do anything that would harm that precious baby?"

She'd smiled. "Of course not, Mother Kane."

"Our Hawaiian *wahines* ride right up until they're ready to give birth, but I think we shall be more cautious where you're concerned, darling Julia. I'll have old Moki saddle you a steady little mare," she declared, dropping a kiss on Julia's brow.

Julia had warmed to the obvious affection in the older woman's voice, and slipped her arm companionably through her mother-in-law's own as they went back down the curving *koa* staircase to the dining room.

Despite getting off to a bad start at the wedding feast that first night, they'd since become . . . well, friends, she supposed you'd say. In fact, in the short time she'd known her, Miriam Kane had been more of a mother to her than her real mama'd ever been!

She and Miriam had gone riding each morning after that, coming to look forward to each other's company and their little forays into the glorious countryside surrounding the ranch house.

With her mother-in-law as her guide, Julia had explored wondrous flows of black lava that looked like rivers of dark chocolate, frozen forever in time. Though rarely given to marveling at Mother Nature's handiwork, she'd been amazed by the delicate ferns that struggled to push their way up through the cracks in that desolate black wasteland to unfurl tender green fronds in the sunshine beyond, in a powerful testament to the tenacity of life.

In other places, cascading waterfalls leaped massive boulders to join crystal pools way below in soapy bubbles and silver eddies, each pool having its own pretty legend of this god or that goddess, and their wondrous or mischievous doings. Julia listened, enthralled, for Miriam's legends—told in lilting English interspersed with an occasional Hawaiian word—were akin to the fairy-tales her mama had told her and her brothers and sisters on cold winter nights as they huddled in their cabin, before Mama'd gotten too worn down from birthings to bother with such foolish things as fairy tales.

On other days, she and Miriam had hitched up their skirts and gone splashing through the warm shallows, leaving their footprints upon pristine beaches of sugary white sand, beaches that embraced azure bays maned with coconut palms and pandanus, or lined with windbreaks of ironwood and sea-grape trees.

In Miriam's care, she'd discovered the delicious taste of sweet wild guavas, crunchy little mountain apples, and tangy peaches eaten straight from the tree, and the pleasure to be had from camping out. They'd cooked heaps of the tiny freshwater shrimp they'd netted while wading in the shallows of a freshwater pool, and seasoned their catch with a few crystals of rock-salt before frying them over an impromptu fire and devouring the results of their labors as if starved! She'd also learned the restful pleasure of lying on her back amidst a carpet of lush grass and staring up at the bluebell sky, doing nothing more pressin' than picking out cloud castles or stately clipper ships from the billowing cumulus!

This past week, however, Miriam had begged off from their daily outings to pay her customary visits to the sick and old folks of the village nearby, most of whom had worked for Jacob Kane at some time or another, or been employed on one of the sugar cane plantations hereabouts. Julia had been genuinely disappointed but had prettily refused Miriam's invitation to accompany her on her good-will visits. Instead, she'd resumed the riding excursions alone, yielding to her hunch that Gideon was meeting his native chit out here on the plains somewhere. She'd decided to find out for herself.

She'd been riding out here alone ever since, ostensibly to watch the *paniolos* roping and branding the three-year calves but secretly trying to catch her husband with the Jordan girl. So far, though, she hadn't caught Gideon doing anything more circumspect than rolling on the ground with a bawling calf, and cussing more than any missionary grandson had any right to cuss!

And then, two days ago, just when she'd decided she was wasting her time—not to mention blisterin' her rump on a saddle, day in and day out!—she'd noticed someone else doing some spying—a man watching *her!* The sneaky varmint had ducked down into the tall grass as if he didn't want to be seen when he'd noticed her looking his way. The same thing had happened the following day, and again this morning, and so she'd decided to follow him, and find out exactly what he was up to.

She turned just in time to catch a glimpse of him before he vanished over a low hill. The set of her mouth and jaw hardened. *Oh, no, you don't, mister—not this time! You're up t' no good, you sneaky varmint—and I aim to find out what!*

Wrenching her horse's head around, she dug her heels into the animal's sides and lit out in the direction she'd last seen the man. She reined the horse in at the top of the rise just as he vanished once again—this time into the rain forest.

Smiling grimly, she cantered the gelding down the verdant, grassy slope to where the trees and forest vegetation began, guiding the animal down a little path that opened out between them, bordered on either side by a tangle of lush vegetation.

The greenery closed around her as if a huge mouth had swallowed her up. It sure was a far cry from the hills she'd grown up in. Exotic and kind of spooky now that she was all alone, without Miriam to point out this plant or that fern, and tell her their Hawaiian or Latin names.

Small, brightly feathered birds warbled and trilled on the still, humid air. Honey-creepers, she thought Miriam had called them. They seemed to swim to and fro through light so golden-green, be darned if it didn't seem like it was liquid, for the towering trees, lush ferns, and leafy creepers tamed and mellowed the sun's fiery brilliance. She glanced up and gasped. *Hallelujah Jesus!* The leafy treetops almost met above the forest floor like a tunnel, only scraps of azure sky showing between them. For a moment, she had the eerie sensation that a trap was closing about her, or a cage. Or jest maybe, the bars of a jail cell?

The farther she rode—the gelding plodding sedately down the meandering track—the denser the vegetation became, the closer and more humid the air, and the stronger her feeling of unease, until, completely without warning, a large clearing opened up all about her. At its heart was a low wall of craggy rocks with a smooth, open area between them. On this raised area, someone had placed strange-looking bundles of *ti*-leaves.

She reined in the horse and sat there in the deafening silence, her pulse throbbing in her ears. Gooseflesh shimmied down her arms, and a slow trickle of sweat slid down her spine to pool at her tailbone. *Great day in the morning, what in the world was this place?* she wondered. *A shrine of some kind, like an Injun burial place? The ruins of a temple where them bloodthirsty kanakas had once come t'pray? Or maybe . . . jest maybe, where human sacrifices had been made to their savage gods?* Yessiree, that was it, she reckoned. Granny'd always claimed she had a touch of the Sight, and right now, be damned if the back of her neck weren't pricklin' something fierce, as if a haint was walking over her grave.

As she slowly skewed sideways in the saddle to scan the foliage that ringed the clearing, her horse snorted and shied, either scenting her own disquiet or reacting to the brooding atmosphere. She glanced over her shoulder to see if there was anyone about. No one. Skittish just the same, she decided, to hell with the man. She'd hightail it out of this spooky damn jungle. Ride—lickety-split!—back out into the bright, safe sunshine of the plains. But just then, a raucous whistle made her head snap around as if jerked by a cord.

Splashes of hectic color filled her pale face, but it was indignation rather than anger that painted them there. *Damn him!* While she'd thought herself following that sly critter, somehow the sidewindin' polecat'd managed to double back and come up behind her! Scowling, she looked down her nose at the man, who was lounging against a lichened tree that had huge lavender sprays of orchids dangling from its branches.

A battered woven hat with a fancy golden-pheasant feather *lei* about the crown was shoved well back on his head. Below it, his face was creased in a cocky grin as he insolently looked her over. His deep-set eyes had a wealth of cunning in their depths—and made her feel bare-assed naked, besides, darn him!

About forty-five years old, she supposed some kind of woman might find his craggy, weathered good looks kind of purty—her kind of woman, come to that! He stood a lick taller than most, besides, and though leaner than her husband, she reckoned he'd stand eye to eye with Gideon, if it came to toeing the scratch.

"How dare you whistle at me that way," she accused, playing the lady of the manor for all it was worth, while trying to tamp down her rising excitement.

Close up, his piercing gray eyes were hooded by a shaggy shelf of brows that had been bleached almost white by the sun. His thick, drooping mustaches were the same color as his wavy hair: dirty-blond streaked with darker nicotine stains. He wore a neatly patched and darned gray shirt with the sleeves rolled up, exposing wiry forearms—sprinkled liberally with glinting blond hairs—that he crossed over his chest. An equally tanned and hairy vee of flesh showed between the unbuttoned fronts of his collarless shirt. His breeches were of worn brown corduroy, tucked into shabby black boots that had seen better days, she noted, while his suspenders were of braided leather. All in all, his rough-and-ready good looks spelled danger with a capital D—and sent a tingle down her spine that'd beat the band!

"Seems to me if you can stare, I can whistle, eh, luv?" he drawled, scowling up at her. "And I whistle when I bleedin' well please."

Her cheeks burned. "Oh, you do, do you?" she countered, eyes flashing as she belatedly realized what he must have said while she was staring at him. "Hell, we'll jest see about that! Do you know who I am, mister?"

She didn't like the slow, sly smile that curled his lips as he answered, "Aye."

"Good. Then you know you're trespassing, too? This here's Kane land, and I'll thank you to get the hell off it, Mister . . ."

"Jordan. Jack Jordan. But, you can call me Jacko, luv." He winked. "All the . . . leddies do." He heaved himself away from the tree and strolled toward her horse, his thumbs hooked casually through his suspenders. His stride was long, loose, unhurried. He seemed supremely confident that she would not ride off before he reached her. And, much as she itched to do just that, for the hell of it, she didn't.

"I'm not your 'luv,' " she bristled, then added pointedly, "If you must call me something, you may call me Missus Kane. Missus *Gideon* Kane."

"May I, indeed?" He smirked. "Ta ever so, luv. That's terribly good of you, old girl. But begg'n yer pardon, mum, if it's all the same t' you, I reckon I'll just call you . . . Joolie," he decided at length.

Why, the son-of-a-bitch was laughing at her! His eyes were glinting like wet stones, his grin broadening into a wolfish leer as he looked up into her startled face and added, "seein' as how we're chums already, eh, *Missus* Kane?" He puckered his lips and made a rude, juicy kissing sound.

"Chums? Why, I've never met you before! I don't know what you mean by chums."

"The hell you don't, Julie darlin'. When a gal follows a strange bloke for three days in a row, well . . . she don't want to ask him the time of day, now, do she, eh?" He winked.

"Me, follow you?" Don't be absurd! I've done nothing of the sort. I saw you loitering by the pond. Since you were acting suspiciously, I decided to follow you and find out what you were up to. When I get home, I'll inform my husband that you were trespassing on Kane land! He'll—"

"Aww, bullshit!" Jordan growled. All traces of good humor gone, he spat into the lush grass and added, "Bugger yer bloomin' husband!".

"Whaat?"

"You heard me, ducks. I know your sort, see? And you won't say nuffin' about havin' run inter old Jack, 'less I miss my mark."

"Why on earth wouldn't I?"

" 'Cos if ye did, you'd have to explain wot you were doing all the way out here, alone, wouldn't yer? And you'd rather ole Gideon didn't know his little wife's been spyin' on him, *right?"* As he spoke, his voice took on a lower, threatening timbre. He put his hand on her knee and squeezed.

His fingers burned through the cloth of her riding skirt. "Get your dirty paw off me," she ground out, forgetting her fancy accent. Her heart was leaping about in her breast like a skewered bullfrog, but it was no more than a token resistance on her part. Overcome by a peculiar lethargy, she stared at him, making no attempt to swat his hand away, nor move out of his reach, let alone ride off. Rather, she watched him like a scared little bitty, frozen in place by the hypnotic eyes of a snake.

"Make me!" he challenged. Reaching up suddenly, he dragged her from her horse to stand in the loose circle of his arms, laughing when she shot him a withering glare. "See, Jules? You an' me, we're cut from the same cloth, we are," he murmured. His eyes feasted on her outraged face as he stroked her cheek, snickering when she flicked her head away in distaste. "I knowed it the second I set eyes on you! You can put on airs, darlin', but inside, where it counts, you're no better than old Jacko. I can smell it on yer, like cheap perfume." So saying, he closed his eyes and inhaled. "Aaah."

Her eyes hardened. Her mouth clamped into a thin, angry slash, she ground out, "Fancy airs? I don't know what you're talking about." But once again, she made no move to escape the hand that rested familiarly on her hip, not even when it began stroking back and forth, brazen fingers grazing her buttocks.

"Aw, come off it, Joolie. I've seen your sort before, ducks, back in Sydney Town. Maybe you're a mite higher-priced than them little lovelies, but you're no foine leddy neither—I'd stake me bleedin' balls on it!"

"Then you'd be gelded!"

"Would I? Come on, duchess. Spill it! Tell old Jack wot yore up to, eh? Start wiv how ye tricked Kane's son inter making an honest woman o' you, eh?" He glanced down at her belly. Flattening his palm against it, he taunted, "Told him ye had his bun in your hot little oven, did yer, darlin'? Made the poor sod pay for his poke with a ring—am I right, luv?"

"I did no such thing. Gideon . . . Gideon loves me," she protested lamely, her momentary outrage ebbing under Jordan's damnably *knowing* grin. Blast his eyes, it was as if he could see straight through her! Could strip away her carefully cultured layers of gentility with those sly gray eyes, to expose the hillbilly gal beneath! "How dare you insinuate otherwise!" she added for good measure.

"Love, my arse," Jack scoffed. "Him sniffing after your skirts—now, that I'd believe. But Gideon Kane *loves* my Em, not you, girlie. I've seen 'em, together, see?"

He winked, leaving her in no doubt as to what he'd meant by seeing them together, and despite everything, his words stung. The silly, fragile hope she'd nurtured—of somehow making Gideon love her—withered up and died.

"You've seen them?" she breathed, and died another little death when he nodded.

"I have. Lots of times. In the forest. On the beach. In abandoned huts—strewth! Like rutting animals they are. They don't care."

She swallowed. "You said, *your* Em? What is she to you, then? Your wife?" she demanded woodenly. It didn't matter who she was, not anymore. Not really, she told herself, fighting tears, trying in vain to swallow the lump in her throat. She was just curious.

"Wife! Nah. Em's me daughter, she is. Emma Kaleilani Jordan. Prettiest little *hapa-haole wahine,* half-white girl, in all the bloody islands she is, if I say so meself. But willful, *oi, oi,* proper willful, she is. Disobeys her old da, she do. I've a mind to teach her a lesson she'll never forget." His pupils contracted and his cold eyes took on an odd, hot glitter when he spoke his daughter's name.

"How touching," she mocked, misreading his expression for one of paternal pride. "Somehow, I'd never have taken you for a doting father."

"Nah? Then what would you have . . . taken . . . me for, then, eh, darlin'?" Jack asked softly, ducking his head so that his hot breath fanned her earlobes, stirring the wispy tendrils of pale-blond hair about her temple.

Despite herself, excitement streaked through her like a bolt of lightning, white-hot and searing. "A coarse, beer-swillin' brute, that's what," she shot back, her voice smoky. She tossed her head seductively, her expression challenging. "A sidewinding snake, half varmint, half polecat. And those are your good points."

He snorted with laughter. "Well, happen you're right, at that, duchess. There's some gels wot likes their blokes as smooth and sweet as butter—and others what likes 'em rough and coarse—the rougher, the coarser, the better! Excites the little lovelies, it do," he added, wetting his lips and eyeing her through slitted eyes.

"The hell you say so?" she grinned. "Well, I purely hate t' disappoint a gentleman, but I ain't one of them."

"Int ye, luv? Really and truly?" Gazing deep into her eyes, he put both arms around her and splayed his fingers over her buttocks. He squeezed hard as he jerked her up against him, laughing at the sudden wildness in her eyes when she found herself pressed up against the swollen ridge at his groin. "Oooh, I'd say you were all that. All that, and a whole lot more, Joolie darlin'."

"What are you getting at, Jacko?"

"That you're a clever li'l bitch. One clever enough t' get herself hitched to that Bible-thumpin' Jacob Kane's son. But—what t' do about it now? Young Gideon and his da control every penny o' that lovely money, don't they?" She nodded. "Papa Jacko could help you to get some for yerself, if ye'd let him?"

"Why would you offer to help me? And why in the hell would I accept?"

"Why I'd help you is easy. See, I've got no more liking for them high-and-mighty Kanes than you have, luv—not since our brave soldier-boy started sniffing after my Em's skirts seven years ago, an' stirrin' up trouble for me in the doing. That son-of-a-bitch—he hadn't been back home in the islands a month when he'd talked my Em into burning me out of my house and home! I seen 'em together afterwards, laughin' at me!"

"And what sort of cut would you expect in return, Mister Jordan?"

"Me? Aw, I'm easy, as blokes go. Easy as pie! I wouldn't ask nothin' you wouldn't be more than willin' t' pay, Miss Julie. In fact, I believe you might be . . . eager . . . t' pay the price I'm asking." He opened his mouth and lewdly waggled his red, fleshy, wet tongue at her. "Must get terribly lonely in that big ole bed, night after night, eh, darlin'? Lovely young thing like you, all alone, while your husband's orf playing with his bleedin' beeves?"

It was Julia's turn to laugh now, and laugh she did, a bawdy, smoky chuckle that smacked of raucous saloons and bordellos, rather than genteel Baltimore drawing rooms. "You're a sly son-of-a-bitch, Jordan! Still . . . I admire a man who gets straight to the . . . point." So saying, she reached down between them, found the bulge at his groin, and squeezed hard.

He winced, then grinned. "And that int all ye'll like about me, neither, lovie," he murmured, husky-voiced in anticipation as he took her by the hand. Casting a hard, hot glance over his shoulder, he added, "Follow me . . ."

Leaving her horse tethered to a bush, he led her down a muddy, winding path, bordered on both sides by leafy vegetation. He didn't stop until he reached the mouth of an enormous lava tube, like a huge cavern, its entrance almost hidden by lush ferns and creepers.

She was smiling like a cat as she ducked dangling vines and sidestepped lofty ferns to follow him deep into the lava tube.

Jack Jordan gazed dreamily into space as he unfastened his breeches and noisily relieved himself against a tree trunk. His gut instincts had been right, he thought with a grin. Hoity Toity Missus Julia Kane had shed her ladylike manners and her haughty ways along with her drawers. She'd been hotter than a bleedin' volcano when he'd had her, clawing and mewling for more like a bleedin' she-cat in heat.

As he buttoned his breeches, he wondered what Kane would have done if he'd surprised ole Jacko tupping his bride, giving her what he'd stopped giving her himself, if half of what Julie'd told him about their marriage was true.

"I had her, Kane," he told the trees. "Ye hear me? Old Jacko tupped your bride good and proper, he did. And you know what, old son? She loved every bleedin' minute of it!" he murmured, and chuckled.

Afterward, Julie had told him about her past, confirming his suspicions that she was not what she appeared to be. Strewth— Jacob Kane'd have a fit, if he knew the sort of woman he had for a daughter-in-law! And he reckoned Gideon'd choke the little bitch with his bare hands, if he ever found out Julie'd tricked him into marrying her!

He was about to go back to the lava tube, and tell Julie to shift her scrawny arse back to Hui Aloha, when the jingle of someone's bell spurs sounded above the call of the honey-creepers and the muffled roar of the distant falls.

Startled, Jack squatted down between some ferns and low bushes and squinted down the path. He groaned inwardly as he recognized the husky rider coming toward him. *Kimo Pakele!* What the blue blazes was the ranch foreman doing way out here? Looking for him? Nah. As far as Pakele knew, he'd been behaving himself! More likely the foreman was chasing down a stray bull . . . the same scrawny black brute he'd butchered last night for his supper. He frowned. It wouldn't do to be caught redhanded with all that jerked beef drying over a smoky fire in the back of "his" lava tube—nor that fresh skin he was working on.

He waited until the *luna,* or foreman, had ridden on—passing not three feet from where Jack crouched—then returned to the lava cave he had called home ever since Emmie had burned his huts down around his ears. His eyes darkened to slate. It was a spiteful act she'd done—one for which he fully intended to bring her to account, sooner or later, whether he was her rightful father, or nay.

Julie was dressed, he saw, though her eyes still held the drugged, glazed look of a contented woman.

"Jacko!" she purred, coming toward him, her hips swaying. She pouted like a little girl. "You were gone ages . . ."

He caught her wrists before she could touch him. He didn't want no one touching him, not even Em. *"Oi! Oi!* You'd best scarper, ducks! Kimo Pakele's snooping about. Go orn, go home like a good little gel, 'fore he finds your horse and starts wondering where you are. And Missus Kane . . . ? Don't forget yer drawers, eh, luv?" he added, nodding at the puddle of lace-trimmed lingerie on the gravelly, gritty floor. His laughter echoed down the cavern.

Retrieving the garment, she stepped into it, lifted her skirts, and pulled her pantalets up as she grumbled, "I don't want to go back."

"I know, luv," he crooned, catching her around the waist and resting his chin on her shoulder. "But it won't be for long, not now we're partners. Remember our plan?"

She nodded. "Yes. But I'm scared, Jacko. What if somethin' goes wrong. We could wind up in—"

"Pipe down!" he hissed, his finger pressed to his lips. "Pakele's nearby, remember? And don't even think about it going wrong. Believe me, luv, it won't, not if we both do our parts right," he soothed her, massaging her shoulders. "Just find the paper for me, find a way t' get Jacob Kane out here, and I'll do the rest."

She wetted her lips. "You won't hurt him, Jacko? I know he's a Bible thumper, but he's been real nice to me."

"Hurt him? Me? 'Course not! Gideon won't hand over no ransom if I hurt his da, will he, you nitwit!"

"Noo, I reckon not. But what about later? When Gideon brings you the money?" She hated herself for caring what happened to her husband when he'd proven he didn't care one little bit about her, but she did. Somehow, she couldn't seem to help it. She'd started loving him the moment he'd promised to marry her, believing he was saving the tarnished reputation she'd lost years before. Countless men had used her, but not one of them had ever given a damn about her or her reputation, till him.

"If we play our cards right, he won't suspect a bleedin' thing. I'll sail to Honolulu with the loot, and then, after a month or two, you can leave your husband and join me there." He grinned and chucked her beneath the chin. "From Honolulu, we scarper t' the land of opportunity—*America!* Now, don't forget t' look for the note I signed. All right luv?"

She nodded, wetting her lips. "I promised I'd find it, didn't I? I'd better get on home now, though. If that damn *kanaka's* looking for me, it won't do for him to find us together."

"You're bloody right, there, luv. It wouldn't do at all! Now, chin up, there's my girl," Jordan urged, giving her a shove in the small of her back. "An' good huntin'!"

With a nervous smile, she left him.

She saw no sign of Kimo Pakele until she was about a mile from Hui Aloha, and was so deep in thought about everything she and Jack had discussed, the plans they'd made, the risks she would have to take to pull those plans off, that she didn't see or hear Kimo's horse until he reined his mount in level with her own.

"*Aloha*, Missus Kane," he greeted, tipping his *lauhala* hat to her. It had a pretty band of ferns and rosebuds about the crown.

"*Aloha*, Kimo."

He frowned. "Is everything all right, Missus Kane?"

"Why shouldn't it be?"

He shrugged. "I was chasing a runaway steer through the forest when I saw your horse. There—uh—there was no sign of you, missus, so I figure, maybe he threw you?"

"No, not at all. I just rode a little farther than I'd planned, and dismounted to stretch my legs. My . . . stroll took me through the forest, that's all." She shrugged, dismissing the matter as unimportant, before adding, "*Mahalo*, Mister Pakele. I appreciate your concern."

"More bettah you stay away from the forest, missus. There's an escaped convict living in the lava tubes there. Besides, the tubes and the sacred altars nearby are *kapu*—forbidden to outsiders and foreigners by the *kahunas*, the Hawaiian priests. Even *Makua* Kane would never think to trespass there, unless the *kahunas* wished it."

"Really?" Her brows rose, as if in surprise. "Well, I saw no signs of any escaped convicts or *kahunas*, so you have nothing to worry about. However, if I had run into Jordan, I'd have been quite able to take care of myself. I was riding long before I learned to walk, Mister Pakele. You need not concern yourself for my safety around horses."

"Maybe, missus, but I think Mo'o—Mister Gideon—he no like you riding way out here, all alone. You get baby to think about, no?"

"As I said, you need not concern yourself further on my account, and I meant it, Mister Pakele," she ground out. "And furthermore, if I hear you've been worrying my husband unnecessarily about my safety, I'll be very angry." She glared at him. "Now, that's an end to the matter. Good *day*."

With a toss of her fair head, she rode off toward the house, leaving Kimo staring after her retreating back.

Jordan, she'd said, although he hadn't once mentioned the runaway convict's name! Now what, he wondered, frowning, was the *haole wahine's* real reason for leaving her horse and wandering into the forest on foot? If she *had* run afoul of Jack Jordan—as he was beginning to think she had—why on earth would she deny it, then angrily insist he not worry her husband with his concerns for her safety? The *haole wahine* definitely had something to hide, he was almost certain, but what . . . ?

It was almost dusk the following day when Jack Jordan returned to the lava caves he called home. As he ducked to enter, he saw a bundle of something wrapped in *ti*-leaves placed in the very center of the opening, and recoiled. *Strewth, no!* A native *kahuna* must have left the bundle as a warning, he realized.

Sweat broke out on his brow and palms. He looked furtively over his shoulder, almost collapsing with terror as a lean, brown-skinned old Hawaiian man, wearing a flowing white *tapa* cloth over one shoulder, stepped from the shadows of the lava tube as if emerging from the dark walls themselves.

"Moki?" he whispered, his voice a croak with fear.

"My name does not matter. It is my message you must heed. I have come to warn you that this place is *kapu*—forbidden to you, Jack Jordan. It is a holy place, one which has been sacred to my people for many lifetimes, a place where the bones of my royal ancestors have lain hidden and undisturbed, protected by the *kapu* sticks, till now. You have defiled their sacred resting place with your presence, Jack Jordan. You have disturbed their bones and their spirits. Like the woman, Kaleilani, whom you once called daughter and sought to defile, these caves are forbidden you! *They are kapu!* Go from here! Go, and guard that you do not break the sacred taboos henceforth, or it will go badly with thee!" Moki's voice, imperiously raised, echoed eerily down the caverns.

Jack needed no second urging. Abandoning his braided leather work, the jerked beef that would have fed him for a month or more, and the last of his possessions, he fled without looking back.

Twenty-seven

"Where are we going, Kaleilani?" Mahealani demanded. "Is it still far?"

"We're going to the beach and to visit Auntie Momi. Remember, I told you? And no, it's not much farther now. Are you hungry?"

The little girl nodded.

"We'll eat our picnic as soon as we get there. And then if you're good, we'll ride the mudslide, just like Auntie Anela and Uncle Kanekoa used to do, when they were little."

"The *holua!* Really? Oh, yes!" Mahealani exclaimed, her dark eyes sparkling. "Pikake and Kamuela love sledding. Why couldn't they come with us, Kaleilani?"

"I thought it'd be fun if we had a day alone together, just you and me. Are you having fun?" Mahealani nodded. "And are you missing your cousins?" Mahealani thought about it for all of a second before she shook her head vigorously. In her excitement, she squirmed like an eel on the saddle. Emma laughed and tightened her grip on the child. "Careful, little *mo'o,* or you'll fall and hurt yourself. I know what! If you'll promise to sit still, I'll tell you a story—my favorite legend about Poli'hau and Pele. Would you like that?"

"Uh huh," Mahealani agreed solemnly. She leaned back contentedly against Emma, one damp pink thumb tucked in her mouth, lulled into a state suspended somewhere between waking and sleeping by Makani's even, rocking-horse gait as the mare plodded sedately along.

They were riding the winding trail that followed the island's coastline, having left the Waikalani Valley at the gulch, where the river, colored dark red by the soil, poured into the sparkling, deep-blue ocean. They'd passed the mouths of several other cultivated valleys since then, all much like their own little valley, where villages of dried-grass huts dreamed in the tropical sunshine, looking like shaggy beige mushrooms amongst the dark-green of the taro patches. In these villages, banana, breadfruit, and papaya trees grew lush and heavy with fruit, and lovely, sparkling streams unraveled, emerald and silver ribbons snaking between green forests of sugarcane on their winding journey to the ocean.

The trail followed the curves of the shore wherever possible, and was fringed with a tangle of guava bushes, Christmasberry and haolekoa, while kiawe bushes, lantana, and sea grape grew closer to the rocky beaches themselves. Sometimes, the trail snaked in and out of a canefield for a mile or two. Then they rode down a red dirt track through an avenue of rustling green, razor-sharp stalks that towered high above them. In a week or two, the canefields would be burned so that only the tough sugar-containing stalks of the sugarcane remained, making the crop much easier to harvest and transport to the sugarmill. When the fields were burned at night, it was a breathtaking spectacle, red and orange flames leaping skyward and roaring up to consume the cane, orange embers swirling and showering down like confetti in the darkness, the blaze silhouetting the plantation workers who patrolled the carefully regulated blaze. Running here and there and waving their arms to issue directions over the roaring, popping, and crackling of the fire, they looked like the celebrants of some ancient ritual in honor of the fire and volcano goddess, Pele.

"Well, now. Where shall I begin the story, I wonder?" Emma

considered aloud, knowing from experience what answer she'd receive.

"At the beginning!" Mahealani crowed as always, clapping her hands in delight and grinning merrily.

"All right, then. Here we go. You can listen, too, Makani, if you'd like," she added politely, "As long as you promise you won't interrupt." Mahealani giggled at the silly idea of a horse interrupting anybody, although the mare twitched her ears and solemnly nodded her head, as if she'd understood every word Emma had said. "Very well. Now, as I'm sure you both know," Emma began, smiling, "Poli'hau is the beautiful goddess of the snows, whose glorious cloak of white feathers mantles the peaks of Mauna Kea, the White Mountain, way up there." She pointed to the snowcapped peaks in the distance that slumbered beneath a head garland of fluffy clouds.

"But *Kumu* Wallace says—I mean, *Mister* Wallace says—that our gods and goddesses aren't real," Mahealani said, turning to look up at Emma's face so she could judge her teacher's reaction to this tidbit. "Mister Wallace says there's only one *akua,* spirit, but that it has three parts—God the Father, God the Son, and God the Holy Ghost. He told us anyone who believes anything else is a 'godless heathen.' "

Emma's brows rose. Her lips compressed in a vexed line. "Mister Wallace said that?" It seemed she would have to have a stern word with Keali'i!

"Uh huh. It was right after he scolded *you,* the last time he came to our *kula*—remember? It was the time he—Mister Wallace—said you mustn't let us count or sing in Hawaiian ever again. And then he said we have to use English *aaall* the time, even if the English words are hard to remember." Pouting, her lower lip jutting mutinously, she sighed as if she carried all the worries of the world upon her small shoulders. "I don't like Mister Wallace. When he scolds us, he makes my *opu,* my tummy, hurt. And when he comes to the valley, all the good feelings inside me go away, Why do we have to do as he tells us, Kaleilani?"

Emma frowned as she considered her answer, silently consigning her well-intentioned but pompous friend to a place somewhat hotter and much farther south than the Sandwich Isles. "Well, one reason is because Mister Wallace is a school inspector. He and other people like him are in charge of the schools here in the islands. I know you don't think so, but we're very lucky to be able to learn to read and count and learn things. Years ago, even before I was born, several very clever people came together. They decided what would be best for everyone in the Sandwich Isles, and our kings agreed that it would be a very good thing for the children of our islands to go to school and learn. And so, we do as they say."

"Even if it doesn't feel good in here?" the little girl asked huskily, her tiny hand pressed to her heart.

"Yes," Emma confirmed doubtfully, feeling both touched and guilty when she thought of the religion, culture, and government her mother's people had already been persuaded to abandon for the American equivalents, in the name of progress and enlightenment. "Even then, darling, unless following instructions could hurt someone in some way, of course."

Mahealani scowled. "Thinking in English hurts me—it hurts my head really, really, really bad."

"That's not what I meant, and you know it, missie," Emma said sharply, trying not to smile. "You have to learn English, and that's that."

"But *why?*"

"Because all of the books you'll study as you grow older are written in English, that's why. And besides, it's the rule, and if none of us obeyed rules or followed laws, and did just what we wanted to do, then things would go very wrong. Some people would do bad things, and then other people would be hurt. After all, even games have rules, don't they, and so must the things we do each day." It was a drastically simplified explanation, she knew, but enough for a seven-year-old to comprehend.

"Hmm. I s'pose so," Mahealani agreed, pursing her lips and scratching her nose. "Kaleilani, was Mister Wallace very cross with you when he left the valley?"

Surprised, she shook her head. "No, darling. Mister Wallace is my friend. He's really a very nice man. And—he wasn't cross with me at all." *Although I rejected his proposal of marriage.*

"Then why were you crying after he left?"

"I wasn't crying," Emma denied, crossing her fingers over Makani's reins so the lie wouldn't count, as she'd done as a child.

"You did, I heard you! You were crying all night, just like when *Makua* Malia died. Did somebody else die, Kaleilani?"

"No, sweetheart, no. Nobody died. It's just that . . . Mister Wallace told me some sad news that upset me. It wasn't about anybody dying, or about us singing or speaking Hawaiian, or anything like that, so you mustn't worry."

"Oh. Was it about the man in the red shirt, then? The *paniolo* who dropped the *po'okanaka lei* that I found in the stream?"

Emma's heart clenched. "The *paniolo?* What—what color was his horse?"

"It was gray, and big."

So, Mahealani had seen Gideon that morning and perhaps, with an intuition far beyond her years, she had guessed he had something to do with her Emma's sadness. *Dear Lord, was there nothing those sparkling dark eyes missed?* she wondered ruefully, remembering the broken garland of velvety purple-and-gold pansies the little girl had found at water's edge below the zigzagging trail leading out of the valley and brought to her.

"Did you like the pansy *lei?* Is that why you kept it?"

"Yes, Miss Ni'ele, Miss Nosy! Now, you've asked quite enough questions for the time being, I do believe! Do you still want to hear the legend, or not? Speak up, mynah bird!" she urged, grinning. "Yes or no?"

Mahealani nodded vigorously.

"All right, then." Emma cleared her throat and prepared to start over. "Well, now, as I was saying, the snow goddess, Poli'hau, loved to come down from the mountains once in a while so that she could go sledding down the *holua,* the mudslide, with the ordinary people. In fact, she loved sledding so very much and went there so many, many times, she became very good at riding the mudslide from the *veeeery* top . . . to the *veeeery* bottom," she explained, gesturing with a graceful hand to show just how long and steep the mudslide was. "But then, one day, another goddess decided to join in the fun! This goddess was very tall and graceful, with long red hair. She wore a head *lei* of crimson *lehua* blossoms and red *ohelo* berries. Can you guess her name?"

"Madame Pele, the volcano goddess!" Mahealani supplied, jiggling about.

"Right again! Yes, it was none other than the wonderful goddess, Madame Pele herself," Emma agreed in the solemn manner of a storyteller. "Now, beautiful Pele also loved to show off and prove how well she could ride her sled down the mudslide from the veeeery top to the—"

"Veeeery bottom!" the little girl supplied.

"Yes! And so, before very long, the two goddesses were trying to outdo each other. 'Look at me! *I'm* the best!' one would boast. And then the other would say, 'No, you're not! *I* am!' "

"Auwe! It's naughty to boast, isn't it?"

"Not really naughty, but it *is* bad manners, yes," Emma agreed, stroking Mahealani's glossy dark hair and smiling down into her earnest little face. "The Bible says we should 'hide our light under a bushel,' remember? That means if we do something good, no matter how wonderful it is, or how proud we are, we should be modest and say nothing that would draw others' attention to it."

The little girl wrinkled her nose. "But that's silly. How will Auntie Anela and Uncle Kanekoa and everybody know how good I can make my alphabet letters or 'member my Bible verses 'less I tell them?"

Emma dropped a kiss on her head. "Because *I'll* tell them all about the wonderful Mahealani and her ABC's, and it won't be boasting because *you* didn't tell them! Now, what about the story? Can I go on, Miss Chatterbox, or do you have yet another question to ask me?"

"Ummm . . . go on!"

"Well, at last the two goddesses, Poli'hau and Pele, challenged each other to a competition. The contest would decide once and for all who could slide most gracefully, who had the longest ride, and so on. But, no matter how many times they rode, and how hard Pele tried to be the best, it was always Poli'hau who was cheered the loudest; Poli'hau who was praised the most by all the people watching them. Soon, Madame Pele grew very jealous of the snow goddess's popularity. In fact, she became so angry, she caused her great volcano to erupt with a mighty roaaar and a terrible rrrummmmbling of the earth!"

"Auwe!"

"Auwe, indeed! Black smoke and ashes poured across the sky until it was no longer blue, but black as the darkest night. Then lava flowed from Pele's fire pit in a great, smoking red river that chased poor Poli'hau back up the mountain to her snowy *hale* in the highest summits of Mauna Kea."

"Auwe! Poor Poli'hau! Is that the end of the story?" Mahealani asked in a disappointed tone. She'd obviously favored the victim.

"No, impatient one!" Emma teased, ruffling Mahealani's dark hair. "Because, you see, beautiful Poli'hau had quite a temper, too—in fact, she was very like someone I know, hmm? Poli'hau was so furious that Madame Pele would try to banish her, she used her own magical powers to cover Pele's fiery lava flow with a freezing feather cape of pure white snow. Then she raised her hands to the sky and summoned the icy winds of the north and the swollen storm clouds to help her. Together, they forced Pele's lava flow to turn back. Then the volcano goddess herself had no choice but to retreat! Her lava, the smooth lava flow that we call *pahoehoe,* swept back down the mountain, through that gulch you can see up ahead," she pointed, "and from there it flowed out into the ocean. When it had cooled, a large, flat point shaped like a *lau,* a leaf, was left. So it was that Laupahoehoe Point was born."

"I'm glad Poli'hau won. I like that story," the little girl declared. "Will you tell me another?"

"Later, perhaps," Emma promised, reining in her horse. Dismounting, she lifted Mahealani down after her. "I'm starved, aren't you? First, we'll eat the picnic our cousin Anela packed for us. Help me carry everything into the shade. And then . . ." she paused, smiling down at the child.

"And then we'll go sledding?" Emma nodded. *"Maikai! Maikai!"*

"Yes! It will be good fun—very, very good fun!" Emma agreed, hugging the little girl and planting a kiss on the tip of her nose.

Her face dropped. "But . . . oh, Kaleilani, we forgot! We have no *papahalua."*

"Maybe we don't have a sled—but we still have something to slide on."

"We do?" The girl's button nose crinkled adorably.

Emma nodded, wanting to smile. "Uh huh. We have *these* to slide on," she said teasingly, patting Mahealani on the bottom.

The little girl collapsed onto the grass, giggling helplessly, her small hand clamped over her mouth to stifle her chuckles.

Laughing herself as she tethered Makani to a bush, Emma unstrapped the saddlebags, swung them over her shoulder, and took Mahealani's hand. "Come on," she urged, pointing to a grassy spot shaded with purple-flowering lantana and long-needled ironwoods. "Last one there's a stinkbug!"

This beach had always been a safe landing place. As Mahealani and Emma rested beneath the shady trees after the long ride and enjoyed their picnic of cold sweet potatoes and her cousin Anela's fried chicken washed down with bottles of spring water, they watched the Hawaiians who made their homes along the shores of the rocky peninsula landing their graceful wooden canoes on the beach. Others were riding long, heavy surfing boards of *koa* wood over the rolling breakers. Boys, girls, grown men and women—no matter their age, all of them were enjoying the swift, thrilling ride to shore!

Below where they sat, several golden-skinned native women wearing vivid satin *pa'us,* with flower garlands crowning their long black hair, raced their horses across the sugary sands to greet returning fishermen with waves and glad cries of *"Aloha! Aloooha!"* They also waved and tossed friendly kisses in Emma's direction, too—greetings that she gaily returned, enjoying the colorful picture the riders made in their flowing riding costumes, and the excitement of their whirlwind greetings, until they'd ridden from view as swiftly and as suddenly as they'd appeared.

She shaded her eyes. Nearby, at the mouth of the gulch, was the village where her mother, Malia, and her aunt Leolani had been raised, and where her grandfather, Papa Kamuela Kahikina, had tended his taro terraces and his sweet potato patches until shortly before his death.

Although she could have been no more than three or four when he passed away—much younger than Mahealani was now—she still remembered him very vividly as a gentle, white-haired old Hawaiian man whose seamed broad face had been lined with the wisdom of age, and whose voice had been filled with love whenever he spoke to her.

She had sat on his knee, or else squatted nearby, to watch while he worked. His gnarled hands had still been deft as he made his feather *leis,* each tiny feather painstakingly arranged and securely knotted to its fiber backing to form an iridescent band of color. Or else she'd watched him weave the dried fiber strips of the *lauhala,* pandanus trees, into a sassy broad-brimmed hat which she could wear to shade her golden complexion, or else fashioned her a sturdy basket, decorated with woodroses, in which to gather flowers to make *leis* for her mother.

As he'd worked, Grandfather Kamuela had talked to her for hours on end, telling her about the islands as they'd been before the arrival of the Englishman, Captain James Cook, and of the missionaries who had come after him from America and changed the lives of the Hawaiians forever, all in the name of their Christian God and civilization.

On other idyllic days, Emma and her grandfather had explored the Point, gathering *limu,* or kelp, or watching the turtles plowing solemnly through the shallows like miniature paddle steamers. Grandfather had never tried to catch them in a turtle net, like the other fishermen. The turtle, he'd explained solemnly to his granddaughter, was sacred to his late wife's family, their totem, or *aumakua.* In respect to Emma's maternal grandmother's memory, he would never catch a turtle, nor eat its flesh. He often waded out into the shallows to net fish, though. He'd spend forever standing thigh deep in the water, head and shoulders bathed by the dying rays of the sun as it slipped slowly over the rim of the world. Motionless, he would wait like a statue carved from polished *koa* wood, until the bronzed whorls and the dark shadows moving beneath the water's surface told him the time was right to throw his net—and haul it in again, heavy with flapping, brightly colored fish.

She sighed, remembering those happy times. Her grandfather, her *tutukane,* had been so very dear to her. He had taught her to be proud of both her Hawaiian and white bloods, and she'd never forgotten his wise counsel. Indeed, she'd drawn strength from remembering the things he'd told her whenever she felt troubled or alone.

Following his death, Grandfather's bones had been separated from his flesh, in the old Hawaiian way, then all except the thigh bone had been wrapped in *tapa* cloth, and taken by a trusted guardian to be hidden in a secret place—perhaps a cave or a lava tube somewhere. From his thigh bone, a *kahuna,* or native priest—acting upon her grandfather's last wishes—had carved the magical fishhook he had wanted to leave his granddaughter, Kaleilani—the same fishhook she'd given to Gideon all those years ago. The talisman, filled with her grandfather's own powerful *mana,* or spirit power, had kept her beloved safe in battle during the War Between the States, she believed.

Her eyes misted over, remembering. *I miss you still, Grandfather. And I shall love, honor, and remember you for as long as I live.*

Soon after her grandfather's death had come another awful time, a night Emma had never forgotten. It was the fateful night when her *makua,* her mother, and Jack Jordan had quarreled even more violently than usual.

On that night, as she had not so long ago, when she'd burned the grass shacks to the ground, she'd awakened in utter darkness to find the man she'd called her father stretched out on the sleeping mat beside her.

Jack had reeked of rum, she remembered, and had been breathing heavily on the shadows, as if he'd run very fast for a very long distance. For the longest time, she'd been too afraid to open her eyes. And then, when she'd dared to peek, she'd jumped in fright, for Jack had been staring down at her in the moonlight that spilled into the hut with eyes that were very bright and glittery. He'd been smiling, but had looked as if he might bite her, she remembered thinking, just as the horrid old wolf had wanted to gobble up Little Red Riding Hood. The five-year-old child she'd been back then had been so scared by his expression, an achy knot had tangled up in her *opu,* her little belly, and her breathing had grown shallow and fast, as if she'd been running, too.

"Papa?" she'd whispered.

"Aye, luv. It's just your ole da. No need t' be scared, Emmie," Jordan had crooned, hearing the fear in her voice. He'd wetted his lips. "Your da won't hurt ye, lovie, you know that," he'd coaxed, squirming his arm under, then around her, and pulling her close.

But . . . she'd not liked having her face buried against his chest, or the funny way he'd kissed her, with his lips pressed so hard against her mouth that he banged her teeth. His wet tongue—stinking of rum and cigars—had poked inside her mouth so far, she'd been afraid it might choke her, or that she'd be sick if he didn't stop soon, and then Papa would be angry.

It had all felt so *wrong*. So very very wrong! She'd wanted her *makua* badly in that moment, but had been too afraid to call out, in case Papa heard. Sometimes, he got so angry with her and *Makua,* she just wanted to shrivel up into a tiny little ball in the corner like a mouse, too small for him to see! To keep from crying out, she'd bit down on her lip and held tight to Grandfather's fishhook talisman for comfort.

And then . . . and then . . . and then . . .

Emma swallowed and sat very still, staring blindly out at the brilliant ocean as she relived that awful night . . .

. . . and then da had slipped his hands underneath her skimpy nightgown and he'd touched her tummy and her chest. He'd stroked her *pua,* her secret girl-place, too, even when she cried and cried and begged him not to. *"Please, oh, please, Papa, don't!"*

But he'd whispered, *"Sssh, Emmie. It's our little secret."* He'd hushed her and told her she'd like what they were going to do together. In a low, whispery voice, he'd told her this was how all good little girls showed their daddies how much they loved them, then warned her she must never, ever tell *Makua* or Auntie Leolani or Uncle Kimo or her cousins or anyone else about their secret games, because then her *makua* would be very jealous, and something terrible would happen.

"Ye mustn't tattle, 'cos telling's bad, Emmie. Reel bad. Little girls wot tell are punished, they are. Punished somefink awful!"

"How?" she'd managed to whisper, terrified at what Jack's answer might be, but needing, somehow, to know, regardless.

"They're sent away, Em. Sent far, far away to the end of the world," he'd said in a doom-filled voice. "Banished to a land where no one loves them anymore."

And then, as he drew her to him, the oppressive darkness had suddenly been filled with light—with light and with screams—and with curses and blows.

Her father had sprung up, cursing foully at her mother, who'd been looming over them with the whale-oil lantern swinging wildly in one fist, splashing hideous light everywhere, her other fist clenched in anger. Tears had streamed down her face as she screamed at Jack to get away from her daughter. She'd flailed at his head with both her fists and the lantern.

"Dirty animal! Filthy offal! Excrement! Your own daughter? Auwe! Auwe!" Malia Jordan had shrieked.

That same night, after Jack had passed out, her mother had bundled her up and carried her far, far away from their grass shacks and their taro and sweet potato patches in the foothills of the Kohalas, traveling on foot for miles and miles without stopping until she'd reached Uncle Kimo's house on the grassy plains not far from Hui Aloha.

There—after allowing a day or two for her bruises to fade—Malia had left Emma in the care of her aunt and uncle, and gone back to Jack Jordan. Soon after, Uncle Kimo had taken Emma to Kawaihae, where they'd boarded the steamer for Honolulu, on the island of Oahu, and the convent of the Sacred Cross. And—although it was really just another island she'd been taken to—the place had seemed like the end of the world to the frightened little girl she'd been then. That first night, shivering and all alone on a lumpy pallet—one among twenty other beds in a long, echoey room—she'd realized that Jack hadn't lied, at least not about something terrible happening if Makua discovered "their secret." Something terrible *had* happened. She was there, wasn't she?

Uncle Kimo had left her with the sour-faced nuns in their musty-smelling robes and what had seemed like a tribe of other children with bright, suspicious eyes. Some of them had been spiteful, too. She'd been terrified of the strange incense smell and of the crucifixes that showed poor Jesus—all hurting and bloody and wearing a head garland of horrid, poky thorns—nailed to a cross. His agonized eyes had seemed full of condemnation to the frightened and confused little girl she'd been then, she recalled with a tremulous sigh. For the longest time, she'd believed that Jesus was angry at her, too. That He knew there was a moment—just a moment!—when she'd *liked* Papa cuddling her, even if she'd hated the other things he'd tried to do.

She'd not seen her *makua* again until nine long years had passed, when her mother had fallen sick and was no longer the young, lovely creature Emma still vaguely remembered in her dreams. The same summer she and Gideon had met . . .

Coming back to the present, Emma blinked away a tear for the frightened, lonely little girl she'd been, hoping Mahealani—happily devouring the remnants of their picnic—had not noticed her upset. All those years! All those wasted, lonely years, she—not the man she'd called Father!—had paid the price for Jack Jordan's wrongdoing, suffering silently under an enormous burden of guilt, for she'd been convinced her wickedness had made her mother so very angry that she'd stopped loving her, and had sent her away to that horrid convent forever.

"Emma Kaleilani's a bad, bad girl, and so are you!" she'd told herself as she played with Emmeline, her faded rag doll—one of several donated to the orphanage by the good women of Honolulu at Christmastide. *"If you're not a very, very good dolly, Emmie, I shall have t' send you far away, forever and ever. Maybe to a norphanage in Sanfrisco or Urope. You'll have to live in a horrid place there and kneel until it hurts, and say your prayers all day and 'fess your sons, and you'll be sorry you were ever bad!"*

No one had explained anything to her. Nor had another word

ever been breathed about what had happened that awful night. She knew now that what her father had tried to do to her was considered too shameful to be discussed by decent, God-fearing folk. Everyone who knew must have hoped that, given time, Emma would forget, but she had not. And, although she knew now that she'd been sent away by Uncle Kimo and Auntie Leo for her own safety—and not because she was unloved or deserving of punishment—she felt angry and resentful nonetheless. Because of Jack Jordan, she had been taken from her mother and robbed of her childhood. *She* had been the one punished, not him!

And so, at fourteen, she'd decided to refuse the offer of a student teaching post at the native girls' school in Honolulu in order to return to the Big Island to care for her sick mother, hoping to redeem herself in her mother's eyes—and, if she were honest with herself, to try to make her *makua* love her again.

But she'd hardly stepped off the boat when Jack Jordan had come after her again. He'd grown craftier now, though, because he'd feared her uncle Kimo and Jacob Kane's threats to turn him over to the authorities, who'd send him back to the prison colony of Botany Bay in Australia, where he'd come from. Or at very least, have him thrown into Honolulu Jail. By the same token, she'd grown older and wiser. That summer, she'd made a point never to be left alone with Jack, until that lazy afternoon when she'd slipped away to meet Gideon, and, head over heels in love, had grown careless.

That last afternoon, as she'd kissed Gideon farewell and planned to meet him the next day, a drunken Jack Jordan had been watching them, lying in wait for her. She'd never gone back to Twin Rocks' Cove again . . . had never seen her beloved again until seven long years had come and gone, and taken with them the last shreds of her childhood . . .

* * *

"Kaleilani, look!" Mahealani cried, cutting into her thoughts. "Over there! The *holua!*"

From where they sat, they could see several children and youths sliding down the muddy ramp of the *holua,* or scrambling up the grassy slopes alongside it, to get to the top.

The mudslide was a long, narrow track, cleared of rocks and vegetation, that ran down one side of a moderately steep hill. The younger children were sliding down it on their bottoms, or else slithering down head-first, on their bellies, while others were riding flat, sturdy wooden boards to the bottom, shrieking with giddy laughter as they went, before clambering back up to the top to try again. Every one of them was covered in mud from head to toe, but clearly having a fine old time.

Emma smiled at the little girl's wistful expression. Drawing her into her arms, she hugged her and kissed her smooth cheek—which was a trifle sticky with sweet potatoes and peach juice—and brushed a strand of long jet-black ringlet away from her eyes. "So. Are you done, *pau,* little one?"

"I was *pau* ages ago," Mahealani said scornfully, pouting so that her lower lip jutted out. "While you were daydreaming, I ate everything!" Proudly, she patted her tummy.

"So I see," Emma pretended to scold, puffing out her cheeks, and Mahealani giggled and wrapped her little arms around Emma's neck, hugging her fiercely. Despite her stern voice, Kaleilani's violet eyes were twinkling. "Come, then. Help me to put away these things, and after we've washed our faces and hands, we'll join the others, yes?"

"Oh, yes!"

Twenty-eight

At Hui Aloha, Julia rose, washed, and dressed lazily, dismissing Pua, the silly serving girl who tapped on her door each morning to ask if she needed any *kokua,* or help, with her morning toilette, with a sharp, "Go away!"

On those few occasions when Julia had accepted Puanani's assistance, the native girl's bright dark eyes had been everywhere, nosy as any mynah bird's as she opened drawers or returned crisply pressed garments to the wardrobe. No doubt the sly little chit was light-fingered, too, and would help herself to anything that took her fancy if it wasn't nailed down, Julia suspected, certain no *kanaka* wench could be trusted with her belongings. Accordingly, she'd opted to tend to her own needs—a decision that Gideon's mama had thought truly admirable, she remembered, surprised to actually find herself smiling.

After getting off to a bad start, she'd found herself liking Miriam Kane far more than she'd ever planned—probably because her mother-in-law's gentleness and sweetness of nature were genuine, she'd discovered, as were Jacob Kane's gruff displays of affection toward her. Fact was, she thought ruefully, it was getting real hard to dislike either of 'em. They were decent folk, and they were so darn *good* to her, Bible thumpers or nay! Great day in the mornin', her own folks hadn't been near as good!

After she'd dressed, Julia dismissed Pua, carefully locked the bedroom door behind her, pocketed the key, and started down the landing toward a graceful staircase that had ornately carved balustrades of polished *koa*. The door to the bedroom shared by Jacob and Miriam Kane stood ajar as she passed it.

Abruptly, she halted, cast a quick glance up and down the landing to ensure there was no one about, then pushed the door inward and went inside.

The room was empty, as she'd known it would be, though the bed had yet to be made. She grinned. Yessiree, bad hip or nay, that old workhorse Jacob Kane was no slug to lie abed till all hours of the morning. Until Gideon's return to take over the ranch, she'd heard that it was his habit to rise at three in the morning to begin his day's work, regardless of whether he was staying at home or out riding the range with his *paniolos,* often not coming home until it was full dark. Small wonder he sought his bed soon after!

Tiptoeing inside the room, she closed the door quietly behind her and looked about.

The faint fragrance of the jasmine Miriam wore in her hair still lingered in the air, mingled with the faint odor of camphor and sandalwood. A beautifully carved four-poster bed of glossy *koa* dominated the room. It was unmade, but a yellow-and-green quilt in pretty Wedding Ring patchwork—a pattern her own Momma had favored, she recalled with a rare twinge of nostalgia—had been folded neatly over a cedar chest at the foot of the bed.

Beneath an open window, where lace curtains fluttered in the breeze, was a dry sink, on which stood an elegant china ewer and matching wash bowl, patterned with ivy leaves. Beside them was a china shaving mug with hunting scenes painted upon it, a pig-bristle soap brush, a cutthroat razor and a leather strop, all those alongside a small crystal bowl that contained service-able bone collar studs and cuff links. On a white lace tablemat lay the ubiquitous Family Bible, bound in leather.

Just as I'd expected! No diamond stickpins or pearl collar studs for these missionary pinch-pennies! she thought, trying to force a grimace of distaste, but failing. Her father-in-law would never fritter his hard-earned money away on diamond stickpins or pearl studs, like other wealthy men . . . but he would give his brand-new daughter-in-law a cheval glass mirror carved from native woods, then sanded and polished for hours on end with his own work-roughened hands to such a fine gloss, you could see your face in the frame, let alone the looking glass proper! Yessiree, Father Kane's idea of extravagance was buying Thoroughbred horses and stud bulls, prime breeding stock brought from the finest ranches of California and Texas, the Pampas of Argentina, and even distant Scotland. His idea of spending was having his men raise a new roof for one of his ranch hand's houses, or giving a gift of money to send some snot-nosed native brat away to Boston for further schooling. These were Jacob's Kane's idea of extravagances! She couldn't afford for it to be hers, though. She had a hunch that, sooner or later, either Gideon or his uncle would find out about her past, and then it would be over for her. Before that day, she needed travelin' money, and a fat nest egg which would enable her to live in luxury until another plump "pigeon" came along. The only way to get that nest egg was by putting Jacko's plan into action.

She turned from the dry sink to the tall boy, and quickly searched each of its drawers in turn, not knowing exactly what she was looking for, except that it was a document of some kind and would have Jack Jordan's signature on it. She found only a neat pile of long johns, several stiffly starched linen shirts, extra collars, stockings, and so on, which she carefully replaced before closing the drawer. She looked about the room and frowned. The dresser against the far wall, alongside the second window, was next . . .

It was in a small, locked wooden box, tucked in the bottom drawer of the second dresser, behind several white nightshirts, that she at last found something interesting. Using the key from her pocket to force the flimsy lock on the box, she riffled through the sheaf of papers within it. Jacob's Last Will and Testament.

Jacob and Miriam's marriage certificate. Gideon's birth certificate. At the bottom was the document Jack had told her to find, folded in half with his name scrawled at the bottom, and beneath it, Jacob Kane and Kimo Pakele had added their own signatures as witnesses. She frowned. It looked like a business agreement of some kind, but why in the world would Jacob Kane do business with a varmint like Jordan? Unfolding the sheet of paper, she smoothed it in her hands, her curiosity growing. "I, Jack Jordan," she read, "an escaped convict of the Botany Bay Penal Colony in New South Wales, Australia, who was transported from my native England and sentenced to twenty-one years at hard labor there at His Majesty's pleasure for crimes that I—"

"Missus Gideon!"

The man's exclamation made her jump, and sent Julia whirling guiltily about to find Kimo Pakele standing in the open doorway. He was frowning, obviously wondering what she'd been doing in the Kanes' room with the door closed.

"Why, Mister Pakele! Just the man I need! Would you just look at this room? It's a disgrace! Do you know what time it is?" she snapped, figuring a blistering offense beat the devil out of a mealy-mouthed *de*fense any day. She turned to the dresser, her back to Pakele, and slipped the stolen paper down her bosom, praying it wouldn't crackle. It didn't.

Uncle Kimo's brows rose in confusion. "Missus Kane?"

"It's nine o'clock, Mister Pakele—*nine!*—and this room's a disgrace! Why, the bed hasn't even been made yet . . . nor the windows opened so that the room may air out, nor the chamberpots emptied! Come. You shall be my witness," she added quickly as Kimo opened his mouth to say something. "Oh, those dreadful girls! They're lazy, slovenly—why, every last one of them should be turned off and replacements hired! I intend to report this disgrace to Missus Kane immediately."

"Pua sorry, missus," the buxom serving girl protested, breathlessly, appearing in the doorway behind Kimo. She thrust past Kimo and almost fell into the room. "I open dis window, yeh?"

"Ha! You're too late to make amends now, you idle wretch. I'll see to the windows myself this time, thank you. Meanwhile, get on with changing those bed linens—and make haste, you lazy girl! I'm sure poor Missus Pakele has any number of other things for you to do in the kitchen when you're finished here, so never mind lolly-gagging. I shan't complain to her or Missus Kane this time, Pua. But if I have cause to reprimand you again in the near future, you may be certain I shall." With that, Julia turned and raised the window sash herself, shot poor, shame-faced Pua a withering look, then sailed past both her and Kimo on her way from the room.

Kimo gave Pua a sympathetic smile, which faded as his eyes came to rest once again on Julia Kane's face.

"And what, pray, are you looking at me like that for?"

"Me, Missus Kane?" Kimo's brows rose innocently.

Her gray eyes flashed. A nerve ticked at her temple. "Don't act so darned innocent. What exactly does that look of yours imply?"

Kimo wetted his lips. "I was wondering why you was lookin' in *Makua* Kane's drawers, missus," he admitted calmly, meeting her eyes without flinching.

She swallowed, but her eyes were hard and pale as glaciers as she countered, "What I might or might not be doing in any room of this house is none of your business, Pakele," she threatened softly. "You seem to be poking your big ole *kanaka* nose into any number of matters here that ain't none of your business."

A thin smile played about Kimo's lips. "You mean, about you meeting Jack Jordan down by the lava tubes?"

A flush filled her cheeks. Damn! The son-of-a-bitch must have been following her! "I don't know about any meetings with any Jordan. I'm just giving you fair warning, sugar. *Stay out of my damned business, or you'll be sorry!* I'll have your hide nailed to the barn door, you cross me, jest see if I don't!"

"Maybe you forget, this ranch *is* my business, Missus Kane.

The ranch, the land, and all the folks who live on her. Me, I take care my family—including the Kanes."

"Aaah, I see." A gloating smile played about her lips. "And Emma, too, I presume?"

To her glee, the Hawaiian actually looked startled by her use of his niece's name. "Emma Kaleilani, you mean?" he stammered.

"You heard me, sugar. What about her and *my* husband? What about their secret little meetings? Or don't they count?" She laughed harshly as he tried—too late—to mask his shock and anger. "Well, well. What have we here, Uncle Kimo? Some ranch goings-on that you knew nothin' about? And you call yourself a foreman! Tut! Tut! Tut! Now, why don't you tell that little tramp to stay away from my husband, old man, *then* you can fret about other folks' doings, hmm?" She smiled sweetly, then swept past him down the stairs with a twitch of her skirts.

Miriam Kane had ridden into the village of Waimea early that morning to visit the families of some of the ranch hands. Gideon had left at dawn for the plantation clinic at Laupahoehoe, wherever that was, to visit some sick old Hawaiian man there. That damned nosy Kimo Pakele would, so far as she knew, be busy with the herds up on the northeast range, once he'd got his employer settled for the day. *The timing's pretty darned near perfect, Jacko,* she told herself silently, *if only I can bring it off.*

It all rested on the whereabouts of good ole Papa Kane now, she mused, pursing her lips thoughtfully as she swept into the dining room.

"Well, well, Good morning, my dear," Jacob Kane greeted her warmly. He was smiling as he rose stiffly from his seat. He dabbed at his lips with a napkin. "How are you feeling today? You're looking positively radiant!"

She halted alongside him and allowed him to kiss her cheek, forcing a tremulous smile. "Yes. I'm feeling well, Father Kane," she murmured, lowering her lashes as if she were saying so only to please him. She bit her lower lip and contrived to look worried. "Indeed, were it not for one distressing little matter, I would feel positively blooming," she confessed, pretending she was unable to meet his eyes. "Mister Kane . . . Father, I . . . I've wanted to say something to you for quite some time now, but the matter is one so . . . so very upsetting to me, I've been quite unable to bring myself to do so."

Jacob frowned. His piercing blue searched her face. "Then perhaps it would be best if you waited to talk to Miriam?"

"Oh, but I cannot! A lady of her . . . refinement. Truly, I cannot."

"Then come, my dear. Tell me what is bothering you. A young woman in your condition has a very delicate constitution. It is vital that you be freed from all worries, both for the child's sake, and your own health and peace of mind. Sit down, do, and tell me all about this 'distressing matter'?"

Tears filled Julia's eyes. She turned from him. "Oh, Father Kane! Now that it's truly come to this, I don't know how to begin to tell you. The shame of it! It's . . . it's about Gideon, you see."

"Gideon?" Jacob's brows rose.

She nodded tearfully. Drawing a tiny handkerchief from the pocket of her gown, she sniffed noisily into it. "I know he told everyone last night that he was riding to Laupahoehoe this morning, but I have every reason to suspect he was lying."

"Lying! But, why would Gideon lie about such a thing?"

"Oh, Father Kane, I don't know how to tell you this, but I suspect that—that Gideon has taken another woman—a native woman—as his mistress," she blurted out. "He . . . he has gone to be with her again, I just know it, and it's d-destroying me. Oh, what shall I do, Father Kane? I love him so!"

Jacob Kane's expression was dark as thunderclouds now as he drew his daughter-in-law against his chest and clumsily patted her back to console her. "There, there, my dear. I'm quite certain you're mistaken about this. Gideon would never—"

"If only I *were* mistaken!" Julia wailed, her crocodile tears soaking his lapels as she buried her face against his chest. "But I . . . I know he has met with her before—on several occasions, in fact, and each time in secret. The night of our wedding *luau,* he left our room as soon as he thought I'd fallen asleep, and went out in the wee hours. When he returned, I could . . . I could smell perfume on his clothes." She shuddered delicately. "Oh, it's no mistake, Father. I know they were together, both then and at other times, because—may the good Lord forgive me—I've followed them! I'm ashamed to say I've jeopardized the life of this innocent child in my womb to ride in search of them, and have seen them together. Oh, Father Kane, they m-meet in the forest, by the old Hawaiian temple ruins. You must believe me!"

"There, there, calm down. You mustn't upset yourself so. Think of the child! I'm sure there's some logical explanation to Gideon's behavior. Come, dry those pretty eyes, Daughter. I intend to get to the bottom of this immediately," he reassured the young woman.

"You . . . you won't tell anyone else? I don't think I could bear the shame were everyone were to know, especially not—"

"Who?"

"It doesn't matter."

"Then tell me."

She turned away and whispered, "Your foreman."

"Kimo. Kimo Pakele?"

She nodded. "Oh, Father, the woman Gideon's meeting is Kimo's niece!"

His white brows rose. "Emma Jordan? You're quite certain about this?"

"I'm afraid so."

"Rest assured, this matter will go no further than my ears, my dear," Jacob Kane promised bleakly, patting her hands.

As Julia dabbed at her eyes and thanked him, she saw how Jacob Kane's deeply troubled, wounded expression belied his firm, comforting words and felt a flutter of misgiving deep in her belly. As he hitched heavily from the room, obviously in considerable pain from his injured hip, it was all she could do to keep from going after him, from telling him it'd all been a mistake or a silly, childish game.

She flicked her head to clear it and hugged herself about the arms, feeling the paper hidden in her bosom crackle as she told herself everything would be fine. After all, no one would be hurt. Jacob would be uncomfortable for a day or two—certainly no more—and then Gideon would pay the ransom Jacko demanded, and he'd be returned to his family. It was only Jacob Kane's money Jacko wanted, wasn't it?

Wasn't it?

Twenty-nine

It was late afternoon before Mahealani became bored with the wild ride down the mudslide. She and Emma were both covered with red mud from head to toe, little more than the whites of their eyes showing as they ran down the beach to wash off in the warm Pacific, then sun themselves on the sand until their *pa'us*, or sarongs, had dried. When they'd done so, they slipped on their prim, ruffled *muumuus*, combed out their dripping hair, and, with Emma leading Makani, headed up the beach hand in hand, chattering like mynahs.

A tall, broad-shouldered man with his *lauhala* hat tipped back was sitting a gray horse on the grassy knoll overlooking the beach, smoking a cheroot as he leaned over his saddle horn. The stallion grazed the sere grass beneath the rustling palms, while its master squinted against the sunlight to watch as the young woman and the little girl headed toward the village in the gulch. Their route would take them straight past him.

Emma's heart gave a sickening lurch of recognition as she drew close enough to make out the man's features. She halted abruptly, holding Mahealani's arm to make the little girl do likewise.

"Gideon!" she exclaimed, her expression unguarded and—for one fleeting instant—filled with treacherous pleasure. "What in the world are you doing here?"

He tipped his hat. "One of our former ranch hands is ill. He's at the plantation hospital back there." He gestured behind him, toward the green, corrugated-iron roofs of the small white-washed plantation clinic, which showed between the treetops. "Since it's too far for my father to ride with his bad hip, I offered to play errand boy, and deliver the treats *Makua* made the old fellow." A sheepish grin lit his handsome, tanned face as he looked down at the bedraggled pair. Emma felt heat burn in her cheeks as he added, "I don't need to ask what you two mudlarks have been up to, do I? How was the *holua*, ladies? Fun?" He winked.

"Oh, yes!" Mahealani cried, her dark eyes shining. "I was the goddess Poli'hau, and Kaleilani was Madame Pele, and I won, every time, and chased her into the sea!"

"We've—er—just finished washing all the mud off," Emma explained unnecessarily, mortified that Gideon had seen her this way—dripping wet, with her hair falling like untidy strands of wet seaweed about her face. Why, the way he was looking at her—clearly trying to contain his amusement—made her cringe with embarrassment. The nerve of the man! After the disgraceful way he'd treated her, she should have cut him dead, should have turned her back on him, walked away, and never given him another moment's thought as long as she lived. What was she doing, instead? Standing there, gazing up at him like some—some stupid, lovesick calf!

"Well, don't let me keep you ladies from your toilette," Gideon said with the utmost solemnity, gesturing expansively at the water as it caressed the sands with lacy fingers of foam. "Were you planning on riding home this afternoon, Miss Jordan? Or staying in Laupahoehoe for the night?"

"We're staying at Auntie Momi's," Mahealani disclosed, smiling up at him shyly, as Emma—in the same moment—crisply insisted, "Noo, we're going home this afternoon, I'm afraid."

"Home? But 'Lani, you *prom*ised! You said we could stay at Auntie Momi's," Mahealani wailed. "She has baby goats, and a donkey, and a mynah bird that can talk! You promised, Kaleilani. You said Auntie Momi was 'specting us!"

Emma—embarrassed to be caught red-handed in such a brazen lie—fell silent and gave a shrug before muttering, "Oh, all right, then. If I promised, then we'll stay, of course."

Gideon shot her a wicked, knowing grin that made her face flame to the hair roots. "Oh, of course. Keeping one's promises is very important, isn't it, Miss Jordan?" There was a world of double meaning to his words and his tone.

Her chin came up mutinously. Lightning flashed in the velvet depths of her violet eyes. "You may not agree, but *I* think so, yes. It's very important."

To her satisfaction, his rueful smile vanished. He had the grace to look repentant. "Then perhaps you'd be kind enough to spare me a few moments of your time? It's very important."

"There's nothing you could possibly say that I'd want to hear," she snapped with a toss of her head that made strands of wet hair flail about her shoulders like whips.

"Then do it to humor me. Please?" he countered softly, looking at her with such a warmth and intensity, her innards turned to mush and her treacherous heart began a mad pounding. Dangerous—oooh, the way she was feeling was dangerous, indeed!

She snorted. "From the rumors I've heard, Mister Kane, I think it's a little late for talking, don't you?—unless it's to offer you my congratulations. I'm sure your mother and father must be thrilled they'll soon be grandparents." She turned away to hide the sudden moisture in her eyes, but could do nothing to conceal the bitterness in her voice. *Oh, how it hurt to say it aloud!* It made losing him to Julia and their child all the more real, inescapably so, in fact. Tears scalded like hot vinegar behind her eyes. She swallowed over the huge lump in her throat. Dear Lord, she couldn't bear to think of some other woman carrying Gideon's child beneath her heart—of some other woman feeling his baby's first, fluttering movements in her belly, or of knowing the pain and joy of pushing that baby out into the wide, beautiful world!

Gideon's jaw hardened. "I can imagine what you must be feeling, Emma."

"It's Miss Jordan to you," she snapped.

"Very well. *Miss Jordan,*" he acknowledged with an unfathomable expression. He chose his words with great care, so that the bright-eyed little imp with her would not suspect there was anything amiss. "However, I still think we need that talk. *I* need it, if you will. I'd appreciate you listening to me?"

Oh, that voice, that voice! Deep and slightly rough with emotion, its timbre caressed her, was almost hypnotic in its effect on her! "Chicken skin" rose on her arms and shimmied down her spine. It took all of her shrinking willpower to stand her ground, when her heart urged her to pick up her skirts, to run away and hide her pain in some safe, dark place. "My answer's still no. I really don't care anymore what would benefit you, Mister Kane," Emma blurted out, her fingers crossed tightly so that the lie wouldn't count. "Now, good day."

Afraid he would see the longing and confusion in her eyes that her brusque tone could not mask, she turned quickly away from him and knelt on the sand, fussing with Mahealani's perfectly tidy hair, straightening the stiffly starched ruffles that edged the square bodice of the little girl's pinafore in an effort to hide her upset before snapping smartly upright and striding past his horse.

With Mahealani's hand gripped firmly in her own, she wound Makani's reins about her fist and, leading the mare, marched the little girl toward the village in the gulch. She towed the child at such a clip, her retreat resembled a Nantucket sleigh ride more than a graceful exit!

Dear God, will it never go away? she wondered helplessly as she fled. Would she always feel this deep, gnawing ache in her heart, her bones—her very soul!—whenever he was near, no matter how innocently or unexpectedly they chanced to meet or what impossible wedges fate had driven between them? Must she forever suffer the—

"Oww!" Mahealani complained loudly, digging in her heels to make Emma slow down. "Kaleilani, don't! You're pinching my arm!"

"Sorry," Emma muttered gruffly, instantly loosening her hold. The very second she'd done so, Mahealani pulled free and skewed around to face back the way they'd come. She wiggled her fingers in Gideon's direction, giggling as she blew him a farewell kiss. *"Alooha,* mister! *Alooha,* horsey!"

From the corner of her eye, Emma saw Gideon flourish his hat and wave.

Ignoring Emma's scowl, Mahealani grinned and waved back. "That's the man who dropped the *po'okanaka lei* I gave you. He's handsome, isn't he, Kaleilani? Just like Prince Charming!"

An unladylike snort erupted from Emma. "That, my dear, is all a matter of opinion. 'Handsome is as handsome does,' your *tutu* Malia always used to say! Now, come along, child, do."

Making a face at Kaleilani's rigid back, Mahealani followed her.

Emma could feel his eyes upon them as she marched away. But, though she itched to find out if her intuition was correct, pride kept her gaze firmly planted on the sandy path ahead.

The sun had almost set that same evening before—dishes washed, floor swept, donkey and goats duly petted, the tame Indian mynah bird coaxed to talk, and a yawning Mahealani put to bed—Emma was at last free to go outside onto the veranda of her calabash auntie's little clapboard house, to enjoy the flower-and-sea-scented air.

It was a beautiful evening. Streamers of gold still looped between the ridges of the distant mountains, while far below, shadows stretched across the floor of the gulch like sleek gray cats. Up and down the grassy banks of the river, whale-oil lanterns and *kukui*-nut lamps were being lit in grass shacks or tiny clapboard houses, their amber light shining like golden fireflies through the emerald dusk.

Mahealani had barely managed to stay awake to finish the

delicious supper of fried *akule,* or mullet, *poi,* and watercress soup that Auntie Momi prepared them before her eyelids began drooping. Emma smiled to herself. The old lady had been so pleased to have visitors.

The widow of Robert Foulger, who'd been manager of the nearby sugar mill until the accident that caused his death, Momi had known Emma's mother's family well, long before Malia and her sister Leolani had moved away—first to the island of Oahu, to keep house for the lawyer, Alexander McHenry, and his crippled wife, Kate, then, after her death, coming back here, to the Big Island, to keep house for Jacob and Miriam Kane at Hui Aloha.

Though not a blood relative, Emma knew she could count on a warm welcome from Auntie Momi at any hour of the day or night, and so she always stayed with her when she came to Laupahoehoe.

There was nothing she enjoyed more than listening to the stately, white-haired old lady speak of the bygone days when thousands of Boston whalers had put into the islands each month to take on water or provisions, instead of the few that came now. Chuckling, Momi had reminisced at some length about the strict missionary fathers' wasted efforts to curtail the sailors' wicked ways with the lovely island *wahines* or to put a stop to their wild drinking sprees and brawls along the waterfronts of Lahaina, Maui, or Honolulu.

As Auntie Momi talked, she bent her head over a quilting hoop, making row after row of tiny running stitches around and around an appliquéd cotton flower or a "fish on coral" design or perhaps a deep-green breadfruit, one of several quilting patterns favored by island seamstresses, who'd adapted the missionary women's patchwork designs to their own, more exotic, tastes, using the materials and inspiration at hand.

"Auwe! Listen to me! How I go on, child!" Momi had exclaimed at length, tucking her sewing into a pillowcase to keep it clean. "I must bore you, telling the same old stories over and

over again, hmm? Oh! The poor little *keikiwahine*, fast asleep already!"

"She's worn out from playing so hard," Emma murmured, laughing as she scooped Mahealani up into her arms. She deposited the little girl gently on the sleeping mat, pulled a light cloth blanket over her, then leaned down and gently kissed her good night.

"Mahealani. Full Moon of Heaven. What a lovely name for a lovely little girl." She and her husband, Robbie, God rest his soul, had had six children altogether, but sadly, not one had survived its first few days of life. They were buried beneath the tombstones behind the little village church.

Emma nodded, knowing the old lady was fond of all children. "Yes. Very lovely."

"She has a look about her, bless her. And good blood in her veins. Mixed, perhaps, but all of it good. Och, aye, pretty—*and* just as smart as a whip, to boot. That's what to look for in a wife or a horse, my Robbie used to say, the rascal!—'brains *and* beauty'—and Mahealani's smart, all right. Just like you, hinny."

"Of course. We're . . . sisters."

"Hmm. So you are. Though how your poor, sick mother could carry for nine months, then deliver a healthy, living child in her condition, I'll never know—especially with only that ne'er-do-well convict wretch for a husband and a helpmate!" Her dark, bright eyes flickered speculatively over Mahealani's face, relaxed in slumber, then she turned and regarded Emma. She frowned, as if she'd remembered something important, but then shook her head and clicked her teeth. "Will you listen to me? *Auwe!* Enough of my jabbering! Robert always said I went on and on, like a loose shutter banging in the wind. I do believe I'll put this quilting aside for now, and turn in for the night." She gestured at her sewing. "This quilt's for you, girlie. For your marriage bed." Her eyes twinkled amidst myriad wrinkles, reminding Emma of a *menehune,* a Hawaiian pixie. The daughter of an island *wahine* and a Scottish sailor father, then married to another Scot for a goodly number of years, Auntie Momi often sounded more Scottish than Hawaiian to Emma, with her "ayes" and her "whist ye's" and her "ochs!"

"I thought I told you, Auntie? I refused Keali'i Wallace's marriage proposal," she reminded the old lady firmly

"Whist, not Wallace, lassie! He's no fit mate for ye. That one's all full o' wind—like a set o' bagpipes. He's way too stiff and starchy for a lively *wahine* like yourself. You need a man who can tame the wildness in ye without breaking your spirit—not a man t' smother your fire like a wet dishrag!" She turned and blew out one of the two chimney lamps that illuminated the room. "Are you ready for bed, girlie?"

"In a little while, Auntie. I thought I'd go outside for a spell first. The sea air smells so different to the air in our little valley."

Momi patted her shoulder. "As you will, then. Just douse the other lamp before you come to bed," Momi murmured, reaching up to embrace the young woman in her frail arms.

"Don't worry, I will. Good night, Auntie. Sleep well, and God bless."

"Good night, darling girl. Sweet dreams!"

As Emma stepped outside, there was a cooling breeze blowing off the sea, refreshing and salty. She inhaled deeply, leaning over the veranda railing as she gazed out at the silver-rimmed ocean, above which the rising moon hung like a disk of yellow pearl. Off in the distance, higher up the gulch, she could hear the shrill, piercing call of *pueo,* the owl, as she hunted, and she shivered. It seemed her mother's *akua,* or spirit, must be very near tonight, watching over her. Yes, surely it was! She could smell the fragrance of her mother's favorite tuberose *leis* on the air, and was suddenly convinced someone was watching her.

"Makua?" she whispered. "Are you there?" She held her breath for an answer, but there was only the reedy chirp of the

crickets in the long grass by the gate, and the soothing sounds of the sea.

Gideon, standing in the deep shadow of the fragrant plumeria trees that overhung Momi Foulger's whitewashed picket fence, felt the old longing build and grow. The ache became an unbearable knot in his throat as he watched Emma reach up and unpin her coil of midnight hair. She shook it free so that it fell about her shoulders in a loose dark cloud, then stretched seductively, her breasts thrust forward, her arms raised gracefully above her head.

Crushing the handful of waxy white and yellow plumeria blossoms he'd picked, he was about to show himself when he heard Emma give a little gasp of delight, as if she'd spotted something pleasing. He hurriedly stepped back, dropping the bruised flowers as she ran down the veranda steps and sped across the lawns, passing by him so closely, he could smell her fragrance on the dewy night breeze.

With little ado, he saw her take her seat upon the worn wooden crosspiece of the swing that hung by thick ropes from the twisted dark boughs of an ancient banyan tree. Humming under her breath—the same lovely old *mele* to which she'd danced the *hula* at his wedding feast, he realized—she began leaning back and forth, letting the ends of her hair trail across the grass below, and working her legs in and out to make the swing move back and forth.

She swung higher and faster, until she became a streaming pale blur against the deepening charcoal sky and the dark-emerald masses of the shrubbery. Starlight threaded her inky hair with silvery highlights, while the moon lent an ethereal blue-white pallor to her billowing *muumuu,* her bare toes, her slender fingers, so that both girl and swing seemed not of this world, but creatures of dreams or legend; a vestal virgin, some gossamer goddess or a nymph of the spring, chaste and unapproachable to any mortal man.

" '*She hangs upon the cheek of night as a rich jewel in an*

Ethiop's ear . . .' " he thought, the quote springing to mind un-
bidden. He scowled. Damn it, Romeo and his Juliet had surely
been no more star-crossed, no more thwarted in their love, than
he and Emma! Were they, too, marked for tragedy? He swallowed at the sobering thought, clenching his fists at his sides.
Dear God, he hoped not! There were so many things he wanted
to tell her, so many things he needed to say. But tonight, her
loveliness awed him. Her beauty tied his tongue and froze him
in place with his hands knotted uselessly at his sides, like a
marble statue.

Since the last time they'd made love beneath the stars, obedi-
ent slaves to their passion for each other, not a single night had
passed when he'd not burned to have her again. If he closed his
eyes, he could smell the musk and flowers of her skin that night,
could draw a breath and recapture the exact scent of her silky
hair, clean and sweet and fresh as dewy orchids after a rainshower, could feel the supple sleekness of her body pressed hotly
against his, the high, round fullness of her breasts rubbing
against his furred chest, driving him wild with desire.

He'd wanted women before. He was no stranger to lust, nor
to its loving counterpoint, desire! But nothing came close to his
feelings for Emma. *Nothing!* And, with his heart's delight denied
and forbidden him, those feelings only flamed still brighter,
burned with a fiercer, scorching blaze that turned fidelity to
ashes and made cinders of the vows he'd given Julia. What about
the vows he'd made with all his heart and soul seven years ago,
beneath a leafy sea-grape tree? he asked himself, time and time
again. Aye, by God, what about those?

Night after night as he rode herd on the Kane longhorns, his
thoughts drifting with the winds, he'd imagined cupping Emma's
slender shoulders in his hands and kissing the downy nape of
her neck or tracing the vulnerable ridges of her spine down to
the firm globes of her buttocks with his lips and tongue, caressing with languorous strokes the svelte, pale-gold line of her

waist, belly, hip, thigh, and calf, then descending to the pretty ankles and dainty feet below.

He'd imagined capturing the dewy flower of her mouth beneath his own and crushing both luscious petals on his lips and tongue to release the honeyed nectar of her kisses, of inhaling the fragrant zephyrs of her breath while his fingers delicately plundered another, hidden blossom, a trembling flower that yielded even sweeter nectar from the secret cache of honey between her thighs.

His thoughts had been erotic, carnal, lusty as any satyr's with the rites of spring, as heady and all-consuming as the most potent of wines. His nights had proven no better, for his sleep had been plagued with fevered dreams of her, in which they'd made love over and over again, until exhaustion claimed them. Yet, when he tried to take her tenderly in his arms, to sleep with her held close to his heart, like water she'd slipped between his fingers and vanished, leaving his arms empty, his heart forlorn.

"*. . . forsaking all others . . . so help you God!*" the voice of his conscience would intone. He'd awake in a cold sweat, his palms and brow clammy, the wedding vows he'd made to Julia still ringing in his mind—but his treacherous body hard and aching for Emma.

In his few hours of free time in the month that followed, he'd given Hui Aloha, his parents, and his pregnant wife wide berth, and begun clearing the piece of land he'd commissioned Alexander McHenry to purchase from the Chinese storekeeper, Ah Woo.

Swinging an axe, he'd first felled the timber, then burned the knotty stumps and dug and dragged out the stubborn roots of the few trees that would have blocked the view from the finished house. When completed, the veranda would afford a panorama of emerald, grassy plains as far as distant, snowcapped Mauna Kea. The ground cleared, he'd singlehandedly dug the foundations for the home he'd once planned to build for Emma and himself, despite knowing with every sod he lifted, every nail he hammered, with every woodshaving that curled from his plane, that he was destined to live there with a wife he neither loved nor wanted, along with a child he could remember no part of creating.

Stripped to the waist under the blazing tropical sun, he'd flexed muscle, sinew, and cord and worked as he had never worked before, not caring that the sun burnished his torso an even deeper bronze, or that the exhausting physical toil drove him to his bed each night with his back breaking, and every inch of his body screaming.

He'd hoped and prayed the hard labor of housebuilding would help to dull his pain over losing Emma, perhaps even bring him a measure of acceptance that would enable him to face the future fate had handed him, but his plan had failed miserably. Despite working from hazy dawn till sultry dusk, despite punishing his body mercilessly while his treacherous thoughts chased each other around and around, like dogs chasing each others' tails, hard work hadn't eradicated his guilt, nor diminished his longing for Emma. In fact, it had only served to deepen it. Time and time again, he'd berated himself for leaving the Waikalani Valley that morning without telling Emma that Julia was carrying his child, and for running home like a coward, and letting Charles Keali'i Wallace do his dirty work for him. He hadn't been able to let things rest, not that way. He owed Emma the courtesy of an explanation, an apology—hell, a goodbye, at very least—if he could offer her nothing more, he'd decided. And then, be damned if their paths hadn't crossed right here, in Laupahoehoe, before he'd had a chance to go looking for her.

When he looked up again, the swing had slowed. Emma was drifting idly to and fro, hair and skirt trailing like streamers behind her as she hugged the rough ropes and gazed dreamily skyward.

In the few moments in which he'd been lost in thought, the

tropical night had fallen, swift and sudden. The flamboyant sunset sky had been transformed, in the twinkling of an eye, to a magician's mantle of deep-blue velvet, spangled with glittering sequins and framed by high, billowing banks of lighter cloud, whose scalloped edges were lit brightly from behind by the moonlight, like the scenery of some heavenly play. The ocean, too, was darkened now, only the surf and an occasional wave crest showing ultra-white and bright against its glassy blackness.

"Emma."

She sat up as if jerked by a cord. "How dare you spy on me! Go away!"

"Emma, please. I have to talk to you."

"No. Go home to your wife, Mister Kane."

Angrily, she sprang from the swing and began striding toward the house. In two swift strides, he intercepted her at the bottom of the veranda steps.

"Emma, please listen to me. I know how you must be feeling, but—"

"Oh, do you?" she taunted, violet eyes blazing like amethysts as she whirled about to glare up at him. "Do you really?"

Her ferocity took him aback. "I—er—I believe so, yes. You're angry—terribly angry!—that I didn't tell you about the baby, or explain why I couldn't divorce Julia, am I right?"

She gave a harsh laugh. "Oh, I'm angry all right. But that's not why, exactly."

His brows lowered, he frowned. "It's not? Then what is?"

She shrugged, her lips forming a queer, twisted line as if she were trying very hard not to cry. "I'm angry you didn't love me enough to put me first! That you didn't say, 'Devil take anything but Emma and me, and the way we feel about each other' when she told you about the baby. Don't you see? I wanted you to say, 'I'm leaving you, Julia. I'm going to start a new life with Emma, because she's all that matters to me!' Like a fool, I waited for you, Gideon. Day and night, through every minute of every hour, I waited for you to—to come back to me. To ride down into the valley and carry me off like my knight in shining armor! But, you never came!" With that, her hand flew up to cover *her* mouth. With a muffled sob, she dashed past him for the veranda.

His hand came out like lightning. Gripping her upper arm, he spun her around to face him. "Don't you think I wanted that? More than anything on this earth?" he growled. "But I can't have it. And I can't have you! She's carrying *my child,* Emma. An innocent child! Decent men don't abandon their children, nor their children's mother. If they're honorable, they fulfill their obligations, however reluctantly. They do their duty. Oh, darling girl, don't you see? If I'd been able to turn my back on my responsibilities, to just—to just walk away without a backward glance, I wouldn't be the man you loved."

"Oh, really?" she jeered, tossing her ebony head. "Then what about your responsibility to me, sir—a prior one, surely, by a span of some seven years? What about that, damn you! And where do I fit in, pray? Under 'One's Responsibilities to One's Mistress?' " she demanded bitterly. "Or is it even lower, under 'A Gentleman's Duty to His Discarded Whore?' "

Gideon's jaw hardened. A nerve ticked at his temple. He wanted to deny it, to tell her how deeply he loved her, the full extent of the agony he'd endured, but he couldn't deny a word. *Would* not, because everything she'd said was true. He'd failed in his responsibilities to her.

"I knew it! You have nothing to say to me, do you, Gideon? But I have something to say to *you!*" she spat. "I say, To hell with you, and to hell with your damned honor, Gideon Kane!" Drawing back her hand, she slapped him hard across the cheek, before flinging herself up the veranda steps and into the little house.

The meaty thwack of the blow was like the crack of a pistol shot on the hushed night air. It seemed to echo long after she'd gone, he thought as he stared bleakly after her.

* * *

A pearly dawn the color of polished abalone shells was washing the sky above the ocean with shimmering silver, rose, and palest yellow, while the land beyond yet lay cloaked in charcoal as Emma left Momi Foulger's house the following morning, amidst the crowing of countless cocks and warbling birdsong.

Mahealani, still half asleep, drooped heavily over Emma's shoulder, deadweight and unwieldy as she carried her from the house to her saddled mare. She was out of breath by the time she'd hefted both the child and the two leather saddlebags, filled with gifts of food, onto Makani's broad back, and managed to mount herself without dropping anything.

Waving Auntie Momi farewell, she clicked to Makani and headed the horse at a brisk trot down the coastal road that would, after countless twists and turns, lead her back to the Waikalani Valley. She hadn't planned on leaving Laupahoehoe this early, until her upsetting confrontation with Gideon, but now that she was up and on her way, riding through the dewy cool of early morning, she was glad she'd changed her plans.

She'd not gone far when she heard hoofbeats behind her. Turning in the saddle, she muttered an exasperated curse under her breath and turned quickly about-face as Gideon rode up alongside her.

He coughed. "Good morning, Miss Jordan. Emma," he added deliberately.

She offered no answer, but stared straight ahead, ignoring him.

"I've just come from the beach. I passed the night there."

"Ah. Then that explains why you look like something the tide spat up, eh, Mistah Kane?" she flared rudely, shooting him a withering side glance.

"I've done some thinking," he added softly, thinking that her face seemed pale, despite her bravado, and that her eyes looked swollen and red, as if she'd been crying. There were faint lilac shadows ringing them, too. Unless he missed his guess, like him, she'd passed a sleepless night. "As I said, I've been doing some thinking, and I've made some decisions, Emma. Important ones, about us."

Silence. If she'd heard him, she gave no sign of having done so.

"Emma, say something, please? Don't you want to know what they are? Aren't you even a little curious?"

"Not even a little." *Damn his arrogance!* Emma thought angrily, refusing to look at him again, knowing she'd succumb to that coaxing tone if she did. *Why does he have to look so bloody handsome?* Despite his claims that he'd spent the night on the beach, his white shirt still looked crisp beneath his black leather vest. He wore it tucked neatly into a wide black belt and wore, too, black corduroy breeches, above polished black riding boots. From somewhere—from some adoring fool of a girl at the plantation clinic, probably—he'd acquired a deep-green *lei* of fragrant *maile* leaves, entwined with a strand of white ginger, which he'd slung about his shoulders. In fact, he looked disgustingly handsome, alert, and refreshed, despite the ungodly hour and the sharp words they'd exchanged the evening before. Not to mention her slap.

"The little lady's still fast asleep, I see," he continued, sensing her momentary weakening. "Won't you let me take her for you? Your arms must be breaking."

They were, and in all honesty, she would have welcomed a respite from holding Mahealani, but she stubbornly shook her head, nonetheless. "No, thank you, Mister Kane. I don't need your help, and I certainly don't need *you*. I can manage very well on my own, so just—just go away before I'm forced to resort to violence again!"

Gideon flinched. Violence, hmm? He could still feel the stinging imprint of her hand upon his cheek and jaw. The little *wahine* might look as if a gust of wind could blow her away, but she packed quite a wallop! he thought ruefully. But in all honesty, her slap had pained him less than her spirited rejection.

For several moments, they rode on in heavy silence, one broken only by the blowing of the horses, the tinkling of harness, and the creaking of leather saddles.

After several minutes had passed, Gideon began, "Emma, I've decided—"

"Oh, have you, indeed? Well, I don't want to hear what you've decided, Mister Kane. Your decisions are absolutely unimportant to me."

"Very well. Then I've been thinking . . ."

"Your thoughts, sir, are likewise immaterial."

He glared at her. "Then may I discuss the weather with you? Or some other, equally mundane subject? The price of matches, perhaps? Or of pork bellies?"

She flushed. "You may discuss anything you please, Mister Kane," she said with a careless shrug. "I can give no guarantees that I'll respond, however."

He nodded. "All right. I'm prepared to take my chances," he agreed huskily, fully aware of the turmoil she must be enduring, and loathing himself for causing that anguish.

He'd promised to come back to her, to make her his bride. He'd returned, all right, but as the husband of another woman. Then, rather than leaving well enough alone, he'd kissed Emma in the gazebo at Hui Aloha while his own wedding feast to Julia was still in progress, then made love to her in a ramshackle hut while promising to divorce his wife, only to let her down a third time. Right now, his poor darling's pride must be in shreds. She needed to berate him, to curse him and slap his face, to pretend she no longer cared for him, in order to save face—and to keep from getting hurt by him all over again.

"She's a beautiful child," he began again, fighting the urge to lean over, draw Emma into his arms and kiss away her fears. He nodded at the little girl lolling heavily against her. It was no lie. She really *was* a beautiful child. The rich, creamy beige of her flawless skin was in sharp contrast to the inky, glossy darkness of her hair and the sharply defined deep-rose of lips and blooming cheeks. In fact, he fancied he and Emma's children would look very much like her, someday, God willing. "Is she one of Auntie Leo's *moapunas,* grandchildren?"

"Noo," she corrected him grudgingly, to his surprise, her violet eyes sliding away, as if she couldn't bear to look him full in the face. "Mahealani's my . . . little sister."

"Your *what?* But she can't be more than seven or eight years old!"

"Six, actually. She was *hanai,* fostered, by my cousin, Anela, and her husband when she was only a few days old. There were reasons her—our—mother couldn't keep her, you see?" she added, sounding defensive somehow. She crossed her fingers.

Gideon guessed she was referring to her mother's lingering illness and her ne'er-do-well father's drinking bouts.

"Sometimes she lived with them, sometimes with my other cousin, Lei, and her husband, Kamuela. She's such a pet. They all love her and make a great fuss over her."

"So do you, I see," he observed.

"How could I not?" Emma asked gruffly, drawing the sleeping child closer and inhaling the clean, childhood scents of ocean, sweet grasses, flowers, and sleep that clung to Mahealani's warm skin and hair. She propped her chin upon the little girl's lolling head. "She's very easy to love."

"In that, she reminds me of someone else," he murmured huskily, his heart in his eyes.

She stiffened. "Aah. You must be thinking of your wife, Mister Kane," she shot back, unable to resist the spiteful gibe, or the chance to hurt him in some small way, as he'd hurt her. She swallowed over the knot in her throat. *Damn him, damn him, why couldn't he just ride off and leave her be?* Her true feelings were still so fragile this morning, so dangerously close to breaking free all over again in a burst of bitter, futile rage that would make last night's little outburst pale by comparison, and do no real good. "I'm sorry. That was both childish and uncalled for."

"Perhaps it was," he agreed, stern-faced. "But it was also quite understandable—and surely no more than I deserve."

Silence—broken only by the birds' joyful matins and the silvery jingling of the bridles as their horses plodded along, side by side—yawned between them once again.

"Emma, you were right," he began tentatively, yet with an urgency to his tone that compelled her to rein in her horse and turn in the saddle to look at him. "You were right about everything. Honor is nothing compared to the pain of living without you. We belong together—have from the first moment we met. Perhaps even before then! We'll go away—anywhere!—it doesn't matter where. We'll leave everything behind and start afresh. The ranch, the Kane fortune, none of them matter to me. You—you're all I care about. Nothing matters but the two of us."

"Don't say that, Gideon. You don't mean it, not really," she said wearily. "You love your family and your land. Do you think I don't know that? And do you think I could still love a man who'd abandon his wife and child? One without principles, without any sense of duty or obligation? Oh, I know I've been denying it—hoping I could somehow change it—but it's true, Gideon. You and I and the way we feel about each other, we're not what's important anymore. And you wouldn't be the man I loved if you could bring yourself to turn your back on Julia and your baby. If—if that's the only way I can have you, then I'd rather not have you at . . . at a-a-all!" She drummed her heels sharply into Makani's sides and sent the mare careening down the trail ahead of Gideon's stallion, hoping he would not see the tears that trickled from beneath her lashes.

"Emma, for God's sake!" He kneed his horse after hers, catching up with her only moments later. She'd reined in her mare, he saw, and was staring up through the avenue of trees and tangled vegetation to the winding trail up ahead, where the track looped in and out of view, following the high coastline. Her cheeks were moist, the tracks of her tears glistening in the first rays of sunlight. Each one was a drop of pure acid that etched his heart.

And then, alerted by her sudden silence, he followed the direction of her gaze and saw what she had seen: several riders with torches held aloft and flags of fire streaming behind them. The spectacular cavalcade made a striking tableau against the lightning charcoal sky, briefly glimpsed, then gone, like a troupe of phantom night-riders, bearing corpselights aloft as they came down the trail toward them.

"Someone's coming." Her anger was forgotten now. Instead, a chill of foreboding filled her.

In almost the same breath, the Spanish cowboy, Felipe, appeared between the leafy trees, a half-dozen other *paniolos* at his heels. Most of them still wore their heavy woven ponchos slung about their shoulders against the crisp night air.

"*Gracias a Dios,* we have found you, Don Gideon!" Felipe exclaimed.

"What's wrong?" Gideon demanded, a chill seeping through him.

"It is your father, señor. Don Jacob is missing! He left Hui Aloha early yesterday morning, and has not yet returned. We have been searching for him since noon yesterday, but have had no luck. Doña Miriam sent us to find you, señor. She is beside herself with worry."

Gideon nodded, grim-faced with concern. The ranch's vast acreage encompassed treacherously steep ravines and barren lava wastes: deadly crevasses roofed with deceptively thin, brittle layers of lava that could crack and send a horse and rider plunging to their deaths; swift-rushing streams littered with boulders; steep valleys and mountains with *palis,* or cliffs, so sheer, even the brave Mauna Kea bronco balked at climbing them. This beautiful land he loved was fraught with many dangers for a cowboy in his prime. It was doubly treacherous for an older man with a bad hip. A cold sweat formed on his brow. His father could have been thrown from his horse. Even now, he could be lying at the bottom of a gulch somewhere, injured and in terrible pain. He could even be . . .

He flicked his head to rid himself of such thoughts. No. Not that. He couldn't . . . wouldn't even consider the alternative. "Did my father tell anyone where he was headed?"

"Alas, no, señor. Señor Kimo and I, we were busy with the branding up on the north pasture when *el viejo,* old Moki, came to ask if we had seen *Makua* Kane. It would seem he left Hui Aloha very early in the morning, and without a word to anyone!"

"Damn it, that's not like him," Gideon growled. His expression was even grimmer now, for it had been his father's hard and fast rule that no one should leave Hui Aloha at any time without also leaving word of their intended destination. And Jacob Kane had never been one to flout the rules, his own or otherwise. "Felipe, have one of the men escort Miss Jordan and her sister home—"

"Really, there's no need, Gideon," Emma cut in quickly. "I can keep up with the rest of you as far as Hui Aloha, if I may? I'd like to help."

He nodded distractedly. The search parties would need feeding as each band rode in. Returning horses would have to be rubbed down, fresh ones caught and saddled. There would be no shortage of work to do before his father was found. They had literally thousands of acres to cover! Finding one man in such terrain was tantamount to finding a needle in the proverbial haystack. He'd need a recent map of the ranch, so he could mark off the places Felipe and the hands had already searched, and to assign those remaining to fresh search parties. There was always something that needed doing at such a time. Another pair of hands would be welcome. "Thank you, Emma. We appreciate the offer. Let's ride, boys!"

Thirty

A side of Gideon Emma had never seen surfaced later that morning, once they'd reached Hui Aloha. He became a granite-faced stranger who snapped orders to left and right like a seasoned general planning his campaign, one whose tone demanded—and received—instant obedience.

With military precision, he organized the cowboys into a half-dozen effective search parties, assigned each one a leader, and showed them on the map which area they'd be responsible for searching. When completed, the search would have encompassed almost every accessible foot of Kane land. It was the best he could do, although in his heart of hearts, he knew it still might not be enough. There were numerous other places where a man might disappear without a trace, with not even his bones ever recovered, narrow, bottomless crevasses, shallow caves cut in sheer-walled cliffs where a falling man might have managed to claw his way, but where no rescuer could possibly follow. It had happened in the past enough times to leave the taste of foreboding in Gideon's mouth and fill his chest with a tight heaviness that could not be lightened, no matter how gamely Felipe and Kimo tried to cheer him.

Oh, to soar like the iwa, *the frigate bird!* he thought when lack of sleep and exhaustion made him fanciful and more than a little desperate by nightfall of the second day. He'd give anything he owned to possess the power of flight for just a day, an hour, to be able to spread his wings and glide on the updrafts, drift on the air currents, and scan the Kane land below for his father. He'd willingly give his right arm to be able to tell his mother that Jacob had been found, unharmed, and banish the awful dread in her eyes.

Emma decided to postpone her and Mahealani's return to the Waikalani Valley for the time being. School was finished until the sultry months of summer were ended, anyway, so they were free to do as they wished until September.

She told herself she'd chosen to stay with her aunt so that she could help out at Hui Aloha until Mister Kane was found, but the truth was, she'd stayed so that she would be close to Gideon. If she was brutally honest with herself, a selfish but very human side of her was secretly hoping he'd do as he'd threatened to do in Auntie Momi's garden: renounce his wife and his unborn baby, his family and his good name, and turn to her for consolation in these, his darkest hours.

And if he does? a small voice asked inside her head. *If he comes to you, what will you do, Miss Emma Kaleilani? What your heart bids you do—or the right thing, the decent, proper thing, and turn him away?* It was a possibility that terrified her, even as it filled her with joy and hope, for in her heart, she knew it was far too late to change anything now. Too many other innocent people would be hurt by their actions if they selfishly grabbed whatever happiness they could and chose to be together no matter what. A shiver ran through her. *No,* she told herself. *However much it hurts, Gideon made the right decision when he chose to stay with Julia and their child. They need him now, more than ever!*

She turned a deaf ear to the plaintive voice that asked, *And what about* me? *What about* my *needs? My* love? *My* broken *heart? My* ruined life?

As it turned out, she need not have worried about Gideon turning to her or the choice she would be forced to make, should he do so. Instead of looking to her for consolation, he withdrew into himself so deeply, she doubted he even knew she was at Hui Aloha at all, and that was even worse. Perversely, being so close to him day after day, night after night, yet unable to touch him, hold him, talk with him, comfort him by some small word or deed, was even worse than being parted.

Not a day passed when his anguish over his father's disappearance was not forcefully brought home to her, whether it was as he pored, hollow-cheeked, over a heavily creased map of the ranch once again, or perhaps as he leaned wearily over the *lanai* railing, running his hands through his unruly jet-black hair in the frustrated gesture she remembered so well, clearly wracking his brain for someplace they might have missed searching as he gazed out at the land, the vast, beautiful land that, like a whale, had swallowed his father whole.

Little by little, Emma saw the hope in Gideon's eyes dim as the hours, then days, came and went with no sign of his father's recovery. But, although she ached to hold him, to pillow his dark head upon her breast and whisper words of comfort to him, she was never given the opportunity to test her self-control, for she was never left alone with him, not for an instant. Julia Kane saw to that.

She sighed, wishing there was something—*anything*—she could do. She couldn't bear to see him so terribly worried and, although in the midst of so many concerned people, so terribly alone as he was in those days. True, his wife hovered about him, red-eyed, wringing her hands and weeping floods of tears, but Emma had seen him gently reject her timid efforts to console him. Instead, he'd offered Julia his stiff back, saying gruffly that he had things to do and that she must leave him to get on with them before seeking out his mother.

Despite everything, Emma had found herself pitying the blond woman over the past few days, for it was so painfully obvious that Julia truly loved her husband—and so patently obvious that he did not return her love, though to Gideon's credit, he never treated her less than cordially, and was always considerate of her well-being.

In the end, it seemed as if Julia had simply given up trying to be a comfort to her husband. She flashed Emma—who'd come up to the main house with the post Alika brought up from Kawaihae each week—a dark look and had asked huskily, "Are there any letters for my husband?" When Emma had answered in the negative, she'd cried, "But there must be! Why is it taking so long!" then rushed up the stairs to her bedroom, where she'd remained henceforth, even at mealtimes.

Strangely, the wretched woman seemed even more overwrought by Jacob Kane's disappearance than was his own wife, if that were possible! So very distraught, Emma observed, that it was Miriam Kane who ended up comforting and reassuring her daughter-in-law, rather than the other way around, while the serving girls who took trays of food up to the younger Missus Kane's room remarked that she ate little, and apparently spent most of her time crying, adding that if *haole*-missie wasn't careful, she'd miscarry her little one.

Poor Miriam. It was to her that Emma's heart went out in those first two endless days when Jacob's whereabouts remained unknown. How could the poor *wahine* endure all of this waiting, hoping, and praying, without shedding so much as a single tear or letting anyone guess by either word, deed, or expression how terribly frightened she must be? If it had been Gideon who was missing, Emma knew she would have been beside herself with fear, grown frantic long before this, sick to her belly and tearing out her hair with a worry that no amount of resolve could hide.

Admiration for Miriam Kane's courage and forbearance grew in everyone's hearts as the third day came without finding him, then the fourth. Throughout those endless hours, the mistress of Hui Aloha carried herself with a regal dignity and quiet strength that were wonderful to behold. She dressed and groomed herself as she had always done—immaculately—with strands of fragrant *pikake,* or jasmine, crowning her dark, upswept hair. And rather than retiring to her room, she pattered busily about the house, dusting and polishing, her toes peeping out from beneath the flowing skirts of her long, ruffled *muumuu*, barefoot in the island fashion. She issued soft commands to her serving girls to help her or Auntie Leolani prepare huge kettles of stew with dumplings or to wash out more tin mugs or to brew pot after pot of steaming tea or strong Kona coffee with which to feed the returning *paniolos*, who'd spent exhausting hours in the saddle, searching for the boss they loved. She served them their meals herself, and as she ladled and they ate, she asked after their comfort, their health, their needs, giving little or no thought to her own.

" 'Nough already, Cousin. Come. More bettah you rest little while," Leolani Pakele scolded her in her lilting pidgin on the third afternoon, gently leading Miriam from her herb garden, where she'd been gathering up horrid, leaf-eating snails with which to feed the chickens. The huge woman steered Miriam Kane to the gazebo where, unknown to the two older women, Emma had fallen into a fitful sleep on a heap of soft pillows strewn across one of the long storage seats.

There were telltale violet shadows ringing Miriam Kane's eyes and a slight tremor in her hands—both a direct result of the woman's exhaustion—Emma noticed as she rubbed sleepy eyes and sat up. From her conversation with her aunt the evening before, Emma knew her aunt was afraid that, without rest, Miriam might sink into a decline from which she would never recover.

"Please, honey girl, try to eat something, if not for me, then for Jacob," Leolani coaxed. "We're so worried about you, and *Makua* Kane would never want you to do this to yourself on his account. Won't you take a few sips of soup, just to please your Leolani? I'll bring a small bowl out here to you. No?" She sighed. "Then perhaps some fish and *poi* . . . ?"

Emma sat up. She saw Miriam Kane standing on the gazebo steps beside her aunt. She was shaking her elegant dark head emphatically about something or other, while Leolani Pakele urged her, "Darling girl—Cousin!—please! You cannot help your husband if you fall ill, now can you? You need food and sleep to keep you strong!"

"If only I *could* sleep, Cousin," Miriam exclaimed, her voice strained. "But you see, I—I fear the dreams sleep brings me."

"Ah . . ." Leolani whispered in understanding, and the expression on their faces as the two pairs of gentle brown eyes met sent a chill down Emma's spine.

Leolani took Miriam in her plump, dimpled arms. She embraced her and fondly kissed her cheeks "My poor cousin. So that explains it. I'm afraid you'll have to be very brave, little *wahine,"* she crooned, rocking the other woman like a small child, "and in the meantime, hope and pray that your dreams were false."

Miriam bit her lip and shook her head. "Alas, I fear they were not. You see, Old Moki has had them, too."

Leolani's blood ran cold. The old Hawaiian man was known for his ability to interpret dreams and, on occasion, to foresee future events. "Nevertheless, until we know otherwise, you must carry on," she said firmly. "Dreams and such things belong to the old ways and to the old gods of our grandmothers. Put such superstitions behind you, where they belong, and say your prayers, girlie. Beseech our Heavenly Father to return your beloved husband safely to you. And, if it is His will, then He will answer your prayers, dreams or nay, and bring him safely home."

She sighed. "I have done just that, so many, many times these past three days," Miriam whispered in a choked voice. "But alas, I fear that this time, Our Heavenly Father has not heeded me! It is not only dreams I've had, you see? It is more than superstition. I—saw something, too."

"Then perhaps your mind played a trick on you, little cousin? It happens sometimes, when we are exhausted and afraid for someone we love," Leolani reasoned, yet her low, sweet voice was filled with unshed tears.

"It wasn't my imagination. I saw him, Leolani. I saw Jacob!"

"When was this?"

Miriam closed her eyes and caught her lower lip between her teeth briefly before she was able to continue. "The very first evening he was missing. I went out onto the *lanai* just after dark, hoping he'd come riding up to the house as always—perhaps with a saddlebag full of flowers that he'd picked for me to string *leis*. It was then that I saw him."

"Ahh. And where was this?"

"He was standing beneath the *ohia lehua* tree, holding a sprig of its scarlet blossoms in one hand and a woven hat with a feathered band in the other. "Haunani, Dew of Heaven!" he called to me. Of course, I was delighted to see him safe and sound! I told myself I'd been foolish to worry so about him and answered gaily, 'My love, you're home so late!" In Hawaiian, he answered me softly, 'Am I? But why are you out here all alone, my beautiful wife? It is already dark and the air is so chill. Go inside, into the light, where you belong.' Well, I laughed and told him it wasn't cold at all. That it was a beautiful warm evening, and that I'd come outside in search of a cool breeze to fan me while I waited for him." Haunani blinked rapidly. Her lower lip quivered. "I told him to come inside and eat, but as I turned away, the strangest feeling came over me. It was as if—as if a cool, damp breeze had kissed my cheek, like the fine, chill rain of the plateaus that gives one goose-flesh. When I looked back to see if he was following me inside, he just faded away, right before my eyes!"

Remembering, Miriam closed her eyes and swayed. It was several seconds before she'd regained her composure sufficiently to continue. "I ran down the steps and stood in the driveway where he'd been standing. But there was nothing there but a sprig of *lehua*." She shivered and hugged herself. "The petals looked dark as—as bloodstains on the crushed coral."

Two pairs of liquid dark eyes met once again in silent communion, sharing a secret too terrible to voice.

* * *

Emma was weeping silently as she waited for them to leave the gazebo, wishing with all her heart she'd been somewhere—anywhere—else, and had not been forced to eavesdrop on the pair.

The search party led by Kimo Pakele found Jacob Kane's body soon after dawn the following morning. They brought him back to the home he'd loved like a mighty chieftain of old, his body wrapped in a length of patterned native *tapa* cloth and draped across the back of Kimo's horse.

His broad face ravaged by grief, the towering Hawaiian foreman was weeping unashamedly as he led his mount and its sad burden to the front of Hui Aloha, halting at the foot of the veranda steps where Gideon, his face implacable, waited alone.

Everyone at Hui Aloha had heard the three shots the search party that found the body had fired into the air in rapid succession, shortly after sunrise. The prearranged signal had been relayed time and time again from the site by successive search parties as they heard it, until those at the ranch house had finally been relayed the reports.

Now ranch hands, carpenters, horse wranglers, laborers, tanners, blacksmiths, and a gaggle of grubby children joined the anxious-eyed serving girls and dairymaids ringing the lawn. Native Hawaiian, Chinese, Japanese, Portuguese, Filipino, white, they stood with eyes downcast, faces filled with sorrow, shocked into silence as Kimo Pakele gently lifted the rancher's body from his horse, and—with tears streaming unashamedly down his face—slowly carried the master of Hui Aloha up the veranda steps, where he placed the body in his son's arms.

His expression unreadable, Gideon turned and carried his father inside. Sweeping off his hat, Kimo followed him in.

There was an unbearable silence in the wake of their disappearance that seemed to last an eternity. Everyone held their breath. The tension grew unbearable as the noon sun beat down upon the tops of everyone's heads. A cock crowed. A baby wailed fretfully. A dog howled, then fell abruptly silent, as if someone had jerked on its chain. And then, just when Emma was afraid she would explode, a high-pitched keening ruptured the hush.

Though they had all been expecting it, the waiting throng flinched as if they'd been struck as Miriam Kane wailed, *"Noooo! Dear Lord, no! Au-uu—we! Au-uu-we!"*

Haunani's wails of grief acted like a floodgate on the emotions of all gathered there. The older Hawaiian women began their traditional show of mourning, weeping and wailing, chanting and tearing their hair from its pins as they rocked to and fro.

This couldn't be happening, Emma thought, feeling numb as she held Mahealani close and squeezed her so tightly for comfort, the little girl cried out in protest. There was a painful lump in her throat. Tears burned in her eyes. It wasn't fair! Hadn't Gideon endured the horrors of the war? Being away from his beloved islands and—yes!—losing her? Hadn't he suffered more than enough torment already? And wasn't his mother a fine, God-fearing woman who'd always helped others? One who didn't deserve to lose the husband she adored? But nevertheless, it was so. And nothing they did could change that.

Jacob Kane, patriarch of the Kane Ranch, a man who'd been as Hawaiian at heart as the native people he'd loved all his life—a man who'd eaten, slept, and all but lived in a saddle since his second birthday—had, or so the party that found them surmised, ridden his horse into a deep pit, one that some cattle rustler or other had dug in the old way that hunters had used to trap a bullock or a wild pig for slaughter.

The unexpected fall had snapped the front legs of Jacob Kane's horse in two, and—in all likelihood—knocked its rider unconscious. When the poor beast, driven mad with pain, had struggled and thrashed wildly to escape the pit, its flailing hooves had crushed Jacob Kane's skull like eggshells, and by so doing, killed him.

To all intents and purposes, the superstitious prophecy that Alika had made when Julia Kane picked the blossoms of the *lehua* tree had been fulfilled. Blood had indeed been spilled, and the cattle baron was dead; the victim of a tragic if unavoidable accident. Or was he . . . ?

By nightfall, there was muttering in the bunkhouse among the *paniolos* and in the little bungalows and grass *hales* among the native serving women and ranch hands that, despite appearances, the boss's death had been no accident.

Thirty-one

The women of Hui Aloha came together that afternoon in the room Jacob had shared with his beloved Haunani. They tenderly washed his body, then dressed him in his finest clothes, neatly brushing the shock of pure silver hair that had been his only vanity back from his brow and temples. When the women were done, the men lifted him into a fine casket of *milo* wood that the ranch's carpenter had made for his own burial, then left his wife and son alone with the body to say their last farewells.

The following morning, Gideon donned the formal dark frockcoat and breeches of mourning. His wife—her pale face ravaged by sleeplessness and weeping, her expression fearful—wore again the widow's weeds she'd only recently abandoned, while Gideon's mother dressed in white after the Hawaiian custom of honoring the dead. Both women sat stiffly on chairs to one side of the casket. Dry-eyed and composed, the trio graciously accepted the condolences of the over two thousand people—many of whom had traveled several miles upon receiving the sad news—who came to pay *Makua* Kane their last respects.

All that day and late on into that evening and again the next morning, they came, and they continued to come, either alone or in groups of two, three, four—sometimes more. Hawaiian, Chinese, Portuguese, Scottish, or German alike, they came, guided by the flaming torches that had been lit and placed around the grounds of Hui Aloha, drawn by their love and respect for the wonderful man who had so cruelly been taken from them before his time.

Either weeping softly, or chanting the *meles* that told of the many good things that Jacob Kane had done in his lifetime, their voices rose and fell eerily in the ancient tongue of the islands as they entered Hui Aloha with its crepe-draped mirrors and windows. One by one, they filed past the casket on the long table in the parlor to pay their last respects to the rancher who had made a difference in all their lives. In the morning, the family—with the exception of Julia Kane, who had declared herself too grief-stricken to make the rough voyage in her delicate condition—and their closest friends and retainers would accompany the casket to Kawaihae, and from there, board the steamer to Honolulu, where Jacob Kane would receive a state funeral. Emma was among the mourners.

"Thank you for coming, Miss Jordan," Gideon murmured as she stood, her dark head bowed, before him. He gravely took the hand she offered him and held it a fraction of a second longer than that of the other mourners. Looking shyly up at him, she could see the pain in his eyes, and her heart went out to him.

"I'm so very sorry about your father," she murmured sincerely, tears about to brim over in her eyes. "He was a wonderful man, and he did so many good things for this island and the people here in his lifetime. If there's anything I can do—either for you or your poor mother—you've only to ask. My auntie Leolani's asked me to stay on at their home for a few days so that I can keep an eye on the house and the serving girls until you . . . until you and the rest of the family get back from Honolulu."

He nodded and cleared his throat. "Thank you, Miss Jordan. It's very kind of you to look after things for us. I hope it will be no trouble?"

Their eyes met, and the yearning, the depth of the need in his, was so potent, so heated and alive, it was as if a sudden gust of hot air had belched out of an oven to scorch her face with its blast.

"No trouble at all, really," Emma mumbled. Stunned, confused, she looked up and caught Julia's eyes upon them, her mouth twisted in barely concealed rage. Pulling her hand from within Gideon's, Emma moved quickly away, mumbling that she felt a little faint. It was no lie. She felt faint with shock, weak with shame and guilt that even here, in this place of sorrow and death—this place where the sharp, sad scent of a thousand island flowers lay like a pall over the air and where Gideon's lawful wife presided as lady of all—she could yet feel the tug of desire in her breasts and belly. What was she? she wondered, disgusted with herself. Some heartless ghoul? A shameless wanton? And yet, she amended, what could be more natural, in all honesty, than to want to celebrate life and creation in the face of death?

She could not sleep that night for thinking of Gideon, seeing his tormented face over and over again in her mind's eye. She considered the words she would say to comfort him, if only he were there and they could be alone together. Tossing and turning on her sleeping mat, in the end, she abandoned all attempts at sleeping.

Flinging aside the sheet, she rose and drew a shawl about her shoulders, then slipped away from the Pakeles' *lanai* and out into the hushed garden, tempted to walk the mile or so to Hui Aloha and see if he was also sleepless and wandering.

The moon was full and bright, a ghostly ship in full sail, scudding across a sky as dark as the darkest *popolo* berries. Her light glinted in the diamond droplets of dew that clung like tears to each blade of grass, each waxy petal, each leaf. The scents of frangipani and ginger, tuberose and jasmine, lay heavy on the sultry air, intoxicating, almost, in their heady quality. Leaning back against the ridged trunk of a lofty palm, she inhaled the glorious fragrances and gazed up at an equally glorious sky.

"All things bright and beautiful . . ." The words of the popular

hymn seemed appropriate, for on such a bright and beautiful, magical night as this, anything seemed possible. Anything at all.

"I wish . . . !" she began, and although there was no falling star, nor any first star to wish upon, her wish was granted nonetheless.

He came like a thief in the wee, dark hours, placing a finger across her lips to silence her cry of alarm when she turned at the scuff of his boots on the grass. He stood there, his dark eyes glittering feverishly in his shadowed face as he towered over her. "I need you, *ku'uipo*," he growled, and she was shocked at the raw hunger in his eyes, the anguish that made his voice a husky rasp as she moved into his open arms.

Whispering his name again and again, she kissed his hair, his cheeks, his lips, tasting the salt of tears upon them. "My dearest dear," she murmured, and framed his face between her hands, "Oh, my love, I know how it feels. Oh, yes, yes, I know! Don't hold back. Let it out, my heart. Let it *all* out."

Drawing him down into the shadows, she loosened the ribbon ties that fastened her nightgown at the throat and tugged it down so that his ebony head was cradled upon her bared breasts. Crooning endearments, she stroked his head, weeping along with him for the father he had loved and lost.

He began to make love to her, deep shudders moving through him as he caressed and kissed her that tore at her heart. Raising the skirts of her nightgown, she drew him onto her body, placing his hands upon her breasts. "Enough, my darling. Come. Love me," she murmured. Parting her thighs, she guided his swollen manhood to the dark triangle at the pit of her belly, urging him to seek his own release. She offered herself, her woman's body, as a balm to his pain, yet demanded no conditions, asked for nothing in return. She had never stopped loving him—*never!*—and tonight, he needed her. For now, that need was all that mattered.

* * *

Even as Emma and Gideon made bittersweet love in a grassy bower, in a ramshackle hut on the outskirts of a nearby village Jack Jordan was fighting for his life, clawing at his throat, trying desperately to tear away the fingers clamped about it.

He screamed in pain and terror as, one by one, the fingernails peeled off his fingers, leaving them raw and bleeding. But still, the stranglehold tightened until he was gagging . . . spluttering . . . fighting desperately for every breath he drew.

Through bulging eyes, he saw old Moki's brown, seamed face—strangely disembodied—floating before him in the shadows. Long, grizzled hair fluttered about his face, like the airborne moss named "Pele's hair," stirred by an unseen wind, while his eyes glowed like sequins, red as any demon's.

"Nooooogggghh!" Jack shrieked. His bladder failed him in a hot, stinging rush. Sweat poured from him, burning his eyes as he battled his unseen enemies, throwing himself first to right, then to left in a desperate effort to escape their—his—its—hold.

"Wot do you want from me, eh?" he whispered hoarsely, spittle gathering at the corners of his cracked lips. "Tell me, damn you! Tell me! I did like you wanted, didn't I? I left your bleedin' burial caves, now leave me be!"

Legs scrabbling for purchase, he tried frantically to escape the *kahuna's* image. Yet even as he watched, Old Moki melted away until only his glowing red eyes remained. The eyes ran together, became a spinning fireball of smoky red, instead; an entity—one not of this world—that hovered, motionless, before Jack Jordan's bulging eyes for seconds that were endless, before it drifted slowly across the hut and out through the open door . . .

"Stop iiiit, you 'eathen savages!" he shrieked. "Leave me alone! It won't work, I tell yer! You can't pray me t' death, you godless bastards, 'cos I don't believe in yer 'eathen sorcery! I won't die, see? I won't! I won't!"

Sobbing, Jack fell back to the earthen floor, babbling like a lunatic. It was almost dawn before he'd calmed down enough to start wondering if it'd all been a nightmare, after all. *Christ bloody Almighty!* It had seemed so real! Still half convinced, his hands strayed to his throat. It felt bruised, but there were no lacerations that he could feel. *Strewth!* His underarms and back were still wringing wet!

Shaking his head, he reached with a trembling hand for the half-empty jug of rotgut he kept within easy reach, and swallowed deeply. The rum's fiery heat slithered deep down inside him, spreading its warming fire throughout his belly. And with the heat came oblivion—until the next time . . .

Thirty-two

"Lady, are you a princess?"

The child's piping voice penetrated the thick fog in Julia's head. She glanced up to see a little girl regarding her solemnly from long-lashed eyes of an indeterminate hue. Ringlets of glossy jet-black hair tumbled down her back in a riot of gypsy curls, while her snub little nose balanced perfectly her full-lipped, rosebud mouth. Frowning, Julia struggled to make sense of what the pretty child had said and remember who she was, besides, but could not. "Wh-what?"

"I said, Are—you—a—princess?" the moppet repeated slowly.

She grimaced. "Honey, right now, I don't rightly know if I'm even *human,* let alone a princess. Why in the world would you ask me a question like that, huh?"

"Your hair. That's why," the child confessed shyly. "It's sooo pretty and golden in the sunshine. I wish I had long golden hair instead of black hair like everyone else. In the fairy tales Kaleilani reads to me, the princesses *always* have golden hair."

Julia wrinkled her nose, wracking her memory for an exception to the rule, but could recall no raven-haired princesses. "Yep. I reckon they do," she agreed. "And they all had 'happily-ever-after' endings, too, didn't they, sugar?" She winked. "But as I recollect, there's likely a wicked ole witch or a mean ole wolf or even a hairy old ogre hidin' right around the corner, just awaitin' t' gobble 'em up, too, so maybe bein' a princess ain't all sugar an' spice. Did you ever think about that?"

Mahealani considered this for a moment, but judging by her doubtful expression, she wasn't about to be so easily put off. "Have you ever seen a big bad wolf, lady?"

"I surely have, sugar, lots of times—the first time when I was jest a little bitty thing like you. There's packs of 'em roamin' the hills where I was raised up. Nighttime, you can hear 'em howlin' at the moon, real mournful like. Makes the hairs stand up on yore neck, it do."

Her eyes wide, Mahealani asked in a whisper, "And were they mean, those wolves?"

"Oh, they sure was, sugar. Mean as all get up, 'specially when they was hungry. They sported the looongest, yellerest teeth you ever did see, and yeller eyes that could jest freeze a body in place, right where they was standin'! Why, a princess wouldn't hardly stand a chance against one o' them gray varmints, golden hair or no! No, sir, no chance at all . . ."

"Hmm. P'raps I don't want to be a princess after all," Mahealani decided at length.

"Well, you sure are pretty enough to be a princess, sugar," Julia murmured, smiling.

"Mahalo nui loa," Mahealani thanked her, and promptly tucked a small pink thumb into her mouth. She sucked on it thoughtfully.

"Come on over here, sugar," Julia urged, patting the gazebo steps beside her. She tucked the shiny folds of her red satin kimono closer about her as she added, "You c'n keep me company for a spell, all right?" The child nodded as Julia grumbled, "This here place is 'bout as lively as a tomb, what with everyone gone." *Tomb?* Hell and be damned, that was a damn-poor choice of words, she thought ruefully, shuddering as she recalled the nightmare that had awakened her in the wee hours and sent her stumbling about the darkened house in search of a drink to calm her nerves.

She'd dreamed Jacob Kane had been laid to rest within a vault of lava rock that lay deep in the rain forest, a place very much like the one where she'd gone with Jacko. Somehow, Father Kane had burst free of his grave and, clad in his moldering shroud, he'd come in search of her, moaning and gibbering that she was to blame for his death. When she'd awakened, crying and shivering, the linens had been soaked with sweat and her heart pounding like a triphammer. She'd panicked and gotten tangled up in the mosquito netting before she'd managed to break free to light a lamp . . .

"You look scared, lady. Is there a mean old witch waiting to gobble you up?" the little girl asked as she took her seat alongside Julia.

"Whassat?" For a second, Julia was still dreaming. She blinked and forced her attention back to the present. "A witch? Weell, now, I don't rightly know about an old witch, honey, but I've a notion there's a young'un who'd like *real* bad to see me gobbled up—an' never mind spittin' out the pieces!" Julia snorted at her own little joke. Heck, after drinking half a bottle of Jacob Kane's apricot brandy, stolen from his hidden store of medicinal spirits, she was feeling no pain, and the idea of Gideon's mistress being a witch tickled her fancy. She laughed throatily again.

"What are you laughing at, lady?" Mahealani asked innocently.

"Why, the whole damn world, sugar. I'm laughin' at the whole—damn—world!"

The child frowned at the harsh edge to the pretty lady's voice. "If it's funny, then why were you crying?"

"Me, cryin'? Was I cryin', too?"

"Uh huh." She nodded solemnly. "You were makin' little piggy noises like this." She wrinkled up her nose and snorted like a little piglet. "Lots of noises. I heard you when I was hiding in the summerhouse."

"Hiding, huh? Who from?"

"Kaleilani."

"Who's she? Your momma?"

"Nuh uh. She's my big, big sister, an' she's my schoolteacher, too. I have to call her Miss Jordan when we're at the schoolhouse, but sometimes, I forget and call her Kalei. What's your name?"

"Weell, Missus Kane always calls me Kulia. She says that's the Hawaiian way to say my real name, Julia."

"I'm Mahealani. That means Full Moon of Heaven. Are you sad because Mister Kane died and went to heaven, Kulia?" Mahealani sighed. "Kaleilani's very sad about it. So're Auntie Leolani and Uncle Kimo, and Pua and Felipe and everybody. Auntie Leo said the king and the royal family will be sad when they hear, too, 'cos *Makua* Kane was a very good man, and their friend. He did lots of good things to help the 'conomy of the Kingdom of Hawaii," she added, obviously quoting a grown-up. She heaved another gusty sigh. "I didn't even know him, but I'm sad, too. I'm always sad when somebody dies."

"So'm I, honey," Julia consoled her, close to tears herself. She slipped her arm around the child's waist and hugged her, astonished by the pleasure the impulsive gesture gave her. She was doubly delighted when the affectionate little girl promptly hugged her back. "Jacob Kane was a sweet old man. A good man, too. It weren't his time t' die—not yet, and surely not in that way!" She shuddered and tears smarted behind her eyes, but then she flicked her head as if to dismiss whatever unpleasant thought had crossed her mind and dropped a kiss on the little girl's head.

"*Makua* Kane's horse falled in a big hole, and he got all broked up," Mahealani explained matter-of-factly, spreading her arms wide to show how huge that awful hole had been. "I falled down last week an' scraped my knee. It hurt really, really bad, but I didn't go to heaven. I just went to Kaleilani. She rubbed some aloe sap on it, and now it's all better. Look!" She yanked up the skirts of her ruffled pinafore to reveal a knobbly little knee that sported a scab the size of a nickel. "Maybe they can put some aloe on *Makua* Kane?" she suggested hopefully.

Julia winced. "You were a brave girl. That knee must have been real sore, honey. But *Makua* Kane . . . Mister Kane was hurt too bad for aloe to help him, or the *kahunas*. He's gone up yonder to heaven now, to be with Jesus and his angels. He ain't hurtin' anymore." *Or more likely,* she amended grimly, *that sweet, kind, trustin' old fool's turnin' cartwheels in his grave after the part I played in his death!* Damn that Jacko to hell and back for getting me into this! she thought, her fists clenched in her lap and hate in her heart. She just knew Papa Kane's death wasn't no accident, despite appearances. Blackmail, hell! Cattle rustlers, hell! what a fool she'd been, to believe Jack Jordan's empty promises that the old man wouldn't be hurt. And worse than stupid to believe he was only after Kane's money!

Mahealani screwed up her nose. "I'm never going to heaven. I'm going to stay right here with Kaleilani an' Auntie Leo an' Uncle Kimo an' Auntie Anela and Auntie Momi—an' Beauty an' Makani an all my cousins, too, forever and ever, amen. And you, too, Kulia," she added generously, flashing Julia an adorable grin.

Julia smiled through her tears, swallowed over the aching knot of guilt in her throat. "Why, thank you kindly, honey. But what about your momma? Don't you want to stay with her?"

The little girl's eager expression became a scowl. "I don't have a *makuahine.*"

"You don't?"

Mahealani shook her head vigorously, spraying loose black ringlets in all directions. "Uh uh. Not anymore. She was very sick for a long, long time, and then she died. But I've got Kaleilani, instead. And before her, I had Auntie Anela and Auntie Lei. They're almost the same as having a mama."

Why, the poor little mite was practically an orphan, all alone in this big, ole world, 'cept for Papa Jacko—and he surely didn't count much for a father. Abandoned by a sickly momma, it sounded as if she'd been passed from family member to family member, probably made to feel grateful for every morsel of food she put in her mouth, too, Julia assumed, her heart going out to the little minx in a way that was quite unlike her.

She stroked Mahealani's dark head, her thoughts made maudlin by the half bottle of liquor she'd downed on an empty belly. She couldn't recall the last time she'd eaten, though she knew it must have been before Gideon and his mother and the Pakeles left for Honolulu for Jacob Kane's funeral. She'd sent the serving girls away until Monday, and the house seemed enormous without them, the ticking of the clocks like the beating of some huge heart. The liquor had helped to blot out the sounds, to numb her conscience, to assuage her guilt. It had also helped her to forget . . . for a little while.

Fresh tears welled as she hugged the little girl to her and thought about her own childhood in the Appalachians. Those years had been far from rosy, with a pappy who could have been Jack Jordan's twin brother. He, too, had had a foxy smile, a pair of wandering hands, and an unnatural fondness for his little daughters—herself in particular. But there was one small difference. She'd had a momma to put food in *her* belly, and a granny to dry her tears once in a while . . .

"Mahealaaani! Where aaare youuu?" called a voice.

"Oh! I have to go now! Kaleilani's coming. She'll find me!" the child squealed breathlessly, jumping to her feet. Her eyes danced with naughty merriment. *"Aloha,* princess lady. I bettah go hide—!"

But before the child could make good her escape, Emma's head and shoulders suddenly appeared over the hibiscus hedge. Julia bristled with rage. It was bad enough the Pakele woman had asked that—that little tramp—to supervise the running of the ranch house in her absence, without so much as a by-your-leave. She wasn't about to have Gideon's fancy woman right here, in her own backyard—no, sireee! Green with jealousy, she noticed that the scarlet hibiscus trumpets looked gaudy and vulgar against the woman's trimly clad figure and neatly upswept hair . . . that her violet eyes were twinkling as she spied the little girl—and filled with love.

"Ah ha! So, there you are, miss! I've been looking everywhere for you, you *kalohe,* you rascal!" Emma exclaimed. Unaware of Julia's presence, she brandished a sheaf of envelopes like a fan. "Cousin Alika rode clear up from Kawaihae to bring us the post this morning. I thought perhaps you'd like to play postman and take these letters up to Missus Kane's house for me. You can put them in the big wooden bowl on the little table in the entryway, if you. . . ." She paused and frowned, unable to see Julia from where she stood. But—recognizing the naughty glint in Mahealani's expression—she cocked her head to one side, planted her fists on her hips, and demanded, "Mahealani? What's wrong with you? What mischief have you been up to now?"

"I finded a princess, Kalei! A real one, with long golden hair just like in the book you read to me. Look! Here she is!" Mahealani exclaimed, clapping her little hands in delight. "Her Hawaiian name's Kulia, and she told me she saw a big bad wolf once, too," she insisted in her own defense, favoring Emma with a defiant scowl.

Her stormy expression made Julia blink and peer at her with sudden intensity, as if she hadn't really looked at the child until that very moment. What had the little imp said? That her Kaleilani and Gideon's Emma Jordan were one and the same. And that she was Emma Kaleilani's little sister? Well, if that was so, then how come the little girl was the spitti—

"You found a princess—ohh!" Emma halted, falling abruptly silent as she rounded the hibiscus hedge to find Gideon's wife, of all people, seated on the steps of the gazebo! Mahealani was perched cozily beside her, her little hand tucked trustingly inside Julia's own, her cheek nesting against the woman's arm as if they'd been friends forever.

Emma swallowed, filled by irrational, jealous feelings she knew were probably childish and definitely should have been

beneath her—but weren't, just the same. The Lennox woman
already had Gideon's name and she would soon have his baby.
Must she try to win Mahealani over, too, with her shallow ploys?
In her opinion—with the exception of her long blond hair, which
had clearly fascinated the little girl—there was precious little
about Julia Kane that resembled a princess. And today, she didn't
even have that much to recommend her!

Julia's hair fell in an unkempt, tangled mane about her shoulders and looked as if it had not been combed in days. Her willowy body was sheathed in a crimson satin kimono, embroidered
with a garish gold-and-black dragon design. She looked, Emma
decided—secretly pleased by the comparison—like the painted
doxies who strolled the wharves of Honolulu by night or called
to the sailors from the upper windows of cheap boardinghouses.
Indeed, scantily dressed as she was—and in broad daylight,
too!—she appeared an immoral, vulgar creature, one who was,
perhaps, even a little . . . *drunk?* Incredulous as it seemed,
Emma sniffed, her nose wrinkling. She was almost positive she
could smell spirits, though it might also have been the reek of
cheap perfume, she allowed charitably.

With her rival's sudden appearance, Julia sprang to her feet.
Her pale eyes were narrowed in recognition and color filled her
cheeks as she glared at Emma with undisguised hostility.

Though she could have stood no more than five feet four
inches tall, the half-breed chit carried herself with the regal grace
and innocent sensuality of an island princess and the quiet pride
and dignity of a queen, damn her flawless hide, Julia thought.
Indeed, there had been times in those awful four days when
Jacob had been missing that she'd been unable to rid her mind
of the image of *Emma* as the future mistress of Hui Aloha, instead of herself, and been furious at how perfectly that—that
fornicating little schoolmarm-cum-*hula-hula*-dancer would
look the part!

Emma Jordan's complexion was beige silk, tinged at the
cheeks and lips with deep rose. Her eyes were a lustrous, long-

lashed violet, slightly tilted at their outer corners. She had a trim yet womanly figure that filled out her crisp, high-necked shirt-waist of navy-and-white-striped Egyptian cotton, which she wore tucked into an ankle-length, dark-blue skirt. She looked cool and beautiful, and jealousy twisted in Julia's innards like a small, sharp blade. She'd hoped that, close up, Gideon's mistress would be plain—or even better, uglier than the backside of a mule—but she didn't hardly come close to bein' plain. Hell, no! Gideon's little native slut was both exotic and beautiful, damn her eyes, with ladylike ways and airs about her, although she was as barefoot as any pickaninny. And unlike her own, the Jordan woman's ladylike manners owed nothing to powder and paint. They had not been picked up in the wings of a Baltimore playhouse as Julia's had been, night after night spent committing fancy lines and high-fallutin' gestures to memory, while that carpetbagging scalawag, Davie Lennox and the Lennox Players, performed!

Julia's heart squeezed painfully, but she mustered her pride, drew herself up to her full height, and cast Emma a withering glare. "What in the hell are you still doing here, you hussy?" she hissed, looking down her nose at Emma as if she smelled something foul. "Your sort ain't wanted at Hui Aloha! Have you no shame? No respect? *Makua* Kane is dead, for pity's sake, and we—his family—wish to mourn him in private. If you had an ounce of decency, you'd leave! Leave this instant!"

Emma's chin came up. And, although her violet eyes flashed angrily, she managed to bite back a blistering retort and instead said, "I'm afraid I can't leave, Missus Kane. Before she accompanied the older Missus Kane to Honolulu, my aunt—Missus Pakele—asked me to instruct the serving girls in her absence and supervise the running of the household."

"Oh, she did, did she? And I suppose she'd set a coyote t' watching the hen house, too?" She snorted. "Clearly the good woman has no inkling of just who—or should I say *what*—sort of woman you really are, Emma Jordan!" Julia accused, her fists planted on her hips. "Or more likely, was too overwrought, under the tragic circumstances, to give the matter much thought!" She tossed her hair over her shoulder and glared at Emma.

"Ah. And what sort of woman am I, Missus Kane? Would you care to enlighten me?" Emma inquired coolly, standing her ground as Julia stalked toward her.

"Aw, come on, sugar. I'm sure you know better than anyone what you are. You sure as heck don't fool me with that 'butter wouldn't melt in yore mouth!' look! You're my husband's fancy woman!" Julia crowed. "His little whore! You think I don't know all about yore goings-on up on the range? You're no better than an alley cat in heat!"

"And what about you, *Missus* Kane?" Emma demanded softly. "What about your . . . rendezvous with Jack Jordan in the forest? Does your husband know about those, I wonder?"

Emma was gratified to see the color drain from Julia's face. It looked as if Uncle Kimo's suspicions had been founded, after all. Guilt was written all over Julia Kane's face.

"See here, now, don't you go comparin' your immoral doin's to the actions of us decent folks," Julia countered, her mind racing. "When I first suspected Gideon was meeting you, I hired Mister Jordan to . . . to follow my husband for me. A service for which I paid him royally, I'll have you know!"

"You thought Gideon and I were meeting each other?" Emma whispered.

"Weren't you?"

Emma bit back a denial. Julia sounded so sure of herself! Did she know about the one night she and Gideon had made love in the line-camp hut? And the second, bittersweet time, after his father's death? Had she *really* hired Jack Jordan to follow them—or was she just trying to throw a smokescreen over her own indiscretions? Emma shrugged her questions aside. It didn't really matter. However she answered the woman, it was doubtful she'd be believed, and squabbling like a pair of mynah birds could serve no worthwhile purpose but to expose Mahealani to an ugly quarrel.

"No answer, Emma honey? Why, whatever's wrong, sugar? Cat got your tongue?" Julia crowed in triumph, certain Emma Jordan's silence was an admission of guilt. "You shouldn't play the cheating game 'less you're ready to lose," she taunted. "Gideon's *mine*, see, and I don't plan on givin' him up without a fight—not to you, or anyone else. I love him, you hear me— and I plan on keepin' him, come hell or high water! It's me and *our baby* he'll come on home to after the funeral, not you. Now, I asked you to leave Hui Aloha, and I meant it, sugar, so hightail your little half-breed ass off Kane land, or else—!"

"I don't have to listen to this. Come, Mahealani," she whispered hoarsely, her face flaming. She was trembling all over with a mixture of mortification, guilt, and honest anger as she held out her hand to the child. "Let's deliver the letters and go home."

"Kaleilani, what's wrong? Your hand is wiggling!" Mahealani asked, looking first at Julia, then up at Emma from wide, frightened eyes.

"It's nothing, *'ipo*. I'm all right," Emma insisted, forcing a smile. "Say goodbye to Missus Kane now, darling, and come along. We'll take the letters inside together, shall we?" Her eyes met Julia's over the child's dark head. "Good day, Missus Kane."

When Emma reached the veranda steps, she couldn't resist a backward glance over her shoulder. Julia Kane was still staring after them. And, to Emma's surprise, her expression was sad and somehow frightened rather than triumphant and filled with loathing, as might have been expected.

Her heart was still thumping over the confrontation as she went inside the house. The serving girls came late today, since it was the Sabbath and there was church to attend in the village, and with Missus Kane and Auntie Leolani gone, the windows had yet to be opened. Hot, stale air billowed around her when she opened the door, though she was too preoccupied thinking about Julia to notice.

To her mind, that awful woman—with her gaudy wardrobe and her bold way of speaking—seemed far too shrewd to ever have let herself be forced into a marriage she didn't want by an amorous drunkard like some naive schoolgirl. Could Gideon have been tricked, rather than compromised? she wondered for the first time. And if so, was Julia truly expecting his child? She doubted it, now that she'd seen the woman close up. From what she could see of it, Julia Kane's belly had been flatter than the proverbial pancake, though surely her condition should have started to show by now?

Absently fanning her sweaty face with the letters in her hand, Emma thought about the child Julia was supposedly carrying. With Jacob Kane dead, the baby had become of even greater importance, for its safe birth would ensure that the Kane line would continue.

Glancing idly down at the sheaf of letters in her hand, she noticed the top one was from Thomas Kane, Gideon's cousin. It had been hastily addressed—in chicken-scratch penmanship and with many blots—to him alone, and marked URGENT in the left-hand, lower corner. The second envelope was embossed with the seal of the law firm of Alexander McHenry and Partners; another was addressed to Jacob Kane, Esquire, from a carriage company in Honolulu, while the fourth, this also for Gideon, had come direct from a local Big Island sawmill. The letters, most of them steamer-brought from Oahu, must have crossed Gideon and his mother on the second steamer as they made their sorry journey to Honolulu for *Makua* Kane's funeral.

She swallowed, Julia utterly forgotten as she blinked back tears. Poor Gideon! How remote, how saddened her beloved had seemed when he rode away from Hui Aloha that morning, his broad shoulders encased in one of the stern black frock coats he hated as he followed the ox-drawn wagon. The cumbersome yet sturdy vehicle would carry his father's flower-draped casket along the rough trail down to Kawaihae, where it would be taken aboard the inter-island steamer and from there, to Honolulu.

As they set out on their sad journey, Emma had watched through the fine misty rain that had fallen, a gentle rain that the Hawaiians had welcomed with soft cries of delight, for, according to island superstition, such a rain meant that the gods had chosen to shower blessings upon the spirit of their *konohiki*, their favorite.

With Gideon—also on horseback—had gone his mother, dressed in a billowing black *pa'u*, or riding skirt, and wearing black *kukui*-nut *leis*, while mourning veils had hid her tear-ravaged eyes. Leolani and Kimo Pakele and Reverend Forrester, along with several of the ranch's faithful *paniolos*, had escorted the casket as outriders. The latter would also accompany the rancher's body to Honolulu as pallbearers, and follow the stately cortege with its plumed black horses and feathered *kahilis*—Hawaiian standards—in solemn procession through the streets of Honolulu to the Kawaiahao Church.

Following the funeral service there—at the same church in which Gideon and Julia had been married in the spring—Jacob's body would be returned to his beloved Hui Aloha, and there surrendered at last to the island soil he'd loved so dearly in his lifetime . . .

Emma sighed as she placed the letters in the *koa*-wood bowl, and turned to leave.

"This house feels so sad, Kaleilani," a small voice whispered, while a small hand tucked itself inside hers for comfort.

She'd all but forgotten Mahealani for the moment, so deep in thought had she been. She crouched down and drew the little girl to her, hugging her close. "Yes, *ku'uipo*. It does feel sad. Did you know that *Makua* Kane built it with his own two hands?" Mahealani shook her head. "I think the house misses him." It was, perhaps, a fanciful notion, but one she felt keenly, nonetheless. Who was to say that homes, like their owners, could not have souls? Mahealani nodded. "Come along now, darling. I think we've had enough sadness for one day. Let's go back to the valley, shall we?" She swept the little girl up into her arms and kissed her as she carried her into the light.

Outside, a vivid rainbow arched across the emerald plains, and the sun—trying very hard to shine through a misty veiling of rainclouds—was dazzling. Shading her eyes, she was suddenly reminded of the conversation she'd overheard between Leolani and Miriam Kane in the summerhouse.

Miriam had said Jacob had urged her to go back "into the light," where she belonged, and Emma'd feared—the fine hairs prickling on her nape—that his words were an omen. Was that why her thoughts kept returning to that conversation, replaying it over and over again in her mind? Something about the light? She frowned. No, that wasn't it. It was something important, though . . . something else. Something not quite right about what Missus Kane had said. But, though she tried to catch the elusive thought, it flitted away like a butterfly, always just out of reach. *Stop trying so hard, and it'll come back to you,* she told herself, and put it out of her mind.

"Will you teach me another *hula* when we get home?" Mahealani asked, skipping alongside her and swinging Emma's hand.

"Yes, but not today, little one." To dance the *hula* required a gladness of spirit and a level of concentration she was far from feeling today.

"Tomorrow, then?" the child wheedled.

"Soon, Mahealani, I promise—but only if you'll promise me something, too?"

"What shall I promise?"

"That you'll stop this running off and hiding from me, as you did today."

"But I like hiding," Mahealani grumbled, pouting, her lower lip jutting mutinously.

"I know you do, but you could get lost, or hurt. Promise me you'll stop, or there will be no *hula* lessons—and no *kulolo,* no sugarcane, nor any other treats."

"Must I?"

"I'm afraid you must, yes."

The little girl scowled, and for just a fleeting moment, Emma could see traces of her father in her little face, before her usual sunny smile returned. "Oh, all right, then, Kalei. I promise."

"Cross your heart?"

"Uh huh. Cross my heart," Mahealani promised solemnly, crossing her fingers within the folds of her skirts just as her cousin, Pikake, had shown her, so that the lie wouldn't count as a sin.

"*Maikai!* Good girl," Emma praised her, squeezing her hand and smiling.

Squirming with guilt, Mahealani could not quite meet Emma's eyes.

Emma had been gone only a few minutes when Julia burst into the house, going straight to the small table and the wooden bowl where the letters were always left. Hands shaking, she sifted through them, but the ransom note she'd been expecting all the time Jacob Kane had been missing—and had dreaded coming ever since his death!—was not among them. *Thank God!* she thought curiously as she held the letter from Thomas Kane up to the light and idly tried to read the contents through the envelope. It was just as she'd feared, she thought, a little drunkenly. Jacko had never intended to kidnap Jacob Kane, nor to send a note to Gideon demanding ransom for his return. He'd intended to kill him from the first, for the simple reason that he hated him, hated all the Kanes. The signed confession Jacko had asked her to acquire explained why. In it, Jack Jordan admitted he'd attempted an incestuous act upon his daughter, Emma Kaleilani Jordan, when she was a little girl. By keeping that damning admission in his possession for sixteen years, Kane had controlled Jordan—but now she had his confession and the control that went with it, instead! She'd force Jacko to take her away with him now, before Gideon returned. After all, the islands were no longer safe for either of them. By sending Jacob Kane off on a wild-goose chase that day, she'd become an accomplice to his murder!

She was about to toss the letter back into the wooden bowl and finish the half-bottle of apricot brandy when the word UR-GENT leaped out at her from the envelope. Frowning, she hesitated. What in the world did Thomas Kane want with Gideon that was so darned urgent? she wondered, inspecting the other letters in the bowl. None of them had been similarly marked. Hesitating only a second, she slit the envelope open with her fingernail, her hands shaking uncontrollably as she withdrew the two sheets of paper inside. She scanned the contents, her breathing suddenly growing labored, for the top page was a note from Thomas, urging Gideon to read the accompanying report at once.

She did so, and the blood drained from her face, for the second sheet of paper bore the motto of a wide-awake eye beneath the heading, *Pinkerton's National Detective Agency,* along with a motto asserting, *"We Never Sleep!"*

She swallowed, panic swirling through her in waves. This was it then! It was all over for her. Thanks to Sheldon Kane's contacts in America, the game was well and truly up. There'd be no money, no life of luxury and ease—she would be back to living off her wits and her looks—and alone. She bit her lip, tried to harden her jaw, but failed miserably. It had been fun while it lasted, but now it was over. *By now, Gideon knew!* The very best she could hope for was to get away, to flee the island before he returned from Honolulu to confront her! But for that, she would need help.

Jacko! she decided, her face contorting as she fought tears. That bastard had gotten her into this. He owed her that much, damn his soul! But first, she had to find him . . .

* * *

As it happened, it was Jack who found her, rather than the other way around.

She had packed everything of value she could carry into two saddlebags—her black-enameled gold bracelets, some rings and pendants, a few pretty pieces of jade set in gold, a necklace of ivory, carved to look like jasmine flowers with matching ear-bobs, and a few silver pieces, including a cup from Gideon's baptism.

She hefted it all to the stables and was struggling to saddle herself a horse when she had the eerie sensation that someone was watching her. Turning, she saw Jacko standing behind her, leaning against the wooden wall that divided the stalls. She let out an involuntary shriek of surprise, for he had changed almost beyond recognition since their last meeting. Gone were the dangerous good looks she'd been attracted to! The man before her was no longer lean, but painfully thin. His face was no longer craggy and rugged, but downright gaunt, and his eyes—Halle-lujah, Jesus!—no man should ever have such an emptiness, such a deadness in his eyes!

"Jacko! You scared me!" she exclaimed, laughing nervously.

"Did I, luv? It looked t' me like you was too busy t' be scared. Going someplace, were you?" He nodded at the saddlebags on the straw at her feet.

"I was coming to find you," she told him truthfully, but it was clear from his expression he didn't believe her.

"The devil you was," he rasped. "Wot's this, then? A little present you planned t' give ole Jack?" He stooped and retrieved a gold bracelet that had escaped a saddlebag, twirling it around his finger like a hoop. "You weren't intendin' t' run out on me, was you, Joolie?"

"No! I swear it! Half of it's yours, Jacko—half of everything I've got, just like we planned! We don't need Kane's money! Maybe it's better it turned out this way? Without—without the money, there's nothing to connect you to Kane's murder."

"Except for the paper I asked you to find."

"Yes, except for that," she agreed shakily. It gave Jack a motive.

"Where is it, Joolie?"

"It's—it's hidden."

"Where!" he thundered. Springing forward, he grasped her chin and wrenched her head around, forcing her to look at him. "I—said—where—is—it?"

"I'll—I'll give it to you, I swear. But first—first you have to promise t' help me! I have to get off the island, Jacko! Gideon's family knows all about me and Davie. They had some detective snoop in' around and—"

"Shut up! I don't give a rat's arse about your problems, do you understand? I just want the paper—and I want it *now,* got it? There's lots o' terrible things can happen t' them wot doublecrosses ole Jacko!" he hissed full in her face, and his pale eyes blazed. "Things like wot happened to Kane . . ."

"Your threats don't scare me!" Julia whispered bitterly. "See, I've got nothin' left to lose! You or Gideon Kane—either way, it's over for me, 'less I get off this island! If you want your precious paper, you can have it—but only if you'll help me get away!"

"Missus Kane! Missus Kane! Where are you, missus?" called a female voice.

"Who's that?" Jacko growled, ducking back into the shadows.

"Puanani, one of the serving girls."

"Get rid of her—get rid of 'em all! Give the bloody lot of 'em a little holiday!"

"But—"

"Do it, blast ye!"

When she returned, she was relieved to see Jacko had calmed down somewhat, and was rolling himself a smoke. The match flared as he struck it against his boot heel and touched the flame to the rolled paper. The horse she'd saddled whickered and moved nervously about.

"All gone?"

She nodded. Judging by their expressions, the serving girls and the ranch hands had clearly thought the young missus had taken leave of her senses, screaming at them all to go home.

"Good gel. Ye know, Joolie, luv, I've been thinking. There's no 'cause fer us t' fight, right? This here's just a little change in our plans, right? You an' me—why, we're a matched team, we are. We belong together, right?"

"Right."

"Sooo, why don't we scarper together?"

"Scarper?"

"Scarper—make a run fer it. You and me. There's a steamer leaving Kawaihae tomorrow, at dawn. The *Hoku*, she's called. We'll be aboard her. I'll meet you at the landing. You bring the paper, and this little lot—" he nodded to her saddlebags, "—and wear somethin' old, somethin' plain." He winked. "Don't want t' draw bloody Sheriff Kokua's attention, now, do we?"

"All right." She wetted her lips. "But . . . where will you be between now and dawn, Jack?" She hadn't trusted him before, dare not trust him now. He was up to something. She could smell it.

"Let's just say I'll be busy till then—busy persuading some reluctant . . . friends t' join us on our little voyage." The grin widened to a leer.

"Friends?"

He nodded. "They'll be our safe ticket off this rock, should Kane try t' interfere. Our passport out o' these bleedin' islands, to America!" In the shadows, his eyes gleamed.

"But what friends?" she repeated.

He grinned, showing stained teeth. "Oh, I reckon you know who they are, princess. Think about it! It'll come to you. To-morrow, at dawn." He blew her a kiss. "Be there."

With that farewell, he chucked her beneath the chin and slipped from the stables.

She stood in the shadows, trembling all over and breathing heavily for several minutes before she could move again.

And then, when she bent to retrieve the weighty saddlebags, she found them several pounds lighter than they'd been before she'd gone outside. Rage filled her. That doublecrossin' son-of-a-bitch! In those few minutes, he'd taken it all!

She could only hope and pray he'd be at the landing in the morning. It was the only chance she had left.

Thirty-three

The decks of the four-hundred ton inter-island steamer, *Kilauea,* were crowded with mats, chickens, calabashes of *poi,* coconuts, Mexican saddles, leather goods, and an assortment of livestock. There were also numerous dusky, dark-eyed children and their mothers and fathers, aunts, uncles, cousins, and grandparents, all of whom had ignored the sternest efforts of the stewards to refrain from running about and making noise. Yet all chatter and merry laughter fell silent, and a path was immediately made through the clutter as Gideon wove his way to the rail. They fell silent out of respect for the Kane family, for Gideon himself, and for the father over whose death he grieved.

He stood there with his hands tucked into his breeches' pockets, gazing off the starboard bow at the green and lovely island of Maui, rising up through the sea spray beyond the foamy line of the reef like a mirage. His expression was troubled.

The snowcapped peaks of Mauna Kea, wearing feathery *leis* of billowing cloud, the silvery waterfalls that leaped from tortured black lava cliffs into the boiling sea, the reddish glare in the morning sky cast by the fiery volcano—all the beauties of his Big Island home—had been left far behind at Kawaihae Landing at dawn, some six hours hence, when he and his mother and their entourage had boarded the steamer, along with the casket containing his father's remains. In a few days, they would reach the island of Oahu, and the capital port of Honolulu, where

Jacob Kane would receive the loving eulogy and extravagant funeral service that befitted one of his stature in the islands, attended by not only old friends but the king and all his court, as well as the leading lights and dignitaries of Honolulu society.

The initial shock and raw agony of his father's death—if not his anger at its brutality and suddenness—had dulled over the past few days. The ache that remained was painful but endurable. Forcing himself to go through the motions of daily life had helped, he'd discovered. He could now function normally, could think about things he'd forgotten since his father had first been missing, simple little things like eating meals and sleeping for an hour or two, at least, both of which he'd done little of in the past week. Even so, the midmorning catnap he'd sought in his berth below deck a while ago had proved far from restful!

Why, he wondered, should this overwhelming sense of unease have come to plague him now as, exhausted, he tossed and turned? And why should the fitful sleep he'd eventually drifted into have brought such strange and fanciful dreams? Was it simple exhaustion, his mind's delayed response to fatigue and grief—or an omen? And what should he do about it? Listen to the voice of his instinct—the same gut instinct that had served him so well in many a tight spot during the war, the same gut instinct that now urged him to turn back, turn back straightway for home before it was too late to avoid some terrible tragedy? Or should he put those warnings from his mind, ignore them, write them off as foolish, morbid thoughts, and go on to Oahu?

The bone fishhook Emma had given him all those years ago seemed to burn against his chestbone suddenly as he gazed at the beautiful island off the starboard bow, the land mass looming bigger and bigger with each passing minute as they steamed past her southwest shores. Still he wrestled with his choices. Soon, Lahaina and his chances to hop another steamer back home would be left far behind, then the islands of Lanai and Molokai would fall behind the *Kilauea*'s wake in turn, and it would be far too late—he knew it, somehow. Time was running out. It was now or never . . .

A freshening breeze blew up out of nowhere in the glassy heat and calm of midday, bringing with it the alluring scent of white ginger. *White ginger! Emma's favorite fragrance.* A vision flashed into his mind's eye of his darling girl by moonlight, her coal-black hair like ebony silk against creamy beige skin, her cheeks tinged with rose, her skin fragrant with white ginger blossoms. But it was no comforting image, for in it, Emma's dark eyes—her haunting amethyst eyes—were brimming with unshed tears! Her lush rose lips were parted in a silent scream: *"Help me!"* she implored him. *"Help me!"*

Horrified, he forced his eyes to stay open, flicked his head to clear it of the frightening image. Looking down, he saw his palms were slick with sweat. More beaded his upper lip. Oh, dear God, how real it had been—how terrifyingly real!

It was then he knew he couldn't take the chance of going on. Right or wrong, he had to go back. He'd never forgive himself if his fears were founded, yet he did nothing!

"I'm sorry, *Makua,*" he murmured in a moment of prayer, his mind made up. He would forgo the remainder of the voyage and his father's funeral in Honolulu in order to return to the Big Island immediately and follow his instincts wherever they led. It was the hardest decision he'd ever been forced to make, one that many people—his mother, included—might never condone, let alone understand. And yet, he believed with all his heart that it was the right one, nonetheless. The dead could wait. The living could not.

Again, the scent of ginger stirred his senses. His jaw set, his resolve firm, he went in search of his mother below.

Lahaina, Maui, was a sleepy village of white-latticed houses with deep verandas that baked in sultry idleness that morning beneath a fierce white sun. The two miles over which the former whaling port sprawled boasted the remains of a royal palace, the old prison—or "Stuck-in-Irons House," as its name translated literally from Hawaiian—and an old fort. Once the chosen site of several Congregationalist missionaries to put down roots and convert the "heathen souls" of the island natives, now only a solitary whitewashed church remained, its spire pointing like a finger toward heaven from amidst mango, breadfruit, candlenut, and fragrant plumeria trees. Above the village, a lingering reminder of missionary influence—the school of Lahainaluna—could be seen upon the hillsides, surrounded by light-green fields of sugarcane.

Springing from the canoe that had come alongside the steamer to take on some passengers and put off others, Gideon and Kimo made their way immediately to the wharf to ask after the interisland steamer, *Hoku*.

"Well, bless me, I regret to say you've just missed her, sir. She sailed for the Big Island less than a half hour ago!" he was told by an apologetic representative of the interisland steamer company, once the man had first offered his deepest condolences. The Kane name was a well-known and respected one throughout the island chain, and Jacob's loss had been keenly felt by all.

"Damn it to hell!" Gideon exploded, slamming his fist down against the shipping agent's desk. "Is there another?"

"Not until next week, I'm afraid, Mister Kane. But the old *Star*'s as ancient and unwieldly as a coal barge—the oldest of our line, to be truthful. If it's an emergency, I daresay a swift canoe might still overtake her? he suggested, brows cocked.

"Good man, Brooks! Find us one for the day's hire, and you can name your price!"

"We'll need paddlers, too, Mo'o," Kimo reminded him.

"Indeed, Uncle. Offer plenty of money for the best on the island," Gideon ordered crisply, reaching into his trousers pocket and withdrawing a hefty roll of American dollars. "American dollars, Spanish *reales*—give them anything, anything they ask

Tell them Jacob and Haunani Kane's son needs their *kokua*, their help—needs it desperately!"

In no time, Kimo and Brooks, the shipping agent, had both the long, narrow canoe and the crew needed to paddle her ready and waiting—a half-dozen deep-voiced, dusky-skinned, handsome native youths with the powerfully muscled arms and shoulders of seasoned paddlers, all eager to help the son of the legendary *Makua* Kane. There was space in the blade-slim craft for two more paddlers. Without hesitation, Kimo stripped off his shirt, and then, despite his great size, the middle-aged Hawaiian waded into the shallows and sprang nimbly aboard her. Gideon followed suit a heartbeat behind him.

"Swiftly, my brothers!" he urged in Hawaiian, stripping off his shirt and stowing it out of the way. Barechested, his muscles rippling and dancing beneath tanned skin, he flexed huge hands, then took up the heavy *koa* paddle and bent his back to the others' rhythm.

Like a bird, the prow of the canoe lifted, skimming swift and sure over the undulating blue of a glassy sea, in pursuit of the leaky *Hoku*.

"Mahealani Jordan, you'd better show yourself right this minute! I know you're hiding from me again, you naughty girl! Shame on you—you promised!" Emma cried, exasperated. But despite her threats, no giggling, bright-eyed little girl emerged from some secret hiding place, and her anxiety mounted, along with her annoyance.

Where in the world could Mahealani have vanished to, on such a damp and gloomy day? She'd promised to teach her a simple *hula* this afternoon, to while away the rainy, overcast hours. Knowing how eager the little girl had been to learn, she was surprised—and disappointed—by her disappearance.

A fine yet drenching rain was still falling as she made her way along the path of flat stones set in the earth. The tiny drops were dimpling the deep-green waters of her taro patches as she padded, barefoot, in and out of the trees and bushes, her skirts hiked up above the long wet grass to keep dry. There was no one about in this weather but her cousin Anela's husband, Kanekoa. The tall, curly haired Hawaiian wore only a cloth wraparound, or *malo,* about his waist, and was carrying a heavy sack of something lumpy—probably sweet potatoes—on his back. A pair of yellow Hawaiian dogs trotted at his heels. He waved and called *"Aloha,* Cousin! Look like we goin' get one bad storm pretty soon, yeah?" to her as he passed, headed for his *hale* farther up the valley, where he lived with her cousin Anela and their two children.

"Aloha, Kanekoa! Yes, I think you're right! Have you seen Mahealani?" she called to him, but he shook his head and she waved him on before continuing her search.

Kanekoa was right about the tropical storm on its way to batter the island. She could feel it in the air—taste it, almost. It had been windy and raining heavily off and on like this for two days in a row now, she reflected. Between downpours, the afternoon air had grown hot and oppressively humid. The endless rain did little to improve one's temper—and even less to ease the nagging headache she'd had ever since Julia had sent them packing from Hale Koa yesterday, that horrid, drunken woman. It would serve her right if none of the serving girls returned to see to her needs, and she was forced to shift for herself!

"Mahealani Jordan," she called loudly in an even sterner voice. "If you don't show yourself right this minute, I'm going to . . ."

Her voice trailed away in shock as Jack Jordan stepped out from beneath the low-hanging branches of a leafy mango tree, only a few feet from her. He was holding a whimpering Mahealani by a fistful of her long black hair, like a mewling kitten held up by its scruff. "You're gonna wot, love?" he sneered.

"How dare you hold her like that! Put her down! You're hurting her!" Enraged, Emma ran at him and battered his chest, trying desperately to free Mahealani from his grip. But with a short bark of laughter, Jack backhanded Emma as if he was swatting a fly, sending her sprawling onto her back in the grass.

"This here int half o' wot I'll do to the pair o' you, if you don't do as I say. Shake a leg, Emmie luv! We're going for a little ride. Just the three of us."

He winked and leered, and a thousand half-forgotten memories poured through her, bitter as bile and far more painful than the throbbing in her cheek. "You don't need Mahealani. Take me, and leave her here!"

"Tch. Tch. Would such a good daddy leave his pretty baby girl behind?" He chuckled. "Nah, Em, nothin' doing. You're comin' with me, and so is she, bless her little heart. See, you're my ticket off these bleedin' islands!"

She saw then that he had a horse and a mule with him—both stolen, surely?—patiently grazing in the black shadows beneath the enormous mango tree. Jerking his head in the mounts' direction, he indicated she should take the horse and then, to her relief, handed Mahealani up before her on the Mexican saddle.

"No funny business, neither, you hear me, eh? Make a move, try t' run, an' I'll see the nipper pays fer it. Got it, lady?"

"I understand," she whispered.

"Marvelous." Jack took the lead, taking the reins from Emma and yanking her poor horse after his mule. He rode quickly to the river that sliced through the valley, heading his braying mule down the muddy, sloping bank, then walking the animal into the water. Emma had little choice but to follow him.

The water reached up to her mount's chest. She was forced to hang on to Mahealani and lean back in the saddle with her legs braced against its neck to keep her skirts from getting soaked.

The waterway snaked between sheer, narrow mountain walls to the sea, glimpsed now through a gray veil of rain. On either side rose steep riverbanks, lush with tall ferns, tangled creepers, and boulders made slick with slippery moss—hardly a foothold to be had anywhere, she realized with a sinking heart. She'd hoped, somehow, to put Mahealani safely ashore and well out of Jack's way once his back was turned, but that was clearly out of the question now.

"No dallyin', Em! You keep acomin'!" Jack barked.

Cursing him under her breath, she took a tighter grip on the frightened little girl and spurred the horse on with a sharp kick. With a whicker of protest, the animal floundered through the water after Jack's mule, snorting like a water buffalo. And then, she saw the direction in which Jack was headed, and her stomach lurched in fear.

The *pali,* or cliff, toward which he was steering his mule was almost perpendicular to the river. Its sheer walls soared up into the mist and vanished among the low-hanging clouds that sagged over the entire valley like a sodden blanket of slate-gray wool. Though she had left the valley by similar zigzagging, narrow tracks hundreds of times before, and thus had no fear of heights, never had she chosen this perilous ascent that began in the river itself! Nor would she have risked taking *any* trail from the valley—known or otherwise—after so many days of fine but heavy rain, had she been given a choice in the matter. The footing would be slippery, hazardous for both mule and horse, and there was every chance the run-off that threaded the *pali* walls with narrow silver waterfalls had also washed out some rocky footholds and portions of the ledges. She swallowed, feeling her stomach churn. Now she understood why Jack had chosen the surer-footed mule for himself!

"Kaleilani, I'm scared!" Mahealani whispered, huddling as close to Emma as she could possibly get and holding on tight.

"I know, darling. But I'll take care of you, you know that," she promised, hoping she sounded more confident than she felt. The Jack Jordan in front of her was a man she didn't know, and one she could not begin to second guess. He had a wild look about him today that she'd never seen before. And, though he'd never had any choice but to dress shabbily, in the past he'd always kept himself and his secondhand clothing clean, pressed, and neatly darned. She'd never seen him unkempt and soiled, as he was now, with red-rimmed, bloodshot eyes and haggard, stubbled cheeks, his dirty-blond hair straggly and uncombed. He looked as if he hadn't slept or eaten in a fortnight, or else was being consumed by some dreadful wasting disease.

"Is it so, what the man said? Is he really my papa?" the little girl whispered behind her hand.

Emma hesitated before answering, "No, darling. Your papa is a wonderful man. He's nothing like Jack Jordan, nothing at all."

Her lower lip quivered. "But Pikake and Kamuela said my papa was a bad man. They said the sheriff put him in jail, but he runned away."

"Did they now? And would you rather believe your cousins or me?"

"You."

"Then trust me, darling. Jack Jordan's not your father. Nor even your grandfather."

"If he isn't my papa, then who is?"

She was saved having to answer by Jack's shout for them to follow him from the water. The horse heaved and scrabbled, its front hooves clattering until it gained purchase on a rocky shelf that was hardly big enough for both horse and mule to stand upright, side by side. It was then that she realized he really meant to do it. *Sweet Mother of God! He intended to climb up out of the valley in this weather, and with daylight fast fading, too! Oh, Gideon, we need you! Help us!* she cried silently.

"Scared, Em?" he asked, his grin showing a picket fence of stained yellow teeth.

"Of course! There's a bad storm coming, the wind's lifting, yet you expect us to climb out of this valley like flies climbing up a wall! Only a lunatic wouldn't be scared."

He threw back his head and laughed. It was then that she noticed the hat he'd worn for as long as she could remember was gone, the one with the golden-pheasant-feather *lei* about the crown—the one that . . . the one that she'd last seen at . . . at . . . Dear God, that was it! That was the nagging inconsistency she'd been trying to remember since the night she'd overheard Miriam describing how Jacob had appeared to her! Makua *Kane had never worn a hat!* His thick silver hair had been his only vanity! He'd preferred to display it uncovered, despite the fierce tropical sun. Everyone had overlooked that fact, assuming— quite wrongly—that the hat they'd found, crushed beneath Jacob's body, must be his own, but Emma knew better. Oh, yes! It had been Jack Jordan's hat they'd recovered, she was almost certain . . .

Of a sudden, she grew clammy with fear. Did finding his hat beneath the body mean Jack had killed Gideon's father, too?

Suddenly convinced that he had, she glanced up, startled to find Jack standing at his horse's head, reins in hand as he stared at her, a peculiar expression on his face.

"That's right, ducks," he said softly, obviously reading something of her thoughts and fear from her expression. "So now ye know I mean business, right? Hand the brat over t' me, and we'll be on our way. You first, luv!"

"Pleeease, Kalei, don't make me! I don't want to go to him! I don't like him! Please don't make me!"

"Mahealani, stop it! Behave yourself this instant!" she snapped, forcing a stern expression as she plucked Mahealani's fingers from her shoulders. Her unusually sharp, schoolmarmish tone served to silence the child immediately, to her relief. She'd been afraid of what Jack might do if the little girl defied him and clung to her. She'd also decided that, all other dangers notwithstanding, the little girl was safer with Jack than with herself for now. After all, he was unlikely to ride his mule off the cliff intentionally, whereas he might well do something to hurt her! "There. Isn't that better? You see, there's nothing to be afraid of. You've done this lots of times before with me, remember? The day we went to Laupahoehoe, to ride the *holua,* the mud-slide? Just hold tight to the saddle horn, darling, and everything will be fine!" she promised as she urged her horse past the mule and up onto the narrow track, praying neither animal would balk. A careless tread, a single, ill-judged step, and she and Mahealani would plunge to their deaths!

The rising wind moaned as it wove its way between the valley walls, a deep, unearthly moan like that of some enormous wounded animal in terrible pain. It sent waves scudding across the surface of the river and the pools, and rattled tree branches, tossing them wildly about. Frightened birds took shelter where they could and twittered anxiously. The sky was an eerie yellow now. The storm was building.

Thirty-four

It was full dark before the steamer, *Hoku,* arrived offshore at Kawaihae Landing, her arrival seriously delayed by a combination of engine trouble and the brief halt she'd been forced to make at midday in order to take on two unexpected passengers. Gideon and Kimo had boarded her from the outrigger canoe in the middle of the ocean, clambering up the rope ladders the crew had thrown over the side like seasoned tars, amidst the cheers and whoops of the other exhausted paddlers.

The sultry humidity and eerie stillness of earlier that day had, from time to time, given way to occasional drenching downpours. He didn't like the look of the yellowish sky as he and Kimo dodged the raindrops that signaled another deluge was beginning and sprinted up the beach to the wood-frame and native grass dwellings which huddled beneath a straggly lone coconut tree. The palm was swaying and shaking like a rag mop brandished in an angry fist, buffeted by the whistling winds and the swirling rain.

To Gideon's relief, Felipe and some of the other *paniolos* were still at the landing, having driven some cattle down to the holding pens in Kawaihae late that day. At first light, the cattle were to be towed out to the anchored steamer by a mounted cowboy hauling on a rope cinched around the animal's long horns to force it to swim. The beasts were loaded onto the steamer's decks by means of slings, and then the hardy little vessel made her return journey to Honolulu.

It was dangerous, difficult work, this cattle lading, but for now, the cowboys were enjoying a well-deserved rest, congregated about a kerosene lantern in the back room of Ah Woo's store, their seats a rickety assortment of wooden boxes. Some braided narrow leather strips into lariats, while others worked on saddles, but all were swapping tales as some sipped their pineapple "moonshine," or smoked and others ate the spicy jerked beef, boiled peanuts, or fragrant steamed pork dumplings supplied by Missus Woo. While his companions followed their own diversions, Alika played his ukulele and sang his mournful lovesongs, yodeling the choruses in falsetto Hawaiian.

"Boss!"

"Señor Kane!"

All the cowboys put lariats and moonshine aside and sprang to their feet in surprise as their boss shouldered his way through the door. He raised his hand to still them.

"No, no, boys, don't get up. I'm not staying. I just need a string of horses and a couple of slickers—"

"Take mine, señor," Felipe offered. "My *remuda,* my string of horses, is fresh and well rested."

Gideon nodded. *"Mahalo.* We're riding back to Hui Aloha tonight. Send someone to Hilo for Sheriff Paka, Felipe. Tell him he's needed at the house as soon as possible."

"Tonight, señor? Is there trouble at *la casa grande?"*

Unsmiling, Gideon nodded. "I'm afraid so."

Wiping his mouth on a kerchief, Felipe's expression was determined in the amber lamplight as he rose to his feet and joined them at the door, "Then I will come, too. Perhaps you will need another pair of hands, *no?* But first, tell me what is wrong, señor? We saw you board the *Kilauea* with Doña Miriam and *los señores* Pakele this morning, and now you are here! How did you—*why* did you return so soon, sir?"

"An honest answer?" Gideon shrugged, a thin, rueful smile curving his lips. In the lamplight, his features looked saturnine and somehow dangerous, or so Felipe fancied. "I don't really know why—unless you'd call it a sixth sense, a gut instinct that keeps nagging something's awry."

Felipe nodded. He had experienced such feelings himself, and over the years had come to respect and act upon them.

"On the other hand," Gideon continued, "how Kimo and I got back here is no mystery! Lead me to those horses, *amigo,* and I'll tell you."

From a distance the following morning, under a slate-gray sky in which lightning flickered from time to time, Hui Aloha looked as it had always looked, her graceful white walls rising up from emerald plains to meet the green-tiled roof that had, over the years, weathered to a charming gray-green. Yet the apparent normalcy of the scene below him did nothing to unravel the knot of dread in his gut that told him, *Hurry! Hurry!*

"Everything looks as it should, I'd say. What do you think, Uncle?" he asked, smothering a yawn. They'd ridden most of the night, stopping only when the thunder, lightning, and rain—and their own fatigue—had made riding impossible, gladly sharing the grass shack and sleeping mats of an old Hawaiian man, and numerous giant cockroaches!

"Listen!" Pakele ordered, and Gideon heard what Kimo's sharp ears had already heard—the distant, angry mooing of cows in the fenced pasture beyond the house. "They have not been milked."

"Could be the storm is making them edgy?"

Kimo shrugged. "Perhaps."

The pair exchanged glances. Well before dawn, then again at sunset, the serving girls, Puanani, Iryn, Mapuana, and the others were supposed to milk the dairy cows that supplied Hui Aloha and her hands and half the nearby village with fresh milk, butter, and cheese. His *makuahine* had always been strict about the milking chores being done promptly, because the poor creatures suffered so when it was not. From the sounds that carried on the chill, wet wind, none of the poor beasts had been milked since he'd left yesterday morning!

"There's only one way to find out. Yee—haah!" Lashing Felipe's spare bronco into a gallop, he careened down the hill toward the house, the two other men riding at his heels.

His heart was thundering with apprehension when he reined the pony into a skidding halt on the coral-chip driveway, for even from here he could see that the place was deserted. A hasty search confirmed his suspicions. The dairy, the tackhouse, the springhouse, the outhouse, the barns—all of the outbuildings were deserted! A search of Hui Aloha proved it was likewise empty. Not a ranch hand nor a serving girl was anywhere to be found! And nor, he realized grimly, was his beloved wife anywhere in evidence. Where the devil had everyone gone? And why?

"Señor! Over there!"

Gideon turned in time to see what Felipe had spotted—Julia, astride a swift bay gelding, leaning low over her horse's neck as she broke the cover she'd taken behind the kitchen building and kicked the animal into a gallop.

Vaulting astride his horse, Gideon took off in pursuit, riding roughshod over the thick lawns, circling the breeding corrals and pens, his game little mount streaking after the bigger horse.

Whatever else his wife might lack, she could ride—that, he had to admit! She leaned low over her horse's neck like a jockey riding the circuit at Kapiolani Racecourse, using a riding crop to force even greater speed from the gelding. Her fair hair streamed behind her as she rode, astride, like a man. Startled, he realized she was dressed in men's clothing, too—a pair of his father's breeches, a shirt, and boots. She also had a bundle lashed to the saddle behind her, as well as bulging saddlebags.

"Julia! Damn it, what the devil's going on here! Come back!" he yelled after her.

Whether the blustery wind kept her from hearing his question or whether she simply chose to ignore him, he did not know, but she neither slackened her pace nor tried to respond. He cursed under his breath—a long, satisfying stream of curses—as he tried to milk still greater speed from the game little bronco.

He finally came alongside her on the crest of the hill where he and the others had looked down upon the ranch house and its outbuildings, bringing her down with a flying leap from his own mount to hers.

He took the brunt of the fall on his right side, landing heavily in the wet grass and mud with Julia—struggling wildly to escape—hugged in his arms.

"Enough!" he gritted, shaking her roughly. "Move an inch, my dear, and I'll forget all I learned about being a gentleman!"

His threat had the desired effect. Though still panting, she lay back in the wet grass, making no further effort to evade him. "You should be after Jacko, not me!" she hissed. "He's the one you really want!"

"Shut up!" he rasped, rubbing his battered side and wincing. Bending down, he grasped her elbow and hauled her roughly upright, growling, "On your feet!"

Troubled pale-gray eyes searched his face. Gideon had never spoken to her in that hard, rough way before, and there was no trace of the cordial yet distant man who'd bid her a polite farewell the morning before in the angry, disheveled man before her. Something must have happened, she decided—and it could be only one thing. "You know. Thomas told you, didn't he?" she whispered.

"Perhaps," he lied, wondering what in the world she was talking about, and how in the hell his cousin Thomas could possibly know about it, whatever "it" was.

"Then he showed you a copy of Pinkerton's report!" she cried, clearly upset.

"Allan Pinkerton, the detective?" he exclaimed. His question was quite innocent. The detective Pinkerton was the only Pinkerton he'd ever heard of, and that from his uncle Sheldon, who'd met the Scot in Chicago before the war. Hadn't Sheldon suggested writing to the man, before he and Julia were married?

"He did show you!" Julia exclaimed.

"Er—I'm afraid so, yes," he hedged. In her guilt, Julia had plainly forgotten the five-day sea voyage between the Big Island and Hawaii, hadn't realized he couldn't possibly have spoken to Thomas in the brief time he'd been gone—had completely mistaken his innocent question for confirmation that Yes, he did indeed know what she was talking about! "However, I'd still like to hear it all from you. The—er—truth, that is." A thin, mirthless smile curved his lips. "Why don't we go back to the house, then you can tell me everything, in your own words."

Thirty-five

"I'm not a widow," Julia whispered.

"Speak up, Missus Kane, I can't hear you!" he snapped, bringing his fist down upon the desk before him with such force, the impact made the inkstand and nibbed pens skitter drunkenly about.

"I said, I ain't a widow. I never was."

"You were never married?"

"Nooo, I didn't say that." She sighed heavily, and her shoulders slumped. "Aw, what's the use? You know it all already. I might as well tell you everything, from the beginning."

"That would be best," he agreed, hiding his confusion.

"I met David Lennox in Baltimore during the war. He ran a theater there that employed a troupe of actors—the Lennox Players, they called themselves. I was . . ." She grimaced. "Well, let's just say I was a hillbilly gal from the mountains, and down on my luck when I met Davie. He—he took a fancy to me. He used t' tell me, 'Julia, darling'—my real name is Julie, but he always called me Julia, see?—he said, 'Julia, darling, you're going to be the lovely Galatea to my Pygmalion, and my very own creation!' He said he'd teach me cultured airs and graces, and how to walk and talk and dress. " 'In short, my dear, you will become—in every way but one—the perfect lady!' he said." She shrugged. "He dressed the part of a gentleman himself, and was forever dropping names, so I believed him. He said his momma was from Boston, but that she'd married a man named Lennox from Maryland. He claimed Sophie, one of his cousins on his momma's side, had wed Sheldon Kane, a rich Yankee sugar planter in the Sandwich Isles, and that her husband's family had money, so I figured Davie for a wealthy man, too, and went along with his plans for me. We were married during the last year of the war."

"Was your husband a soldier?"

She shook her head. "When the South was defeated, Davie got drunk one night. He broke down an' told me he'd invested every red cent he owned in the Confederate cause! He'd never had more than two cents to rub t'gether, he claimed, but now he was penniless, 'cept for the pretty trinkets he'd bought me, and what little I'd put by when he was flush. Soon, he began badgering me to sell those, too! Right there and then, I'd had enough. It was time for lil' old Julia t' light out, lickety split. So, here I am, just like Pinkerton's report said."

"Then David Lennox is still alive? You're still married to him?" he asked, scarce daring to breathe as he awaited her answer. Upon it hung all of his hopes, his dreams, for the life he'd always planned, with Emma as his bride, for if Julia was still married to Davie, and Davie was still alive, she could not be married to him, too!

"Hell, I don't know about now, but that smooth-talkin' son-of-a-gun was alive and kickin' the last time I saw him!" she admitted ruefully, rolling her eyes and pursing her lips.

Thank God! Oh, praise be to God! he cried silently. Relief flooded through him so strongly, his knees almost buckled. It was as if some enormous burden had been lifted from his shoulders. He was a free man, he realized. A bachelor once more. He'd *never* been married to Julia, not in the eyes of the law!

Though his father's death still weighed heavily on his spirits, the future no longer seemed as bleak and meaningless. It held a ray of hope and sunshine now, the promise of happiness to come, once time had eased the grief. *Devil take Julia!* He had to find Emma straightway—had to tell her he was free! Free to love her. Free to make her his bride! Free to have children with her! Free to spend the rest of his life with her! They had plans to make, wedding plans! Just as soon as a decent mourning period was over, they'd—

"Gideon!" Julia repeated for the second time, clearly irritated.

"What is it?" he asked her distractedly.

"I said, you should be frettin' after Jack, not all this . . . hoopla!"

"Jack?" Stormy dark brows crashed together in a frown. "What the devil has he to do with this?"

"You didn't let me explain. That's where I was going when you jumped me. To find him!"

His heart skipped a beat. The ominous feeling had returned, slamming like an anvil into his gut. "Why?" he demanded hoarsely. "Why were you looking for Jack Jordan?"

"Because he's gone after them, don't you see? He means t' use that woman t' get off this island!"

His gentian eyes flashed dangerously as he reached out, took her by the wrist, and jerked her toward him. "What woman?" he rasped, his breath hot in her face as he spat the words at her like bullets. His grip tightened so painfully, she wanted to cry out, but didn't dare as he added, "Tell me you don't mean Emma?"

"Yes, yes, I told you, that woman! Jacko killed your father, Gideon. He as good as told me so! Now he's scared and he's ready to run. She's his safe passport off the island, onto a steamer or a schooner, don't you see? If you don't hurry, he'll get away with it!"

"But meantime, what am I to do with you, my darling wife?" His caustic tone made color flame in her pale face. She looked flustered now, bewildered and unsure of herself, yet he felt no pity.

"I . . . don't know. I guess I was hoping . . . I was hoping you could find it in your heart t' let me go," she said huskily. "You have to believe me, darlin', I love you! I never dreamed Jacko wanted your father dead, I swear it! I—I liked the old man, truly I did! It was—it was the money I wanted—only the money—right from the very first night! Jacko swore he wouldn't hurt him if I helped him. He said he planned to kidnap your father and keep him in the lava tunnels until you brought ransom money. He said we'd take the money and go to America, build a new life together. I believed him, so I said—I said I'd help."

"I see. And exactly *how* did you help him, Julia?" Gideon asked in a voice as bleak and empty as a windswept Siberian tundra. "Tell me that."

The chilling quality to his voice made the fine hairs rise on the back of her neck. "I—I—!" Sweet Jesus! She couldn't get the words out!

"Go on."

Her eyes filled with tears. "I—I told him . . . I told Father Kane that I'd figured you and the Jordan woman were lovers. I said you'd gone to meet her that very morning, at the lava tube—the same morning you went to Laupahoehoe. I begged him to talk to you, to make you stop seeing her. He told me not to worry, and then he . . . he left."

Her confession made him sick to his stomach. It was all he could do to keep from striking her. "Your lies sent him to his death. An innocent old man who'd grown fond of you!"

"Yees," she admitted, almost inaudibly.

"Then how could you ever think I'd let you go, my dear, knowing what you did?" His eyes were cold with fury, his grip on her wrist like the steely teeth of a bear trap.

Judging by his murderous expression, she thought with a shiver, he might snap her arm in two like a brittle twig, then break her neck with equal ease. And if he did, no one would care. She swallowed. "Lord knows, I ain't deservin' of much mercy, but please, Gideon, *please* let me go!"

"Sheriff Kokua is on his way up here from Hilo. He and my father used to hunt wild pigs together up in the mountains, did you know that? When my father was missing, he personally

searched for twelve hours a day, every day, until he was found.
I suggest you see if you can talk Paka into letting you go, my
dear!"

"The sheriff!" Appalled, she looked over her shoulder, as if
expecting the Hawaiian lawman to burst through the doors in
that very instant. Grasping the cloth of Gideon's shirt, she
begged him, "Please, Gideon, don't let them take me to jail! I'd
die in there, all locked up!" she whimpered. *"Please!* I'll do
anything!"

"It's not up to me. The law will have to decide what's to
become of you—and I do believe they'll have a noose waiting
for you, rather than a prison cell. Kimo?"

"Mo'o?"

"Get her out of my sight."

The ranch foreman grinned nastily. "My pleasure, Mo'o!"

"Wait! Take your hands off me, you big, ugly *kanaka!"* Julia
protested, her face chalky ever since Gideon had mentioned the
noose. "Gideon, you must listen to me. Even if—oh, Jesus!—
even if I'm goin' to hang, there's something you have to know
first . . ."

" 'Nough talk. Let's *hele* on, Missus *Lennox,"* Kimo panted,
trying to subdue the struggling woman. Wrapping his hefty arms
around her tiny waist, he lifted her clear off the floor and began
carrying her toward the door.

But as he tried to pass through it, Julia hung on to the door-
jamb, digging in her heels. "Wait! You have to listen! It's about
Jacko. He's gone after the little girl, too! He plans to use her
and the Jordan woman to get off the island!"

"Wait, Uncle." Gideon raised his hand to halt the Hawaiian,
then strode across the room to stand over Julia. Black brows
quirked, he demanded, "What little girl?"

"Mahealani! You know, the pretty little girl with the ringlets?"

"Emma's sister?" He frowned, confused.

"Uh huh. Though she's not her sister, not really," she babbled.
"She's her daughter. The Jordan woman's—and yours."

"What!" The single word exploded from him.

"You heard me," Julia continued, her tongue running away with her as disbelief filled his face. "You only have to look at her t' tell, if you don't believe me! She's the image of you—her pa!—when her blood's up! Oh, Gideon, you have to find her! You know how Jacko is with little girls. How he was with your Emma. He's sick, twisted, just like my pa! And believe me, honey, they may get older, but they never change," she added bitterly. "For that little gal's sake, if no one else's, go get her!"

Gideon felt cold—cold as he'd not been since the bitter northern winters of the war. Cold with sick dread. *"How he was with your Emma!"* Julia had said, and there was only one thing she could have been implying. A memory of Emma at fourteen swam into his memory, her violet eyes haunted by some secret sadness he had never understood—till now—though he could remember his own youthful determination to erase that sadness. "Where did he go?" he demanded flatly, his thoughts and emotions in chaos. *Emma, oh God, my poor little Emma, what did that bastard do to you? What did I abandon you to? She'd borne his child alone, for Christ's sake—a precious, lovely daughter!—and he hadn't guessed, not for a second!* "God damn you, where was that son-of-a-bitch headed?" he snarled. "Tell me, or I'll choke it out of you!"

"He didn't say, I swear it! But—I'd bet money you'll find him wherever you find Emma. And she said—" she looked away, reluctant to admit she'd sent Emma and the servants away, "—she said she was going home."

The Waikalani Valley was a good two hours ride away. "Bring the horses!" Gideon barked. "I'm going after him!"

"No worry, I'll get the *lios*. What about dis *wahine*, Mo'o?" The foreman looked as if he might gladly snap Julia's neck himself.

Gideon hesitated only a second. "First things first. For now, leave her. There'll be no rock on this island she can hide under if anything happens to Emma or the child. On that, she can rely! We'll take care of Missus Lennox later."

Julia's face was still white as chalk as Gideon thrust past her. In the hallway, he turned and asked, "One thing more, before I go."

"Yes?" she whispered.

"That night in Honolulu. Did we . . . ?"

There was a flicker of regret in her eyes. A moment when she might have—could easily have—lied, but thought better of it. "Never, Gideon. I swear it."

He nodded once, curtly, and was gone.

From somewhere in the house, a clock chimed noon.

Thirty-six

"We can't go on, Jack!" Emma yelled. "The wind is rising. It'll pluck us off the ledges! And the animals are scared!"

A thunderbolt clattered loudly across the sky, followed by a brilliant flash of lightning that lit the valley below like a magnesium flare. As if to prove her claims, Emma's horse chose that moment to scream loudly, snorting and shaking as it backed away from a narrow, crumbling section of ledge, refusing to go on.

Determined not to look down at the ribbon of river below, or at the wildly tossing trees that looked more like dollhouse miniatures from this height, Emma slashed the reins across the poor beast's backside and dug her heels in. "Yeeahh! Get up there! Come ooon!"

But the terrified beast refused to budge.

"Get that nag movin'!" Jack roared.

"Don't you think I'm trying? It won't go, I tell you!"

"Then lead it!"

Biting her lip, she closed her eyes and slithered from the horse's back, walking sideways, pressed up against its belly, as she inched her way toward its head, praying it wouldn't move. It didn't. Gripping the reins just a few inches from the horse's mouth, she tugged. "Come on, boy! Good boy, that's how, just a little farther." To her relief, the horse responded, first gingerly testing its footing, then following her lead, though it rolled its eyes back at the way her long hair whipped about in the moaning wind.

"Up ahead!" Jack shouted. "There's a cave, looks like! We'll wait out the storm there!"

Her knees almost buckled with relief.

It was late afternoon by the time Gideon, Kimo, and Felipe reached the Waikalani Valley. The storm was at its height, and broken branches and swollen streams and rivers had delayed them. Now a shrieking wind lashed the hems of their slickers back and forth against their boots like whips, hurling stinging particles of grit, shredded leaves and rain into their faces, stealing their breath away and making it difficult to stay astride their mounts.

The sky was the color of a new bruise, livid and puffy, while the thunder and lightning had increased their violent, noisy battle about the mountain peaks. The wind still moaned like the mournful call of the conch-shell trumpets, signaling the warriors to rally under the standard of Kakailimoku, god of war. Never, in his fifty years, had Kimo ever seen a storm to rival this!

"Auwe! Great Kanaloa and Kanehekili are warring! The old gods of the winds and the thunder are angry that we make them no sacrifice," he observed, shouting the words over the drumming sheets of rain. He was only half joking. Nor was he the first Hawaiian to embrace the newer Christian God, while retaining more than a passing respect and affection for the old gods of nature; nor would he be the last. "In my mother's time, it was forbidden for anyone to speak during such a storm, for fear it would anger the great ones."

"If you ask me, your *makuahine* had the right idea!" Gideon growled, frustrated and angered by their slow progress. Spurring his already exhausted mount on, he pulled ahead of the others, knowing he was risking his neck to ride at such a speed in such weather, with the going soft and treacherous, and the light fading, to boot, but he dared not delay.

Only when Emma and their daughter were safe in his arms would he surrender to exhaustion. *Please God, he was not already too late!*

The cave was a small one, perhaps man-made, hollowed out from the sheer wall of the *pali,* the cliffs, but it was a shelter of sorts and would keep the wind and rain off them. Fiercely clutching Mahealani to her, as if she feared the little girl might try to escape, Emma ducked and stumbled inside. Anything was better than being astride her terrified mount on that narrow, slippery path in that endlessly shrieking, moaning wind, while lightning and thunder flashed and crackled overhead!

"What will happen to the horses?" Mahealani whispered, her voice choked with tears.

"Don't worry. They'll be fine on their own," Emma lied, not at all certain they'd be anything of the sort. She shivered. Pulling Mahealani onto her lap, she held her, rocked her, stroked her hair, her shoulders, her back, trying to keep the frightened child warm. The mercury must surely have dropped several degrees since the rain started falling in earnest, and the little girl's teeth were chattering. Wishing she had a shawl or something of her own she could remove and wrap around her, she cuddled her close, kissed her, and whispered, "Try not to worry, darling. I'm here. Everything's all right. Sleep, if you can."

Jack Jordan's bulk blocked what little light remained, then he ducked and crawled into the cave, fumbling about on hands and knees in the gloom to clear a place to sit. His clumsy movements disturbed something—small rocks, perhaps—that skittered dryly about.

With a curse, he dug into his pocket and withdrew a box of matches. There was a rasp, a hiss, the sharp stench of sulphur, then a small flame cast a small puddle of light over the cave floor.

"Holy Christ!" Jordan whispered, his face a horrific mask, lit from below by the tiny, wavering flame.

In the second before the match burned his fingers and he tossed it aside, Emma glimpsed what he had glimpsed: a heap of yellowed bones strewn across the cave floor and the tattered remains of the *tapa* burial cloth in which they'd been wrapped, then hidden here, after the ancient customs. Her grandfather's bones had been hidden in just such a fashion.

"You don't have to be afraid, Jack," she said softly. "The dead can't hurt you. It's the living the guilty must guard against!"

"You shut up!" Jack roared over the loud, undying moan of the wind. "I ain't scared o' no bones—an' I ain't scared o' no heathen witch doctors, neither. I ain't gonna die, so just—just shut your bloody yap, or I'll shut it for yer!"

But he *was* scared—scared witless—and they both knew it.

"You are crazy—*pupule*—Mo'o! You can't go down into the valley until this storm is over. It's suicide!" Kimo shouted over the sounds of the tempest.

"*El jefe* is right, Don Gideon! To attempt such a thing can only bring tragedy! Please, do not try it! The ranch, she needs you, with Don Jacob gone!"

"And what about Emma?" he growled. "She needs me, too. I know it—in here, and in here—as surely as I know my own name!" he added, touching his chest and his hard stomach. "We've been denied each other long enough, damn it. Seven years—a little lifetime! I won't stand idly by and let Jack Jordan take her from me. Step aside, Felipe!"

"Alas, I am sorry, señor. I have other orders . . ."

"The devil you do!"

"Felipe's right, Mo'o. He has other orders. Orders from me,

as the foreman of the Kane Ranch. This is for your own good, Mo'o."

"Whaat?" He turned just in time to see Kimo's massive fist come out of nowhere, heard the crack as it connected with his jaw. Then a bright white splash of stars filled his vision, and everything went black.

She must have slept fitfully, for when she awoke, she could hear someone chanting in Hawaiian, and for the moment she couldn't recall where she was, or with whom. Mahealani lolled heavily against her, deeply asleep, to her relief, as the eerie, whispery voice rose and fell, changing registers in a way that made "chicken skin" tingle down her arms, Silently she translated:

> *Tie him, tie him!*
> *Drag him down into the underworld.*
> *Place a cord about his throat*
> *And pull him down,*
> *Down into the nether kingdom,*
> *Down to the dark realm*
> *Of great Milu, take him!*
> *There, where endless*
> *Fire awaits him,*
> *And endless night,*
> *And barren is the land,*
> *And the springs are dried up*
> *And all is misery—*
> *Feed him to the dark one, here,*
> *At the pit of Milu—*
> *Make sacrifice to Milu!*

The prayer—for such it was, though one she'd never heard before, and hoped never to hear again!—was an evil prayer of the sort used by a *kahuna-ho'ounauna,* a soul entangler, to bring about the death of a chosen victim. The voice seemed to come from the dry heap of bones in the corner of the cave, as if by some clever sorcery they had been given life and, with it, the breath by which to speak.

Slowly drawing the sleeping child onto her lap and praying to a far newer God that she would not awaken, Emma watched, transfixed, afraid to blink, afraid even to breathe as an orangy-red glow appeared above the bones. It expanded, became a ball of pale, shimmering fire that hovered in the same place for endless moments, before it drifted across the cave and out, into the wild night, leaving only a sharp odor in its wake. *Akua'ele, the fireball, harbinger of death!*

Frozen numb by fear, Emma jumped violently as Jack suddenly let loose with a shrill peal of cackling, mirthless laughter.

"Ye see, Emmie? You see! It's not just me—you saw it, too! How d' they do it, Em?" he babbled. "Ropes? Mirrors? Lanterns? *How?"* When—still in shock—she didn't—couldn't!—reply, he screamed, "Answer me, damn you!"

"I can't explain it, because I don't know how. It's just . . . it's their power."

"Power, my arse! It can't be power, 'cos they don't have any bleedin' power—it's all a trick! Like the tricks the bloody abbos used t' play on us white men, back in Botany Bay. Did I ever tell you about Botany Bay, Emmie? We had men die, we did, lots of 'em. Some starved t' death. Some were 'anged. Some died o' the bloody flux—an' some died just 'cos one o' them blackfellas pointed the bone at 'em, and told 'em they would! But I know the truth, I do. The voices, the fireballs—" he lowered his voice and whispered, "—none of it's real. It's all illusion! They want you to *believe* it's real, but it ain't," he babbled. "And as long as you don't believe, *it can't hurt you."* He giggled as if he'd uncovered some great secret. "And *I* won't die, neither."

"Then—then why do you fear it?"

"Wot? Wot's that? Fear?" he echoed, mimicking her voice. "Jack Jordan don't fear nothin', gel, you hear me?" he roared. "Nothin'! I'll kill any man—or woman—says he do, see if I don't."

In the silence that followed his passionate denial, Emma could hear the low, droning moan of the wind as it searched the valley walls, trying to fit itself inside the cracks and crevices and niches in the rock. It whistled through deep clefts, soughed in narrow chasms, moaned and shuddered through the black and bottomless lava tubes, then finally erupted onto the plains, belching free in great, hiccupping groans and ghastly shrieks and hisses, to tear the leaves and small limbs from the trees and bushes and scatter handfuls of pebbles like so many dice.

On the narrow ledge outside the tiny cave, the horse screamed in terror, stamping fearfully to and fro, back and forth, desperately seeking a safe path, an escape, but finding none. Lightning flashed, followed immediately by a deafening clap of thunder that went on and on, lasting longer and sounding far louder than any hitherto. From inside the cave, they heard the rattle of loose rocks, a great thud, then another shrill equine scream as the horse lost its footing and toppled over the narrow ledge and into the river far below.

The scream was one Emma'd never forget. "That poor horse is gone."

"Wot?"

"I said, the horse is gone," she repeated. "Let me go and see if I can do anything to save the mule."

"Mule?" he echoed flatly.

"Yes, the mule. Your mule."

In the fading light, she saw his disinterested expression grow sly. *"Oi! Oi!* Wot's this, then? You, see to my mule? Not bleedin' likely, gel! You stay away from my mule—and stay away from them saddlebags, too!"

"It's not your saddlebags I care about, it's that poor animal!" she retorted sharply. Gently transferring a sleeping Mahealani

from her lap to the ground, she rocked forward onto her hands
and knees and began crawling from the cave.

"Get back here!" Jack roared. "I know what you're after, you
thieving little bitch!!" He lurched after her, his hands going to
her throat, fastening clumsily around it.

"I'm not after anything, you lunatic," she cried, batting his
hands away. "I just want to see to the mule! Let me goo!"

"I warned you, Emmie! I told ye t' stay away from my—
aaaggh!"

Mahealani chose that moment to sit up, to stretch like a kitten,
and yawn hugely.

Jack had completely forgotten the child. In his confusion, he
saw only a dark form rising from the ground in the general
direction of the bones. A hunched, dark form that reached small
hands in his direction as if to grab him by the throat as it uttered
an unearthly moan! And, despite his bravado, he was desperate
to escape it!

Thrusting Emma aside, scrabbling over her to save himself,
he backed away, incoherent little gurgling sounds coming from
his mouth.

"Jack, be caref—"

"Stay away from me!" Back, he stepped, back, back, pushing
her aside to get past her, stepping on her fingers, treading on
her hair. He took one step—two—then three—then—!

The fourth carried him farther than he'd ever intended;
straight over the crumbling lip of the *pali,* then down, way down,
cartwheeling head over heels to the cold, dark river below, and
still beyond, to the fiery realms of Milu!

"Mooo—kiii!"

Jack Jordan had been wrong about the power of the *kahunas'*
magic. Once the sacred *kapus* had been broken, one could deny
its power, but could never escape it.

* * *

Emma awoke the following morning with Mahealani nestled in her arms, to find a golden dawn breaking. Sunshine bathed the valley and cast dazzling light everywhere, even illuminating the shallow cave with its radiance. The storm had passed on.

Remembering the bones, she gasped and looked gingerly about her, but there was nothing to see but a few loose rocks and a layer of grit and reddish dirt. A shiver crawled down her spine. Had she and Jack both imagined the bones in the midst of that dreadful night? And if they had, had they also imagined the *akua'ele,* the fireball? She did not know; perhaps she would never know.

Looking down from the cavemouth with the little girl at her side, she could see the damage the storm had left in its wake: broken trees, flooded riverbanks, a hut that had been washed away, and its wreckage caught between some rocks—even her schoolhouse was gone—yet none of that mattered. They were alive, and safe, and somehow, they would get down.

"Emmaaa! Mahealaaani! E-e-maaaa!"

"Kaleilaaani! Mahealaaani!"

With a cry of delight, she picked up Mahealani and hugged her tightly, filled with relief, with happiness. That was Gideon's voice calling—Gideon had come for them!

"We're down here!" she yelled, tears of relief spilling down her cheeks as she stuck her head out of the low cave, like a turtle poking its head out of its shell. "This way!"

"We hear you! Stand clear of the ropes!" his deep, wonderful voice responded. "And Emma—?"

"Yes?"

"I'm a free man, and I love you! Will you marry me?"

"Marry you!"

"Yes!"

"Will you still pull me up if I say No," she teased, laughing through happy tears.

"Not a chance!"

"Kalohe! Then I suppose I've no choice in the matter. I'll have to say Yes!"

"Is everything going to be all right?" her daughter asked, tugging on her muddy skirts and looking up at her anxiously.

"Oh, yes, darling, yes!" Emma reassured her. "From now on, everything's going to be wonderful!"

Thirty-seven

The feasters fell silent as Emma, still dressed in her ivory silk fitted *holuku*, her feet bare, began to dance. A ripple of approval ran through the gathering as they saw the *hula* she had chosen, for it told of a man and a woman's desire for each other, comparing her beauty and his strength to the beauty and strength of nature all around them.

As she danced, her hips sensually swaying, her graceful arms weaving patterns in the air, Gideon rose from the matting and took his place beside her. Also barefoot, and clad in the white breeches and white shirt in which he had been married, island-style, he danced the male part in the lovely old *hula*, the pair moving to approving cries of "Yeehaah!" and *"Hele* on, Mo'o!" from the *paniolos* and ranch hands surrounding them. They made a handsome couple in the flickering light of the torches, she delicate and lovely, he tall and darkly handsome. He carried himself like a warrior of old, his head held high and proud, his broad shoulders thrown back, his bold, masculine foot-stamping, and his arrogant strutting movements forming the perfect counterpoint to Emma's delicate, feminine movements as they danced side by side, turning and dipping in the ageless rhythms and perfect harmony of the forbidden *hula*.

> *Lovely is my sweetheart,*
> *As she dances*
> *In the morning light.*

> *O, she is a graceful thing!*
> *Her breasts are pearls,*
> *Full and rounded,*
> *Her body shapely*
> *As the sleeping hills.*
> *Her tears of happiness*
> *Are the soft mists*
> *That veil the uplands,*
> *Gentle, my beloved's voice,*
> *As the breeze*
> *That cools my cheek.*
>
> *Strong is my beloved*
> *When he comes to*
> *Me by moonlight.*
> *In his hands,*
> *He holds my heart—*
> *For him alone, it is beating.*
> *He, the comely,*
> *He, the strong one!*
> *Like the mountains,*
> *Ever steadfast.*
> *In his arms*
> *There is my harbor*
> *In his kiss,*
> *I find life's meaning . . .*

The guests fell silent, and there was more than one moist eye
among them as Emma and Gideon danced, their dance of love
reaffirming the vows they had taken that morning in the little
white-steepled chapel of Waimea, with the Reverend Cornwell
presiding. It had been six months since Jacob Kane had been
laid to rest in the small graveyard at Hui Aloha, alongside the
tiny infant he and his Miriam had lost. And, despite spending
seven years apart, those six months had proved the longest sepa

ration Emma and Gideon had ever endured. Both bride and groom had incurred the good-natured teasing of family and friends by arriving at the church some two hours early, rather than a fashionable few minutes late.

After their dancing had ended with the bride and groom shamelessly joined in a kiss, the guests responded with whoops and cheers and rushed forward to congratulate them before the small string orchestra from Honolulu took the place of the native musicians and the strains of a waltz floated out over the darkened plains.

After an hour or so, there was a lull in the entertainment to allow those dancing to refresh themselves and rest a little, and the *ho'okupu,* the traditional gift-giving, began. The wedding gifts were as diverse as the guests themselves, reflecting both American and Hawaiian cultures. There were lengths of the finest *tapa* cloth, beautifully printed with vegetable dyes in gorgeous designs, carved bowls of rich, glossy *koa* wood, and platters of the same, scrimshaw combs and a scrimshaw sewing box for the bride, and, for the groom, a fine new saddle that a grinning but bashful Felipe—the new ranch foreman since Uncle Kimo's retirement the month before—modestly confessed he'd made himself, as well as traditional American wedding gifts of crystalware, silver pieces, and fine embroidered linens. Auntie Momi Foulger proudly presented the newlyweds with the beautiful quilt on which she'd been laboring for several months. It had an off-white background with a deep-scarlet, appliquéd-cloth pattern in the breadfruit design—a symbol of fertility, the guests reminded each other, grinning knowingly and nudging their neighbors. Around the intricate central pattern, rows and rows of tiny running stitches had been painstakingly worked. It was these that gave the quilt its beautiful, billowy quality.

"It's just beautiful, Auntie Momi!" Emma exclaimed, ducking down to kiss the old woman on both cheeks and hug her warmly. "I'll treasure it always. *Mahalo nui loa! Mahalo . . .*"

"Och," Momi exclaimed, embarrassed by her praises, "I

doubt you'll have need of its warmth, not with a fine mon like Master Gideon here t' keep you warm!" She cackled with laughter, sounding a little like one of her own laying hens.

"A truer word was never spoken, Auntie," Gideon promised with a grin, likewise bending down to kiss the old lady's cheek: "And if I have my way, it'll burst into flame one fine night!"

"Oh, you," Emma scolded. She blushed yet was smiling nonetheless as she clung to his arm, evidently reluctant to let him go, even for an instant.

Gideon dropped a kiss on her brow. "Missus Kane, dearest, if you'll excuse me for a while, there's a small matter I have to see to."

She grimaced. "Not ranch business, today, Gideon?"

"Aah ha. That would be telling, my dear," he said mysteriously.

"But . . . can't it wait just a moment longer? I want to give you my wedding gift first."

"Here?" he exclaimed, leering at her with a wolfish gleam in his dark eyes. He growled and curved his fingers into claws. "In front of everyone, my wicked *wahine!?*"

"Oh, stop it. This is a—a serious moment," she scolded him primly, her lovely face stern beneath upswept black hair that was crowned with a heavy circlet of jasmine flowers, white rosebuds, and baby's breath. "Here. This is for you, with all my love." She solemnly handed him a roll of thick buff-colored paper, yellowed and water-spotted and musty-smelling with damp and age. It was elaborately tied with a length of white ribbon in which had been tucked a posy of creamy plumeria buds.

Cocking a dark brow at her and pursing his lips, he loosened the ribbon and unrolled the fragile document, scanning it by the light of a nearby torch. His eyes were moist when he looked up at her again. "This is the grant to your *kuleana,* your land!" he exclaimed, his voice husky.

"Yes. I had Alexander McHenry add your name to the title.

It's my wedding gift to you. The Kane herds will have more than enough water next year. All the water they need!"

Words failed him then. His heart bursting with joy, he simply whispered her name, like a prayer, and wrapped his arms around her as she stepped into them. For several minutes, he held her as if he'd never let her go, too overcome to utter a single word.

"Auwe! 'Nough already!" scolded a stern voice. "Dis no way for a respectable married couple to behave! *Auwe!* Shame on you!"

Embarrassed, a startled Emma and Gideon broke apart to see Auntie Leolani standing before them, her enormous body swathed from head to toe in yards of flowered calico, her broad, handsome face wreathed in a smile. When she saw their startled expressions, she threw back her dark head and laughed uproariously. "Oh, you two, Auntie only teasing! No more shame you *honi-honi,* kissing! Dis your wedding day, after all! Go ahead, honey girl. Kiss him some more!" Chuckling, she sailed off to delight the crowd with one of her *kalohe*—naughty—*hulas,* for which she was justifiably well known. Though the *hula* had been banned by the missionary fathers, and though it was illegal to perform it—even punishable by imprisonment or fine—that night, on the lawns of Hui Aloha, with the guitars and ukuleles playing and the stars shining down, it flourished grandly!

It was some time before Gideon was able to evade the well-wishers and his suspicious bride to slip away from the *luau.* He headed for the stables, surprising Mahealani and her cousins, Pikake and Kamuela—two of Leolani and Kimo's grandchildren—playing *kimo,* jackstones, on the flat pathway by the kitchen building.

"What are you three doing here?"

"Kamuela's cheating," Mahealani said matter-of-factly, pointing accusingly at Kamuela. "But me and Pikake are playing *kimo.* Would you like to play with us?"

He smiled. "Later, perhaps, poppet. I have to go somewhere for a little while. Would you like to come with me?"

"Can I? Can I really?" Big, dark eyes wide and shining, she looked up at him hopefully, crowing with delight when he nodded. "Of course."

"Where are we going?" she wondered aloud, but as she snuggled up against him, her little cheek pressed trustingly against his chest, he knew his destination really didn't matter. She just wanted to be with him.

"I've planned a surprise for Kaleilani—your *makuahine*."

Mahealani sighed. "I still call her Kalei, most times. I just keep forgetting!"

"It doesn't matter. I'm sure she doesn't mind, little one," he told her, turning Akamai's head to the east.

"Do you mind that I don't call you Papa?" she asked in a small voice.

"Well, I hope you'll want to one day. But until then, no, I don't mind at all. You can call me Gideon, or Uncle. Whichever feels right."

She sighed happily, reassured by his answer. It seemed she'd put the frightening night when Jack Jordan had abducted her and Emma in the past, where it belonged, and he was more than satisfied. Some wonderful day, his little daughter would call him Papa, and love him as wholeheartedly as he'd come to love her. He'd move heaven and Earth to make certain she did! Until then he intended to provide the security her life had lacked thus far—perhaps, he thought ruefully, the only thing it had lacked. She had never lacked loving. In his opinion, Emma had made the supreme sacrifice by letting her cousin Anela and her husband raise their small daughter, forgoing the precious years of her babyhood in order to keep her safe from Jack, and concealing her condition so cleverly before the birth that everyone had believed the baby girl Malia and Jack Jordan's miracle child.

At that moment, the "miracle child" seemed about to tuck her thumb in her mouth, then thought better of it so that she could pipe, "Uncle Gideon?"

"Yes, darling?"

"May I help with the surprise?"

"Well, let me see. Do you know how to strike a match?" She nodded solemnly. "How to light candles safely?"

"I don't like to burn my fingers, but if you show me how, I'll try."

"Then I wouldn't dream of doing it without you," he told her solemnly, kissing her button nose. "After all, you're my little girl, aren't you?"

Her delighted, gap-toothed grin was more precious than gold.

"Why ever didn't you come to us, child?" Miriam Kane murmured, touching her new daughter-in-law's cheek with affection. "You didn't have to be all alone with Mahealani. We would gladly have helped you—both you and your poor *makuahine,* God rest her soul. She and Leolani really were both part of our Hui Aloha *ohana,* family, after all!"

"I was afraid you wouldn't approve of me, *Makuahine,*" Emma murmured, resting her cheek on Miriam Kane's shoulder as the older woman took her in her arms and embraced her. Softly, she added, "And ashamed, too. I thought you would think badly of me for having Gideon's child. The nuns said . . . Well, they said a great many things."

Miriam released her and held her at arm's length. "Poor Kaleilani! You've had so much *pilikia,* trouble, in your short life, haven't you! Small wonder you were always such a serious little thing—the image of my darling granddaughter! My heart went out to you that awful night when Kimo brought you to us, girlie! Your beautiful violet eyes were just brimming over with tears, but your poor uncle Kimo was too furious at Jack Jordan to even speak, let alone try to comfort you! If it had been in my power, I would have taken you in, raised you as my own *hanai* daughter, foster daughter, in the old way. But . . . Jacob thought it best you be sent away, beyond Jordan's reach."

"That was the night Uncle Kimo came to ask Mister Kane for his help." The night she'd never forgotten. And never would.

Miriam nodded. "I never asked for details, but I had my suspicions, nonetheless. And then, soon after Kimo had taken you to Honolulu, one of my serving girls saw Jack Jordan in the village. She said he looked as if he'd been run over by a stampeding bullock and warned us he was muttering threats against Jacob." Miriam laughed, her eyes taking on a faraway light as she remembered that time. "My husband was a gentle, God-fearing man, Emma, but he could also become a raging bull if the moment called for it! He could never stand by and allow a man to harm an innocent child, or strike a woman, or even hurt an animal—at least, not without paying the price for it." She shrugged. "After Nani told me about Jack's bruises that day, I guessed Jacob had decided to use his college boxing skills to help the good Lord along! He also 'convinced' Jack to sign a confession admitting he was an escaped felon—a Botany Bay runaway—so that he could hold the confession over Jordan's head whenever the rogue started acting up and preying on his wife and child." Miriam shivered. "The Bible teaches us to love our neighbors, as well you know, my dear, and to turn the other cheek when we are wronged. But it also says 'An eye for an eye.' With Jordan dead and gone, and that Lennox woman locked up, the world is a far safer place for us all, I do believe."

"Indeed it is. But I can't help thinking how Jack must have feared and hated your husband all those years for the power he held over him," Emma observed with a shudder, remembering the feral glitter in Jordan's eyes when he'd spoken of Gideon's father.

"Oh, yes. He hated him enough to take my Jacob's life . . ."

A knot of tears gathered in Emma's throat. Now it was her turn to embrace her mother-in-law, and embrace her she did, squeezing her tightly. They had grown close over the past months, and would, God willing, grow even closer in the coming years.

Miriam Kane sniffed back her tears and dabbed at her eyes. "There, there, enough of this nonsense! *Auwe!* Jacob wouldn't want this sadness on your wedding day, and nor do I. Go! Go and visit with your guests, my daughter. Look over there! Alex McHenry's coming this way. I expect that dear man will want a waltz with the bride!"

Emma smiled. *Alexander McHenry.* It was the name she'd thrown in Jack Jordan's face the night she'd burned the grass huts to the ground, after Jack told her he'd destroyed her letters to Gideon. *Her real father's name.* A lonely, grieving man, he'd reached out to the beautiful native serving girl who'd loved him for comfort, after losing Katherine, his wife of many years. *She* had been the result, and the serving girl had been Malia Kahikina, her mother. Malia had never told McHenry that Emma was his daughter, and although Emma had told Gideon her true parentage, she had decided she would not tell McHenry. It could serve no purpose, and some secrets were better left untold . . .

"Och, there they are—the two bonny Missus Kanes! May I claim a dance wi' the bride, my dear?" McHenry asked with a gallant bow.

"You may indeed, sir," Emma laughingly accepted with a gracious incline of her head. She smiled at Miriam over her shoulder as Alexander McHenry took her hand in his large, bony one and led her to join the others. She was dancing a second waltz and conversing gaily with the lawyer when Gideon returned.

"There now! I believe your husband wants t' cut in, my lassie," Alex observed with twinkling eyes, turning her briskly to the music and away from Gideon. "But I dinna think I'll let him! It's been many a year since I've danced with a bonnie lassie!"

They were both laughing when McHenry led her to a smiling Gideon's side several moments later, "There she is, laddie," the older man declared, placing Emma's hand in his. "Safe and sound. Take good care o' her, whist ye."

"I intend to spend the rest of my life doing just that, sir,"

Gideon assured him, leading his bride away from the lawns and McHenry with a haste that bordered on uncivil.

"Wait! There are guests I haven't spoken with yet!"

"Believe me, they'll understand. Besides, I've already made your—our—excuses and apologies."

"Excuses? Apologies?"

"For leaving the *luau*. You see, I have something to show you."

"Oh?" She looked intrigued now, he saw, like a little girl promised a surprise. Like their beautiful daughter. "What is it?"

"You'll see soon enough. Come on! Last one to the stables is a—"

"Stinkbug?" she supplied.

"Something like that," he agreed, grinning.

Epilogue

"Come on! Give me your hand and follow me—and mind you don't trip in the dark. Better yet, I'll carry you."

After leaving Hui Aloha with its torchlit gardens and lively music, they had ridden for some twenty minutes across the hushed, moon-drenched plains when Gideon reined Akamai in beneath a spreading *ohia lehua* tree. Its leaves were edged with silver in the starlight, and the same ethereal light danced in his dark eyes as he grasped her by the waist and lifted her down from the horse to stand beside him.

"Stop that! I can walk perfectly well, I tell you— Ooh! Put me down, *kalohe,* you rogue!" she wailed. "Oh, Gideon, stop! We mustn't go inside! It's trespassing?"

Ignoring both her struggles and her flailing legs, he swept her up and carried her between two large rocks set some feet apart on the grass. "I'll be the judge of whether we're trespassing or not, Missus Kane," he said firmly, turning her sideways to maneuver between the obstacles. "Mind your skirts on the gates, now."

"Gates?" She glanced over her shoulder as he carried her toward an unfinished two-story house that rose from the crest of a gentle rise, and frowned. Raw beams and planks of lumber gleamed palely in the moonlight. Indeed, the neatly aligned rows of rafters and their supporting timbers were like the rib bones of an enormous skeleton—that of a whale, perhaps, carried miles inland and upland by some enormous *tsunami,* then beached, high and dry, on this site. She sniffed. The pleasant aroma of fresh wood shavings and well-seasoned timber hung on the warm, dewy night air, but . . . there were no gates, not that she could see, and she said so. "What gates? I don't see any gates?"

He grinned down at her. "That's because you're looking with your eyes, my dear."

"Ah, me! So I am. A foolish habit, I admit," she observed tartly, and punched his chest. "What else would I be looking with, you silly man? My knees? My elbows?"

"With your *imagination*. What else, my dear Missus Kane?" he taunted. There was laughter in his voice as he carried her the last several yards, puffing and blowing noisily as he bore her uphill across rough grass, between several more *ohia lehua* trees in full bloom, pretending to groan under her weight. He came to a halt at the front steps of the unfinished structure. There, he set her down with a loud, false sigh of relief, and turned her to face back the way they'd come.

"There! Squint just a little and tell me if you can see them now?"

"Them?"

"The brace of graceful iron gates at the end of the coral driveway, my dear! Surely you can see them? They came all the way from New England, just for you. There are posts of white coral blocks standing on either side of them, like sentinels. Aren't they just grand?"

Shooting him a wary look, she nodded and agreed that they were, indeed, the very best gates she'd ever seen, and didn't he think it was high time he allowed Doctor Forrester to examine him? It didn't do to argue with a madman, the nuns at the convent had always cautioned.

Noting her expression, he grinned even more broadly and declared, "And now, the *pièce de résistance*—the house itself! Upsadaisy!" With a dramatic flourish, he swung her up into his arms once again and bore her across the wide threshold, planting a smacking kiss on her lips before he set her down.

"Do come inside, my dear," he invited her huskily, his gentian eyes lambent with desire as he led her through a long, broad entrance hall—or rather, what would someday be an entrance hall, when the house was completed. Halting at the foot of a gracefully curving staircase, he bowed gallantly, indicating she should lead the way up it as he added, "I do believe the master's been expecting you, ma'am."

"Oh, Gideon, you idiot!" She giggled at his silly formality, reaching out to finger the untied strands of fragrant jasmine, entwined with sweet-smelling *maile* leaves, that hung down on either side of his snowy-white shirt—traditional wedding *leis* for a bridegroom. Her fingertips drifted across the broad chest beneath them, and her smile deepened. "I'm afraid you're quite mad, my darling," she murmured, casting him a coquettish glance from beneath the sooty fans of her lashes. *"Pupule! Crazy! Let's go now, before the owner comes and finds us here, hmm? It is our wedding night, after all?"

"But the owner's already here, *me ke aloha.*"

His voice was low and caressing now, like a hot, dry wind that fanned her senses. He casually slipped his arm around her neck, the ball of his thumb caressing her bare, downy nape as he murmured, "And—as I said before—he's been waiting for you, beloved. Waiting half a lifetime, it seems!"

Her delicate brows rose in astonishment. Her velvety eyes widened. "This is your house?" she squeaked.

"No." He shook his head. "Not entirely mine, sweetheart. 'Ours' would be a better description—though to be honest, I'd stopped hoping you'd share it with me someday."

"And you've been building it all by yourself?"

"Six months—and it's still unfinished, board by board and nail by nail, just as I always planned. Remember, my love?"

Her expression softened. Did she remember? Oh, yes, she remembered—remembered all too well the proud young man he'd been back then, and the way his boyish face had grown animated as he described the wonderful home he'd build for them to share someday! *"I'll build us a fine, new house of our own from the best koa-wood. It'll be a house with a long veranda where we can look out across the plains . . . and remember when we first made love by the light of the full moon."* She remembered those precious, stolen moments as if they'd happened but yesterday! In fact, she'd even named their daughter for the wonderful moonrise on which she'd been conceived—Mahealani, Full Moon of Heaven. "I can't believe you remembered! We were little more than children back then," she exclaimed softly, touched.

"Perhaps. But old enough to know we loved each other—would always love each other—even so." He drew her hand to his lips and pressed his mouth to the tiny hollow of her palm, before kissing the tip of each finger. As he did so, his eyes held hers willing captives.

Emotion filled her breast—a swelling, heady joy that was as potent as wine. She was the first to look away, and did so with flaming cheeks. Innocent as his kisses had been, she'd nevertheless felt them everywhere. They'd prickled across her scalp, tingled down her spine, fluttered in her belly, sizzled in her veins!

"Lead on, milady," he urged in a husky whisper.

Mutely and with no further urging, she started up the stairs, her fingers skimming the newly sanded balustrade that felt smooth as silk and strangely provocative to her touch.

On the landing, which was still open to the deep-blue vault of sky above, she glanced up, almost dizzied by the glorious view. The stars were huge and glittering tonight, like enormous silver moonflowers just waiting to be plucked and strung on gossamer thread to make a heavenly lei. *Hokulani, Star of Heaven.*

Her heart skipped a beat, then righted itself. Trembling with emotion, she turned and took Gideon's hand between her own, far more aroused by his seemingly innocent caresses than she cared to admit. Drawing his calloused hand up to her face, she rubbed her cheek against his knuckles like a kitten, uttering a contented little purring sound. "Nothing's changed between us, has it, Gideon, despite all the years we've spent apart?" she reflected, happiness filling her with an exquisite glow. *Gideon was her husband now, and she, his wife. Nothing could ever part them again!*

He pursed his lips. "I disagree. Some things have changed."

She grew very still. "Oh? And what are they?"

"For one, that I love you more on this, our wedding day, than I loved you then," he murmured, and she almost swooned with relief. Smiling, he traced her adorable little nose with his fingertip. "And for another, that you're even more beautiful now than you were the first time I set eyes on you."

"Impossible," she whispered huskily, moving closer to him, letting her hips, then the fullness of her breasts, brush up against his lean, hard body. He sucked in a breath, and the moonlight slanting through the open rafters danced merrily in her own eyes now as he stiffened ever so slightly in response to her nearness.

"Impossible?" he echoed hoarsely.

"Absolutely. You were *madly* in love with me, even then," she declared smugly.

He grinned. "And I still am, you heartless minx. Even madly-er!"

"Madly-er, indeed. Just listen to him, and he claims he's a college man, too!" she declared, rolling her eyes. "There's no such word."

"There is now, mistress schoolmarm. I just invented it."

"Ah. And what is its meaning, pray?" she challenged, eyeing him archly.

"That no one—I repeat, *no one*—has ever loved a woman the way that I love you, Missus Emma Kaleilani Kane. And that no man has ever made love to a woman the way I intend to make love to my bride tonight."

"You do?" she echoed shakily, his promises inciting delicious, dangerous little tingles inside her. She felt suddenly weak-kneed and breathless.

"Indeed, yes," he confirmed with a fierce ardor to his tone that made her hot and cold all at the same time. "So, let's adjourn to the master suite, shall we, my dear?"

"The master suite? How very grand!" she murmured shakily, raising the ruffled train of her ivory satin wedding *holoku* by its finger loop to take the arm he so gallantly offered her. Breathless with anticipation, she followed him down the landing.

Sawdust lay like a fine powder everywhere. Curls of wood shavings were heaped neatly in corners, while sawhorses stood where dividing walls would someday stand. But in Emma's mind's eye, she could see the elegant entry hall below the spindle railing as it would look completed. The crystal prisms of a beautiful chandelier would be ablaze with reflected candlelight, while elegantly gowned visitors from Honolulu or as far away as Hong Kong or San Francisco or even Boston danced to the strains of an elegant waltz.

Off the hallway would run spacious, airy drawing and dining rooms with French windows that reached from ceiling to floor, furnished with cool wicker and rattan furniture, and a few fine *koa* pieces, too; gracious rooms where island society matrons would flock to take afternoon tea, and where literary and political lights would gather to discuss world affairs, or simply to gossip about the latest island scandals. And, in one of the bedrooms leading off this very landing, their darling daughter, Mahealani, would sleep soundly each night in a four-poster bed that her grandfather, Jacob Kane, had made with his own hands, adrift on a billowy mattress stuffed with the softest *pulu*—the downy inner part of the fern.

And—by this time next year, God willing—she was almost certain there would be a rocking cradle in the third bedroom, the nursery, next door to their own. A place in which to sit and rock *Tutu* Miriam Kane's new grandchild—a little replica of Gideon this time, she hoped, if Auntie Leo's calculations were accurate, a handsome son with his papa's black hair and gentian eyes whom they would christen Jake Alexander Hokulani Kane, after both his grandfathers, and for his parents' starlit wedding night, on which he was conceived. Why, if she closed her eyes, she could almost see him, the spitting image of his older sister at the same age, cooing and gurgling as he bounced on his *tutu* Miriam's knee . . .

"You've grown very quiet," Gideon observed, breaking into her thoughts. Taking her elbow, he turned her gently to face him. He searched her face. "Are you plotting some mischief or other, *ku'uipo,* sweetheart, or is something troubling you?"

"Noo. I was just thinking that this will be such a beautiful house. And quite . . . grand, too."

"It will be more than a house—it'll be our *home,* Emma. Yours, mine, and our children's, and their children's. There's nothing for you to be afraid of, not anymore. It's over. Now, come here, wife. Come and look at the view from your veranda."

He led her through the enormous master bedroom and out onto the *lanai* by way of elegant French doors that were flanked by wooden louvers and shutters.

The veranda was broad and long, encompassing the entire side of the upper story. Emma gasped in delight as she stepped out onto it, for Gideon must have left their wedding feast at some point to come here and light the dozens of white-ginger-scented candles that floated in wooden basins of water. The tiny flames shimmied in the water, danced a graceful *hula* in the softest of fragrant breezes, like myriad fireflies in the shadows.

With a contented sigh, she leaned back against his chest. His strong arms encircled her waist, and he angled his head to kiss her throat before resting his chin in her hair.

In intimate silence, they gazed out across the darkened, sleeping land to the distant sea, where the surf cut a narrow line of bright white against the night, and where the restless tides ebbed and flowed unceasingly upon the shores of a small bay that was dear to both their hearts.

There, two black rocks rose from the water, the same two rocks that ancient legend claimed had once been an Hawaiian princess and her handsome commoner sweetheart. The lovers had chosen death together, rather than separation, and by so doing, had won the blessing of the gods.

"Oh, Gideon! It's our bay I can see from here, isn't it? Our own, special place!" she breathed, deeply touched that he had planned all this in secret, with her pleasure in mind. "Thank you, my love! Thank you for everything!" she exclaimed, turning to smile up at him.

He returned her smile. From the moment he and Emma had met all those years ago, they'd ceased to be two separate people. Their love had been the bond that made them one; a glorious bond that would, God willing, last forever.

" *'While I yet have breath within me/I shall not be parted from thee/ Sweet one, I will not forsake thee!'* " he quoted from the *mele* she loved.

"Never?"

"Never, *me ke aloha.*"

Taking her in his arms, he held her to his heart for a long, long time. And when—much later—he began making love to her, it was with unhurried, lingering caresses that made her cry her pleasure to the very stars.

There was no need for haste, after all, Emma thought dreamily as she lay in her bridegroom's arms. They had a lifetime ahead of them.

"Ha'ina ia mai ana kapuana."
The story is told.

Author's Note

This Stolen Moment is a work of fiction. All names, characters, and incidents in this novel are either the product of my imagination, or are used fictitiously, except where obvious historical references are made.

For those of you who are familiar with Hawaii and the history of this beautiful state, you will recognize the location of the Hui Aloha ranch as Waimea, Hawaii, where the world-famous Parker Ranch—once, if not still, the largest, single-owned cattle ranch in the world—is located. It is a glorious place of mist and rain-swept emerald hills, of vivid blue morning glories and Hawaiian cowboys who are as unique as the range they ride. But please, don't take my word for it. Go there! You'll fall in love with the Big Island, as I did.

To all of you who have written to me in the past, I treasure each and every one of your letters. *Thank you!* If you'd like to write to me but have not yet done so, I would love to hear from you at the following address:

Penelope Neri
Zebra Books
850 Third Avenue
N.Y., N.Y. 10022

I do hope you enjoyed reading this book. I'm looking forward to hearing from you with any comments or questions you may have. Until then, *Aloha!*

—P.N.

YOU WON'T WANT TO READ
JUST ONE — KATHERINE STONE

ROOMMATES (3355-9, $4.95)
No one could have prepared Carrie for the monumental changes she would face when she met her new circle of friends at Stanford University. Once their lives intertwined and became woven into the tapestry of the times, they would never be the same.

TWINS (3492-X, $4.95)
Brook and Melanie Chandler were so different, it was hard to believe they were sisters. One was a dark, serious, ambitious New York attorney; the other, a golden, glamourous, sophisticated supermodel. But they were more than sisters — they were twins and more alike than even they knew . . .

THE CARLTON CLUB (3614-0, $4.95)
It was the place to see and be seen, the only place to be. And for those who frequented the playground of the very rich, it was a way of life. Mark, Kathleen, Leslie and Janet — they worked together, played together, and loved together, all behind exclusive gates of the *Carlton Club*.

Available wherever paperbacks are sold, or order direct from the Publisher. Send cover price plus 50¢ per copy for mailing and handling to Penguin USA, P.O. Box 999, c/o Dept. 17109, Bergenfield, NJ 07621. Residents of New York and Tennessee must include sales tax. DO NOT SEND CASH.

TODAY'S HOTTEST READS
ARE TOMORROW'S SUPERSTARS

WHAT'S LOVE GOT TO DO WITH IT?

Everything . . . Just ask Kathleen Drymon . . . and Zebra Books

CASTAWAY ANGEL	(3569-1, $4.50/$5.50)
GENTLE SAVAGE	(3888-7, $4.50/$5.50)
MIDNIGHT BRIDE	(3265-X, $4.50/$5.50)
VELVET SAVAGE	(3886-0, $4.50/$5.50)
TEXAS BLOSSOM	(3887-9, $4.50/$5.50)
WARRIOR OF THE SUN	(3924-7, $4.99/$5.99)

Available wherever paperbacks are sold, or order direct from the Publisher. Send cover price plus 50¢ per copy for mailing and handling to Penguin USA, P.O. Box 999, c/o Dept. 17109, Bergenfield, NJ 07621. Residents of New York and Tennessee must include sales tax. DO NOT SEND CASH.